"A gripping story of adventure, casual treachery and intrigue, and the redemption of an emotionally and morally ruined soul. .... *The Lost City* shares something of the same timelessness [as] Thomas Hardy's *The Return of the Native*, one of the great creations of terrain as a character in English fiction."

—*The Guardian* (London)

"Shukman proves himself a master of driven narrative and psychological drama.... At times the prose has the terse muscularity of a Hemingway adventure, at others an almost biblical thunder, underscored by touches of Graham Greene.... This is Shukman pushing his talent to the edge."

—*The Scotsman*

"Haunting. . . . Shukman has a phenomenally well-developed sense of place. . . . But what's perhaps most impressive here is the way that he seems able to make everything symbolise something larger than itself."

—*The Independent on Sunday*

"A powerful debut. . . . Shukman skillfully blends his genres: political intrigue, drug lords, and South American militia . . . while the poetic prose harks back to Conrad's original jungle quest, *Heart of Darkness*."

—*Daily Mail*

"[This] is the closest to the sensation of a rainforest jungle adventure that you'll get without buying a ticket to Chachapoyas."

—*Time Out London*

"Shukman, a travel writer and novelist, has brought together all the vital elements for a good tale. . . . But it's more than just that. The road traveled here is of course our short stint on the planet, the perils and tedium symbolic of life's trappings and *The Lost City* that elusive paradise. And Shukman has pulled it off magnificently."

—*Evening Herald* (Dublin)

Henry Shukman

THE LOST CITY

Henry Shukman has worked as a trombonist,
a trawlerman, and a travel writer. His fiction
has won an Arts Council England Award and
has been a finalist for the O. Henry Award.
His first poetry collection, *In Dr. No's Garden*,
won the Jerwood Aldeburgh Prize and was a
Book of the Year in *The Times* (London) and
The Guardian. He lives in New Mexico.

THE LOST CITY

THE LOST CITY

A Novel

Henry Shukman

Vintage Contemporaries
Vintage Books
A Division of Random House, Inc.
New York

i.m. HMS 1965–84

Nature's first green is gold,
Her hardest hue to hold.
Her early leaf's a flower;
But only so an hour.
Then leaf subsides to leaf.
So Eden sank to grief,
So dawn goes down to day.
Nothing gold can stay.

—ROBERT FROST

Part One

LOWLAND

1 · Caballo Muerto

1

This wasn't a country you would visit unless you had to, if you were born there, say, or were sent in to check up on some account. I mean country in the broad Hemingway sense: terrain, land, *country*. The mountains rising ghostly and huge on one side, the strangely cold ocean on the other, and in between a strip of desert so barren not even cactuses grew. Half the year a blanket of low cloud covered the desert, the infamous *garúa*, shouldered off the back of the Humboldt Current which came up glacial from Antarctica. The other half, blazing equatorial sun fired all things into immobility—the piles of gravel and sand by the never-improved highway, rubbish at the roadside, mummified dogs, old men waiting, waiting. It was too hot to move. It was enough to get through the day. To reach six p.m., when the red balloon of the sun regularly settled on the rim of the Pacific, felt like an achievement, a deliverance.

For six months the unrelenting fog hung a hundred feet overhead. No wind stirred. A fogbound desert—hot, drizzly, mind-achingly grey. Grey sand, grey rocks, grey sky, grey concrete in the cities (there were two), grey rain when it fell, grey dawn, grey dusk, grey days. Grey ocean even: in that season the Pacific lay lifeless and limp, more like a mass of gelatine than water, with barely the energy to slap at the long grey beaches. They weren't waves, let alone breakers. Lakeside ripples. Slap—then a little slurp—then slap again. Water the colour of slate.

Two rivers, the Caballo Muerto and the Malcorazón, broke westward from the mountains to run through the country. They were freaks, spindly and seasonal, but much fêted. All other rivers that rose in the mountains went eastward into the jungle. Only these two made the perverse pilgrimage to the Pacific. They descended tremendous canyons of sandstone, dropping thousands of feet in a few miles, from the glinting peaks beyond the reach of cloud to the long decline of the desert, where they formed shallow wide valleys and their riverbeds became highways of gravel threaded with rivulets that snaked and criss-crossed each other like leather thongs. Even the water was leathery here—nothing endured the heat without transformation. Lower down, nearer the coast, the canyons became suddenly green. Banana trees bushed in the valleybeds, fields of alfalfa blazed under the sun and along either rim eucalyptus trees shivered and smoked, the colour of old copper.

Just north of the northern river a dirt track forged straight at the mountains then petered out in a path which soon forked and lost itself among the rocks of the foothills. Farmers used the track, piling ancient pickups with towers of bananas and pineapples among which they perched, struggling to keep the loads from tumbling as they swayed down to market.

Late on a Thursday afternoon toward the end of the *garúa* season an empty truck made its way up the track. From above, all you saw was a plume of dust travelling along with a kind of self-absorbed determination, as if an animal were furiously burrowing its way just under the surface, an invisible point churning up a wake of dust. Then a little black dot showed at the front of the cloud, trembling in the distance. It grew slowly, coming straight up the hill; the only moving thing in the landscape. Then it stopped. It seemed to grow broader. A tiny human figure emerged. Then, as if in slow motion, the truck turned off the path, described a large lazy circle, rocked back onto the track facing the opposite way, and trundled back in the direction of the distant ocean.

The man who had got out pulled on a rucksack and took a step to balance himself. He was a young man who stood still, watching the truck drive away. Its gurgling engine soon faded in the crunch of wheels on dirt, then that too was lost and all that remained was a low hum, until even that became indistinguishable, and the man knew he was alone. The dust kicked up by the truck dispersed, leaving a faint blemish low in the sky.

The young man turned and looked up the hill. A mile away stood a red cliff, the beginning of the mountains.

The air was dusty, clean-dusty. Clean in a different way from the high mountain air. Thick, sure of itself. Clean like a parade ground on the morning of a big day, before anyone was up. There was something about it—it invigorated you. Perhaps it was just the relief of having got away from the coast, from the torpid ocean and the dull concrete city, the ugliest the man had seen in a long time.

He set off right away, glad of his boots, an old army pair. The leather had outlasted three complete sets of stitching. They were the most comfortable footwear he had ever known. There's no happiness like a good pair of boots, he thought as he walked. Boots, if they were just exactly right for you, changed the way you felt. In fact, there was no happiness like marching alone up a track toward evening in the desert. His limbs tingled. For a while he didn't care if he ever found what he was looking for, if he had to give it all up tomorrow. Nothing mattered but this march through the wide-open air of the desert hillside.

The good feeling suggested he was on the right track. He had an urge to stop and make a sketch, and that too was a kind of affirmation.

When the track ended he branched off to the left. It was harder going now, on the loose sand and gravel. He tried to plant his steps on the broken rocks lying here and there for better purchase. The slope steepened. He slowed his pace and kept up a steady mild pressure, his heart knocking. He looked at his watch: half an hour of daylight left though you would never tell by looking around. Night came without warning here. You noticed a hard-to-define dissolution in the air, as if the light had broken into particles. Then it was only a matter of minutes before the dark poured out of the solvent air, as if those particles were the first fragments of coming night.

He strode more quickly. He didn't want to get caught by nightfall without a camp, and he wanted to make camp at the foot of the cliff. His steps grew louder, rattling on the sand and gravel. No other sound. Just his footfalls. There might have been no other living thing in the world.

He was sweating hard by the time he got to the top of the slope. He was impatient to get the pack off his back and start looking around, but he made himself keep walking until he found a space between two rocks that would make a good camp: level ground, and only a few stones littering the dust. He slid the pack off. At once his shirt felt cool on his back and his body seemed to lift an inch clear of the ground.

A breeze sprang up. Perfect timing, he said to himself, thinking the breeze would cool him.

The nearest boulder was about his height, of pale yellow rock. He walked round, scanning it from top to bottom. Part way round, on the side facing the open west, where the light was still strong, he saw what he was looking for. Low down, around knee height, a pale carving of a star. The lines had been carefully chipped out, not hastily scratched. They formed eight radii. He ran his finger along one line, across the little bump of the centre, then sniffed his fingertip and caught the dry-plaster scent of stone.

He placed a rock on top of the boulder and made his way further round, stooping and scanning up and down. On another smooth rock face an animal had been carved, some quadruped. A llama, a cow, a dog, a jaguar—it could have been any of them.

Then he saw a kind of face, square with a wide-open mouth and four fangs. It was fainter than the other carvings, but unmistakable.

For a moment Connolly seemed very close. He had been right here, certainly.

His mind reeled: no one knew how old these carvings were. They had waited, a message on a rock to be received thousands of years later. Who had last bothered to come and see them? Connolly. He had found them for sure. What did they mean? *We are here.* Nothing more. A cry of loneliness. The spill of red rocks in the big red land on the big planet spinning in emptiness, and on them, this sign.

Excitement gave way to a plunge of sadness. He felt that something had been missing from him for a long time.

Self-pity, he told himself, stop it at once. But it wasn't just self-pity. It was sadness too, that Connolly really had been here, and never would be again. He was on his own, Connolly had gone. He exhaled sharply and almost sobbed, but stopped himself. He mustn't let it start.

He fetched his sketchbook and started drawing the designs. The late light showed them up in clear relief, and on the page in thick charcoal they looked good: so simple, so stark, the eye that created them had seen the world so clearly. He thought about beginning an attempt on a chart of the site, using his green graph paper, but it was too late, the light was going and the wind would flap the paper about. Camp was the thing to attend to.

Trees he couldn't see in the valleybed would have blackened by now. It was a matter of minutes till darkness fell. He unbuckled the straps of his rucksack, relieved to be busy, and forced himself to think only of what he was doing. He pulled the tent out, shaking it loose from its pouch. It snapped like a sail. He realised he was going to have to pitch it not only in the wind, but on loose dust. He fumbled in the bag of pegs and attempted to fasten down a corner of the jumping, shifting sheet. The peg went straight in: no need to bang it with a rock. And as soon as he let it go, it leaned over in the dry sand and the tent slipped downwind, pulling the peg with it. It flipped over onto a rock.

He left it there and fetched big stones, bringing them over one by one. He knew he didn't need the tent, it seldom rained here, but he wanted a real camp. He had carried two logs all the way up in the backpack and was planning on a fire. A fire and a tent. And tomorrow while he was sketching things out it would be good to have a base. A tent was a mobile office, as well as a study, a bedroom. And he liked his tent: green impregnated canvas, the old two-pole style: a triangular home. A man on his own in the world needed a tent, the home of the wanderer. Except he wasn't a wanderer but a quester. Or else nothing but an escapee, a deserter.

He didn't care what he was. What mattered was that he was free. He had brought himself here, to northern Peru. He had done it. That was what mattered. Connolly had told him: think of the high, man, what could compare to stumbling into a lost city, the old centre of a forgotten empire? A week or two from now he'd know.

For several weeks he'd been on the loose in the unknown continent. He'd bought a one-way ticket. He had known the moment he entered the door of the dingy office block behind Oxford Street, one of those buildings with a hundred business names taped up by the door, that he was doing the right thing. Things were salvageable after all. Life was broader than you thought. One of the men in that shabby little office smiled and took his envelope full of notes: £270. Which left him a little short of £700 in the bank. The travel agent nodded and counted. You ever coming back? he asked, laughing. The joke of a man who had his daily work to attend to.

A blue ticket, filled in by hand: London–Lima. Lloyd Aero Boliviano, whatever that was. A flight into the unknown, with his own private thread of purpose wrapped about his hand. Just enough. And now the thread had become a rope and was holding. He mustn't let it go.

In the dusk he fetched the tent back. The wind ripped right through the spot he had chosen. He got the corners weighted with stones then bundled his way inside with the poles. The tent took on a flowing loose shape. He crawled out carefully, conscious of the need for doing everything right if you were alone in the world, and on a trail.

He sat and waited. Maybe the wind would die. He remembered that happening before: a wind that got up at dusk and died soon after nightfall.

He unstrapped the two fire-logs from his rucksack then

unpacked the things he would need: sleeping bag, notebook, fat paperback with a torn cover, candle-stub, a jar lid to stick it on, sketchbook and the pad of graph paper.

Things seemed quieter, more orderly now. Camp was made. Only food remained. The tent fell silent, flapping occasionally. He crawled out and stood up and looked about: yes, the wind had become a warm breeze and you could tell that even that would die down soon. The wind had been night itself blowing in.

2

Jackson Small was his name. He was twenty-one.

He emptied a can of tomatoes into a pan. Behind him the tent glowed like a lantern, lit by the candle within. He sat by the fire stirring. Gradually he became aware of the smell of heating tomatoes, and of a light sizzle coming from the pan. He tested the temperature by licking the knife tip, and once they were on their way he broke in two of his eggs. Poached eggs in tomatoes. He would never have thought of that back in London, but once you were out in the world almost any food tasted good.

He became mildly bored. This was the time when he wanted company. He thought of John Connolly again, and experienced a sudden worry, a foreboding. Connolly had last come down here two years back, and had always meant to come again.

To cheer himself up he thought of Frank Parker, who'd left the regiment around the same time he had. The two of them had had one hell of a lunch in Langan's once they were both out. And rightly so. Even he had had his brass handshake. But if he had known then what was to come, that he was starting out as he would go on—anyway, that was behind him now, he mustn't think of it. Parker used to call him Sinbad in Belize. Sin the Worst. It was a joke. Because of him and Connolly.

Then he thought of his father, their last lunch together in the Eagle and Child, his father's favourite pub in the City. What's the big idea? his father had asked. A wild goose chase?

The mere prospect of leaving had glamorised everything: the yellow ashtrays gleaming in the pub's stolen daylight, the dark wood tables freshly wiped down by the barmaid, a fingerprint of swirled droplets left behind.

Normally Jackson was immune to his father's ageing, but that day, with the knowledge of a lengthy parting ahead, his face had looked overweight and gaunt at the same time, the cheeks hanging down in tapering sections, the eyes harried and dark.

A great hiss came from the kitchen. A slab of meat being thrown on a skillet? The sound went on, adjusted its pitch, and Jackson realised it was a tap running.

Didn't I tell you about it in a letter? From Belize? I knew a chap over there who was full of it all.

Why couldn't he talk plainly to his father? He tried, every time, and every time his words formed themselves into stock phrases.

But lost cities, old boy? His father had blurted out his high-pitched laugh reserved for friendly scoffing.

One lost city. La Joya. There was this civilisation in the cloud forest, the Chachapoyans. All the chroniclers talk about them. That chap in Belize, my friend out there, Connolly, you remember, he showed me the ropes. We visited a lot of ruins together.

His father had let out a sound that was both a grunt and a laugh.

It sounded lamentable. A man with nothing to his name, running off like this. But the only thing that had lifted him out of his blighted months in London had been picking up the old copy of Prescott's history of the conquest of Peru that Connolly had given him. He'd been encouraged to rest, to take it easy. But it had been bad advice. He needed the opposite. At the Royal Geographical Society he'd found the village of Choctamal on a Peruvian army map. It had been good, too, to go to the British Library day after day to read about the region. Through those weeks and months it had brought him back to life.

His father sighed wearily. It can be hard leaving the army, he said. But it's over a year now. You need to put all that behind you.

A wave of doubt or fear moved through Jackson. The army had been his father's idea from the start. After the calamitous, precocious sprees that had destroyed his school exams, he'd had no choice.

Never been so grateful for anything. Army taught me how to live, his father added, draining his gin.

This was where his father was happiest, with his face sagging into the tinkle of ice and gin.

Outside a flock of pigeons gusted before them as they walked back to his father's office, the older Mr. Small flapping his arms into the sleeves of his coat. The afternoon was cool and clouded.

You know, there isn't that much to life, Jackson, when all is said and done. We may think we want this and that—big things—but in the end it's the little things that matter. Day in, day out. Your focus gets smaller.

Those were always the best moments of their lunchtimes, the stroll back to the office with that after-lunch glow that made the two of you feel like masters of life. They had fallen into step.

His father's voice went low, adopting a throw-away note. Best thing is to settle down and get on with it.

Jackson had watched his father cross the road and disappear into a doorway, the revolving door spinning slowly after him, and wondered why he did not have a similar office to go into.

He lifted his pan off the fire with his shirt cuff and ate fast. The food went down hot and clear to his stomach where it burned out more space. It was mostly gone already and would never fill him. He realised he had forgotten about the crackers, fetched them, and made himself slow down.

After supper he filled his smaller pan with water. The embers were winking like the lights of a city, and hissed when he set the pan down. He rolled a cigarette, then lifted one of the logs, figuring there was just enough glow on it, and leaned the tip of the cigarette against the dimming wood. A flood of lightheadedness moved through him. He shifted off his rock and lay back on the ground. How did you describe something like this, he wondered, and who to? He thought of his mother. He could see her frowning over a letter at her kitchen table, clutching her dressing gown together at the neck and thinking he was a fool, not understanding him at all. It was beyond her that he should be in South America, supposedly looking for a lost city. How could South America possibly be relevant? His father would say, Splendid, a toast. He would be pickled already and worried somewhere in the back of his mind about his son: not quite above board.

But he was away from all that. All he had to do was keep his mind on the tasks at hand.

Into his thoughts stepped the light crunch of footsteps. He thought nothing of them. They ceased. He lay still on his back, wondering what stars would be out if you could see them. Then he snapped himself upright and turned round.

A man was standing at the reach of the fire's glow. Jackson stared at the half-lit figure for a moment, his heart knocking.

Pase, he said out loud. His voice sounded strange. He might have been talking to no one. *Adelante*.

He couldn't see the face. An Indian. He wore the short baggy white trousers and smock of the highlands. A long cloth belt trailed down one side. Jackson was relieved. An Indian would have his own business.

Adelante, señor, he repeated.

The man came forward briskly with the light foot of the mountain Indians. He was an old man, his face heavily wrinkled, and he wore a poncho of indeterminate colour, much faded, ragged with moth holes. He had a bundle tied to his back.

He held out his hand in a closed fist—a gesture of humble greeting. Jackson held the fist. It was light and cool. The man slumped down on the other side of the dying fire. Only when he dropped to the ground, his legs collapsing beneath him like folded crutches, did Jackson see the other, smaller, figure standing some way off, where the light illuminated nothing but a pair of glazed eyes.

Ven, Jackson called, pronouncing it *beng* in the local accent.

It was a boy. He advanced a few steps then stood still, mouth half open, and stared either at Jackson or at the fire.

Ven, Jackson repeated, beckoning.

The child swayed slightly. He too wore a poncho, and carried something in the crook of his arm.

The fire pulsed silently. When the boy stepped forward his small feet crunched neatly on the desert. He dropped into a crouch near the old man, and at once began stroking what he was carrying, which Jackson now saw was a cat, its small head protruding from the side of the boy's poncho. The boy scratched the head and the stiff ears.

The presence of the cat vaguely unnerved Jackson. Why bring a cat through the desert? Cats weren't pets out here. They were even less domestic than the local dogs, who were left to scavenge the garbage dumps and alleys, alternately tossed scraps from doorways and driven off with volleys of stones. Cats fared even worse.

Would the cat like to eat? Jackson asked.

The boy hugged the animal close and averted his eyes, which switched off like two lights.

Jackson pushed his dirty pan across the sand toward the boy. There was nothing left but maybe lickings for a cat. The boy remained hunched over, listening but apparently determined not to look. Then quite suddenly he grabbed the pan and set it down between his knees. The cat emerged from among the folds of the poncho and shivered in the firelight. It was a small tabby, very skinny, its ribs visible. It took a couple of shaky steps, stretched, yawned, shook itself, then contentedly buried its head in the pan.

Would you like tea? Jackson asked the old man.

He added more water to the pan on the fire, sprinkled in more tea from a plastic bag, two spoons of coarse sugar from another bag. You took it off just as it began to boil properly and let it stand: the camp method. The leaves would sink and you could pour the liquid off.

The man said, *Cigarrillo.*

Jackson handed over his tobacco and papers. He saw then that the man had lost all the fingers of one hand. It was a stump like a wooden club.

Jackson took back the tobacco. I'll do it, he said.

The Indian watched. Jackson was aware of the fineness and

paleness of his own fingers, the wisps of hair on the knuckles, clearly not those of a *campesino*. He had a short beard too, from not having had the opportunity to shave. None of the Indians could manage that.

¿Estados Unidos? The old man's voice was sibilant, light, the voice of a man who worked in the fields.

Inglaterra, Jackson told him.

The old man gave no sign of having heard or understood. *¿Inginiero?* he asked.

Jackson shook his head, licked the cigarette paper.

Minero entonces. Miner then, as if the matter were concluded.

Jackson handed the cigarette across the fire and steered a log back into place with his boot, pushing it under the pan, which tilted up.

The log crackled appreciatively. He let it burn a while then held it for the Indian to light up from. He got the cigarette going with a single powerful draw.

The man was barefoot. Usually they wore sandals made of old tyre treads. His feet were crossed in front of the fire. You would not have thought them feet. They were gnarled and calloused beyond recognition, knotted like old rope, like the tree roots people sold at the roadside in the capital, dried and varnished for suburban commuters and tourists.

Without moving his feet the old man reached for a twig and drew three circles on the ground with it. He said, *Perú, Inglaterra, Estados Unidos*, pointing to them one after another.

Jackson nodded. How did you correct a map like that?

They fell silent. One of the logs hissed. The man smoked his cigarette with his good hand. They were an odd pair, these two. The old man's feet gleamed in the firelight and his face was a mass of wrinkles with the two darknesses of the eyes. The boy sat on his haunches, mouth agape. In the fire-glow Jackson could see that his lips were cracked and peeling from the Andean sun, his eyes shining like marbles. He sat staring in a state of either fascination or torpor.

After a while the man looked at Jackson so that the glint of fire-light was visible on his black pupils.

Muy guapo, he said to Jackson: very handsome. His mouth opened slightly in a kind of sneer. *Eres muy guapo, hombre.*

Jackson looked away. His heart started pounding. He fought down the feeling, and waited a moment.

So you're looking for gold, the Indian said.

Jackson shrugged. There were always stories of lost gold in this country.

More or less, he answered. From here I go to Chachapoyas.

Mucho tesoro allí, the man said. Much treasure there.

¿Verdad? True?

Of course. Otherwise why would the *señor* be going?

Jackson smiled. I'm looking for a lost city.

Las ciudades perdidas, the Indian said, using the definite article, as if he had heard of them. Over in Chachapoyas.

Chachapoyas was across the mountains in another world.

The pan rattled softly. Jackson stirred it with the knife. With the only light coming from below, from the fire, the interior of the pan was invisible: a blackness against whose wall the knife knocked, carried round by the current he had started. *Tap-tap.* He let it dangle lightly from his fingers. This was how the Indians did things: lightly. They held objects lightly, walked lightly, almost floating over rocks and forest floor, they even climbed mountains lightly.

Jackson had to guess when the tea was done. He pulled down his shirt cuff and picked up the pan by the edge and splashed out a cupful into his tin mug. He set it down in front of the old man.

The Indian sat quite still, his face bronze in the firelight and lined with shadow. He didn't touch the mug.

Té, Jackson said. *¿Le gusta?*

Le gusta el té, the man stated, not understanding: you like the tea.

Jackson drank from the pan. He had to blow a lot and wait.

The Indian didn't touch the cup.

¿Cómo se llama? Jackson tried.

The Indian said nothing.

Jackson waited a moment, then said, *Me llamo Sinbad.*

The old man smoked, uninterested.

Jackson stood. He needed to pee. He would leave the pan to cool a moment. His legs were stiff in a good well-walked way. He went behind a rock, treading carefully, blind in the complete darkness. When he let his stream go it rustled on the dry ground.

A faint chink sounded from the camp—the Indian putting down the mug, probably.

When he got back, the Indian was drinking from the pan. The white cup was standing on Jackson's side of the fire.

Jackson picked it up, still full.

The man said, *Para el señor.*

Deference, blind and unquestioning. The señor must have the cup. The lowly Indian could drink from the pan. Jackson shrugged and raised it to his lips.

Nothing like tea. He had once stopped his platoon to make a cup in the middle of the Belize forest. No sooner had they begun to drink than mortar shells started coming in. Guatemalan rebels. Somehow he had been sure, with the tea's confidence inside him, that some other platoon was taking the fire. Not one of his men even looked jumpy. They all sat slurping from their canteens until they finished. The shelling ceased and they moved on. The tea had saved them, they agreed afterward. If they had started scrabbling around and running for it they might have been noticed.

The Indian asked for another cigarette. Jackson rolled one and the man put it inside his smock like a valuable.

Where are you headed? he asked.

Guadalupe.

It was as he had thought. The old man was making for the town a few miles down the valley.

Buying and selling?

The old man hid his face in the pan of tea.

It must have been quite a route he had come down, scaling the cliffs of the high canyon. But there were always paths in impossible places out here, relics of the Incas' network of roads.

He felt he ought to conclude things somehow, send him on his way or offer him a bed, had he had one. But there was nothing you could do with a stranger who drifted in after dark for no reason that he would make clear.

Jackson announced: Well, I'm going to bed.

He drained the last drops from his cup, tied up the food bag, placed it in the pack and carried the now light pack into the mouth of the tent, leaving the pan and cup and spoon out by the fire. He took his knife into the tent with him. The man would be gone in the morning. He would be selling guinea-pig fat and the little mountain chillies. It was odd that he travelled alone but for the boy. Normally the Indians went with a mule or a llama at least. But after all, he himself was alone too. Perhaps the man had a grand-daughter in the town who was marrying. Something like that, something simple. There were no complicated reasons in this country.

Jackson lit the candle and unlaced his boots. He felt uneasy with the Indian just outside, but it had happened before like that. It was the fire that drew anyone who happened to be passing through an empty land at night.

In the morning Jackson would get to work, marking down everything he could. It was incredible what you could do if only you had the will. Every city had an office of the National Institute of Culture, for example, where a *superintendente* would sit smoking—Marlboros if he could afford them, Broadways if he couldn't—who would gladly let you rifle his drawers full of maps and plans of the known archaeological sites, peering over your shoulder and asking questions like, were you married and how much did it cost to get to London. Life was like that. It offered you one little discovery, one insight, and it was up to you to follow through. He had visited four sites so far in the northern country. All he had left was the hardest part, up in the mountains. He tried not to think about it. If he did he would not sleep. If it happened, if he found the lost city, it would be like raising Atlantis from the waves. Just as Connolly had said.

He unbuttoned his shirt and pulled on a singlet for the night: no mosquitoes in this land of dust and rock. Here, he thought, dust took the place of water. You washed pans with it, it lay in plains like lakes where the hills came down, it fell into ripples, it flowed down the mountains. He stifled a thrill at feeling the cool cotton of his sleeping bag against his bare limbs. Something about it made him think of his sister. He had had his last lunch with her the day before he flew. He already had his ticket then; his traveller's cheques folded in his jacket. He had planned a fine farewell: lunch at Simpsons or the Red Fort, but she had had only an hour and told him he'd be needing his money. He sent the waiting taxi away and they ate in a pub off the Tottenham Court Road round the corner from her office.

At least have a good time, she said. It doesn't matter about anything else. You need to put everything behind you. You need to learn how to do that.

He hadn't known what to say.

And it doesn't matter if it turns out to be a wild goose chase, she urged. That was the family line: he was on a wild goose chase.

Just enjoy yourself. Don't be too—too serious, she said with a smile.

Outside the Indian coughed, a low sound, delightful to the ear when you were tucked up in bed. He reached for the big book and slid it under his rolled trousers to amplify the pillow. Books, clothes: it was good for things to have two uses. You needed a fraction of what you thought.

A wave of exhaustion moved through him, an irresistible fatigue. It surprised him. He found he couldn't move his feet, nor his legs, so profound was his weariness. His head swam. He tried to lean over to blow out the candle but all his muscles seemed to melt into the ground. He dropped into an abyss of unconsciousness.

3

Something heavy was lying on him: furs, animal skins. His arms struggled against them, broke free, forced them down to his waist, and he kicked his legs clear. He began to pour sweat, as if every pore had been waiting for the open air. He was somewhere very dark. He was quickly soaked.

He sat up. Something hit his head from behind. A ram, butting him senseless. It was coming again. He lay down out of its way. His head sank into something soft: foam, or a pile of clothes waiting for the laundry. Somewhere a cat might like to sit. His head sank and sank.

When he woke again his trousers were round his ankles, his shirt bunched round his neck. He was outside his sleeping bag, half on, half off it. He was warm, terribly warm. In panic he reached behind his back. His underpants were still on. He ran a hand over his buttocks: smooth as a baby's, no telltale crust, he was all right. He sat up. His head reeled and he dropped back.

Walls of pale green around him. He tried to sit up again, shifting his legs, which were stuck as though in a viscous liquid, pushing himself onto his elbows. He spilled forward over his legs, eyes closed, and dragged himself toward a crack of light. He pushed his head out, the rest of his body bent double behind him, still in the green oven. The open air was cool on one cheek, the ground warm against the other.

The third time he woke, his jaw hurt. He shifted his head but that only made it worse. He lifted his face and realised he was sleeping in the open. A fierce ache wheeled around his brain, like a sling that had been waiting to strike. He pulled himself to his knees and discovered he was half naked. Squatting, he managed to tug up his trousers before a spasm of retching caught him. Bile splashed on a rock, strings swung from his lip. He shook them loose and heard someone groan, the sound resonating in a cave. Must have been him. He got to his feet and fell against a boulder, clutching at it to keep himself upright. That was the way. Get the sleep and pain to drain out of his head. He turned himself round, got his back against the rock and stayed there, giving his weight to the stone. His legs bent but didn't give.

A pan with a black bottom stood inverted a few feet away beside a fire pit. A tin mug lay on its side. High above, in the white sky, two birds turned slowly like lazy flies. He had an idea: a cup of tea. Tea would help. That was the next step.

Two charred logs lay by the ash pit. Suddenly, as if he had fully recovered, he lurched to the mouth of the green tent standing nearby, fumbled at the door flaps and stuck his head inside.

Gone. All gone. There was his sleeping bag, and his boots lying apart on their sides, the remains of a candle also. Nothing else. The tent had been cleaned out. He backed out. A spoon gleamed in the dust. He ran off past the boulders of the encampment, took a few heavy steps downhill and stopped. The whole silent valley lay before him: empty. Nothing moved. Just rocks and the pale sand reaching away to a white wall of sky. He looked up again. Only one bird was up there now, turning on its slow circle like the hand of a clock.

He searched among the rocks. His pack had gone and everything in it, the books too, everything but his sleeping bag, the tent itself and the pan, mug and spoon.

His feet hurt. He found his boots, sat on the ground and laced them, and let out a shout. Then he remembered and reached down inside his left sock to feel the once-crisp, now soft edge of folded paper: his emergency hundred-dollar traveller's cheque. At least that was still there. He shook the sleeping bag. Nothing fell out. He crawled into the tent and ran his hands all over the crumpled ground sheet, pushing it flat so he could see what was on it: nothing. Outside the door he found a half-full water bottle. Further away a can of tomatoes lay on its side, its contents spilled on the ground, already colourless.

What about the camera? That had gone too. What would he do? He'd have to make do with his sketches and rough maps. Thank God he had sent some films home already.

It was best not to think. He would make tea, then he would think. He poured water into the pan, rinsed it, poured more. He fetched kindling, found the matches in his pocket, built a base of small pieces of wood, laid the remains of the two charred logs over it, gave them time, watched the flames begin to lick. Then he realised that not even the little bag of tea was left. The old man hadn't been inscrutable, he had been stupid. An exercise book and some tea, a passport, a half-read novel without a cover: all useless. He let the water heat anyway, he'd sip it from the pan. He retched again.

He too had been stupid, apparently. You could trust or not trust. On balance it was better to trust, he thought. Either way, a random stupidity could fall at any time.

His watch had gone and without the sun nothing gave away the time, no shadow, no brighter patch in the sky. The even sky above, the deathless, lifeless desert all around.

Far away down the hillside, Jackson couldn't say how far, he made out something blue, or black, a dark shape quivering in the heat. At first he thought it must be a vehicle. Or a dead animal. He began to walk toward it. He imagined a dead cow bent up on the ground, though he had not seen a cow in weeks, except one tied up in a suburban garden of all places, a sleek zebu munching on a lawn.

More likely it was a dead horse.

The object was closer than Jackson guessed. It ceased to be blue as he approached and became dark green. Jackson broke into a run, almost tripping over, even now worried someone might conjure the thing from under his nose.

It was his rucksack. He stood it up and tugged open the mouth with both hands: empty, a litter of sand. He scrabbled through the side pockets, found a pencil stub, string, the broken lighter—the old man must have tried it.

Jackson picked up the rucksack, lifting it high above his head, and brought it down with a thump on a rock. It lay limply where it landed. He walked in a circle, kicking aside loose stones. He let out a wail, dropped to the ground and clutched his head in both hands.

When he looked up, the boy who had been with the old man was sitting a few paces away on a rock.

Jackson's chest was heaving. Every time he wiped the sweat out of his eyes with his sleeve it ran into them again. His breathing came and went noisily. He waited for it to quieten.

Where is he? he said.

The boy looked straight ahead, his nostrils twitching.

Where did he go?

Jackson's mind was racing. Of all the dumb things to do, to rob him and then leave the boy. What did this mean? Why leave the boy?

Hombre malo, the boy said. His voice was fine, clear, like a chorister's—a choirboy seated there on a rock in the desert. *Hombre malo*. Bad man.

Jackson squatted in front of the boy and put a hand on his knee. The leg was so slight, so light. Jackson couldn't help feeling a flutter of something like pity.

Where did he go? he tried again. Which way? Up or down?

The boy shrugged.

El viejo, he's not your papa?

The boy shook his head.

Who's your papa?

The boy remained silent, just breathed and stared at his hands in his lap.

Do you have a papa?

The boy barely shook his head, a mere twitch of negation.

Where's your mama?

The boy didn't respond at all.

Jackson felt ridiculous, squatting in the middle of nowhere and interrogating a small boy about his family. He exhaled sharply and patted the boy's leg as a way of removing his hand.

So he's your grandfather?

The boy shrugged, hands limp in his lap. He's not my grandfather. *Señor Papaluca es hombre malo.*

Papaluca?

Sí, señor.

Where did he go?

The boy said nothing.

Why is he bad?

The boy shrugged decisively. *Es así.* That's how it is. Or: that's how he is.

Jackson blew out his lips. He climbed on a boulder and gazed down the hillside. The whole slope sparkled like water, like jewels. He hadn't noticed the sun coming out. The *garúa* season was supposed to be drawing to a close, but he hadn't expected to witness it. He considered that he still had his notebook and the money in his sock, and his sleeping bag and tent, as well as his cooking pot. He'd have to be careful about the lack of a passport.

He called to the boy, What's your name?

Ignacio. The answer came clear and quiet in the stillness.

Well, come and help me.

He walked back up the hillside to the camp. The boy followed at a distance.

It took a while for Jackson to lose the feeling that there must be something else he could do, some other action to take under the circumstances, but finally he packed up what was left, dropping it into the gaping rucksack, whistled to the boy, and headed off down the hill again, with the rim of the pan digging into his back. He felt better as he started to walk, noting that he was still alive, that the old man might easily have killed him, might even have intended to. The drug, whatever it had been, left a kind of coolness in his limbs as it dissipated. The more he came round, the cleaner he felt.

He stopped and looked back. The sun sang on the rocks. The boy had just detached himself from the scattering of prehistoric boulders, and was following, stepping down the slope with the light bouncy tread Jackson in his heavy boots envied. The boy had pulled his hat low over his ears and was holding something in the crook of his arm.

2 · Vulture City.

1

The *garúa* came back. It rolled in across the sea, a milk-skin of cloud that turned the sun overhead into a papery blur.

Jackson had bought the boy a comic book. The two of them lay reading on the roof of the Hotel Las Americas. From the steel hut housing the stairwell in a corner of the roof Jackson could hear now and then a door's clunk echoing below, followed by the sound of footsteps. But otherwise at two in the afternoon the city was in its torpor. In the canyons of the streets all the traders had rattled down their shutters, the *micro* buses had been put to doze in yards, and the pedestrians had gone out of the daylight. Although there was no sun it was still hot—a heat without teeth but with firm gums. You had to sit it out. Nothing moved. The car horns had fallen silent. The streets were closed up as if for a holiday. A pall of stillness hung over the afternoon. And the *garúa* hung like a shroud over the grey desert, the grey city.

Among the broken crates and brown newspapers strewn in the gutters three floors below, a litter of black banana and mango skins, and plastic bags that had once held fruit juice, released an odour of sweet rot into the air detectable even here, thirty feet up on the hotel roof. Now and then a bare-ribbed dog moved among the rubbish, paused to sniff. Jackson could see over the rooftops of the city, some hung with ghostly laundry, some littered with rusty junk, but most bare. In a far corner of the hotel roof an old mongrel bitch sat scratching herself, grunting with the effort.

Above, against the white sky, vultures turned like tea leaves in a just-stirred cup. They had forsaken the glinting landslides of rubbish on the nearest hills to inspect the city's carcass. It was a dead city in the wastes of afternoon, disturbed now and then by the throaty gurgle of a truck pluming up from the concrete grid of streets. A dirty geometric city—the reverse of what the natives would produce: their haphazard villages were immaculately clean, they swept the very dirt outside their huts.

Jackson moved from the parapet wall to his shirt, which lay spread out on the cement. He had a book with him, but the enervation of the afternoon made concentration hard. The stillness was absolute. Just he and the boy slumped on either side of the square roof, both of them reading, or trying to, he a book and the boy thumbing slowly through his comic. Periodically he would hold it up close to his face for a long time.

He had done that when Jackson first gave it to him, and Jackson had had to show him which way up to hold it. This had depressed him. At the time, he had just bought the boy a banana *licuado* and had noticed something like a smile, a sigh of satisfaction, after the boy had sucked the straw to a dry crackle. That smile had been virtually the first expression to cross the boy's face. He was no more demonstrative than the ancient idols in the museums, with their long cheeks and vacant eyes. And then he had gone and held the comic upside down. How was Jackson supposed to reach across such a gulf of miscomprehension? And the boy wouldn't leave him, or offer any explanation why he was with him.

Now he seemed to have got the hang of cartoons at least. No matter that he couldn't read the captions. He'd make what he wanted of the story. He sat back against the parapet wall, his legs drawn up close with the magazine resting on them. The trousers, shortened by the posture, barely made it over his knees. The boy's legs were dark, smooth, thin, in a way, elegant.

Jackson attempted and failed to get absorbed by his book. He felt both lethargic and excited. There was something thrillingly dismal about being stranded in this strange city, so stiflingly warm, so still, and about being a passportless foreigner in the uniform drabness of this desert. The thrill, he assumed, was largely just to be where Connolly had been. He had unquestionably found a site Connolly had visited. Those geometric incisions on the rocks were precisely the ones Connolly had sketched, and which he said he had seen in the highlands. As was that jaguar-face with the fangs: proof perhaps that the Chachapoyans had held an empire that reached into the lowlands. Supposing he did get into the mountains and bush-whacked into the cloud forest, did find the right ruins, found the appropriate carvings, what then? But the point was to walk, machete in hand, into a lost city.

Ideally, he would have gone back to the rocks near the Caballo Muerto and finished documenting the site. But now, without enough money in his money-belt, it would have to wait until another time.

The kid was silent, happy just to sit around saying nothing, more or less doing nothing. It was alarming. And there was the question of his clothes. For some reason it seemed wrong to Jackson to let the child wander around town in his stiff Indian mountain clothes. They were all he had—a pair of bellbottoms nine inches too short, made of stiff fabric which had not been washed in so long it had acquired a colour all its own, a composite of beige, grey and brown, and a loose smock which would evidently, judging by the inside of it, have once been white, and on top the poncho, a thing of dusty hue and weak brown stripes. His hair was a mess of stiff thatch. All in all he was surrounded by stiffness: the chap-like trousers, the ancient firmness of the poncho, the bunch of hair. The boy fitted into the dry landscape like some feral animal, a creature bred for it.

The first day in the city they had gone to a Western clothes store where Jackson purchased purple nylon slacks, a yellow T-shirt and sneakers for the boy. The store was a shabby chain called Palacio

Torres, and the entire wardrobe cost seven dollars. Only afterward did he ask himself why he had bought them. The answer wasn't obvious. The boy's highland clothes had probably lasted him two or three years already, night and day, and would probably be good for the same again until he outgrew them. They built durably in the Andes—houses, tracks, religions, clothes, none had changed since before the Incas, since no one knew when.

But it had seemed important to Jackson that the boy have new clothes. Perhaps it was just lack of imagination: what else could he do for him? Or inconspicuousness. They stood out enough as it was, a tall gringo with an Indian boy. How much more if the boy went about in costume too.

Several times Jackson almost went to the police. Not to report his stolen belongings—what could that achieve?—but to hand the boy over. Presumably he had to be missing from somewhere. Somebody somewhere must be aware that he was gone. But each time he baulked.

He thought of going down to the market and handing him over to the first sympathetic-looking market woman. Or he could try the bus station, hoping to find a driver who might happen to recognise the face from some mountain village, or at least the region of the boy's dress. Except that he suspected the clothes were generic Andean, could come from anywhere up and down the mountain range. But whenever he thought of parting with the boy something held him back—not exactly pity or sympathy, more an attachment to the absurdity of the situation.

And he had been thinking about his choices: he could blow all the money he had left in getting down to the embassy in Lima in the hope of being issued with a new passport. He didn't know if they would do that. He could call home and ask them to wire him some money—except he couldn't possibly face asking. Or he could just press on, on a shoestring, find out if the city was really there, push himself onward and through and finally break out, maybe, into some kind of daylight for good.

But sooner or later he knew that he would have to bow under the yoke and do the thing he had been avoiding.

2

Jackson had met Connolly on his first tour. Connolly had been at the garrison in Belize for two years. He was a quiet man and kept his distance from people.

On leave Connolly liked to visit ruins. Often he'd cross the border into Guatemala, where he would talk to the local farmers and get them to take him to whatever ancient houses, *casas antiguas*, they knew of. He started to take Jackson along with him, and the two would find their way to what looked like rocky outcrops in the hills, hidden by foliage, but which would turn out to be carefully fitted masonry once they began cutting and pulling away the vegetation. It was exciting, not so much for the stone walls and overgrown plazas themselves but because people had built them. Ancient people had once been here; these were their remains, hidden for hundreds of years. Jackson and Connolly would grin at each other, their pulses racing, as they uncovered them. Then they'd set to sketching the ruins on graph paper, attempting to photograph them and trying to fix the coordinates and record just where they were. Jackson would also draw pictures of them in charcoal or pencil. Sometimes he'd get carried away and do more drawing than anything else.

But these sites were titbits for Connolly.

Connolly's favourite books were Prescott's pair, recounting the conquests of Mexico and Peru, and he would read passages aloud to Jackson. That's real writing for you, he'd say. There's no adventure story like these.

Nor was there anything like adobe at night, with earth above, around and under you, while a peasant family slept under goat-wool blankets. In each village there'd be a little church with a tin-capped pair of steeples, red mud walls, a lofty cross on the pitch.

On one trip they walked into a sleepy plaza swimming with the shadows of eucalyptus trees. Jackson was all for taking off their rucksacks and resting in the shade, but Connolly said it was better to present themselves at once. He was right too. Children with wide black eyes and snot crystals under their noses from the altitude came out to stare at them, giggling and holding their hands up to their faces as if shy. Soon they had a posse of children following them, making the arrival of the two gringos alarmingly conspicuous.

A man in a bowler hat and an old green suit approached them, an Indian, his face folded and dark. *Buenos días, señores*, he offered, welcoming them formally in a depressed-sounding drawl, as if it were burdensome to speak.

He took them to the *corregidor*, who was just then conducting a council meeting in the old Palacio de Justicia. Five men in dusty suits and crumpled bowlers were seated at the end of a long bare room, smoking cigarettes. On the floorboards between them stood an unlabelled bottle of clear liquor. They offered Jackson and Connolly a shot from a glass that had been doing the rounds. The shadows of trees outside twitched across the dusty floor, turning the dust silver. Sunlight drew beams across the blue smoke of the cigarettes and, with the glow of the *aguardiente* in his chest, Jackson felt the afternoon become charmed. The crowing of roosters, the sudden flare-ups of barking from the village dogs: there were no sounds here save natural ones, no light save candle and kerosene, moon and sun.

The *corregidor*, with short silver hair and bony cheeks, spent a long time inscribing their names in a ledger. The other men gathered round to watch the solemnities of the pen. Then he offered the two foreigners his daughter's empty house for a few days.

The house was a small adobe on a cobbled lane. It had one room, two doors, a window and two small beds in opposite corners. You fetched water in a metal jug from the chilly stream at the back. Jackson stripped off in the sunshine outside and splashed himself down, then dried off with a thin towel. Afterward he spread out his sleeping bag on his bed, feeling thoroughly delighted. This was the way to live—trekking across highlands with a friend who knew the ropes, being four years older, all of twenty-three. Connolly knew how to live. He did not let small things get him down.

You never heard him complain. If buses were late or roads closed or truck tyres punctured; if you did not know whether a region was safe, Connolly was not put off. He suggested you go all the same. It would take a lot to make him change his plans; equally it might take very little. One day it might be raining in the mountains and he might suggest you stay in a café all morning drinking soup and coffee, smoking Marlboros.

Jackson lay on the bed in the small house, relaxing in his cleanliness after the day's hot walk, basking in the glow left on his skin by the icy stream water. Connolly was sitting up against the wall on his bed, smiling at him, with a big old book open on his knees. He tossed Jackson a cigarette, and after it a book of matches. Something happened to Jackson then. For a second it was as if he had been in this sunlit room before with this man. The way Connolly smiled at him from across the room, while he too smoked: there was a knowingness in it. He knew Jackson inside out, and Jackson was happy that he did. It hit him then: perhaps what he felt for this man was something like love.

From the open window soft sunlight flooded the room. But all the power had gone out of it for the day. Jackson felt slightly sad for the sun. But up here in the highlands, all that mattered was happiness. Judgement abated. You loved whom you loved. Human life made its simple sense because no one got in its way. The *corregidor* and his family, his plump whispering wife who bustled in with glass bowls of corn stew and flat bread, the pleasure of smoking with the door of the house open to the evening as the sun turned the walls orange and the moon rose like an aluminium coin—you knew these pleasures lay in store. While you waited there was peace in your midriff.

There's silver in that hill, the *corregidor* had told them when he showed them the house, pointing at the hill behind. I own it and if I had mining equipment I would excavate. You don't have equipment, señores?

No, but why not come back one day and get rich? It was possible.

But Connolly had other ideas. Listen to this, he said from his bed, and read from the book in his lap. Page two hundred and seventy-one, footnote two. You see? It's just a footnote. *The Inca kept Chachapollo maidens in his harem, renowned for their harmonious voices and fair skin. Chachapollo is said by García de Vega to have been a principality in the northern kingdom, once powerful, adorned amid its mountainous cloud forest with temple-cities of great splendour, which the Incas had sacked by the time the conquistadors arrived. No trace was ever found of this once great people, except for their single mighty fortress, Kuelap, which had evidently availed them little against Huayna Capac's forces. Their fabled wealth appears to have eluded Inca and conquistador alike.*

Prescott, Connolly said. See what I mean? I'm going back, I really am. You better come too. It'll be the find of the century. What do you say? I tell you I got to it last time, just the edge of it. A huge city, a metropolis miles wide. La Joya. No one has ever found it.

Connolly had been in Peru the year before, looking for the Chachapoyan ruins. He had been down three times in all.

He and Connolly lived well side by side. After they'd been to archaeological sites Jackson would tear the pictures he'd made out of his sketchbook and give them to Connolly, who would pin them to the wall above his bed at the barracks in Belize. Sometimes he did watercolours too. The thought of going down to Peru to search for a lost city with Connolly was dizzying.

For the next two days they explored a big old temple two hours' walk from their borrowed house. Jackson did a series of sketches that were his best yet. He could feel something magical in the geometry of the stones, in the broken pyramids with their corbelled steps, and under his pencil and pen the place seemed to grow more palpable. He began to feel that there was a mystery to the old edifices, some secret of space and shape unknown to Western architecture. They affected the mind more deeply than you'd think possible.

He sat watching the distant hills beyond the ruins bloom yellow in the late sun, then turn to smoke. They seemed to crumble like sponge cake, as if some giant's fingers were breaking them up, releasing something like a fragrance of herbs that he sensed in his lungs. Then the giant breaking the hills was Jackson himself; he had giant hands, and they reached out and touched the hills. He tried to shake off whatever strange mood had come over him, but it wouldn't go. A glassy vision took hold of him. At the same time it was as if a fire had been lit in his chest. The wonderful feeling welled up and glowed in him.

When the time came to go back to the lowlands, over the border into English-speaking Belize, Jackson didn't feel disappointed. The descent enchanted him: the smell of rain in the jungle air, of hot-house verdure, rotten fruit, rivers, of pigs in their little mud yards. Trucks would go by stacked with bananas on their way to market. There was music again blaring from every open shop, from the windows of the slow trucks. He was only nineteen; if he had learnt to live this well already, what might lie in store later? The two of them were young men who did not weigh more than they could lift. The slog through the rain of childhood was worth it, it had brought him to this.

In Belize, nothing much had been happening. There were two monthly exercises in the jungle, and some parade work, but the colonel didn't ask more than was necessary. Jackson and Connolly had their moments. Sometimes they went out to the cays for a night. Jackson had never known a friendship like it: adventure, courage, and a kind of mutual goodwill, unspoken, non-exclusive, that filled him with confidence. Once Jackson had a brief romance with an English girl on Cay Caulker, and that too seemed blessed by the friendship with Connolly. He slept with her in a bamboo shelter on the beach, and he was able to make love without hesitation, without question, because of Connolly.

Then Jackson got hurt. They were on exercise along the Guatemalan border and hit on separatist rebels. Jackson happened to be on patrol with Connolly. They found a kind of crater to take cover in. Connolly reckoned it was an old Mayan plaza, just a small one. They were there when Jackson's leg got hit, by a piece of shrapnel, it turned out later.

Connolly had the field radio. He'd call for support in an hour or two, when things had quietened. Connolly shouldered him down the embankment then scrambled back up to keep an eye out.

Life or death, Jackson thought later, could boil down to a good recognition signal. Did you hold a rifle vertical or horizontal over your head. It was bad to make it diagonal, you might miss that in the midst of action. It was easy to make a mistake under duress. If you had been wounded and were lying behind a fallen rock and mortar shells were coming through the jungle, sending shrapnel bouncing off the rocks and showering you with leaves and bark and, meanwhile, the rain was pounding down, pouring over your face into your eyes, so that if you suddenly heard a crack and turned to see a figure snaking toward you on hands and knees, you blasted it before you knew what you had done, what with the pain making you crazy and unsure if you still had your leg or not. Before you knew it, your finger had squeezed, obliterating all risk with a burst of automatic fire. And it might be that even as you did it you had a dull misgiving in the heart of all the confusion and pain.

Jackson heard a rustle up above, where Connolly was, then silence. For a moment even the insects went quiet. Somewhere an animal fluted. In the far distance he could hear the hiss of cicadas. Gradually the tide of forest sounds flowed back in.

His leg was so numb he thought it had gone. He was abominably hot. But his leg was cold, cold. Night came. Another rainstorm arrived, a great roar overhead. For a while the canopy held it off, then it found its way through, and the ground became misty, pummelled with bouncing rain. Jackson was soaked in an instant. He wondered why Connolly did not come back down. He wondered when someone would come. He thought Connolly had left the radio on, had talked to base and someone would soon be flying in for them. In which case they ought to get going to meet the chopper at the river.

Then the roar of rain stopped, though the drops kept on clattering from the treetops. Where was Connolly? The drops stung Jackson's face. He imagined he was already back in bed, dry and warm. A woman was at his side. Who was she? Why was she holding his wrist? Would she give him a hot drink, a cup of tea?

He listened for a long time, then called out Connolly's name. War, if this was war, was strange. Stealth was everything. As a result, you could easily believe nothing was going on, that it was all in your mind. You could steal through the jungle and not encounter a whisper of an enemy.

No reply.

It was long past time to move. His leg was completely dead, until he started to crawl, whereupon his knee scalded him like boiling oil. But he had to get up the bank. Ground-thorns cut his knuckles, but he kept his rifle clutched tight, clawing his way up, dragging the useless leg.

Connolly was lying halfway to the top. Jackson fell on him telling himself he was alive, right up until he rolled Connolly over and his head fell back and there could be no doubt. A wave of elation swept through him at first. Connolly was taking him on a new trip. The elation was paper-thin and crumpled. Jackson retched. Connolly was soaked through. His cheek was cold. The ground reeled at Jackson and struck his face.

There was the pain in his leg again, and the coldness. He pulled himself up and sat with his back against Connolly, until he lurched away from the body and retched again.

Things like this are awfully hard, the colonel said. No comradeship like that of active service. First tour too. And you're young. All that guilt you're feeling. It can be awfully confusing. You were both coming under heavy fire. Whatever you thought you did, I can assure you, you didn't. It was their rounds the doctors found in him.

Jackson was in a glassy daze. He heard what the colonel said from the other side of his desk, and saw right through it. It was obvious the man said what he did for Jackson's benefit.

That's why we're sending you home. Get you sorted out. Compassionate leave for you, old chap. Close to family and friends. They'll sort you out in no time. Sunday evenings in the pub, all that.

The colonel's eyes moistened. He was saddened by what had happened, as well as by the thought, probably, that here he was living out his later days so far from home.

Have a pint of Hook Norton for me. Do you know it? Last of the smalls, they call it. Just right for you, eh?

Jackson swallowed. He did not want to risk speaking.

When he arrived at Heathrow he was sickened by the gloss on everything: on the floor tiles, the glass walkways, the magazines racked at the news-stands, the new cars outside with their boots cocked for luggage. It seemed that everything shone. Grief glistened on all things. His shoes squeaked. His legs felt cold. The bad one had stiffened again. Outside, the air gasped with steam. You could feel London like a distant thunder through the mist.

His father met him. Come on, Jacko. Jackson had not noticed him at first, standing beside the old brown Rover at the train station. A TC, the fancy model, but old now, old and sagging on its springs like a carriage. Come to take you home, son. Hop in. Give us your bag, there's a chap.

He had a smart black case. There was nothing in it worth transporting across the ocean. As he lifted the bag into the jaw of the car's boot he felt that it was the case of death and he had brought death with him.

His father chatted idly on the drive. They could use a stretch of the M25. Just finished the roadworks last month. Home in half an hour. You'll see. Jackson did not speak. The word *M25* caused him to shake with panic. What had he come back to? What had he come back as?

The wipers whined on the windscreen. That was England, whining wipers and cold windowpanes. And always feeling your clothes were not warm enough. Battling against draughts, always losing. Poor Connolly: the words drifted into his dead mind from somewhere, as if he had been conversing with someone. He doubled up, weeping into his hands. He heard himself. His sobs were whining too, like the wipers, and his hands were cold, he felt the dampness falling onto his trousers, and hated that he couldn't stanch it. His father's hand was on his shoulder. Jacko. Old boy. It's OK, he said as if to an animal, in a high, soft voice. But Jacko was not available for comment. What could be worse? Crying in the passenger seat of his father's car as they turned onto the new M25 in rainy October. Why had he had to come back in October, when the world was dying and he would die with it? Why was he being so weak? Poor Connolly: something else, think of something else, he must get this jag under control before they got home—a friend was a friend and war was war, the army was the army and you were a soldier, enough of this. He wiped his face on his sleeve, extracting a long thread of snot. He tried to wipe that away with the other sleeve, and only got both sleeves wet.

Here you go, his father said. A handkerchief appeared in his lap. You clean yourself up.

As soon as he saw his father's wife it started up again. He fled upstairs like an adolescent daughter, he thought, and buried his face in the pillow under the mock-Tudor beam of his bedroom. Metal window frames, radiators, thick white walls: he couldn't bear any of it.

Downstairs and out of the front door, up the gravel drive past the gate that was always open except when they went away to Cornwall in the summer, down the road through the rain and along the grassy verge. His leg was still sore, he felt it now in the wet, a dull ache. Long wet grass soaked his trainers in no time. His shirt darkened with rain. If he kept going he would reach the Four Corners. He might have a whisky or three. They would take dollars, surely. He passed a gate into a field. A field put to grass. That was what he needed. Not a bloody pub. He hopped over the gate and waded into the grass. The rain came down softly. In the distance he could hear the soft purr of cars on the bypass, unzipping the air.

He lay in the grass, spread-eagled himself face down, and pressed his face deep into the wet stalks. You could smell the mud. It was a good smell, a clean, honest smell. He breathed it in, breathed and wept for the wonderful, neglected smell, grateful to it for being there.

They found him as it was getting light. He woke to see men in yellow anoraks, and blue lights at the edge of the field in the grey dawn, the grass grey now and the sky bruise-mauve, and still the rain falling. His father was there too. Come on home, Jacko. But he didn't want to go home. Please, he said, and spoke without crying.

He spent the next three weeks in the centre. Daily consultations and group therapy. The doctor gave him boxes and boxes of little pills. A weekly check-up, a few months on the pills, and he'd be on his way.

But the regiment wouldn't have him back, not after a collapse like that. He found himself thrown back into the world with half his severance pay.

3

Later that first day, after the robbery—Jackson thought it must have been around noon, then looked and saw that it must have been much later, with the sun glittering above the hills, and realised he had forgotten about losing the morning—later, he saw another dark shape ahead. This one turned out to be his spare trousers. They lay in the dust as if hurriedly removed. He flapped them, gritty in his hands, and dropped them in the half-empty rucksack.

Funny how rock glittered in the desert, whereas up in the highlands it was dull and camouflaged. Down here the earth dazzled you like water. There was a painting in it somewhere.

When they left the valley of Caballo Muerto he had been afraid Ignacio wouldn't keep up with him. Quite the reverse. The boy skipped ahead tirelessly, often so far ahead Jackson thought he had gone off on his own. Then he would come upon him sitting on a rock, staring into space, dry as a bone, looking just like he always did—lips apart, eyes big and glazed and seemingly fascinated by nothing. How could these people do it, sit endlessly in the heat like lizards, while Jackson was sweaty, out of breath, his legs stiff?

Further down, he again found Ignacio sitting on a rock waiting for him and holding Jackson's black notebook, dusty and scuffed, in his lap. He took it from the boy's small hands.

Where did you find it?

But Ignacio didn't say. Only that Señor Papaluca had stolen it. *Lo robó Señor Papaluca.*

He asked where Papaluca was from. The boy waved an arm up toward the mountains and sang, ¡*Allá, allá!* with a falling second syllable like some bird's falling cry. Up *there*, up *there* . . .

They got to the bleached mud village of Guadalupe in the late afternoon. The sun blazed gold on the straw roofs and the walls were orange-gold like the walls the El Dorado–seekers had dreamed of. Ignacio led him off down a back street of rutted clay and stepped through a gap in a wall into a yard where an old woman sat in a spread of thick cotton skirts beside a limp fire. Smoke trailed into the air.

The old woman tipped back her head, as if wearing bifocals, revealing a chicken neck looped with chins, and said something in a whisper of Quechua. The boy went and sat in the shade of the wall. Jackson, feeling suddenly irritated by his helplessness, followed him, unable to think what else to do.

There followed a perplexing late afternoon and evening. It wasn't clear how the boy knew this household, or even if he did know it. Various people came and went, and to Jackson's several attempts to find out about the old man he received only mutterings and once, from a bright-faced man, an eager but impenetrable laugh.

Jackson wandered around the village attempting to make enquiries. It was hard. The village was half deserted, a place of unimaginable torpor, its spirit beaten flat by the desert sun, by poverty, by hopelessness. It might have been this way for hundreds of years. He had been struck time and again by the tidiness of Indian villages in the mountains. Down here it was as if the influence of coastal whites and their broken labourers had infected the spirit. Caballo Muerto was the right name for the region. Dead Horse Junction. A hopeless frontier stop, pitched on the far shore of meaning, a place some pioneer had ridden to only to die beside his gaunt horse, which in time died too.

Jackson wondered if this, precisely, was part of what he had come for himself—to pitch himself against meaninglessness. To find a place that matched his grief which had already changed, moved apart from him, turned into a distant weather, constant but remote. He knew it made no sense, had been beyond the evidence. The edge of his shame had dulled too. It was of no conceivable use here.

He longed for the rows of corn and potato surrounding the high villages, where men wrote out in straight lines on the curving earth their acceptance of the conditions of life. Those were good people to be among. One felt forgiven. Or no longer felt the need for forgiveness. He was glad he would be going back up there soon. Now it would have to be very soon, with his funds so limited.

In the village shop he bought a tin of corned beef for Ignacio's cat, and once they got down to town he let it sleep in the hotel room with them. It curled up by the boy's head at night, evidently a sick cat, uncurling only to stretch and lick its paws. Once in the middle of the night, sleepless, Jackson became aware of a gentle snoring in the darkness. He looked at the boy's sleeping face thinking it must be him, but in fact it was the cat purring. It opened a big eye and stared, aware of Jackson but not bothering to direct its gaze at him. Jackson had been touched. It struck him that that was all the boy had—the cat's pleasure at being with him.

What he wanted to do was leave Ignacio and go and talk to someone about him. But who, and could he leave the boy alone? Could he trust him with what was left of his own belongings, and also not to disappear? He knew, everyone knew, about the street kids of Latin America. He felt responsible already. But what did a passportless foreigner do with a stray orphan? He had found a certain pleasure in paying for the boy's fare on the pickup ride down to the town, and in buying him meals. The money felt well spent. He imagined paying for two seats on the bus up into the mountains, and that too seemed like a pleasant gesture in store.

Jackson's sister had a baby girl whom he had held now and then, but other than that he was pitifully unused to children. Children were everywhere, all over the world. They were the single most decisive fact of life on earth. Yet he had never really been with a child himself. Except when a child himself. Which wasn't the same thing at all.

Once, early, in their hotel room, with Ignacio on his own narrow strip of a bed just beyond the night table, Jackson lay on his bed with his sketchbook trying to get the precise shape of the rhomboid Inca arches. He drew several of them, while dawn turned the thin curtains a perforated blue. He heard the boy roll over, and by the sound could tell he was awake. He closed his book.

Thinking that the early morning might provoke a new candour, Jackson began in his soothingest voice: So tell me, Ignacio, where were you born? Adding, by way of example: I was born in St. Albans.

No sé, came the reply, swift and quiet and convincing. I don't know.

Jackson waited a little in the murk. *¿Y su mamá?* You don't know who she was?

Nobody told me, he said. Señora Papaluca, she made me work hard.

But she wasn't your mother?

No, señor, he exclaimed.

She was the wife of Señor Papaluca?

No sé. Could be she was his wife, his mother, his aunt, his sister. I don't know, señor.

Una vieja? Old?

Sí.

Jackson turned his head a little, but hearing the loud-seeming rustle on the pillow, he held still. Outside a bus gurgled thunderously in the depths of the street. He waited for it to dwindle.

And how long did you live with them?

No sé.

Which month did you arrive there?

No sé.

Where did they live?

Pachacamac.

Pachacamac de Santa Cruz?

In the mountains. In Ayacucho.

Ayacucho is far.

Ayacucho was in fact very far, some seven hundred kilometres to the south.

Sí, señor.

Jackson sighed. Don't call me señor. Call me Jackson. Or Sinbad. Whichever you like.

The boy was silent.

Jackson rolled over and let out a groan, which he hoped would sound informal and reassuring. He lay facing the boy, staring at the frayed, thin curtain.

What were you doing up there?

¿Qué?

Why were you up at Caballo Muerto?

¿Caballo Muerto, señor?

The place where you found me. Where I had my tent.

Sí, señor.

What were you doing there?

The boy, supine under his sheet, tipped his head toward the window. Señor Papaluca is a bad man, he answered.

Jackson waited. Nothing more came. What were you doing with him so far from Ayacucho?

The boy shrugged slightly, enough to make the sheet whisper. Then suddenly he broke out in a high defensive whine, a plaintive Andean style he must have learnt from some guardian: It's not my fault. *No es mi culpa.* Señor Papaluca was taking me down to the coast to sell me to the Indonesians, to a man with a ship who lived in a palace full of boys like me. He would make us work all day and night and give us only one bowl of rice a day and one cup of water.

Ignacio fell into sulky silence. He mumbled, *No es mi culpa*, again, then rolled completely away from Jackson and pulled the sheet up to his ears.

Jackson lay still, feeling stung. He didn't know what the boy really thought, but he understood what he meant.

I know it's not your fault. I'm glad you're here. *Soy feliz.*

He meant it. He had no idea how much of the boy's garbled talk was his own invention, how much the old man's, but he decided to believe the import of it.

Ignacio stayed as he was, sheet clamped over his ear. Jackson assumed he could still hear, and went on: You're brave. How did you get away?

Ignacio said something indistinct.

What?

He repeated grudgingly, a little louder: I ran. In the night.

It seemed too simple, too obvious, and Jackson experienced a wave of suspicion. He said: Why didn't you run away sooner? But even as he asked the question he guessèd the answer.

He wasn't surprised by the boy's reply: How could I?

The two of them, *viejo* and *niño*, would have been always staying with friends of the old man. A wave of pity ran through Jackson's chest. Ignacio knew he couldn't cast himself loose on the land all alone. Or didn't want to. He needed an adult. He had been waiting for an escape route, and Jackson had been it. And of course the old man would have had no time to waste searching for the boy. He would have wanted to get away as fast as he could from the man he had poisoned and robbed. Jackson wondered how long the boy had been waiting for this chance.

As soon as he felt the pity, he also felt annoyed. Why him of all people? This was really the last headache he needed. And why just at the time when his own hassles had multiplied tenfold, when he had just been forced against the ropes?

It was obvious he must clean the boy up as soon as possible then get rid of him, deliver him to the proper authorities. The idea offered an illusion of resolution for a moment, until he remembered this was Trujillo Province. There were no proper authorities. Who knew what might happen to the kid if the police, for example, got their hands on him?

Now and then over the weeks, when things were going badly, Jackson would comfort himself with the thought of going home. Wasn't his real goal to get through this task in order to be able to go home with a clean slate? Wasn't that why any man did anything?

But now the thought of home offered none of its comfort, only its dread. To go home now would be nothing other than to fail, once and for all.

4

The boy sat in the corner of the hotel rooftop, ponchoed, hatted, catted. Jackson was trying to read and it was hard to concentrate with him there. He was a continual reminder that things were different now. The easy days were over. Jackson hadn't realised until now that before he had been able to delay as much as he liked. Now the clock was ticking.

The rooftop was stultifying beneath the lid of warm white cloud. Jackson dozed, woke up, read a little, dozed again, then woke up sweating and alarmed.

The boy was still in the corner. He was smiling. The comic lay on the ground, and he was talking softly to the cat in his lap, laughing at something, running his hand along its back.

In the late afternoon the air didn't exactly cool down but you could tell that it had come off the heat. The vultures had moved on. Noise had returned to the city below, a pleasant collective babble of shopkeepers and stall owners setting up for the evening, calling happily to one another after their long siestas, in good moods, with the evening ahead of them. One sensed that at last the long months of the *garúa* season were really drawing to a close, and everyone knew it.

Time to go down. In the street the vendors were out in force, but the crowds had not yet arrived. It was a good time to be out and about, before the show really got started, when the set was still fresh. The revived streets basked in shade and bustle.

The boy stopped at a bamboo stall overladen with plastic toys— boats, aeroplanes, fire engines, tennis racquets, even a cricket bat, all made of plastic. Anything and everything to do with play. The child stared at a lime-green kite hanging in front of the stall.

The woman behind the mass of cheap goods studiedly ignored them, staring off down the street.

You know what that is?

Ignacio nodded. He glanced at Jackson. Then, perhaps feeling he needed to convince him, he mumbled, It's a kite.

Exactly, Jackson said, overenthusiastically, then felt self-conscious.

Halfway down a quiet side street a gang of boys in tattered shorts were running around screaming, dumping water on each other from plastic bowls. They had found a leaking water main that let out a tired plume which bubbled up to ankle height then sank into a brown puddle where the boys stooped to fill their weapons.

Ignacio stared at them from the corner, took a few magnetic steps in their direction, paused.

Jackson chatted to a woman who was selling a pile of oranges. She had a broad felt hat, a dimpled smile and deep crow's feet. The top of her stall was a blue sheet which released a gentle light, softening her face. Jackson felt awkward because of the boy, yet slightly proud too, and noticed he was talking louder than normal, feeling Ignacio's presence just behind him.

Just give me three little *soles*, the woman pleaded, tilting her head to the side, enjoying a charade of pitiful bargaining.

Jackson gave as good back, raising his eyebrows in mock horror. Three *soles*? He made a gesture of tugging out his pockets. How can I give three *soles* for five oranges?

So give me two *soles*, the woman said.

For how many oranges?

The woman clucked, seeing that he had preempted her next line.

He usually didn't like to bargain. What was a penny or two? But he felt differently now, both because of his limited funds and because of Ignacio. As a temporary surrogate guardian he felt obliged to participate in the mechanics of the society, of which haggling was an important part.

The woman sighed and moaned, and said, Ay gringo, you're robbing me, and tipped five oranges into a blue plastic bag.

Jackson handed over the money and thanked her.

No hay porqué, guapo, she said. No need, handsome. She settled her gaze down the street.

Jackson turned round to move on. The boy was gone. He stepped back, whistled and looked either way down the rows of stalls. He called out the boy's name. Hearing his own voice in the busy city alarmed him for some reason. He looked at the woman.

Where did he go?

Who?

The kid. Did you see?

The woman shrugged. *No sé, señor.* I didn't know he was with you.

Jackson took a few steps, ran a few more, then turned and ran the other way. He called out again, imagining that he ought to feel self-conscious in front of all the vendors, surprised by how little he cared what they thought, surprised by something like a sad pleasure at finding himself so concerned, and briskly walked two more blocks, then jogged back all the way to the orange lady, where the street seemed oddly empty now, and on another half block to the next corner.

Ignacio was leaning against the concrete wall of a shop, holding a plastic bag in his hand.

Jackson's heart was knocking. Where did you go? You mustn't go like that.

The boy lifted the bag by way of explanation. I was waiting for you, he said softly.

Jackson touched the boy's tiny shoulder. Come on.

They walked on toward the plaza.

It's dangerous here, you never know, Jackson began. So where did you go? he tried, out of breath, hot and sweaty in his shirt.

The boy lifted his plastic bag once more and said, For the cat.

The bag held something compact and heavy.

As they walked out into the blaze of brilliant buses swirling around the plaza with its five green palms and six white busts of the forgotten illustrious sons of the town on their columns, Jackson thought he understood the extra dimension that parenthood must add to life. A needful young thing dependent on your care made your own troubles seem to diminish, so you could step over them easily. You learnt to dwarf them, you became taller.

He took the boy by the hand and they climbed on board one of the roaring *micro* buses labelled "San Lorenzo—Playa": to the beach.

3 · Consular I

1

From the city the coastal desert stretches northward in a strip of unparalleled aridity where rain is seen once a century. Nothing for hundreds of miles except the odd concrete town and the mummies in the museum of Chan Chan, a long-deserted city of mud, or rather clay, for mud is soon fired here. Hunched figures with little spills of dust around their ankles, they sit in their glass sepulchres, grinning vaguely at their feet, gazed at now and then by the rare tourist.

Then the land changes. The cold Humboldt Current, knocked offshore by Cabo Blanco, releases the land from its cape of *garúa*; a big river coming down from the north feeds an enormous delta; the ground is carpeted in acres of glossy banana—the world's largest plantation. The coast is lined with fishing villages, their reed pirogues upended on the beaches by night, bobbing in the surf by day. Here and there a port crumbles by the sea, its tin roofs interspersed with verdure—palms, papaya trees, the ubiquitous banana. Down at the quays a handful of mildewed steamers are tied up, tramps manned by slow Panamanians in grease-toiled shirts who loiter on deck on holiday from the engine room, while local stevedores, bare backed, steer enormous pallets of boxes, gas cylinders, sacks of fruit, banana fists, into and out of the holds: strong men bronzed by the sun, who hoist their loads in time to salsa music screeching from tinny radios. Everything you would expect of a tropical coast.

After a hundred miles of this lively impoverished world—green land, blue sea, semi-naked people hacking with machetes in cane fields, washing at village taps, clacking down dominoes on road-side tables—you come to a sprawling Pacific port in a new region. Here the great container ships—tower blocks in miniature—glide with silent momentum up the docks between warehouses as big as football pitches. Their tiny crews appear on the bridge in whites— ruddied, bearded men from Norway and Rotterdam—and watch with mild surprise the old black cranes come creaking down their tracks into position: not like Tokyo, where they unload in half a day. May as well get to know the sights, boys, the captain says, we'll be here three days. But other than a few beers at the vel-veteen bar by the port gates—a mile of concrete wasteland away— and a half-hearted flirt with its chubby girls in miniskirts, and perhaps a little business in the back room, they decide: Nah, why bother? I'll wait for Colón or Miami or Honolulu. The country's supposed to be safe, but you never know.

The Paseo Maritimo is lined not with the restaurants and night spots of other esplanades, but with concrete two storey office blocks, most of which have no front wall on their bottom floor— cavernous holes occupied by ironmongers, grocers, mechanics, juice-makers and bare cafés that specialise in glasses of ceviche. The aromas of cilantro and lime, seafood and beer, mingle with the exhaust fumes of the busy street that winds along the seafront.

There's a little bay that fancies itself picturesque, despite its *fe-rreterías* and *talleres mecánicos* and constant traffic. The municipality erected a stone monument of a man staring vacantly into a pool with a net dangling at his side, entitled *"Monumento a los Pescadores,"* and it was dutifully numbered on all tourist maps, which further honoured this part of the town with the legend: "Locals haunt for seafruits."

A copy of this map lay on a table in the Cevichería de la Cruz. The man sitting at the table with the map mopped his brow with a napkin, which broke into shreds on contact with his forehead—a large forehead that extended back into his scalp. He grabbed a handful of napkins impatiently from the dispenser on the table and swabbed his head again, then his neck too.

The woman who worked behind the counter, composed of two large refrigerator units that rattled and whined, turned up the dial for the ceiling fan. The man heard the click and looked round. He said, *Gracias*.

She nodded over her shoulder. Whereupon he smiled at her.

She looked away. The man had a bad smile. Local people always looked away when he smiled. Probably they were worried about getting the evil eye. It was a smile that did nothing for him except reveal the unsightly gaps between the front teeth, and show up a hollowness, a soullessness around the eyes, giving him a vampirical look. You could see it cost him an effort.

He looked better when he turned back to the map on his table and settled his features in their customary frown. Before him stood an as yet untouched glass—like an old-fashioned ice-cream flute—of marinated fish, and a brown bottle of beer sweating in the heat. He picked up the bottle and guzzled. The thing about somewhere like this was you could drink as much beer as you liked, first because the heat made you drunk anyway, or at least useless and fuddled, and second, you sweated the alcohol out as fast as you drank it. And third: why the hell not?

Brown had been sent down to the coast by the consulate in the big city in the northern mountains. Many times over the last year he had looked forward to just such a trip. He had imagined something like Acapulco in its hilly bay. It's a terrible curse, he reflected, to put your trust in other places. Even now, sweating in the Cevichería de la Cruz, he was doing it again. This time he was longing for the mountains, for the apartment he called home, with its view of dull khaki hills and afternoon clouds, and having to close the window at night because of the cold.

You would have thought a man would be cured of this disease by ten years in the Foreign Office. Apparently not.

María, he called out. They were all called María. Or else Carmen. Or María Carmen. It was a game he had: how many times could you be right if you just blurted it out.

The woman, who was busy chopping limes, looked up. She was young, plump, with bad skin but a brave, heartening smile. She said, *¿A quién busca?* Who are you looking for?

He apologised then realised he had forgotten why he had called her. The reason had melted in the heat. He plucked up a new one: *Una cerveza más*, he said, holding up his half-empty beer bottle. As she turned away he hurriedly poured the remainder down his gullet. And he ought to eat something—have a pick at that glass of fish. He hadn't eaten today and it was already noon. Yet he had no appetite.

A tall man in a blue short-sleeved shirt and cream slacks walked in off the street. He ought to have looked well-dressed. If he had been a local he would have done: the trousers would have been pressed, the shirt ironed, the whole ensemble lifted fresh from its laundry wrapping. But this man was not a local. He was visibly a gringo who had lived in the heat too long. That was what the heat could do. You lost things in it, one by one, until finally you lost yourself. Grime, dust, what looked like oil here, egg there, had all left their traces on the man's outfit. Added to which, instead of the customary loafers of a tropical *homme d'affaires*, he wore ancient trainers.

Brown looked at the man as he entered and nodded slightly, turning on a quarter smile. He thought this must be the chap. He certainly could have been German. But Brown didn't want to make a fool of himself. It wasn't that the two of them really needed to be secret, but on the other hand, there was no need to be overt. And if it was the man, he ought to be able to pick up a noncommittal greeting.

The man was tall and slim, but ungainly. When he pulled out a chair for himself at Brown's table, there was something awkward about the movement, as if he were too big for the little object and might easily break it. He sat himself down and crossed his legs and you noticed then that he had large, heavy thighs. He was altogether a heavier, clumsier man than many more corpulent figures: a big man disguised as a slim one.

So far he had only glanced briefly at Brown. Now, seated, he raised a finger at the woman behind the counter and ordered an orange juice. Then he squared himself to the table, rested his elbows on it, forearms vertical, and set his cheeks in his hands. He's a giant, Brown thought.

So you've got a problem? The man spoke in a deep smooth voice that would have been reassuring in a doctor, say, but was somehow menacing in him. He had a faint German accent, tempered presumably by years among foreigners.

Depends how you look at it, Brown answered. He hadn't meant to sound snappy, and let out a short false chuckle. We need to get something up into the mountains, to the Chachapoyas region. But it's tricky, Brown said with resignation. It's like groping in the dark down there.

The woman brought over the orange juice. The German gave elaborate thanks and bowed to his glass.

Ya, he said with light enthusiasm, after taking a sip. But I thought you had people up and down the Andes.

It's not so easy for us. They tend to confuse us with Yanks. English-speakers and all. Brown smiled.

The big German raised his eyebrows and shoulders in a ponderous shrug.

We heard that you have a couple of chaps down there, Brown said, with a rattle of a giggle, trying not to sound aggressive. He did sound aggressive. He smiled to smooth things over, but the German only grimaced. We really need someone outside it all, as it were, but up in the region. We need to get something up there, like I said.

The big German shrugged. It's simply a matter of transportation?

We actually need to *place* this damn thing.

Well, you'd have to have your own people do that. What is it?

Brown smiled again at the German, who looked down at his juice glass.

He swigged on his own fresh beer. It's about the size of a paperback, he said. Like a small radio. A pocket transistor radio. I was supposed to be hearing from someone.

Just then Brown didn't actually imagine that he ever would find someone to plant the device. It was a hopeless scheme, he had thought so from the start: a beacon to let them get a fix on the drug baron's airstrip, which somehow had eluded all the Americans' best equipment, and perhaps on his headquarters. Except he undoubtedly wouldn't have only one headquarters, nor probably even a main one, but many scattered through the mountainous jungle.

The German raised his eyes and looked at Brown, then dropped them to his hands folded on the table. The two men drank in silence.

Brown said: There is another thing. We could be interested in that judge of yours. The one who helped you out with the chappy in jail.

The German laughed and looked out into the street. As if he's ours. He took a long swig of his juice.

Brown coughed. About the other matter. And he slid his briefcase from under the table, extracted a brown envelope.

The German sipped his juice through a straw, turning the plastic tube dark. It's a bad part of the country, very difficult.

Brown kept his hand on the envelope. He looked up at the big face of the German, smiling slightly.

Who knows, my friend, if things go wrong there, you'd be lucky to face a judge these days. The German turned away toward the street, and said: Judge Montoya. Remember it is not an entirely uncivilised country. A little civilisation is a dangerous thing. Not everyone has a price. You'll find him on Calle Montalbán, Chachapoyas.

If it comes to it. Just in case. Brown lifted his hand from the envelope, which the German ignored.

Two foreign girls walked slowly past the restaurant. They were talking animatedly, and when they glanced in they happened to be smiling. They were pretty, both of them. Could have been English, possibly, or French. Long skirts, long hair: not hippies, just travellers.

At the sight of those faces Brown's heart sank. Reflexively he smiled at the German, to give the impression that he too was having a good time. But it was obvious the two women were having a better time than he. They had things to look forward to. He felt a bitter envy. They were holidaying round the continent like all the other backpackers, then after three months of fun and adventure, they'd go home feeling worldly, to interesting jobs or university degrees. They were kids playing at adulthood. Brown had a depressing sense that his good mood was gone for the day.

Now he just wanted to get home. What did he care about this ad hoc spooking? They had only asked him for one reason, because he was single. A man without strings, probably miserable, probably ready to behave shoddily. He was the only family-less man in the little consulate.

He called for the bill. The German slid the brown envelope into his own briefcase and the two men left, each going in opposite directions along the seafront.

Brown had planned to go for a good long walk about the city, but as he drifted along he couldn't remember why. Bugger this, he thought, and hailed a taxi back to his hotel, where he installed himself in front of the cable TV in the bar and watched an American film, before a protracted early dinner.

Lying in bed that night he thought: the problem is, I'm bored. He felt better identifying his malaise. How did you cure boredom? You did something new. He had an idea: he wouldn't fly back to his home in Santa Cruz, he'd take the train. No one would miss him if he came back a day late. It was one of the sights of the country, the train that climbed ten thousand feet, zigzagging up the Andes. It was the kind of thing travellers did. He felt a random affection for travellers. They took their time, giving themselves to a country. Perhaps those two foreign girls would be on the train. He could buy them a meal in the buffet car, maybe show them around once they reached the city. After all, he knew the country. He had been here two years. There was no telling what could happen. Which one, he asked himself, knowing it would be the gold-haired one. Then he wondered: but if I *am* going to see them tomorrow, it would be a good idea to be nice and relaxed. Not to have any desperation hanging about him. There was only one way to be sure of that.

He climbed out of bed and dressed rapidly, fumbling with his belt buckle.

An unoccupied taxi came by as soon as he stepped out of the hotel, which seemed like a good omen. A moment of bashfulness hit him when the driver asked where he wanted to go. He managed to bury it: he was a man, a man has needs. It was just that the driver happened to be a youngish fellow who probably had a wife and a toddler or two at home. It would have been easier with an older driver.

Wherever the *chicas* are, he said.

The driver's face broke into a grin. Ah, he said. *Bueno. Vámonos.* And stepped down hard.

On the dashboard a little icon of the Virgin of Guadalupe glowed in a frame. Brown felt better, on familiar ground. It might have been vice but he knew the ropes. The trinket-rattling taxi ride, the plump girl with a crucifix, the thrill when she unzipped her skirt. He knew where he stood.

The next day the train left two hours late. As it finally lurched out of the station his bag fell off the luggage rack onto his head. There was no sign of the two girls. Nor did the windows open. If they had, they would only have let in clouds of diesel smoke from the ancient orange locomotive that jerked the train up the hillsides. A whole day and half a night of it. As for there being a bar, let alone a buffet car—nothing but four crowded carriages inherited from Mexico, which had inherited them in turn from some old U.S. branch line. He could make out a stamp in the metal floors of the ramps between cars: Dayton, Ohio.

2

The consulate didn't open till ten. One morning a few days later Brown came from behind the desk with the latest two-day-old *Times* in his hand, and set it on the coffee table by the chairs where people could wait for their visas to be issued or refused. Through the frosted glass of the front door he saw the dark shapes of two visitors arriving. The buzzer went off as they opened the door. They had been talking but went quiet as soon as they were inside the small carpeted room.

He smiled at them. It was the two girls from the coast.

Morning, he said, and carried on fussing with the newspapers, arranging them in overlapping rows. His heart started thumping. He could feel the two tall happy women standing behind him. He left what he was doing and walked around to the other side of the counter, closing the flap. Then he took up his post, hands on the top, and said, What can we do for you?

He decided he ought to remove his hands—the bitten nails, the freckles, the funny white flecks that had developed in the equatorial sun.

The two women were both wearing jeans today. One, the one with dark chestnut hair—*castaña*, the locals would call her, a pretty word—had bright, slightly buggy eyes. Not exactly buggy, but large, shiny, as if you could see a little too much of the eyeball. But she was pretty, and she was smiling at him—an odd smile, self-assured, but somehow a little too bright, almost insincere.

The other one, meanwhile, the blonde, or part-blonde, had picked up the new *Times*, and was reading the front page, with the paper still folded as he had left it.

She wasn't really blonde. Her hair looked rusty brown now. Had she dyed it? Somehow he didn't think so. It was hair of a shade and lustre that would change with the light, he guessed.

Actually, said Chestnut, slowly and deeply, in answer to his question: We were just wondering if we could read the papers.

Haven't seen one in weeks. She spoke with a pronounced Australian accent.

Help yourself.

Brown turned to a pile of post some way up the counter. He was first in this morning, and rather than taking it back to his office, he settled at a table behind the counter, leaving the women still in view. He could hear them muttering to each other, papers rustling. They were sitting in the chairs.

He cleared his throat, then thought it sounded like he might have been obscurely ticking them off, and said out loud, Just passing through?

We're not exactly passing through, said the chestnut one, in her slowed-down Aussie drawl. What? she added, turning to Blondie.

Blondie: I'm heading south. Down to the beach. Then the mountains.

The blonde had an American accent. She was probably in her mid-twenties, he guessed. Hair randomly variegated, from golden to sunny to lustrous brown, her face a pleasing sandy colour, friendly. She had blue eyes. Or were they green? Brown felt a pang on looking at her. She was, surely, just the kind of woman he wanted, who any man in his late thirties would want. You could tell she was bright just from her face. Bright and forward-looking and relaxed and intelligent about the way she led her life. American girls often were. They took their lives in their own hands—that was what they had been brought up to do—and made the most of them on their own terms. Not like us Brits, Brown thought, lugubriously fulfilling the duties of our moribund society. That was what a man like him really needed—an invigorating American girl.

But the thought merely depressed him, so far was he from getting anything like that.

Brown: South? The mountains? You better be careful, he said. It's no joke down there right now. You're all right once you get to Lima.

Blondie: I'm not going to Lima.

Oh?

The supercilious British interrogative. Get a grip, man, get a grip.

So where are you going?

To my uncle. He lives down there.

Brown couldn't resist another peek. He turned his head, still bowed, so it appeared that he wasn't breaking his concentration on his important work. Long hair, glowing with health and hope.

Down where exactly?

Chachapoyas.

He started, gave up his pretence of work. Your uncle lives in Chachapoyas? Three or four hundred miles south of here? That Chachapoyas?

She nodded. Is there another?

Has he been there long?

Thirty years, came the reply. She rested the newspaper on her lap and raised her eyebrows at him. He loves it, she said.

Ah yes, he murmured, accompanied by a clever little chuckle, though why he should have thought this necessary he couldn't understand.

He's not in the town but up the Tingo valley.

Don't know my geography too well, but I do know that's quite a place to live. He laughed, hoping they would too, but they didn't. What keeps him there?

His wife, his chickens, his kids, his pigs, his farm. Lots of things.

Brown raised his eyebrows. But then a vague recollection stirred. Is he the chappy . . . ? he began, hoping he would not have to go on, that she would jump in. She didn't.

He struggled on: Who whatever—the whatsit . . . ? He stopped there, thinking it might do for a friendly communal chuckle.

The two girls sat looking at him, their faces lifted expectantly.

The *castaña* broke the awkward silence. Your uncle keeps a low-ish profile, doesn't he?

Silence fell. The three of them rustled their respective papers. You could hear the hum of the consular air-conditioner. It was an awkward scene: he trying to work; they using the waiting room as a library. No one spoke for perhaps ten minutes. Brown went out to make a cup of coffee, feeling slightly overawed. She was actually on her way to Chachapoyas. How maddening that he didn't simply have the little device and couldn't just give it to her and say: Could you give this to my friend so and so? No one would look twice at a backpacking girl. But it was out of the question, of course. And anyway, he hadn't even heard from a man he was hoping might plant it.

Finally he heard the blonde say, Don't you think . . . ? and the answer, You're right, and the two of them got up. The dark one sent him a little wave and said, Thank you.

He rushed to his feet, almost stumbling over himself as he paced round the side of the counter.

Here, have a card. At least you'll know how to get in touch. Should anything come up. If you ever need help or anything. Don't hesitate. He gave it to the fair one.

And that was it, they were gone.

That was how the public treated the consulate. A place to come and use whenever they liked, a little piece of terra firma always available to them. It wasn't right. If he had his way there'd be a lock on the door.

4 · Beach Life

1

Jackson and Ignacio found seats near the front of the bus to the beach. The boy set his plastic bag on the floor between his feet. Jackson noticed that he couldn't take his eyes off the bus driver's podgy brown hand as it clunked through the gears. The long stick puffed every time it moved, and when the driver tapped the red button to change the compression, the engine pitch dropped with a long hiss.

Independence comes young here, Jackson thought. He and the boy were two males. If Ignacio wanted to travel about with him that was his business. Jackson needn't worry about it.

The sweat on Jackson's skin cooled in the breeze that moved through the bus. He untied the sweater from his shoulders and pulled it on. The weave felt good against his bare arms. It was nice to add a layer of clothing for the evening. He felt homey and comfortable with the warm seat throbbing, and the bus wheezing and lurching through the streets toward the ocean side of the city.

They got off on a track of packed dirt. Small wood and tin houses stood here and there, and some of the lots were overgrown with ground creepers. They walked between the houses down to a flat wide beach of grey sand. Ahead was the ocean, grey and calm, unrolling itself in mirrored ripples that slapped on the beach. The wavelets disburdened themselves of their message—*slap*—then inhaled as they withdrew. That was all they had come to say, right across the widest ocean for that one stark monosyllable.

The evening clouds formed an arch in the sky through which, as if looking out of a cave mouth, you could see a landscape of mauve like the first glimpse of the firmament at the end of the deluge. The sun showed as a smooth red ball, giant, slightly misshapen. It hovered just above the graphite horizon, casting a bloom of red shadow on the gelatinous water. Some way up the beach a cluster of the local fishing craft, rush canoes with curved prows, stood upended in the sand like a curious stand of palms. Out to sea one fisherman was still at work in his boat, standing up, visible merely as a vertical stick attached to a horizontal stick.

The wooden structures along the beach were cheap restaurants. There might have been eight or ten of them. They had signs which weren't lit and were hard to read in the last of the daylight.

Ignacio put his plastic bag down on the sand, glanced at Jackson uncertainly and stepped toward the water. He paused, looking back over his shoulder, then sprinted to the wet sand. When he got there he let the little waves ripple over his new shoes, standing in the running froth. He bent down and scooped up a handful of spume. Jackson saw him stare at it, holding it up close to his face.

Jackson moved toward him, bringing the bag with him, and sat down where the sand was still dry. The boy pulled off his clothes and shoes, leaving them in a neat pile a little way up the beach, ran to the surf and squatted down, allowing the waves to break over his dark back. A dark figure in the dark grey water.

Sitting still, fingering the sand, picking up handfuls of the fine, cloying dust, Jackson became aware of a pleasant aroma of cooking. He looked around trying to guess which restaurant it came from. They all seemed too far away, with their terraces on stilts over the upper beach. While Ignacio played in the water Jackson picked at the opening of his plastic bag. The smell became stronger.

Inside was something wrapped in newspaper. He pulled at the wrapping and revealed the golden skin, traced with black, of a roast chicken. He picked up the bag, held it open. The bird was still warm. It must have come from one of the town's rotisseries. Ignacio could only have stolen it.

How could he have done this? *No hay que robar*, the phrase came to mind. He must tell him. Jackson felt somehow belittled.

When he looked up, Ignacio had retreated from the waves and was staring at him.

¡Ven! Jackson called, beckoning with his whole arm.

The boy didn't move.

¡Ven!

Ignacio kicked at the sand and sauntered back toward him, past his heap of clothing, wearing only a pair of black shorts, his arms glistening as if with oil. He could have been a child in India strolling up from the Ganges.

Look, Jackson began, we can buy food, there's no need. We could get into trouble. And yet he could barely suppress a smile.

The boy stared at him, big eyes shining in the fading light, and suddenly Jackson felt they must leave this dark land, get back to the high sunshine. Neither of them belonged in this heavy clay land. It could do one no good to linger in this greyness. Maybe he would after all do the things he had been putting off. Maybe, now that his resources were so straitened, the time had come.

All along the beach the lights of the little restaurants had come on, a train of stars, only serving to show up the presiding murk of the scene. The sun's dim ball had gone. The ocean was turning to black.

Ignacio stood still, staring at the ground like a cliché of a guilty schoolboy.

Está bien, Jackson said, looking away.

The boy went and fetched his clothes, pulling them on over his still-wet body. In the desert you could dress wet and be dry in a minute. The air drank up moisture like fire.

In the last of the light Jackson could make out some kind of commotion further along the beach, a cluster of people and what sounded like a wave of applause. There might have been a fire up there. A point of light showed, and sometimes the legs of the gathered figures flickered across it.

Jackson took Ignacio's hand, surprised by how low he had to stoop to find it. With his other hand he gave the boy back his bag. They started walking toward the little throng. The boy fell into step beside him.

It's a lot for one little cat, Jackson said.

She's not little.

It's still a lot.

She's hungry. She eats and eats.

And doesn't get any bigger?

No, señor. She gets much bigger. And the señor engineer is too busy planning his mines to feed her.

Jackson chuckled. The boy's hand had become light in his and he sensed that this was a kind of joke. And it was pleasant, anyway, to be thought anything as cogent as a mining engineer, even by a boy.

I'm not an engineer, he said.

Ignacio was silent, probably assuming he was lying.

Or a miner.

The crowd turned out to be smaller than it had looked—just a handful of people scattered over the beach outside a restaurant called El Cantinero. A small fire fluttered lamely on the sand, fuelled by old boards. A group of fishermen stood apart, arms folded, watching the crowd, who were mostly foreigners. Several blond and brown beards could be seen, and likewise some of the women had hair that was not black. The gathering was loose, as if most of the people didn't know each other and had merely been drawn by the fire, by the beach, by the ocean. Periodically a boy came briskly down the steps from the restaurant and distributed bottles of beer, waiting patiently beside each customer seated on the sand while they unfolded their bills, bent close to read them, then handed them over. The boy efficiently gathered up handfuls of empties embedded in the sand at the end of each trip.

The whole thing seemed wrong, a misplaced beach scene, a Bacardi moment lifted from Montego Bay or Copacabana and deposited here on the edge of a grey desert, between grey dust and grey water, with the only settlement around being a pale-grey city full of impoverished humanity. By no stretch of the imagination could this be construed as a holiday scene, a happy beach party.

Jackson stopped a little way off, puzzled. He hadn't been waiting long when the occasion for the gathering sprinted into view out of the darkness. On the firm sand down near the water a young man in bathing trunks, skinny, who looked like a local, with cropped black hair, came running very fast. Almost as soon as Jackson became aware of the running figure, the man performed a high skip, raising his arms above his head, and dived toward the sand, flipping over in a lightning cartwheel from which he flexed himself into a chain of backward handsprings, the fall of hand and foot, hand and foot making light precise *chips* on the sand, and finally flew up, body straight, arms rigid at his sides, and quite slowly, gracefully turned a backwards somersault, his body stiff as a board.

The acrobat landed perfectly, without taking a step either forward or back, rooted as surely in the sand as if he had been born to tumble like that.

The spectators clapped, except for the Peruvian fishermen, who turned away and sauntered off. The tumbler moved to the fire, breathing hard, the firelight picking up a glint of sweat on his upper lip. He sat down cross-legged, elbows on his knees, and took a sip from a plastic cup buried in the sand. He was an attractive man, with a well-shaped part-African head.

Ignacio said, Why doesn't he do it again? Tell him to do it again.

He's probably tired.

The boy looked up at him. Have you ever seen that before?

No. Yes. Only on television.

Jackson waved the restaurant boy over and ordered a beer and a Coke. The waiter stooped to pick up an empty, then scurried off up the beach.

The acrobat was poking at the fire with a fresh piece of wood. He set it on top. The flattened flames soon began to curl around the edges. In the flare, a woman's face some way back from the fire glowed orange. She had sun-bleached shoulder-length hair and a strong shield of a face like a bronze mask, and she was looking straight at Jackson.

Jackson attempted a smile but was too surprised by the woman's gaze to carry it off. She smiled back anyway. Then she said something to a brown-haired girl beside her, got up and sat down beside the acrobat. She spoke to him and he laughed.

The fire let out a volley of crackles.

It became clear that the gathering was composed of several pairs and threesomes. One man with a straggly ginger beard, in white cut-offs and a much-faded Princeton singlet, strummed idly on a battered red guitar, singing so softly that his words, and even the nationality of his tongue, were inaudible.

So the cat's going to get it all, Ignacio? Not a mouthful for a hungry human?

The boy touched his bag uncertainly.

Where did you get it anyway?

In the city, the boy said evasively.

Jackson suggested they eat fish in the restaurant. Neither of them had eaten since that morning. But just as he was getting up, the boy said: Here, señor, let's eat, as if he had understood none of Jackson's earlier hints and the idea had just crossed his mind. He added, Why buy fish when we have this?

Jackson pulled off a leg for each of them. While they were eating, Jackson glugging from the neck of the cold beer bottle between mouthfuls, Ignacio chewing noisily with his mouth open, then swigging from his Coke, the acrobat called across the fire: Hey there. Where you from?

As Jackson began to answer, the man stood up and moved closer, along with the blonde girl, and at the same time the brunette in the shadows got up too. All three of them settled close by.

That was wonderful, Jackson said.

I keep my hand in, the acrobat said, in Spanish. I came down here with a circus troupe from Venezuela, that's my home, the city of Mérida in the mountains. Beautiful place. You ever been?

Jackson shook his head. If I ever get out of this country maybe I'll take a trip there. He dug at the sand with his chicken bone.

The acrobat introduced himself as Celer.

Sela?

That's right.

How do you spell that?

The acrobat told him.

Jackson smiled. That's Latin, you know. Quick. Speedy.

Hey. Celer broke into a big grin and shook Jackson's hand firmly. A scholar.

Just school. We had to do Latin.

The acrobat laughed delightedly. So anyway, why wouldn't you get out of here?

Jackson twisted his beer bottle in the sand and shrugged.

If you keep your nose clean you should make it. Celer looked at Jackson, eyes glittering.

Jackson felt a weight gather in his chest.

Just then Ignacio walked over and said to the acrobat, Will you do that again?

Celer smiled up at him. Did you like it?

Teach me.

That's not so easy, you know. Then he said to the blond girl: Kids are good at this. Watch.

Celer lay back on the sand with his knees up. OK, he said, broadly. He reached for Ignacio's hands, placed them on his own knees, gripped the boy's shoulders and hoisted him straight up into the air, upside down. Straighten your legs, he said.

The boy's nervously buckled legs opened out into a handstand. His trousers dropped around his thighs, revealing thin and perfect limbs the colour of tin, upside down in the night, curved like some cryptic symbol.

Easy, no?

Ignacio said nothing, suspended above the sand.

The acrobat adjusted his grip then suddenly flung the boy up, spinning him over in the process, and caught him just above the ground by his hips. The boy, surprised to find himself on his feet, broke into a big grin. Again! he cried.

They repeated the manoeuvre, the boy acting his part readily. As soon as it was over, he giggled and said, Again!

Later, later, the acrobat said. So you like gymnastics.

The blonde girl, sitting off to the side, clothed in a thin skirt of pink cotton, drew in her knees. Is he your son? she asked Jackson, in perfect English. She had an American accent.

Jackson was a little surprised by the question. He seems to have adopted me, he said, draining the last plunge of froth from his bottle, and dug the base into the sand.

Did you meet him here?

A hundred miles away.

The young waiter brought them new beers, his arms flashing in the firelight. Night had settled completely, the sea an invisible presence from which the thin lines of white emerged.

So who is he? she asked.

He's Ignacio. Jackson shrugged. I wish I knew. Seems to be an orphan.

He felt strangely restless and nervous. I'm Jackson, by the way. Who are you?

Sarah, she said, with a shy kind of smile. Just got down here the other day, me and Daphne here. She gestured at the brunette. We've been making our way south.

The boy was turning somersaults now with the acrobat supervising, teaching him to get up without using his hands. They both watched Ignacio attempt a backward roll and collapse in a knot of limbs.

You see why kids are good at this, Celer called. They can't hurt themselves.

The boy was already on his feet, ready to try again.

You're from England? the girl asked.

Mostly. You?

Connecticut. And upstate New York. What does *mostly* mean?

I've moved around.

He felt he was lying. But he didn't like to mention the army to other young people. They had opinions. Nothing much, he added.

Sarah introduced her friend Daphne, an Australian. She sent Jackson a confident, winning smile that made him feel more at ease, cocking her head slightly. G'day, she said, as if to prove she really was an Aussie.

Another man in a long striped shirt, gentle-faced, came and joined them. It seemed they had become the centre the scattered gathering of lost souls strewn on the margin of the land had been waiting to find. Nearby, people fell into travellers' talk of a kind for which Jackson had little taste. Hotels, restaurants, planned routes—the talk of people who made journeying the point of their departure.

The gentle-faced man was different. He was Swiss and had heard of some Garden of Eden hidden in the Andes, a secret monastery for which he was searching.

I spent six months looking around Lake Titicaca, he informed them. Just now I am having a break.

You've stopped looking? Daphne, the Australian, asked.

No, no. But I believe the monastery is in the mountains. I was called back down to the coast for a while. By the sea.

Maybe for the last time? she said.

Yes. He laughed lightly. I hope so. I think soon the time will arrive for me to be there.

Jackson wondered what exactly the man meant when he said he had been called. What will you do if you find it? he asked.

When I find it. I'll stay. What else?

And never leave?

You can't leave. Why would you, once you find it?

To see friends, family, I don't know.

I have said my farewells. In a way we can't imagine we will be with our loved ones too, up there. He shrugged, his face full of patience. It was enviable, Jackson thought. Faith was like determination. It made a person look ahead, onward, never back. It made you ride the crest of life, ride your energy as fast as it would take you. Maybe what he himself had once had was faith. He had always thought it was courage, or purpose, even love. But after all how could you have those things without faith?

What about money?

I sold my apartment, my car, everything. I have nothing. Nothing but this body. He gripped his shins and grinned self-consciously.

You're on a quest, Daphne said.

He nodded. I guess, he said with an American intonation perhaps acquired from some former travelling acquaintance. Except, you know, I feel I have already found what I am looking for. Once you find the way to where you need to go, you have already found what you need.

So then why go to this secret monastery at all? Daphne asked.

He chuckled and paused. Because that is the way. Going to the monastery is the way. He shook his head. I used to be a stockbroker in Zurich. I made good money. I had bikes, always BMWs, a nice apartment, a beautiful girlfriend. And I was miserable. I was never happy. So I give it all up and come to Peru. On my very first day here I meet this guy, you know, long hair, hippie dude, who used to be a monk. He looks at me a long time, like he's really studying me, then he smiles. I think you've been called, he says. You're looking for the monastery in the sky. But no one can tell you how to get there because no one who has found it has come back.

He paused a moment, then continued: Some people say the Himalayas are masculine, their spirituality has gone out into the world. But the Andes are feminine, they keep their secret knowledge to themselves. You have to come and find it.

They were all silent. An unusually large wave perforated the stillness. A beetle whirred among them, hovered above the fire a moment, then whirred on.

You see? the Swiss man said. He doesn't ask where he is going, he just goes.

Who? asked Daphne.

That beetle. He just goes and goes until one day he can't go anymore.

Aren't we the same?

Only we don't know it, he concluded.

Ignacio and the acrobat had moved away onto the open beach

to continue their exercises and balances. Occasionally Jackson would hear Celer clapping and saying, OK! Yes!

To which would come the boy's faint response: *¿Correcto?* Right?

Bueno, would come the confirmation. It was a relief for Jackson to see his charge enjoying himself independently.

So that's me, the Swiss guy went on.

Another pool of silence arrived on the broad beach in the night. The clouds must have lifted because you could see the black hills pricked here and there with a star, some farm high up a hillside.

Sarah, the blonde—except she wasn't exactly blonde; from certain angles in the firelight her hair even looked dark—seemed different from the usual backpackers Jackson had met. The only comment she'd made in the course of the guide-book talk earlier, uttered with a tinkle of a laugh in response to another remark, had been that concrete was the marble of modern Peru.

After a while Jackson became aware that only she and he were not talking. She rested her chin on her knees contentedly, smiling faintly, gazing into the fire, apparently lost in her own thoughts. Perhaps, Jackson thought, she had some local lover, maybe the acrobat, and was sitting here content and replete. He experienced a pang of jealousy, but couldn't say if it was for her or her lover or for something else.

Then he realised that she was in fact gazing not at the fire but at the boy and the acrobat playing together. Perhaps she was wondering happily about the acrobat as a father, enjoying the sight of him frolicking with the boy.

The Swiss man cleared his throat and stroked his wispy beard. He gave Jackson a long look, then asked, So what about you? Why are you here?

La Joya.

La Joya?

I'm looking for a city, the Chachapoyans' biggest city.

Shouldn't be too hard to find then.

It's a lost city. In the cloud forest, in the mountains. No one's ever found it. It was all there, thousands of people, acres of terracing, roads, temples—and sculptures, plazas, everything. And it's still there. Some of the smaller sites have been found, but this one is different. This is the one the nineteenth-century explorers were all looking for, not to mention the conquistadors. Some say it was the original El Dorado.

How do you know it's there?

All the chroniclers talk about it. And a friend of mine saw it. He got to the edge of it, some kind of outpost with a fort on a cliff, and from the cliff he could see the city reaching away under the trees. He said it was obvious from the lie of the land. A big bowl in the mountains, just the place to build a city.

There was silence for a moment except for the crackling of the fire, and the deep quiet boom of the small waves, a sound full of power far in excess of the little surf coming in.

And you know where it is? the Swiss man asked.

I know which village it's near, within a few days' hike. I'll set up there and keep searching until I find it.

There was more quiet. Then he asked: Why didn't he explore it more? Your friend?

He had to leave. He was always planning to come back and do it properly, but he couldn't.

Why?

Well, that's another story, Jackson said.

Can we have the highlights?

Jackson coughed quietly. At least it sounded quiet out there on the wide beach under the wide night sky. He died. He was killed.

I'm sorry, the Swiss man said.

They were all silent a moment.

Sarah said: My uncle lives up near Chachapoyas.

Jackson glanced at her. He does?

She nodded. I'll be heading up there soon, in fact, to stay with him. I don't know exactly where this place is but the mountains around there aren't too safe just now, you know. You can't really go there. These warlords, drug lords, they rule it. It's wild country. My uncle's OK because he's outside the worst part and everyone knows him.

When will you be going?

Depends.

Jackson guessed it depended on Celer.

He shrugged. Well, I should be OK. I can look after myself, I hope.

He had an instinct to pat his shirt, as if to show he was carrying a weapon. And wondered then if perhaps he really ought to be, at least a handgun. Except that he had already decided long ago that he wouldn't.

Sarah tilted her head to the side and said, It feels so good to be back. I can't believe it.

You've been here before?

She nodded, still smiling, hugging her pleasure to herself. I used to come every summer. Sometimes I feel this is where I really grew up. My uncle sort of tutored me one year while there were difficulties back home. Whatever. He didn't exactly believe in education. He used to be a hippie, I guess. There's a few up there. Now he's a farmer. The simple life, that's his thing. Back to basics. But anyway, she said, I was thinking, my uncle actually has this friend in town up in Chachapoyas who kind of takes kids in. At least he used to. A priest. If this kid really is an orphan and has nowhere to go, you should check him out. Padre Beltrán.

Jackson nodded. Thanks. Maybe.

Seriously. This is a terrible country, as you'll have seen, for kids on their own. So many of them. You've seen all the kids down by the plaza? She shook her head. I mean, you can't get sentimental about it, that's the way it is here, but if you can do anything about it, why not?

Travelling, Jackson was thinking, did funny things to people's personalities. It allowed them to adopt personas they would soon discard in favour of others. He didn't quite believe that the woman was speaking with her natural diction now. Which also confirmed his hunch, although he had seen them exchange only one private remark, that she might be hanging out with the acrobat, and was basking in the first glow of fulfilled lust.

What about you? he asked. What are you doing here?

Me? I'm being a beach bum. I don't have to be back in college until September, and I'm doing my thesis anyway next semester.

Which college? If she was doing a thesis she must be a postgraduate, Jackson figured. She must be at least twenty-four or so, he thought: a little older than he was.

It's in Connecticut.

That must be nice. Woods and the sea.

She shrugged. I don't see much of it. Spend all my time hunched over a microscope looking at little baby flies. I'm a biologist, a geneticist. At least I will be if I ever finish my doctorate. Anyway, I needed a break, and my tutor is on sabbatical, and I haven't seen my uncle in years. It seemed like the right time. Down through Baja, Central America, and now here I am. Pure indulgence. Some lovely grass now and then, and plenty of gorgeous beaches.

She ran her fingers through the sand between her feet. And now I'm not too far from family again. Can't wait actually. You can have too much of beaches, even if you haven't had a holiday in years.

How long will you stay? Jackson asked.

I don't know. My uncle has this strange household. He has two wives. They both live with him and they all get along. It's the happiest household I know. A dozen kids, I lose count, plus they always have extra people coming to stay. They all sleep in hammocks in this big giant room like a longhouse. It's the local way, he says, the natural way. He has this feud against the nuclear family, he thinks it's the root of all evil. Individualism, greed, ambition, all that stuff we love.

The Swiss man cleared his throat. It's interesting. How did your uncle come down here?

With the Peace Corps. In the sixties. He fell in love and never went back. He says he's really just a draft-dodger.

The Swiss man nodded approvingly.

Where are you from again? Jackson asked her. I mean originally?

She glanced at him. Her eyes were unusually bright in the firelight, as if talking had brought them to life. When their eyes met Jackson felt it in his stomach.

Upstate New York is where I grew up, she said. I had an ordinary East Coast upbringing. Good school, good college. Brown, as a matter of fact. Ever heard of it?

Jackson shook his head and swigged from his beer.

After she finished speaking he was aware of a difference in the air. It was as if for a moment he was conscious of the beach not as a beach but as an accumulation of billions of individual grains of sand; as if for a split second he had been able to sense the individual existence of every one of that vast array of sand-stars. The sky had somehow drawn back. He felt the space between beach and sky like a vault.

2

When Celer and Ignacio returned, Celer suggested they all move into the restaurant. Jackson was pleased that Sarah came too. The three beers had gone to his head enough to lend enjoyment to the act of walking up the sand-smoothed steps—smooth and dry like driftwood—and into the restaurant, which was little more than a wooden deck with a cooking hut on one side. He was happy too to be sitting beside her at a table of sun-bleached wood. It felt right and comfortable to be off the beach now. Ignacio automatically dragged a chair up beside Jackson and promptly put his head in Jackson's lap, uninvited and unprecedented, and fell asleep.

Above the next table hung the restaurant's single light bulb. Only one other table was occupied, by a middle-aged couple having a heated discussion which involved much slapping down of glasses. Later, when the barman changed the tape from Spanish ballads to salsa—by which time Jackson had drunk another two beers and had shared a shot of the local firewater with Sarah—he blithely asked her to dance, not really expecting that she would accept, but she did. He was surprised by the light feel of her rib cage, how slender it seemed, and by how easily he could enclose her in his arms. He had not noticed until now how fine her shoulders were or how brown, how well-defined her physique. The whole front of her body was warm against him, her back firm, strong but light; light as if all her bones were made of something strong but weightless. He couldn't remember enjoying dancing with a woman so much.

She asked if he enjoyed beaches late at night, and he understood that the question might be an invitation, that the two of them could go back onto the beach together later.

A new song began with rich piano chords. He waited with one hand on her forearm to see if she wanted to keep on dancing, and of her own volition she folded herself against him again. The singers entered a thick powerful refrain that repeated itself several times before releasing the singular male vocal on its own path, singing, *Le gusta quien le gusta,* You like whom you like, before it made its way back into the waiting arms of the general chorus. She floated in his arms like a Latina, using the song's rhythm to provide a cushion of air for her feet. He never saw her face, lodged beside his shoulder, but somehow he could tell she was smiling.

When they got back to the table Ignacio was curled up on the floor, fast asleep.

Is he all right there? Sarah asked, gesturing at him.

Not really. He'll be worried about his cat.

He has a cat?

He stole this chicken here for it. He pointed to the bag on the floor.

Neat. She smiled, then turned away and went and sat by the acrobat.

Jackson drained his drink and settled beside Daphne, the Australian, feeling momentarily glum. Daphne leaned her head on her palm and asked, So where are you going next?

I've got work to do, he said. Then, feeling he was bragging, added, Sort of.

Where does it take you? she tried again. Up to these ruins?

He felt a need for caution. Travellers had nothing to do but travel. If you weren't careful you could get yourself saddled with them for thousands of miles. It wasn't that travelling was boring exactly, but they were happy to get company for those long bus rides, those lonely slogs about a new town with a heavy pack on the back looking for a *hostal barato.*

He shrugged and said, Maybe Lima first.

Her eyes lit up. Yeah? Me too. Lima then Cuzco.

Just as he had thought. He smiled at her. It was hard not to. Her relief was palpable. It was lonely to be cast on a strip of sand thousands of miles from New York, from London, from Sydney, from anywhere civilised, to be living in steel buses and concrete hotels with a gaunt wall of mountains rising beside you one way and the emptiest of oceans rolling away the other. No phones, no faxes, no Fosters. Nothing but a huge land of iron.

Lima, she said, like it was the promised land. Can't wait.

He asked her: What made you go travelling?

Daphne screwed up her well-sunned face. If you grow up in Australia you just have to. You're so far away.

Did you want to?

She paused, smiling. You know, it must sound idiotic but I don't think I ever asked myself that. I just knew I always would. She shrugged. It's OK. I've seen a lot of cool stuff, and you learn to look after yourself, so that's good. Yeah. And when I eventually get home it'll be great to see everyone.

And you'll never have to go away again.

Exactly.

They both laughed. A moment's silence fell.

Jackson was restless. Across the table Sarah turned to Celer and laughed at something he'd said, which Jackson hadn't caught. He couldn't help wondering if she was not yet attached to him, but only flirting. Most travelling girls were unattached. Tonight might be a chance for him or the acrobat, assuming the acrobat was interested.

It was burdensome to have to leave the gathering, but he couldn't see what else to do.

He said to Daphne, I think I better take him back now.

He was unsure what to do, unsure what he wanted. Sarah seemed to have implied they could hang out together later, but he couldn't see how to arrange that, what with the boy. And anyway, she was sitting with Celer now.

I think I'd better take him back, he repeated, nodding at Ignacio.

Jackson was half attracted by the notion of letting the boy sleep on the floor while he made a night of it, and half bothered. The boy worried him altogether and until he worked out what his responsibilities were it seemed safer not to risk doing something that might be irresponsible.

But when Jackson got up to go, Sarah got up too and walked to the bar. He saw her writing something on a piece of paper with a pencil. She came up to Jackson and said, You're going?

Jackson hesitated, then leaned forward to give her a kiss on the cheek. He smelled what he had been smelling on the dance floor, some face cream or sun cream, a fragrance of cleanness, of health.

She said softly, Here's where I'm staying. Why don't you put him to bed then come by later? We can go out again. I'll wait up. The night doesn't have to end. She flashed a smile at him.

Jackson felt exhilarated then depressed. What was he supposed to do about the boy?

On the bus back into town Ignacio sat upright with the chicken in his lap.

The cat was lying curled on the end of Jackson's bed. It got up and stretched its small flimsy body, trembling, racked by a snort of purring.

When Jackson came back from the bathroom he found the boy kneeling on the floor at the end of the bed, pulling off stringy pieces of chicken and feeding them to the cat, who sat comfortably on its hindquarters, chewing exaggeratedly with its eyes closed.

Jackson felt awkward, like he was intruding. As quietly as he could he closed the door and moved onto his bed. The springs squeaked, then he lay still. Neither the boy nor the cat seemed to notice him. The boy whispered to the animal and gave it another piece of meat, then lay down on his bed.

When the cat had finished eating it quivered rather than scampered across the floor, all shivering fur and bone, all ribs, taking giant awkward leaps as if it had been given paws one size too big, as if it couldn't control the tremendous scope of its limbs. It flowed in one movement up onto the bed and onto Ignacio's stomach. He was wearing only a T-shirt but lay quite still, undisturbed by the pounce. The cat made a couple of pretend leaps at nothing, then lay on its back and proceeded to bat the boy's fingers. Ignacio batted back at the cat's head, making little noises of attack, until the cat got his hand in its teeth and rested with its jaws wide apart, as if caught mid-yawn.

Jackson made an unnecessary fuss of his bed, flapping out the thin cover and walking all the way round to stretch it smooth over the corners. Underneath the unease he had been feeling, he found he felt unaccountably good, as though he had recently heard good news but couldn't think what it was. He put it down to the beers.

Without undressing he lay on his bed and switched off the lamp. The room barely darkened. A light in the street outside illuminated the thin blue curtain, revealing its stippling of holes. The boy lay still, but Jackson became aware of the rhythmic thrumming of the cat's purr. He turned his head carefully to the side. The cat was sitting above the boy's head on his pillow, gently working its claws into the material, eyes half closed. It blinked at him and fluffed itself up, for all the world like a fat parlour cat.

A cat's life 'was so simple: a full belly and the day's work was done. Company helped but was incidental.

Jackson's heart was beating hard. He tried counting his breaths to pass the time, lost track, got bored and finally sat up as quietly as he could and waited in silence. The cat had gone quiet, the boy seemed to be asleep. He stood still a while then stepped around his bed toward the door. He was nervous and now realised that what was making him nervous was not the excursion he planned to make, but a simple decision he had been putting off: should he lock the door after him? To shut Ignacio in seemed wrong. On the other hand, he might wake up, find himself alone, and leave. Jackson didn't like that prospect either.

He opened the door and stood by it, listening. Behind him the room was filled with the thick silence of sleep. He shut the door, walked down the hall on the balls of his feet, kicking along the hisses of sound, then paused at the stairs, still wondering if he should go back and lock the door, but instead walked on down and out into the night.

3

Back in London, three weeks before he left, a strange thing had happened. An old major had tracked him down and invited him—had in fact insisted on his coming—for a drink in the Ritz.

The Ritz bar was more like a tea parlour, with chairs of yellow silk and little mahogany tables, and a high sky-blue ceiling. Jackson spotted the major from behind, bending over the low coffee table at which he was seated in order to put something in his mouth.

What ho, Jacko, the major said mirthlessly.

Jackson let out a dry laugh, part sigh. As he sat down he asked, What could you possibly want with me?

What? The major came as close to springing up as he could without leaving his seat. Then he looked to his side and waved at a waiter, who banked off into the distance as if he knew what to do.

Hear me out. You're just the chap I want.

A bottle of champagne arrived, along with a plate of canapés.

Jackson eyed them. This is a turn up. Army entertaining in style. Well?

He sensed Major Buckley would have preferred some chit-chat first, rather than have to launch headlong into business.

Not strictly army, Buckley said. Where you're going happens to be interesting to certain people in HMG.

Jackson swigged from his glass, the drink vanishing in effervescence on his tongue. He computed what HMG meant. Then he said, Who told you where I was going?

What? *Regimental News*, Buckley said, with mock-consternation. It's hardly a secret.

It was true: sometime back Jackson had had a call from a Sergeant Pindy—or perhaps Pindhi—from the regiment's rag, asking him what he was doing these days. Wanting to have something to report he'd told them he was organising an expedition to search for lost ruins. The voice on the phone had asked for a few specifics, which he'd given, although at the time he hadn't known if he'd ever set out.

Jackson had last seen Buckley two years before. In the interim he had turned himself from slight bulkiness to middle-year corpulence. His eyes sparkled fiercely, unpleasantly, from too many boozy lunches perhaps, and he had balded badly.

So?

On the ground, Jackson. Nothing beats it for recce. You'd be helping us and helping yourself.

Who's us?

I've got in with some interesting chaps since the old Bedford days.

And how would I be helping me? And if I did what?

They can be generous. You'll be needing funds. To hire help and so on.

The last thing I want is to draw attention to myself.

I'm not telling you how to do it, just that it'll be easier.

I've got everything planned. I don't need—but how to do *what*?

That valley you mentioned to the *News*. Just happens to be right next door to the private domain of a Mr. Carreras. He's a drug lord, own militia and everything. He seems to be turning into some sort of political leader up there now, bringing the different groups together. We'd like more of a sense of what he's up to. Tingo, that's the name. Near Chacha-something-or-other.

Buckley tipped his flute high to drain it, then poured them both more.

Jackson sighed heavily.

What's the problem? Buckley looked genuinely aggrieved. You help them, they help you.

The problem is, I'm all right.

You think you are.

What's that supposed to mean?

Come on, Jacko. The regiment's been the soul of discretion. We kept mum about you and old Connolly. We all knew. Some people weren't too happy about it.

Jackson's heart sank and he said nothing.

We wrote you glowing references too. Not even your own family ever knew what really went down. Now did they?

Jackson's eyes landed on Buckley's. The pupils were pinpricks. Jackson found he could not remove his gaze from them. His face grew hot. After a moment he closed his eyes. It seemed to be the only way out of the stare.

Look, you can walk out of here right now. Or we could put everything behind us once and for all. Just think about it. There's a chap in the consulate out there. I'm going to give you his name.

Without a moment's hesitation Buckley set down his business card by Jackson's glass.

On the back, he said. Obviously, there'll be guineas for you. By the way, are you serious about these ruins?

Jackson took a deep breath. He could see what Buckley was doing now, trying to be friendly and informal, as if the business were over. He drained his glass. Course I am.

Buckley flicked up his eyebrows. Perfect cover.

Why the hell would I want a cover?

Buckley spluttered a laugh and lifted his glass. You're a good soldier, Jackson, I was sad to see you go. Still am. It's American territory, of course, Buckley went on. Truth is, the Yanks can't send anyone down there, not on the ground. Wouldn't stand a chance, what with what the vietnamistas have been up to.

Who?

The DEA chopper pilots. The Nam vets the Agency uses. With experience of jungle action. They've been burning crops left, right and centre. It's just a piece of fortuity. Right time, right place, right chap. If you want it.

Buckley poured out more drink, letting the bubbles subside slowly.

Jackson almost smiled. Buckley hadn't been too bad back in the old days. Now, in stiff blue suit and silk tie and gleaming brogues, there must surely still be something left of who he had been.

I think I'm OK for guineas, he said. But thanks anyway.

When they left the bar, he noticed that Buckley still walked with that curious stiff walk of his, slightly stooped and pensive. A lot of well-to-do Englishmen had odd walks, Jackson reflected. Sooner I clear out of here the better, he thought.

Buckley stopped at the kerb on the corner of St. James's, where a taxi waited. Like a lift anywhere?

And why didn't they use pronouns?

It's nice of you to think of me, Jackson said, and clunked shut the black taxi door for his old major.

Buckley opened the window and looked up at him. I know you won't forget how good we've been. Wouldn't it be nice to draw a line in the sand?

The vehicle grunted off into the traffic. As Jackson watched it disappear past the railings of Green Park his boots seemed to sink into the pavement. There was no escaping anything in this life, wherever you went, whatever you did.

4

Sarah was staying in an apartment in the colonial blocks of the old city, above an arcade. He found it easily. One orange lamp illuminated the far end of the street, casting a fluid sheen on the old uneven paving within the colonnade. A black iron gate with wire-netting on the inside, instead of a door; the bell buzzed loudly, and when he let it go it made an electric click which echoed in the stone alleyway beyond the gate.

No one around. A curious, quiet, pretty part of town, the one part with any grace.

He waited. A church bell clanged.

Then he heard a knock up above. He stepped back, out of the arcade.

She was at a second-floor window. Hold on, she said, and closed the shutter.

Her footsteps echoed in the corridor, she herself was invisible in the darkness. Then she was at the gate, clicking two locks, opening it slowly—he could see it was heavy—holding a hand behind her, palm flat, ready to steady the gate as it swung shut, not to let it bang. The whole neighbourhood, the whole inner city was asleep.

Jackson was nervous now. Nervous and downcast. It was partly about money: he was getting through what little he had so fast. This night was going to be extravagant beyond anything he could afford. And here he was now with this woman he hardly knew.

She gave him a warm hug. Her body hot, warming him, and soft. They walked fast down the street, then right for two blocks into the floodlit plaza.

Jackson hailed a cab, a small green-and-white vehicle with no glass in its windows. The driver was talkative. He had few teeth and spoke in a growl, a man prematurely in his fifties. She named a bar. They drove down block after block of small concrete homes, all shut up.

Three times the driver suggested he take them to some *sala de fiestas* where the *rumba* was *preciosa*. Lots of people there, señores, he advised them. Trust me, you don't want to go to—but then he would lose heart, and drive on swiftly, the half-attached exhaust rumbling beneath them.

They passed a long strip of bars, all thumping and booming with live music.

What is it with this town? Jackson said, expecting no answer, getting none.

Sometimes the whole country seemed like one big party. Especially in the thick of the hot nights. It was a hard feeling to pin down. You just knew that out there in the night women were dancing in flimsy dresses, men were guzzling cold beer, taxis were cruising with their radios thumping. Summer came and never went, the year-round season when the days were a hammering down of heat, the nights a balm of shirt sleeves, arriving not just as a relief but a celebration. Spring here had nothing to do with buds and blossoms, but with watts and dance sweat. Something went loose in people's minds, and all they wanted to do at night was party. It was too hot for anything else.

They went back to the beach. One open-air restaurant still had its light on; they bought a quarter of rum and two cans of Coca-

Cola. They settled on the beach and mixed the rum in the cans, knocking them together with a dull clank.

This is the life, she said. Makes you wonder what the hell we're all doing with our lives.

Tell you the truth it doesn't do it for me here, he said. So big and gloomy. I can't wait to get back to the mountains.

God, I know what you mean. Clear air, simple people. The quiet. I love it up there too. But this is good for me. It's just what I need.

She seemed excited. Her voice was slightly higher than before, and a little breathless. He wondered why this place was just what she needed, but before he could ask, she jumped up and pulled off her skirt and her shirt. She had a black swimsuit on underneath, made of some shiny material that glistened in the light of the bar behind them. Her limbs shone too, darkly tanned.

Come on, she said. Time to freshen up.

She grabbed his hand and pulled him down the beach. He disentangled himself from his clothes and they ran across the sand toward the quiet thunder of the surf.

The water was thick like oil in the dark, moving in plates, giant scales, each one edged with a white fringe. It was warm glutinous water, unrefreshing, vaguely alarming. It didn't matter what monsters might be in it, Jackson thought, it was itself a kind of monster.

They wallowed in the shallows, Sarah laughing and splashing him, Jackson vaguely fearful of the big, dark ocean just there. And he felt he ought to move closer to her, but he couldn't.

Afterward when they sat drying off, side by side, he couldn't bring himself to touch her either. An appalling shyness seized him. He not only couldn't reach out and touch her, but sitting there with his knees drawn in to his chest, for a while he felt he could not make any move at all. It was as if all the alcohol had evaporated. The vault of the sky overhead, the great ocean beside them: the two of them might have been the only people on earth. Yet he felt paralysed. Then strangely he began to sense that she was content just to sit side by side in silence. After a while a good feeling strengthened, and he didn't even want to think about anything else, in case he started worrying again.

She told him she was getting over a long relationship, and that seemed a way of offering him shelter for not having made a move on her.

These ruins you're looking for, she said. Why are you so sure they're there? And why are you so into them?

That friend of mine I mentioned. I guess it's all to do with him.

He really found them?

He said he did. I want to find out.

For you? Or for him?

He didn't respond. He didn't know what to say.

It was an abortive date. He had the sense that it was too much too soon: they weren't ready to be half naked and alone on a beach at night. He felt too that there was more in store. In a little while he walked her back up to the road. There were no taxis, no buses. They began the long walk into town.

He told her he was getting over some difficult things too.

That's OK, she hummed, and kissed his cheek.

Up on the main road he flagged down an ailing truck carrying a load of pigeons in crates. The birds cooed and gurgled as the truck bounced along. The two of them sat side by side on an empty sack, shivering.

5

Jackson found it hard to sleep. His body was flooded with a happiness he couldn't understand. He liked hearing the occasional rustle from the next bed as the boy or the cat adjusted themselves. He understood again that his shame and regrets were unnecessary. It was possible to erase them, not to care about the past because it didn't exist. He wondered why he didn't always feel like this, and congratulated himself on slowly learning to live moment by moment, to adopt the great lesson of a journey. And on having taken the step of leaving, of coming here.

He lay awake thinking about Sarah. He could still feel her close to him when they danced, the warmth of her skin, the weight, or lack of it, of her body. With his arms round her he had had the feeling that she was hollow. Or permeable. As if he could have put his hand right through her. Yet there her warm skin was. And the rest of the café had become brighter and somehow softer, and smaller. It had seemed as if the walls and floor, tables and chairs, and all the people, some sitting, some dancing, receded from the two of them. He had felt as if he had broken down some barrier, and a life he wanted was no longer out of reach. But on the beach—for a moment he worried again that he should have done something. But then a good feeling welled up that he hadn't. That seemed to mean even more. It was hard to explain.

It seemed impossible he would wake filled with uneasiness the next morning, yet he did. He had slept only lightly, and awoke to dismay. When would he try at least once for something he really wanted? He had known how to do that when Connolly was alive. Ever since then it had been one mistake after another. Probably he had just let another golden opportunity slip through his fingers.

He decided today had to be the day to do something. First about the boy. He thought of nuns in their white-walled confinement, of policeman-soldiers with their patent leather holsters and Spartan offices; then of his own lack of a passport, shortage of money. He could no longer put off what he had been avoiding. He was down to twenty-seven dollars. He would have to get in touch with that contact of Major Buckley's. It filled him with unease, but he couldn't see what else to do. He simply couldn't wait.

He and Ignacio ate breakfast in a cavernous café with blue plastic tables and an ancient vaulted ceiling. Two fat women ran the place. They found Jackson and the boy inherently comic. They could barely suppress their giggles when they brought out plates of *huevos diablados* and a mug of hot milk for Ignacio, coffee for Jackson.

Is there a telephone kiosk nearby? Jackson tried asking the younger of them, a plump woman with a downy moustache. Her face shone with a film of kitchen grease.

A smile broke out on her cheeks and she turned round, started to call back to the kitchen, stopping in mid-sentence as she skipped up the steps.

A moment later the other, older woman emerged, dressed in a white housecoat, her hair pulled back in a bun, amplifying the full width of her face.

¿Qué? she asked from the steps.

He repeated the question, smiling to offer her a cover in case she collapsed in laughter too.

She retreated into the kitchen, and the two of them talked back there for a while. Then the older one emerged again with a plastic basket of tortillas wrapped in grease paper, which she deposited on the table without a word.

The boy explained in his best Spanish, quietly, what the señor wanted to know.

There was a phone store a few blocks away, it turned out. On the way back to the hotel, Jackson ducked into it. An old man sat behind a table at the end of a row of small cubicles. Jackson gave him the number he wanted, then took the boy with him into the cubicle the man directed him to.

Brown?

The receiver was old, heavy and black.

The man at the other end cleared his throat and said in a calm English voice, Ah. Yes.

Major Buckley gave me your name.

You must be Mr. Small. I wondered if I'd ever hear from you.

I have twelve dollars to my name, Jackson blurted into the receiver, surprised by his own sudden desperation at the sound of the English voice. I nearly got killed by some crazy old guy with a boy. The boy's still with me. I'm about to spend my last *soles* on a bus ticket.

You think they're tracking you?

What?

With the boy?

Who on earth would do that? Jackson shrugged, as if the man might see. Jesus, this is Peru. All I know is I've got no money. That old man robbed me.

There was a pause.

What do you want me to do?

The man was silent. The line hissed. Then he said: As it happens there is something you could do, yes. If you were asking. But this isn't some squalid quid pro quo. He paused again. Anyway, it's convenient. As it happens.

There was silence.

Where *are* you?

Jackson didn't reply at first, he wasn't sure why. Trujillo.

That's good.

Why is that good? Jackson wondered.

And you're going up to Tingo? Into the cloud forest?

Yes, but I need to get the money together.

Of course.

The man spoke like posh army men did, but he didn't have the right accent. Jackson could detect something not quite like them in the intonation. He wondered if he always spoke like that, or was putting it on because of the army connection.

Well, for what we have in mind—it's just to pick something up and place it somewhere, nothing to it—I think we could stretch to a grand. Dollars.

Jackson sighed. All right. All right. He didn't have any choice. He could hardly haggle.

There's a hotel called the Panama. Go at two. I'll give you the address. Ask for Jorge. He'll sort you out and tell you what to do once you're up in the right province. You do plan to *go* there?

Jackson didn't answer. It was like being spoken to by a school-master. His heart sank. To be signing up with these people again. Not to be free of them. Never mind what it would mean to have a covert mission where he was going.

Don't get yourself in trouble. It's not pretty up there, by all accounts.

Jackson hung up feeling disgusted with himself, and only when he was half a block away did he realise he had forgotten to men-tion his passport. But nothing could induce him to get·back on the phone.

The Hotel Panama had a swimming pool at the back. A handful of people were scattered on sunloungers, and one man hung in the water with his elbows over the side of the pool.

As soon as Ignacio saw the water he pulled off his shirt and kicked off his shoes. Jackson was about to stop him when he thought to himself: why not? Maybe it would allow him to talk freely to whoever Jorge was, if Ignacio was amusing himself in the pool.

Ignacio stripped down to his shorts and ran straight at the blue water without stopping, and also without making any kind of extra leap, he simply ran into the water. His dark head vanished in a sparkle of spray. Then he kept bouncing up and down, his head emerging and sinking again.

Jackson watched. He hadn't known until then that Ignacio could swim. The boy kept ducking under and breaking out. It looked like he was letting himself sink to the bottom, then springing back up. Then he didn't emerge for a while, and when he did he gasped and sank under again in a cloud of bubbles.

Jackson fumbled with the buttons of his shirt then whipped it over his head, and tugged off his trousers as fast as he could. He didn't have trunks but dived in in his underwear. It took only one lunge off the bottom to propel the boy to the side, where he held him while he clung on and caught his breath, spluttering and coughing. Jackson pulled him out and sat beside him on the concrete, one hand on his back as the boy sat there hunched over, his chest heaving.

The boy's face hung down and he stared at the paving. Jackson thought he could see the fear and shame in it.

It's OK, he said. You have to learn, that's all. We all have to learn. It takes time. You didn't know.

He must have come from some high village, so high the water was far too cold for anyone to think of swimming.

The boy was still gasping, only now it was hard to tell if he was out of breath or sobbing.

It's OK. I'll teach you. You want to learn? It took me years to learn, but you're fast, you'll learn fast.

Gradually the boy quietened and Jackson ruffled his wet hair and put an arm round him. Come on. You want to have your first lesson?

The boy nodded without looking up. Jackson took his hand and helped him climb down into the water. First he taught him to hold onto the side and kick, then to lie flat on the surface, with Jackson's hands under his little torso, and kick while Jackson moved him along. Then they added a little paddling with the hands.

You're good. You see? A little practice and you'll learn in no time.

A man in the far corner of the patio, wearing shades and a *guayabera* shirt, seated at a table with a cup of coffee and a pad of paper, had been glancing at Jackson now and then. He pushed his glasses onto his forehead now and openly stared for fully two or three seconds, then picked up his coffee.

Jackson said, We'll dry off in the sun.

They went and sat on a lounger not far from the man. There was no one else nearby.

Jorge? Jackson called to him.

The man raised his eyebrows. *¿A quién busca?* Who are you looking for? He had a deep gravelly voice, and sounded like a local.

Jorge, Jackson repeated.

The man didn't answer. He sipped from his broad white cup, then set it down. With an inclination of the head he beckoned Jackson over.

So you're Señor Brown's friend? It's very simple. Sit down. No. Tell the boy to stay.

Ignacio had got up from the lounger.

Jackson tutted at him, and he sat down again. He pulled out one of the heavy iron chairs for himself at the man's table.

The man at once slid an envelope from under his pad. Here, this is for you.

It was a small envelope, and Jackson couldn't help feeling just how little he was gaining for what he was about to do. He felt as though he were giving up his freedom for a crust.

So what do I do? he asked before taking it.

You get to Choctamal on the twentieth. You find it in the Tingo valley south of Chachapoyas. A small village. There someone will have what you need. Is a beacon. They tell you where to put it. Is simple. No problem.

Jorge smiled, and two sleeping dimples formed around his mouth. I thought it would be easy to find you. A young *inglés*. But I didn't expect you to have this boy. I didn't think was you.

By the time Jackson led Ignacio back to their clothes, waiting on a chair on the other side of the pool, they were both dry, ready to dress.

Later, Jackson lay on his bed and sent the boy up onto the roof with the cat. He opened the window and lay still, listening to the traffic picking up once more in the streets now that the day had passed its zenith. There ought to have been something comforting in the recovery of life and industry, in the sounds of humanity rousing itself from its afternoon torpor, but there wasn't. Just the same old things going on yet one more time.

He opened the envelope he had been given and counted out $950. Someone had taken a commission. He felt weary and heavy. He had just over three weeks to get to the village. At least it was where he wanted to go. At least they had been right about that. That much was good. He still had the worrying problem of his passport, but he wasn't going to wait any longer. He needed to get into the mountains.

He tried telling himself that perhaps it wasn't so bad after all. He might be truly being helpful. And they—whoever exactly they were, but presumably military intelligence, eager to ingratiate themselves with the Americans—were helping him after all. But he wasn't convinced. It was leverage, it was indebtedness, it was the past and its shadow. The thing he wanted to escape. He had the depressing sense that all along he had known he would do it, too, because of Major Buckley's implicit threats.

Two flies were buzzing around the light bulb, even though the light was off, as if they were waiting for it to come on. They travelled their odd courses, bouncing off invisible angles in the air like billiard balls in perpetual motion. Somewhere there was a mosquito. Jackson caught sight of it, a skittery dot, then lost it. The whine of a mosquito, he thought, was the only thing that gave it away at night. Once a curious shiny fly appeared on the wall beside him, travelling in quick jerky zigzags, as if hunting desperately for something; then it too vanished.

Who cares about the little fly, he thought, with its tiny transparent wings and diminutive green body? It has no parents it knows of, no friends. Yet it goes about its life. Was that a high aim—perfect self-sufficiency? Yes, he thought. But it was no good quietly tending your stock and being secretly miserable. You had to be happy.

What would Connolly have said? Don't look back. Onward, onward, there's no other way, mate.

Time to write a letter, he thought. A letter to whom, though? The only person he wanted to write to was Connolly, and that was obviously out of the question.

Ignacio came back to the room.

Come on, we're off, Jackson said. Pack up.

The boy had gone straight to the window and was kneeling in front of it struggling with the strings of a kite, which had got in a formidable tangle. Jackson hadn't noticed the toy before. He frowned.

Where did you get that?

Every time the boy succeeded in unravelling one knot he would move his fingers down to the next snarl only to find it more impregnable than the last.

The boy looked round. What, señor?

That.

The boy didn't answer. Instead he asked, Where are we going, señor?

On, on. Put that in a bag.

The boy wanted to carry the kite, a big green diamond of plastic sheeting, probably an old fertiliser bag, but Jackson showed him how to snap its cross-poles out of the corners and roll it up like an umbrella. With that in one hand and his cat cradled in the other, and with a red knapsack on his back that Jackson had bought for him at a stall, in which his Andean clothes were bundled up, the boy followed Jackson down the echoing stairwell and out into the street.

They walked over to where Sarah was staying first. Jackson buzzed on the bell several times. Eventually a window high up opened and an old woman wailed, *No está, señor, no está.*

He thought of leaving her a note but didn't know where to put it so she'd see it.

Tell her, he called up, the *inglés* has gone to Chachapoyas.

The old woman said something that he didn't catch, and closed the window.

5 · Night Ride

The bus growled toward the black wall of mountains.

Beneath the low roof of cloud the vehicle of sky-blue tin, crammed with ragged humanity, traversed the flat grey land like the wastes of Creation's second day, when God had parted the waters and installed the land but nothing more. Land and sky were a dim bivalve opened just wide enough to admit the vehicle's passage.

A man four rows ahead had his transistor turned up so loud it was all screech and jangle. He leaned one ear against the window and pressed the radio to the other. He must have been deaf. If not, he would be before long. The axle interminably cleared its throat beneath the floor, making it hot. Some windows were open and could not be closed, some were closed and could not be opened. The tattered, chequered vehicle shuddered on.

At some point Jackson woke and found the boy asleep with his head in his lap, one bare shin projecting across the aisle, shoeless. The sight stirred pity. He could see the shoe lying beneath the next seat forward across the aisle. He wanted to retrieve it but did not want to disturb the head sleeping in his lap. He couldn't decide what to do, poised in a caring indecisiveness in which finally the care overwhelmed the indecision.

Later he was overtaken by panic. A night like this could be the night on which one would die. This crowded canister of steel could be the carriage of death, ferrying all its unwitting occupants into the void. It could even be the night one had already died. The night might know no end. The thought stirred a kind of excitement, to be growling across emptiness with no known goal. Wasn't this the right way to travel through life? Wasn't this in fact how life was?

In the darkness outside black bulks of rock moved. You could see the truth that although God had ordered the chaos he had done it imperfectly. Chaos was still the raw matter of creation. The endless toing and froing of the waters, the great chunks of black rock—God like an inexpert gardener had fenced in a rockery here, penned in a forest there, but the forest climbed up into the crevices, the waters stirred constantly, and the clouds shifted uneasily across the peaks. Where was man's proper place? A gypsy, a nomad, caught in an endless migration from nowhere to nowhere.

⚓

At Miami airport, where Jackson had changed planes on his way over nine weeks earlier, he had been surprised to remember so much—the duty-free boutique with the purple neon sign, the crummy food stalls selling hot dogs and nachos, the black-mirrored faux-foyer of the airport hotel and, more than any of that, the colourful clothes. Guys in orange, black, blue *guayaberas*, in big straw hats, patent-leather shoes, silk and satin shirts open to the navel. Not to mention the women. This was the big stop for the islands and the slice countries, each with their own little piece of the continental pie. Right away you could feel it was happier than the north. Something in the air, a friendly madness as if you had landed in a cartoon.

He had found himself thinking of Connolly. He and Connolly had come here together now and then on trips out of Belize. They'd drunk beers at that dingy little bar with the small, fuzzy TV, had had glasses of shrimp during a stopover. It had always been a good place for them—either on their way to some brief adventure during a leave, or else getting back to base after a blow-out and looking forward to getting in shape again, to camp routine.

He remembered the last time, when they had sat up in the bar on the roof of the hotel drinking Michelobs and watching the jets take off for destinations all over the continent. Connolly had talked about Chachapoyas again, how one of these days he'd be going back down there. It seemed to be his ideal place on earth. The last time Connolly had returned, he had found the ruins he was after, and came back with money to throw around. They'd had some big nights out on the cays, buying steak and lobster at the beach restaurants for any traveller who cared to join them. There was prosperity down in Chachapoyas, if a man knew where to look. Whatever frustrations life had, their solutions were to be found there. It was like an attic where all that was best in life had been stored.

Jackson could remember being captivated. Everything had seemed perfect just then—the golden scimitars of beer, the silver jets tipping up like toys on the runway streaking off for who knew where, and the promise of criss-crossing the sunny globe with a true friend. They could go anywhere, once they got out, take on any kind of work. They were strong and young, worthy of their promise.

Connolly had his theory about the mythical El Dorado really being the vanished civilisation of Chachapoyas Province. His dream was one day to prove it. Can you imagine, he used to say, what it would be to stand in the very heart of a forgotten civilisation, knowing all their bones and the bones of their dogs and llamas and chickens and turkeys were buried under your feet, along with who knew what treasures? And no one had been there since them?

This old civilisation was yet another promise held out by the sunny side of the globe. It didn't exactly matter if this or any other El Dorado really existed; Jackson had felt that he already had found a kind of El Dorado, sitting above the golden runways on the brink of the many departures he might one day make.

And not long after, there'd come that night in the forest in Belize, and everything had been so different.

But here he was now, at last, going to that very place, endeavouring to do the very thing Connolly had done, and more. It was different to be doing it alone, of course. But he was glad of the boy, who kept him distracted.

Somewhere in the middle of the night the bus engine cried and groaned through the gears, and collapsed in a series of falling yelps.

Jackson tried to see what was going on, but the vehicle was enveloped in a cloud of dust. He leaned across the sleeping boy to look down the aisle, saw a red light in the road ahead, a barrier, a clutch of soldiers. The bus came to rest with a hiccup.

He shook Ignacio awake. The boy felt for the cat hiding inside his poncho then blinked and sat up. Jackson put his finger to his lips. Then, not sure if that was a universal sign, said, *Shh*.

A man in a dirty white shirt two rows ahead looked round at him.

Jackson leaned back against his window, waited a moment. Then, not sure if *shh* was a universal signal either, he whispered to the boy: Don't say anything. Sleep.

Then he burrowed his head down deep against the arm rest, leaning away from the aisle, and pulled the boy half on top of him. He covered his legs with a blanket he had bought at the market in Trujillo.

The engine chortled away, idling, the tone adjusting as the driver reached across to lever open the door.

A light came on. Jackson had been hoping that wouldn't happen. He hooked a hand inside the boy's armpit to hold him in place. He was expecting to hear an exchange of words with the driver, but there were no voices. Perhaps the driver had climbed out himself, and no one would come in. He couldn't afford to look.

Then just a row or two away he heard a deep, smooth military voice saying, But this is out of date, señora.

And a woman answering, *Yo no sé nada de eso*. I don't know about that. This is my identity, my identity.

At first it was reassuring to hear the military voice, the voice of a man who knew that what he was doing with his life, the way he used his mind, body and days, was good. You could feel that in the army. But he himself was outside it now. He was in some no man's land. He didn't even have a passport.

With one eye open Jackson saw a black polished boot plant itself beside his row, and at the top of a green trouser leg he could see the muzzle of a revolver. The leg and foot paused then stepped on toward the back of the bus. They took a long time coming back, as they must do, the bus having only the one door at the front. When they finally reappeared they stopped. Jackson watched the boot turn toward him, and a second shuffle into sight.

The same smooth voice said: *Carnet*.

The boy lifted his head off Jackson's shoulder. Jackson lay stiff with the blanket up around his ears. He pulled in a stertorous breath.

Papa está enfermo, the boy said. *Enfermo*. Sick.

¿A dónde van? came the voice. Where are you going?

Chachapoyas, the boy muttered apologetically.

Jackson closed his eyes. Why watch after all? He was powerless. Events must take their course. Then he opened them again. The two boot toes still shone in his direction. Then one by one they turned away.

When the bus roared on he raised his head enough to catch a glimpse of a concrete hut, an open doorway, a bare lamp-lit room, and a clutch of soldiers outside, machine-guns slung over their shoulders, dark-faced.

He waited a while, thrown back and forth by a series of bends, then eased himself up and looked at the boy.

Gracias.

A hint of a smile broke the boy's solemnity.

You're good, Jackson said.

The flesh twitched either side of the boy's mouth and his eyebrows seemed to rise. Then he looked down at the floor, as if unwilling to get caught out in a smile.

After that Jackson could not sleep for a long time. He thought about Sarah, and wondered if he should have stayed, should have found her again. The further the bus rode into the mountains the more it seemed to be she who was keeping him awake. He couldn't get her face out of his mind. Her eyes and cheeks seemed superimposed on everything he saw, like an image etched on a veil. What did it mean? As the night wore on he began to wonder if he should do something about it. But what? He realised he wanted very much to see her again. Perhaps it was possible. She would be coming into the mountains before long, she'd said, to see that uncle of hers. Maybe he could try and find out who the uncle was, and where he lived.

And he worried about what he had signed up for with Mr. Brown. It wasn't just that he didn't want to be beholden to those people. It was what they had asked him to do: be deceitful. No longer would he honestly be pursuing his quest. He had a secret agenda—and he didn't even know what it was. But undoubtedly he would have to deceive people. It compromised the journey; he was no longer acting in innocence. This was his chance to put things right, and he was sullying it before he'd even reached the cloud forest.

Then to wake to the first lick of the sun's tongue: in the swirl of black dust to his side there was a gulf of space, a chasm. Its far wall caught a shaft of golden light as if on a movie screen. The heave of a bend pressed his forehead against the dusty pane, the weight in his lap shifted and was gone, and a wall of funnelled clay appeared. High up, ridges stood edged with filaments of light, and ahead, straight up the aisle of the bus, beyond the driver's bouncing head, he saw a black mass of rock: the shadow of the mountain they were fighting to climb.

The boy was sitting up, staring ahead. But in a moment he

tipped his head back, mouth agape, wobbling with the jounces, neck stretched taut, and slowly closed his eyes like a dying man.

Jackson woke later to a golden cloud of dust and smoke. His window had yellowed overnight. He was powerfully hungry, and looked forward to finding his way through the cool air of a mountain morning into a cafeteria with *lomo saltado*, coffee and tortillas.

His watch said six. He lit a cigarette and put his knees up against the seat in front. The passengers had all finally quietened in the hours before dawn, all radios extinguished, lulled finally like babies by the mighty gurgle of the diesel, by the heat of the grinding axles rising from under the floor. The boy's legs stuck out under his own, while his head was thrown back over the arm rest into the aisle, his mouth still open, little upper teeth just showing under the lip.

Jackson had misgivings about taking the child even further from wherever his home might once have been. He had already made up his mind that he would try to find the priest that Sarah had mentioned. But was it right to deliver him to an unknown priest in a small town in the remote mountains, sixteen hours from the nearest city?

They rode along the edge of a steep slope. He could see a track snaking down in a ribbon of switchbacks, pale against the hillside. Three grey blocks stood on the plain below. At first he took them for buildings. Then he saw they were buses, lying on their backs like dead beetles, their story clear.

Finally the bus wound over the brow of a hill and the little town lay ahead, glittering on the brown earth of a broad basin like a spill of mineral ore, the very ore perhaps that had once given rise to the settlement in the first place. The town blossomed out from the pale cord of the track leading to it.

An ancient bulb-fronted truck passed them with a demonic rasp of its engine. Jackson, leaning his forehead against the window, saw that its wheel arches were completely eaten away by rust. It was hard to imagine what held it together. In the back of the truck, wrapped in blankets of every hue, sat a tightly packed confederation of Indians. As their truck guzzled down the stony road they hunched against the wind, their white felt hats wedged down on their heads.

The ragged bus passed the first dilapidated walls and vacant yards of the town's edge. An air of expectancy filled the vehicle. People rustled their plastic bags and tied up their blankets and complained at their children, as if now that the elixir of travel had worn off they were all waking up to the hopeful hangover of arrival.

A woman shook a bulging burlap sack whose contents moved of their own accord, muttering. When she set the sack down in the aisle, a soft crowing sounded inquisitively from within.

Soon after, they pulled up in a market square.

Part Two

HIGHLAND

6 · Mountain Padre

1

Trees. The shivery eucalyptus trees of the Andes, copper green beside copper-green rivers, the colour of factory run-off, thick with ore. The trees were wonderful. They stood in long lines along lonely roadsides like avenues, as if planted deliberately. Padre Beltrán saw them often on his solitary travels in his jeep. The *padre agrónomo*, people called him. He took credit for re-introducing quinoa to a whole section of the country—the flat-topped eastern hills, where the land was an array of giant anvils raised up to the sky, beaten by sun by day, by night poured over with molten moonshine.

Beltrán lived in Chachapoyas, once famous for its silver mine. He was a quiet man, good-humoured and philosophical. The years under the high-altitude sun had turned him bright red, so he looked permanently shocked. His life was simple: a bare flat in town with tiled floors, metal sink and single bed, a small office, also his sitting room, that he staffed by himself with the help of TAD, the Telephone Answering Device, which had stopped working around the same time the telephone line gave out, and a spare room with three sets of bunks where the boys he took in slept.

He had lived in Chachapoyas for over twenty years, and had known as soon as he moved here that it was the right place for him. Small, it bustled all day long, especially at either end of the day. But its bustle was its own, it was self-sufficient. After a certain point in life, it was the self-sufficiency one came to value most.

The train used to clunk out of the big dilapidated city to the north once a week, arriving at midnight the following day, pausing for an hour before continuing its crossing down to the capital. Then they suspended the service. They built a new road in the seventies, when the country enjoyed a brief false boom. It came glinting across the northern desert between a pair of corroded crash barriers, but vanished after only a couple of dozen miles. There was also once an airstrip. But pilots complained of the awkward approach, a plunge over a steep hill, and the strip had returned to weeds. Now only the police helicopter used it.

Despite the cloth, Beltrán no longer considered himself a man who necessarily believed in God; he just knew God. Sometimes in town he would see God in the market, with all the blue plastic sheets over the stalls and the bowler-hatted women sitting amid giant heaps of avocado, orange and banana. You might see a dog slip beneath a stall, skipping its hind legs over the crossbar of a trestle table, and meanwhile be hearing the constant babble of soft, breathy, Andean voices like a stream jumping over rocks, and God might tap you on your shoulder, and make you not just see and hear, but feel all of it. You would have to agree he was right to do so. He would draw your attention to himself, which was the same as the human bustle. Or you'd find him in the smell of fruit, when it seemed the air in the market was so sweet you could only have walked in the back gate of Eden.

Beltrán had not always lived alone. Nor was he a local. He had grown up in Salamanca, and as a young man won a scholarship to Princeton, where he met the daughter of a wealthy retired admiral, niece of a soft drinks manufacturer. She was rich, pretty, and guided his hand up her skirt on their second date. They were married when he was twenty-two, she twenty-one. He turned down lucrative postings within the provinces of her family's wealth, and instead took her to live in Georgetown, and enrolled in medical school.

But you've just finished at Princeton, her relatives cried.

But he wouldn't be swayed.

She miscarried twice, then gave birth to a girl who died at five weeks, just after learning to smile. After three months, his wife, separate, inconsolable, left him for her father's Pennsylvania farm. Beltrán suffered the worst period of his life. After months immobile on friends' couches around Washington, an old tutor set him up as assistant to a doctor down in the Bahamas.

It was there Beltrán met Father Jerome, the hermit of Cat Island. He was an Englishman, a Franciscan, and had built himself a little hermitage out of local stone. Every time their rounds took them to Cat Island, Beltrán would climb the long, hot slope, and sit with the hermit in his diminutive cloister. One day Beltrán spent an afternoon up there alone. You could see the sea on both sides of the island, green on the leeward, dark blue and glittering on the windward. It came to him then what he must do: go back to Spain, to Toledo, and enter the seminary.

That was nearly three decades ago. Today Beltrán had his clean, tiled flat, the office, the Nissan jeep with its two giant spare wheels on the back. Every time he turned off the Pan American highway and rattled up the tracks toward the villages, something in him settled. Some men were made for cities, others for the country, he thought. Beltrán's eye would graze the hillsides, guzzle the high ridges black in sunlight, gorge on the long moors that fell away in ravines so profound you couldn't see the rivers in their beds, though sometimes you could just hear their hiss. When he drove west, his heart went out to the volcanoes of the cordillera, toy white cones on the rim of the world.

Then by evening he'd be rattling into some earthen village where the lamps were being lit beneath the high sky. A woman with black plaits hanging to her waist and a face like crumpled brown paper would give him chickpeas and a stiff unleavened loaf still warm from a clay oven, then llama blankets and a clay shelf to sleep on. In the villages where there was a padre, Beltrán would stay with him.

How's my little *gringuito*, the Catholic missionary in the village of Bolívar would say, because of Beltrán's time in America, and because of his small stature. They'd talk till late in the glare of a paraffin lamp.

Beltrán looked neither forward nor back. He had made his peace with the past. There were so many babies, so many solitary mothers, too many beaten ones. He sometimes thought love, as it was known, was the cause of most human ills.

2

Tuesday began badly for Beltrán. Normally he didn't set an alarm, because the church began its daily broadcast of religious music at seven in the morning. Loudhailers mounted on the corners of the old edifice would jangle and crackle, so at first you had no idea what the noise was, until a choir of voices launched themselves over the distortions of the instruments. It had been his idea, a way of reminding the town of the constant offer of salvation. It was never too late.

Felipe, the altar boy, an orphan from Celendín, used to switch on the tape. If you lived or worked within five or six blocks of the church—anywhere in the town centre—you went through your morning chores under the carollings of Beltrán's metallic angels.

But this day Felipe had evidently neglected his first duty. He had probably sneaked out last night to drain the empty bottles in the crates at the back of Agustín's cantina. Beltrán knew he did that. But there would be no mileage in confronting him. Good guidance was a pillar that drew people, not a fence that enclosed them.

The music didn't start till seven forty, when Felipe had probably rolled into a sunbeam on his pillow.

Beltrán felt something was wrong when he heard it. He sat up at once, as he always did, and without hesitation set his feet on the cold floor. He pulled off his nightshirt (an old Brooks Brothers button-down missing three buttons) and stood up. He rushed through his ablutions, grabbed a small loaf, stuffed a spoon of marmalade into it, and lurched down the long rickety wooden staircase attached to the side of his abode, its only means of access (which one day, he was sure, would be the death of him). He struggled to gain entry into the pocket of his cassock where he kept the key of the church's side door, and slipped into the susurrating interior just in time to see a bulky, stiff, middle-aged lady come bustling up the aisle.

Señora, he called.

So began his first parish duty of the day: listening to Señora del Cabo's catalogue of matrimonial woes.

The padre glanced anxiously at his watch. As soon as he decently could he broke away, and once again mounted the perilous steps to his apartment, where a man stood with his back against the wall, holding a white felt hat in his hands, wrapped in a pall of gloom Beltrán could almost see, for all the world like a man waiting to see a dentist or a lawyer.

But why didn't you take a seat? A million apologies for making you wait. Let me offer you a cup of coffee, a pancake.

Without waiting for a reply, which in any case would not be more than a mumbled *Pues*, his visitor being a humble peasant, Beltrán filled an aluminium saucepan from a hose that entered his home via the window, tipped with a copper clip-valve, and fired up his Primus stove. He could smell the man from across the room. It was a strangely welcome odour after the mix of cheap perfume and sweat coming from the woman he had just been listening to in the church. Or maybe it had been expensive perfume, he had no idea, except that he preferred the pungency of the peasants, which could take your breath away but was wholesome as straw. In fact it was something like straw, a dry fierce aroma that attacked the back of the throat.

It's not necessary, the man said in a muffled, lugubrious tone, which Beltrán knew to be his visitor's habitual voice, referring to the refreshments.

But of course, Señor Cruz. I'm so glad you have come. Do sit, do sit.

Beltrán pulled out a chair at the little steel table, which Cruz reluctantly took. As the water boiled and the batter bubbled, the farmer sat in silence. Two of the boys, Xavier and Tomás, came out of their bedroom, their eyes big and black in the morning light. Beltrán shooed them outside, telling them to go and play for half an hour. They solemnly obeyed, and tramped down the outside stairs, still half asleep.

With cups and plates put out, and a little can of condensed milk punctured ready for the coffee, Beltrán seated himself opposite Cruz, murmured a grace, then announced: The point is this. Can we get enough people to our side? If we can, we can drive the *tráficos* out for good. But only the people can do it. That means you and me and others. Go and persuade your friends.

The little speech surprised both himself and farmer Cruz. The words seemed to have ambushed him, jumped out by themselves.

I am determined to help, he found himself adding.

Cruz stared into his coffee and stirred it slowly. He shook his head. Things are bad, señor. They keep coming by our *chacras*. I can't tell them to go away or they will shoot me. Then where will María and Gloria and everyone else be? I don't know what choice is left. There are two who come by every few weeks and stay at the farm. They have guns, padre. They bring in guns. If I don't take them across the pass I don't know what they'll do. It's not so simple, padre.

Of course not, Beltrán said. But with prayer all things are possible.

Riding a sudden invigoration, Beltrán lifted his tin cup and declared: To liberation. No consequences.

He would think about that morning afterward, wondering what had come over him. Perhaps it had been listening to Señora del Cabo yet again, a member of the town's petit bourgeoisie, who grabbed one petty dissatisfaction after another, and then meeting with Cruz, the solemn, hardworking peasant.

Cruz smiled sheepishly, puzzled, then realised he was expected to raise his cup too, did so, and the two men each sucked noisily at their respective drinks.

On the radio a quavering tenor was singing "Miserere" to the accompaniment of a symphony orchestra reinforced by rock drummers. The music irritated Beltrán, and he got up and snapped off the old transistor on the windowsill.

For a moment his room was filled with a delicious quiet. He picked up his pen with relief and smoothly completed a sentence of the letter he was composing to his father in Spain. He wrote to him once a week, his mother having died four years ago. Then the little monkey Felipe turned on another tape of church music that boomed through the loudspeakers out onto the streets.

Ah, what are you *doing?* Beltrán muttered, and glanced at his watch. Eleven fifteen. Well, it was true he had said the tapes could run until noon. Maybe it was time to repeal the order. But at least the music might remind a few of the townspeople of his presence among them. If the squatting monster of the church, three times the height of the rooftops over which it presided, didn't do that already.

The music annoyed him because it seemed irrelevant and trivial. He was a man with more important things on his mind than experimental schemes in religious education. He would go and find Felipe and tell him: no more music. Only now and then, when I say so. He would switch from blanket to guerrilla tactics, sudden surprise reminders.

Father dear,

For once the risk of boring you with more tales of small-town life is appreciably reduced. Things are changing here, I feel it. It has been a busy, busy week. One of the local farmers came to see me this morning. Carlos Cruz. I am urging him and the others to make a stand against the tráficos.

What can we do, though? Cruz asked me.

If enough farmers come to our side, we could arrest the traffickers one by one as they come down the valley to town, I suggested.

But how? They have Kalashnikovs. What do we have? And what would we do with them then?

Send them to Cajamarca.

And what would happen to them in Cajamarca? asks Cruz.

They'll be jailed. We must get them beyond the local policia, who have long since been bought off, as we all know.

He shakes his head. Padre, what makes you think the police there will be any different from here?

Of course I have no answer.

One moment—I think someone's at the door . . .

Beltrán had got into the habit of writing to his father as if he were talking with him on the telephone.

The doors were terrible. In the windy weather of July—a metallic month up on the mineral hills, a month of chrome sunshine and visits by the jet streams—the doors moaned like animals. When he opened the door to his office–sitting room, postcards would jump off the mantelpiece in excitement. When he released the catch on the window frame, the pane would either fly out of his fingers—he never could get used to its not breaking, but instead coming to rest at ninety degrees to the wall—or else would require a feat of pushing, as if something alive were pressing against it. And outside the window, he might see birds riding up against the wind and dropping down again as if they had been thrown up in handfuls.

Nobody there, just the wind, which has been prodigious the last two days . . .

From what I hear, the entire valleys of the Tingo and the Ucayali are now given over to the bad crops. Cruz lives near the valleyhead. Once you cross the pass there you're in bandit territory: no go at all. It's all down to Carreras. His stronghold is between the Tingo and Marañón rivers. It's always been no man's land, cloud forest. Never

sees the sun, hundreds, thousands of kilometres of uncharted jungle.
No wonder he chose to plant himself there. You've heard of him from
me before. Lives in sin with three of his daughters, so they say.
Gesualdo Carreras. He lives as he pleases. Now he is getting in league
with the guerrilleros too. Just the other day they invaded a village
east of here, shot the corregidor and his family. Sometimes they prefer
stoning. They'll use stones torn from the walls of a village church. Just
like the terrible days before, with the Sendero terrorists. I fear it could
all start up again. Carreras lets them do as they wish. They help him
and he helps them.

What will we be able to do? Who knows? These men, they
understand little save the bullet and the buck. And one needs the latter
for the former.

Wondrous weather we've been having lately, by the way. Showers
of gauzy rain, showers of diaphanous sunshine. From my window just
now I can see the rooftops below, wet and gold in a burst of sunshine.
The leaves of the vine are brilliant green, illuminated from the far
side. And the mountain, our little town's guardian, is just now a sleek
well-groomed thing, glorious in her ancient repose. (Forgive a little
flush of poetry.) Anyway, I spoke too soon: the sun has gone in again.
Now the mountain is a brooding heap of brown and grey, the rooftops
dull like the ocean on a cloudy day. When the town is looking that way
I always want to smoke. Which I won't do in public. The padre
oughtn't to behave like the vaqueros and tráficos who darken our
cantinas.

But enough. I will fill you in later. In the meantime, do not fear, I
will be cautious. Wish us Godspeed, and may God bless your weary,
beautiful bones. (I hope you are having less rheumatic trouble now it
is summer with you.)

Con abrazos.

7 · *Mountain Town*

1

Dusty plaza in the morning. Dusty high town, a rough sea of terra-cotta roofs with two crooked belfries rising up like buoys, each topped with a cap of green copper. Music blaring from tinny loudspeakers, screeching and wailing.

The plaza was almost empty—one vendor with a tray of cigarettes and sweets at the corner, a few men seated on the edge of the raised area of paving in the middle. It was an unusual plaza, three-sided with the dirt road running across the top of it and the church closing it off at the end in a solid wall of orange stucco. A deep tank of stone. Perhaps because it was closed on three sides it did not function as magnetically as most plazas. A policeman in fatigues and white T-shirt sat slumped on a bench under the red awning of the *policía*.

Jackson found a little café where an old woman was frying meat. The street outside was rich with the fragrance. Inside, in the dark just by the door, the woman laid the strips of meat in her black tub of oil. As the flesh went in it would sink and rise again, buoyed on effervescent clouds of tiny bubbles. The woman smiled, aware that she was being watched by Jackson and Ignacio as she worked. She moved with great economy, planted still on her stool while her arms did all the work. She fished the meat out of the oil with a sieve, loaded it into sliced buns, then spooned in a red sauce. Jackson ordered two.

There was a hotel on the plaza. A boy of eleven or twelve came and sat at a table in the courtyard taking down Jackson's details in a ledger. Jackson dictated them, patting his shirt pocket to indicate that the required documents were in there, and saying, *Está bien*, when the boy asked to see his passport. *Todo correcto*, he added. I'll give you the details.

The room was high up, with an uneven wooden floor, something like a mix of a garret and a mess room overlooking a parade ground.

Jackson bought the odds and ends he would need around town. The search for a new machete was easy but finding a compass took him to several shops. Eventually he located an old tin one in a shop whose chief purpose was hard to determine. The shelves of its cavernous interior were stocked with many coffin-shaped tins of pilchards, and an array of green bottles of different sizes, all of them empty. A new sickle and hand-plough shone on the wall. He tried out the compass in the shop and it seemed to work, but when he took it outside, having paid a dollar for it, and tried again, it wouldn't give him the same north twice. But he didn't go and ask for his money back; perhaps he might recharge it, he thought, if he could find a magnet, and perhaps it was better than nothing. Anyway, to attempt to get a refund might be complicated.

He liked the diminutive mountain town already. It was good to be back in the high, clear air.

Avoiding the pilchards, he bought several tins of sardines from another busier shop, along with rice, sugar, tea and oats, and a small torch with a magnetic handle, and batteries. He would have liked decent imported batteries, but they had only the cheap domestic brand. He also found an old kerosene stove that came in a tin box, on which the storekeeper had it displayed. Jackson tried the pump and screwed and unscrewed its two valves, and it felt like it would work. The shopkeeper wanted twenty dollars for it. Jackson said he would take it as long as the man let him try it out that night, and bring it back if it didn't work. He agreed, and threw in half a litre of kerosene in a plastic bottle.

He bought new T-shirts, a pair of canvas gloves, a simple camera, extra film, and a cheap watch.

Sooner or later he thought he would try and find the priest that Sarah had mentioned. But now that the time might almost have arrived, he could hardly bear the thought of parting with Ignacio.

Jackson was woken by a rapping on the door. He lifted his head, unsure at first where the noise was coming from.

The hotel room was dark but for a strip of light along the bottom of the window shutter. On the boy's grey blanket the cat lay stretched on its side, its claws splayed as if it had been dreaming of hunting.

He was about to get up when the door croaked open and a woman put her head round. She stayed there a moment, then mumbled, So this *is* the right room.

At that moment, in the semi-dark of the shuttered morning, he recognised who it was and sat up straight.

My God, he said. How—

There's only about two hotels. It wasn't hard to find you. A gringo with a local boy?

It was Sarah. The strangest part was that instead of feeling shocked or alarmed, a smile rose to his face. He had just been dreaming about her, although only now did he remember the dream, and then only vaguely. But because of the dream it didn't seem odd that she was here. In the partial light her hair looked silver, moonlit, and her face was both dark and somehow filled with a light of its own.

It's not exactly early, you know, she said. I thought you'd be up by now. I'm hungry. Want to meet me downstairs? I just got in last night.

Jackson rubbed his face and wondered how he looked. In his

semi-awake state he almost told her he had just been dreaming of her.

Whatever. Sounds good. You got here last night? He shook his head and smiled. I can't believe you found us.

The presence of Ignacio in the room allowed Jackson to be less nervous. He wondered if it was the same for her.

Instead of leaving she, stalked lightly into the room and un-hitched the window shutters. One of them banged back against the wall and Jackson felt a cold breeze on his bare shoulder. Sunlight fell on the wood floor. Perhaps this was the way an American would act, casual and confident, not worried about other people's reactions to their behaviour. He liked it, he felt comfortable with her in the room.

I was coming up anyway, and I was thinking about him, Ignacio. I thought I'd see if I could catch you. Big day today, she whispered.

What do you mean? He found himself whispering too, even with the light streaming in.

She nodded at Ignacio's bed. I want him to meet Padre Beltrán.

That priest? Better let me get dressed then.

I won't look.

She went and picked up the cat, draping its length over her hand, and took it to the window over the plaza.

He felt self-conscious as he listened to himself dressing—the rus-tle of the sleeves as his arms went in, the flapping of his trouser legs, the zip. While he sat tying his boot laces he heard the plop of the cat dropping to the floor, and looked up. She had opened his sketchbook on the windowsill.

Hey, he called.

The boy quietly sat up in bed and sloughed off his blanket, already fully clothed in poncho and pantaloons. He had reverted to his mountain outfit.

Sarah turned a page in the middle of the sketchbook, then turned the page back. She held the book up, spine horizontal, for an upright double-page spread. The paper fluttered in the breeze. She turned so the window light fell on it, studied it a while, then put the book down again on the windowsill to examine it more closely.

This is really something. I can't believe this. When did you do this?

It's just sketches.

She held the page for him to see. This one. You did it just the other day?

He shrugged. Must have been.

You did it in town, right?

A smile threatened to surface on his face again but he fought it back.

The drawing was one he had done the previous evening, of an old woman at the side of a mountain road glancing at the viewer from among her bundled belongings. Jackson liked it, governed as it was by the indomitable face of that old woman, which he thought had something of the mountains in it; as if she was her own kind of mountain too, amid the mountains that were her home.

When did you do this?

I don't know. Yesterday. After the bus ride.

The bus up here?

I saw her on the way up, had an idea, and that's what I did. They're nothing. Just doodles.

Doodles? And all these ruins. She flipped through the book. Ruin after ruin. These are beautiful. The trees, the stones. I love these. How did you do all this shading? They're so good. You make them look so good. I always thought ruins were basically boring. Anyway, I don't believe you.

He laughed.

You pinched this off someone. Or your little boy did.

Sure.

OK, so why do they all say *S* in the corner? Look at this. She flipped through the book. They all do. *S May. S June.*

It's a name I sometimes use.

You've got two names? She let out an incredulous laugh. I don't believe this. She rolled her eyes and sat on the foot of his bed. What's this other name then?

He told her and she laughed. Now that she'd retreated from the window where the light behind had hidden her face, he could see her properly. He wasn't struck by her beauty, more by the fact of her: here she was, fresh and real. The sandy colour of her face, her eyes that seemed blue, but when the light fell on them were revealed as possibly green, her messy hair, the general mix of prettiness and rough-and-readiness: there was a lot about her to like. Jackson even found he particularly liked the suede jacket with tassles she was wearing. Or rather, he liked the way she wore it, thoughtlessly. He had seen her in it before. It could have been a plain old anorak for all she cared. There was even a hint of self-neglect about her, which he found appealing, as if her mind was on more important things than her looks.

Perhaps it was an American thing. She didn't seem aware of how she looked, of what she was showing of herself. For example, sometimes her shirt rode up revealing her beach-like belly with its slightly turned-out button. It was a small thing, especially when you had been living on and off in your swimsuit for weeks, as she had, but still it showed something nice about her.

The wind streamed in through the open window. It was a bright, windy morning outside. The air changed in the high bare hotel room. For a moment he felt that this room was his garret, high among the rooftops of a town where he lived, with its beams running down diagonally at either end, and the sense of being removed from the bustle below. She seemed to light up the room. She was light made flesh: that was the thought that came to him. But why? Why was he so happy to see her? Why didn't he even mind her being in the room first thing in the morning, uninvited, someone he barely knew? Yet it was as if he did know her. He looked away, hoping to reorder his feelings.

She sat half twisted for the light, with the sketchbook still open in her lap, shaking her head gently at it, half smiling.

Why do you like drawing all this archaeology? How did you get into it?

It's beautiful. I don't know. It makes sense. The way they built makes sense. You said you were hungry. Have you had breakfast? he asked. Shall we do that?

2

Although the little town was set among the hills of the altiplano, and one snowy peak hovered a little way off, it had found a small plateau on which to spread itself, and whichever direction you walked from the plaza, after a few blocks you found yourself going downhill.

Only one street had ever been paved, the main road from the coast, which entered the outskirts of town as a rough track, picked up a coating of pale asphalt crayoned with tyre tracks, and snaked among the town blocks until it reached the iron-roofed market hall, which it had been aiming for all along. Here the potholes that had started to ambush it back by the cemetery wall like old mortar-fire overcame it, pummelling it into a dirt street, busier, more crowded with stalls, than the comparatively cool and quiet chambers of the market building itself.

Ignacio walked between Jackson and Sarah as if he were their child, and they protectively, happily flanking him. Jackson felt self-conscious and tried to break the spell of his own embarrassment by asking what Ignacio wanted for breakfast. But that only made it worse, as if he were relishing his paternal role.

Mercifully, the boy just shrugged and stroked the head of his cat, protruding from the hole in his poncho.

Ever since arriving in Chachapoyas the kid had been particularly dour and silent. Jackson had recklessly told him he might be going to stay with an uncle. The boy of course knew he had no uncle here, and said as much. Jackson said the man was like an uncle.

The boy had ignored him much of the previous day. Now, in the morning, as they walked the market-filled streets, the boy seemed to sense he might be about to have his last breakfast as a free agent. As it was about to happen, Jackson found himself questioning the wisdom of it. How on earth had this responsibility dropped on his shoulders, to determine the life of this child? The boy had presumably grown up in a village, with the run of the mountains. He might have had a hard time but at least he had been free to have his own kind of hard time. He hadn't been nailed down and forced to imbibe a culture not his own. Maybe Jackson was conspiring to murder the boy's identity, forcing him into the old imperialist dogmas. But it was easy to remind himself of the child brothels, the child assassins reputedly used by coca lords and the guerrillas. Surely a child should be protected, no matter how.

It was a long time since Sarah had been in the town but she thought she remembered a restaurant a few blocks below the market. They walked down a cobbled street out of the bustle. Here the houses of pocked and graffiti-scrawled lemon-yellow stucco no longer had upper storeys, and two or three in each block were ruins, with vacant doorways and windows without glass.

In the dark of Sarah's remembered café a bulky woman wrapped in layers of skirts and cardigans, wearing a bowler hat with a piece of rope as a hatband, was frying meat. Deep-fried mutton seemed a staple of the little town. Unless it was llama or goat meat. When she had done a round and set the stiff, grey scraps in a blue bowl, she would stir up a dish of batter. Then she'd dip a loop of wire into the batter and drop it in the hot oil. Soon a thin gold disc would form in the dark oil.

Mmm, said Sarah. Deep-fried pancakes. They'd never believe it back home.

They sat at a table with a plastic cloth. The low room had been limewashed sky blue. Two religious pictures made of velvet and framed in gilt hung at either end, in partial darkness.

A younger woman served them. The coffee was weak, sweet, flavoured with cinnamon. The boy kept his head down and tucked into his portion seriously. She came over to sift him extra icing sugar from her sieve. Then Jackson bought the boy a second round of pancakes without meat this time, just sugar. He ordered a separate saucer of meat for the cat. The cat sat on the end of the bench beside the boy, eating thoughtfully.

A truck pulled up outside the café door, stopping right in front, darkening the room, and grumbled to itself. Through the doorway Jackson could see strings of dirt flung up over the metallic paint on a big wheel arch. The thudding of a stereo ceased, and the engine was switched off. The street fell back into quiet. A child cried somewhere nearby, a cock crowed.

The truck doors thumped shut. A police captain in khaki and mirror sunglasses stepped into the little restaurant. He was followed by a *campesino* in a straw hat and purple shirt, who came in scratching his groin. Both men had a dusty well-travelled look about them, as if just returned from some venture in the hills.

Buen día, señora, the captain called.

The woman emerged from the kitchen and stopped. She wiped her palms on her cardigan, but made no move toward the two men. *Capitán*, she said.

Where is he? the captain asked.

The woman stared at him, saying nothing.

Where is he? he repeated.

He wasn't a big man, but he stood very erect, his chest held forward. He cocked his head to the side patronisingly.

The woman wiped her hands again. Meanwhile the larger, older woman who had been making the pancakes by the door got up off her stool heavily, and went out.

The policeman sighed. We better have some breakfast while we wait. Can you fix us some breakfast? He raised his eyebrows and they held each other's gaze.

Jackson watched, with his fork dipping down to the plate in front of him. Sarah, beside him, did not look up at all, and the boy, seated opposite with his back to the newcomers, continued to eat in his noisy Andean way, slurping in his mouthfuls of sugar-dusted pancake.

The woman marched briskly to a table against the far wall, wiping down the plastic cloth and rearranging the bottles of hot sauce and coffee essence that stood in the middle, bustling into activity with an alacrity she hadn't shown until now.

The two men glanced at Jackson and Sarah but didn't greet them, not even with a nod.

Jackson saw the woman bring out two glasses of hot water and place them on the table. She disappeared and came back with a basket of flat rolls.

As she was leaving the room again the policeman, who had not moved, who was still standing near the door, said: *¿Sol y sombra?*

Ya viene, the woman said. Just coming.

Sarah bowed her head to her food and kept quiet.

The newcomers ignored the table the woman had laid for them, and stepped up to a counter at the end of the room. The captain removed his red-banded cap. Slowly, ceremoniously, he lifted one boot and set it on a wooden rail low down, then rested an elbow on the counter.

An elderly man shuffled out from the kitchen. Good morning, Captain.

Sí, Agustín.

The old man set out two rinsed, wet glasses. Dextrously, though with trembling hand, he poured from two bottles at once into the beakers—a brown liquor and a clear. Together they misted in the glasses.

Sol y sombra, poured *a la vez.* As you like.

The captain snapped a pocket on his shirt and pulled out a cigar. Then he pushed back his cuff and consulted his watch.

Where is he? he said, shaking his head. We haven't got all day.

He tapped the butt of the cigar against the watch-face then dipped it mouth-end down in his glass. He twirled it round the drink, letting it tap dully against the sides.

Outside, a demonic cackle suddenly boomed across the town, then settled down into a scratchy hiss. Out of the hiss came a screech of poorly recorded organ music, into which a wail of voices leapt, a sanctimonious chorus singing a hymn.

The captain stopped stirring his drink with his cigar. *Dios,* he said. Not again. I thought he might spare us today.

He popped the damp cylinder in his mouth, sucked at it noisily, then struck a large waving flame from his lighter. A cloud of blue smoke rose above him. What do you think? he asked, without turning back to the barman. Should we allow it to go on?

Agustín, who wore a loose white jacket over a ragged brown shirt, cleared his throat with a rattle and asked: Allow what, captain?

It's a little much, don't you think? That damned church music all morning?

The elderly Agustín picked up a glass and briskly wiped it with a rag. In a sing-song sigh he said, Padre Beltrán's music, and shook his head.

Sarah had been keeping her head lowered to her plate. Jackson could feel her unease. Perhaps she knew of this captain, or perhaps she had a general fear of the local police. Perhaps they didn't like her uncle, were enemies of his.

The padre thinks we should stay in the Middle Ages. Get all the peasants to grow potatoes and corn and ride donkeys. No TVs, no Toyotas, no telephone. What do you think? Is he right?

The barman Agustín had filled a tray with tumblers. When he lifted it onto a shelf, it rattled alarmingly.

I agree with the captain, he said, setting it down.

The captain picked up his glass and gently swilled the honey-coloured liquid.

Here we are, some of us, trying to bring good things to this little dump of a town and what happens? The people don't want our help. Why not? Because the padre says it's bad to have hi-fis and electricity for everyone. And every morning at seven—you can set your watch by it—there's that music of his. And then like today, he does it again and again. What do you think, Agustín? Is that music?

Agustín said, That's hymns, sir.

The captain muttered, Hymns, and tipped up his glass, draining it in one go. Ah well.

He reached into his trousers and left a coin to ring itself down on the counter.

The *campesino* followed him to the table the woman had prepared. Once they had settled in their chairs, into the glasses of steaming water the woman had put there the policeman poured clear liquid from a bottle which he pulled from his fatigues. He topped them up with the coffee essence on the table. Eggs and pancakes arrived for them, which they ate quietly, without talking. Every so often they drank noisily from their laced coffees, letting out sighs of satisfaction. The captain attempted unsuccessfully to stifle a belch.

Jackson noticed that the captain would steal glances at Sarah while he bowed to his breakfast. The *campesino* glanced back over his shoulder periodically to look at her too. Finally when the officer was done with his food and had relit his cigar with his gold lighter, he stared openly at the three of them. He pushed his sunglasses up onto his brow and wiped his eyes. His eyes looked younger than Jackson had expected.

Señores, he said with a nod in their direction.

Jackson nodded back.

All right? he barked across the room.

Bueno, Jackson answered.

Señorita. All right?

Sarah looked up. Thank you, yes, she said.

What are you doing here?

Visiting, she said.

He shook his head and tutted. *Cuidado*. Things aren't like they used to be. Problems today. Bandits. *Bandidos*, he said broadly, raising his eyebrows.

I'm just passing through, Sarah added.

But don't worry, the policeman went on. We'll look after you. No problems for you. But this is not Cuzco or Lima. This is the frontier. *La frontera*. You have to be careful. Where are you staying?

Near the plaza, she said.

That's good. Near the *policía*.

Just then a man in a dusty suit stepped off the street into the cafeteria. He stopped, glanced at the police captain, and ducked out again.

The policeman's *campesino* was out the door in an instant. A shout came from the street. The captain followed. At the door, he turned back into the room.

All right, he said in an efficient tone to the woman, who was standing still in her apron. We take care of him, don't worry.

Sunlight caught one side of the policeman's face. His long moustache glistened and the stubble on his jaw glittered. He was about to say something, but there was a thud followed by a grunt from outside. He reached for the holster on his hip, let out a plaintive and tired *Ay* and left.

The big truck whined into life again and with a click of its gears moved off, revealing once again the sunlit street.

Ignacio was staring at the open doorway.

Let's go to the priest, Jackson said.

It's always like this round here, Sarah said. It's normal.

The woman came and took away their plates then returned with a cloth and frantically wiped at their tablecloth. *Ay*, she too muttered.

Sarah ruffled Ignacio's head. Let's find you a home, eh? *¿Qué piensas?*

Ignacio glanced at her then touched the head of his cat, nestled on his thigh.

When the woman came out again she had taken off her apron and wore a white sweatshirt and a pair of blue jogging pants. There was something unsettling about seeing her in these informal Western clothes. She disappeared up the street without a word, and in the end, after waiting ten minutes, they had to guess their bill and leave the money under a plate.

3

A small wooden door hung in the corner of the plaza just beside the church, deep in shade. The top third of the door was wire-netting, through which Jackson could see an alley hung with geranium pots, clean, orderly, well-swept, though the pots were all manner of containers—unlabelled cans, cut-off plastic bottles, buckets, jam jars, mugs without handles—and had been attached to the wall with wire and nails. It was touching to see them there, so many of them, to see the little alley so well cared for.

Sarah put her face to the grille and called out: Padre?

Behind them, on the opposite side of the plaza, stood the *policía*, a broad low yellow building vaguely reminiscent of a small European railway station. Beneath its awning a young policeman loitered, watching them. He wore a white singlet and fatigues. It was past ten o'clock now, the night's cold had passed. When Sarah banged on the wooden door and called again, Jackson felt a little embarrassed under the soldier's watchful eye.

Ignacio stood close to the door as if afraid of not being allowed in.

At the end of the alley a shutter flew open on a window two storeys up. A spectacled face appeared. *¿Sí?*

It was an unusual greeting, somehow more thoughtful than the standard *Buen día*.

Padre, Sarah called. May we come up?

The man adjusted his glasses with a large hand and let out a short high laugh. *Momentito*.

From beside his window a green string ran down the wall through a row of hoops. The padre pulled on it, tugging up two or three arm's lengths of string before a little click sounded just the other side of the door.

Push, he said, miming the action with his free hand.

They walked into the fertile shade of the green alleyway. Up above, they heard a knock and a hurried exchange of whispers, then a long silence broken finally by a light scuffle. A door opened, and a short plump man in a baggy green cardigan emerged at the top of a precarious-looking wooden staircase, with his arms spread wide. Come on up, come on up.

Sarah went first. She took the first steps then hesitated. The whole wooden structure leaned alarmingly from the wall to which it was attached, and groaned to the side as she climbed.

Don't worry, the man called. I trot up and down every day. He stepped back to show off his belly.

A boy of ten or eleven appeared beside the padre and stood on tiptoe to look down over the railing. He was dressed like a European, in a white shirt, but he was an Indian boy, with a dark slope of a face and deep black eyes.

Jackson waited at the bottom with Ignacio while Sarah went up.

As soon as she reached the top, the Indian boy came running down and disappeared down the alley.

Come on, all of you, it's fine. *Sí, sí*, he said, beckoning with his whole arm.

The staircase creaked and sagged under Jackson's boots. He leaned against the rough stucco as he climbed. Ignacio skipped up ahead of him, taking the steps two at a time.

At the top, Beltrán was staring at Sarah. Now let me see. Good Lord, it's Señorita Sarah. Daughter of our dear Don Alfredo. How is he? All well, I hope? It's not a good place to be right now, the Tingo valley. Is he all right? And you? What an honour. What brings you here? And you? he asked, turning to Jackson.

The padre was a podgy man with a smooth chubby face, glasses and a short silver moustache. There was an air of repose and comfort about him. Beneath his cardigan he wore a large white shirt with a button-down collar. He had the voluminous jowls, Jackson thought, of a celibate prelate—something almost of the eunuch about him. He stood before Sarah, an inch or two shorter than her, opened his arms wide, and said, *Ah, desde chiquitita*, tilting his head to one side as if he remembered her only from her childhood, not from her more recent visits.

Then he bent down, hands on knees, and said, And who is the señor?

This is Ignacio, Sarah said.

The boy stared at the face looming close to his, then glanced at Jackson. The padre laughed and straightened up, patted Ignacio's head neither too gently nor with the patronising vigour typical of some men. He shook his hand. *Don Ignacio. Mucho gusto.*

Beltrán addressed himself to Jackson again. An Englishman. And what brings you to our far-flung province?

Jackson was briefly at a loss. Before he could answer Beltrán went on: And what have we here? He bent down toward the cat in Ignacio's arms. Who is this?

Quietly Ignacio answered: *El gato.*

Sí. El gato. I see that. But doesn't he have a name?

That is his name. Ignacio became confused. That is a name, he said.

I see. He stood up again and said to Sarah, And how is dear Don Alfredo? I have been thinking about him.

He turned to Jackson. Do you know Alfredo, her father? He is our local Rousseau, our Thoreau of the hills, a farmer-philosopher. A true philosopher lives by his philosophy, as he does. Isn't that so?

Actually, he's my uncle, Sarah said. But yes.

Excuse me, excuse me, he said in faltering English. Of course. It has been so long since I've seen any of you. Much, much too long.

He looked Sarah up and down, and drew her into another big hug, as if the earlier one had been invalidated by his mistake.

But I have been worried for him. Really it's not a good place to be, the Tingo valley. Is he all right? Well, come on in.

Padre Beltrán was not only a rotund man, at once solemn and jovial, Jackson thought, but also slightly cowed-looking, in spite of his bonhomie. With his glasses and precise Castilian, he seemed unusually urbane, a reassuring figure to meet in the mountains. As soon as he spoke he became unaccountably cheerful. The sombre look on his face as he listened would be replaced by an animated smile.

At first Jackson took this to be an affectation. One-time cosmopolites who settled in backwaters, he thought, would pick up some bearing or demeanour from ages ago that they believed sophisticated or shrewd or capable of putting people at ease, and work it to the bone. They had nothing else in their repertoires. But gradually he saw it was unaffected. The padre's face ranged through the broadest spectrum of expressions with no trace of self-consciousness.

His apartment, attached to the back of the church, was quite bare. Through an open doorway Jackson could see a single bed and a desk covered with books and papers.

Beltrán noticed Jackson glancing that way. That is my sitting room and my bedroom, he said. And my office. It has a staff of one, he added with a chuckle. Me. It is hard to run an office when the telephone lines have been down for more than two years. But what can I get you? Coffee? Bread?

Without waiting for a reply, Beltrán filled a pan and set it on the stove.

We just had breakfast, Sarah said. Thank you.

Nonsense. I'm so glad you have come. Do sit, do sit.

Beltrán pulled out two chairs at the little steel table in the middle of the room, and fetched a third and fourth from a room next door. While the water heated, he got out a can of condensed milk then seated himself beside Ignacio.

Well. Are you from near here? he asked the boy.

Ignacio didn't reply.

Jackson coughed. I found him. Or rather he found me. In the desert, down near Chiclayo. I think he'd been—well, taken from his home. I don't know though. He escaped the people he was with and sort of came to me. I haven't known what to do with him. Jackson spoke quietly and quickly.

Beltrán's eyes hovered on Jackson from behind their lenses. So you thought to bring him here. All the way from Chiclayo. I must be acquiring a reputation as a home-giver.

Beltrán turned to the boy. Have you ever slept on a top bunk? You could have the bunk above Felipe's. What do you say to that?

The boy said nothing, but glanced at Jackson.

The cat is his? I'm afraid it wouldn't be able to stay.

He loves that cat, Jackson began.

But fleas, disease and so on. Cats are carriers of ills, you know, here no less than in fair Venice.

Ignacio watched the conversation closely and hugged the cat.

Beltrán looked at him and smiled. I think you understand more than you let on. Well, we'll see.

I go where he goes, Ignacio asserted.

Beltrán shrugged and smiled. And where are you from?

The boy looked down under the table, slouching back in his seat with the cat in his lap.

You don't know?

From the south.

Ignacio del Sur, then. Welcome.

The priest got up and went to a cupboard, where he found a small flat loaf, which he cut open at the sideboard and loaded with a spoonful of *dulce de leche*. Here, he said, handing it to Ignacio. See how you like it.

And you? What could bring an Englishman to our forgotten town?

It's a long story, Jackson said.

We have time.

Jackson expected to feel self-conscious as he explained. But in the little apartment at the back of the church, among the mountains, the story of Connolly's quest for the lost Chachapoyans, and his own, sounded strangely plausible.

Beltrán shook his head. How on earth did you, or your old comrade, get interested in all this? I thought I was about the only person on earth who cared about it. But come. Let me show you something.

✦

The padre led them back down the stairs. In the alleyway, he rummaged in his pocket and pulled out a large iron key.

Behind a heavy wood door was a dark barn-like room. The open doorway cast a lozenge of light on the stone floor.

El Museo, Beltrán announced, and lit a candle.

As his sight adjusted to the gloom Jackson made out two glass tanks standing on packing cases, opaque with dust. In each of them was a wizened crumpled human figure, wrapped in dirty cloths. The two faces jumped out of the murk, pale like an ore in rock. They showed off their mouthfuls of yellow teeth in gums and lips that had thinned to paper. The eyelids had sunk into dim cavities.

History incarnate, Beltrán said. Or rather prehistory, he corrected himself. The Chachapoyans had no writing. But look.

The priest stepped close to one of the tanks. See her hair.

Jackson was surprised to hear the feminine.

The hair, which lay around the corpse's neck in the bundled remains of a plait, was the colour of rust.

See? the priest said. It is true, the Chachapoyans were a fair race. They did not have black hair. How could this be? The only blond races on earth come from Europe. Could the Vikings have found the mouth of the Amazon, as some have claimed, and sailed up the river across the continent? Others say they were Phoenicians, who were great seafarers. But would they have been blond?

Could I come back and draw these two? Jackson asked.

These two old friends? Of course. Beltrán shrugged. Anyway, here is proof they existed. But what happened to them? There is mention in the chronicles of their war with the Incas. But where did they go? Who knows? It is like shining a light into the night sky. All you can see is the beam, illuminating nothing but air.

They left their cities too, Jackson said.

If we could only find them. So far no one has found more than a fort here, an outpost there. I'll tell you a story.

He fetched a cracked earthen jar off a shelf.

This comes from a village to the south of here, on the altiplano, a terrain of big bare hills. All the villages are made of adobe, of course, and the chief crop is potatoes. I had hopes, I was going to make them all plant quinoa, the Incas' miracle crop. If only they could break their reliance on cash crops and the potato, they would survive whatever the world market tipped their way. I was an idealist. You can't imagine how it felt to roll into those villages in the late afternoon with the children scampering along behind my jeep, the straw roofs shining and amid the houses the church still propped there like an ark waiting to ferry them off. The Franciscans built the churches in the 1590s, the oldest in all America. They're wonderful. Three times the height of the houses, big walls of mud with heavy beams holding up the roofs. Some of them no one had been inside for decades. I'd have to prise the nails out of a board holding the door shut, creak it open and get that smell—clean sand, clean dust. I was in love with those churches. I'd get the people to help me do repairs. And we'd have Mass in those ancient places, that dark peace undisturbed so long. The candle flames dancing about, the shadows of a little group of worshippers jumping over the walls, the smell of incense and candle wax, dust and peace.

I was interested in the region's past. I knew the Chachapoyans had been here until the Incas came, then the Spaniards. I had heard rumours about the Cities of the Jaguar, and La Joya. I put out word that I was interested in archaeology.

You know what was remarkable? It worked. First, they started to grow quinoa alongside their potatoes. Scurvy became a thing of the past, and the quinoa grew well; this is its native soil. It's a beautiful sight, a steep little field like a patch of fur in the breeze, a deep red, and packed full of nutrition. And the boys and the farmers used to bring me pottery and carvings they ploughed up in the fields. Like this. See? This is a jar, of course. I have many like it. But then they stopped. One of their witch doctors said they shouldn't disturb the belongings of the ancestors. That's how it is here. Anything you try to start comes to nothing. Eventually they stopped growing quinoa because they couldn't sell it. I told them the whole point was to eat it, not sell it.

The padre shrugged. Then one day a farmer from the Tingo valley, a day's drive from here, came to see me. I hear the padre is interested in antiquities, he says. He leads me up to the market where a truck is parked. He heaves out two sacks from the back. Look, señor. He opens one up and I just about jumped out of my skin.

Beltrán gestured behind him, at the mummies in the cases.

It was these two. But he wouldn't tell me where he got them; I couldn't get it out of him.

Beltrán shrugged. Forgive me. Here I am talking and talking. Come. Let us go back for some fortifications.

He led them back upstairs, and installed them again at the table, this time with a bottle of pisco.

You've got me talking. He smiled. It's a long time since I had company from the *grand monde*. He poured out shots of the spirit.

Here, it's hard enough to get anything to work today, let alone dig in the past. And it's worse than ever. If there are any lost cities, they're likely to remain lost. He sighed and lifted his glass. Anyway. To lost peoples. Why not?

Jackson and Sarah sipped their drinks. Beltrán threw his pisco down.

Excuse me rattling on. Still I haven't let you say a word.

Beltrán topped them up and poured himself another shot. He paused and sighed. Yes, the *padre agrónomo*. They still do grow quinoa in some villages, you know.

He drained his little tumbler again and encouraged the two of them to do the same.

Jackson watched. The priest seemed agitated. Perhaps he had been feeling the lack of Western company, or perhaps something was on his mind.

Beltrán shook his head. But it's sad these days. Just the other day another of the farmers came to me. He's being forced to help these gun-runners now. If he doesn't, he fears for his family. It's lawless, it's hopeless. I even went down to Trujillo not long ago to talk to the bishop about it. He just shook his head and muttered what difficult times these are, and the Church must forgive. Sad times, sad times: that's all the bishop would say. I think the bishop himself is a sad man. How does a man get like that? By making the wrong compromises. We all have to learn the compromises we should and shouldn't make.

Anyway, one last thing. The padre fixed Jackson with his eyes. I do not advise you to go looking for La Joya. If it is there at all, it is in such a remote place there are only two or three *campesinos* who could guide you. Excuse me, one of them was killed last month—a young man too. So there are two at most. One you cannot approach, he has become a henchman of Señor Carreras—of whom I assume you have heard—and the other is uncertain. He claims to be resisting what he calls powerful temptations, but I don't know whether to believe him. He can tell I am not sure. Once he knows I doubt him, what sway I have is lost. You see, there is a war going on here, the same there has always been, for the human soul. Even in the little villages with their infernal superstitions it is being waged.

Beltrán filled his shot glass to the brim once more, and although his hand shook only a little as he picked it up, it lapped over his fingertips.

So I don't know who you can trust to guide you. But worse, these are bad times. You cannot imagine. Last month an adulterer was dragged into the plaza of Pachatin, only an hour from here, and stoned to death. Stoned. In front of everybody. They call it justice, revolution, Marxism. As if Marx would ever have condoned medieval brutality like that. Yes. It seems the bad times are returning. That is what we dread most. Then they got the woman. First they cut off her hair and then—excuse me, señorita, he said without looking at Sarah—they cut off her breasts, and then they heated a hand-plough in a fire. I won't go on. She was dead in an hour, thank God, but what an hour.

The region is going mad. Carreras is a drug lord pure and simple, but he lets these rivals fight it out—the guerrillas, the Marxist terrorists, the *traficantes*. Carreras keeps them at loggerheads, as you say. So then he is the one in control. They say he murdered his brothers and now sleeps with their daughters. Who knows if it is true? But it might be. He has houses in Lima and Miami, he has friends in the government. The police are no use; they are in his pay too. The local captain is his proxy, you could say. I don't think that if you go looking for the city of La Joya you will find it. You're not the first to try. Why should you, a young adventurer with nothing but his bold spirit on his side?

He looked sharply into Jackson's eyes. Jackson winced as those hard pupils settled on him, as if the padre was searching to see just how bold his spirit was.

But I do think that if you venture out of the valley of the Tingo, beyond the pass, into the cloud forest round Choctamal, you will not come back.

Beltrán cleared his throat.

But forgive me, time has flown. I must let you get on. You will probably wish to visit the little fiesta tomorrow. And you can see our own little Chachapoyan ruin. Perhaps you can tell us what it is. We will meet later, I am sure. And Ignacio will visit again tomorrow? Please be careful, both of you. Oh yes, I almost forgot, tomorrow morning you must come to the opera.

The opera? Sarah said.

We have our little opera season here. Once a week we play a film, I have a friend in the capital who sends them to me on the truck, and we show them in the parish hall on Wednesday mornings. Come.

It's a film? Sarah asked.

Yes, an opera film. We are having an opera phase. We try to keep civilised here. Tomorrow is *The Magic Flute*. He smiled. Ignacio can help me and Felipe with the projector. Would you like that?

Ignacio stared first at him, then at Jackson.

The padre added: And I never even knew you could get operas on film.

4

Chachapoyas. Tuesday night.

I feel like writing this diary again. It's been a while.

The relief of being up here again. It's indescribable. I guess it'll be short-lived but I don't care. I love it. This is what you do on the plain that opens before you after a big break-up: pause for breath, as and when you can. You go away. You get a change of air. It's like a relief between marches. (But what drives the march? That's the question, and the solution probably, to the whole messy game. A game you find yourself caught in, though you never asked to join. And you have to discover the rules by yourself as you play.) Sometimes, like now, a gamble pays off out of the blue. This trip is so helping me.

There's a guy I've met. He's strange. He's doing strange things, has done strange things. Like he was in the army. I mean—of all avoidances. But he's bright. He thinks for himself. I like that. Funny how some people can just interest you. For no apparent reason. He's not living like anyone else I know. Though he's foreign too, which may be part of it. English. I think that counts as foreign. He's looking for these ruins he's heard about. Up in the cloud forest. In an area near where Uncle Alfred lives. I think we're going to go up there together. We might. We could. I'm kind of excited. I was anyway, to be going up there, but even more so now. There's something peculiar about him, I don't know quite what.

I guess the strange thing is not whether he's bright or unusual or

talented (which he is: he draws beautifully, though he hardly seems to
know he's doing it, and doesn't think anything of it), but the way we feel
together. I mean the way the two of us feel. Not like it was with Hayden.
It's subtle but there it is: it's as though we understand each other without
saying a word. It makes me feel calm and excited at the same time.

The landscape here must be part of why I love it so much: severely dry,
bald as a monk's head. This town is still not so easy to get to. Here and
there you can see where the railway used to run, a pencil line drawn over
the hills which might be erased at any moment, winding along troughs
and gulfs, stitching in the southern edge of town.

It's a good place to have come. I love the remoteness. You feel you have
escaped something, just to be here.

Sarah met Jackson in a café the next morning. They had a cup of coffee while she tried to persuade him to come to the padre's film.

I've got things I should do.

What things? Come on. You're a visual guy. It will feed your vision. I promise.

It turned out she was right. Jackson was spellbound, sitting on his hard bench in the empty hall. There were only half a dozen other people press ganged in by the padre, who had been hoping for more, to judge by the number of benches he had set out. The film played on a bedsheet hung from a wire. The projector clicked and rattled as the bands of gold and blue light twitched in the mote-thick dark overhead.

The film director spent a long time studying the faces in the opera audience, as the orchestra ran through the overture. Normally one might glance round an audience and notice none of the individual faces. Now they all looked so different from one another. They were like paintings, portraits to gaze at as the music cantered along.

Then the action started. As the actors in their rich costumes sang, the director closed right up on them so you could see the muscles of their necks working. It was irresistible. It wasn't just the colours, the movement, the joyous music running like a brook through the dark hall, it was the intelligence—he couldn't think what else to call it—of the man who had made the film. The camera moved with such good sense, as if there was a point to every shot. He wasn't just reporting, he was arguing, proving something. If you tried to track down what he was saying, you couldn't, but you could still feel it.

Jackson came out stunned and confused into the brilliant mountain daylight.

He frowned. What was that? That was unbelievable. I didn't think I liked opera.

At once he wanted to run and grab his sketchbook. But what to draw? He wanted to see if he could capture that same kind of intelligence on paper somehow. Why not? It was no one's possession. You didn't have to have been to college to recognise it, evidently. It was some kind of horse sense. It seemed to make the sun shine in your mind.

They left Ignacio to help clear up the hall with Beltrán, and Jackson promised to come and see him later on.

5

That evening, in the faint light of a half moon, he and Sarah walked up over a rise at the edge of town and came upon the fiesta of San Agustín. Rough canvas stalls covered the field, all lit by kerosene lamps within so they shone like lanterns. Beyond the tents, each with the rushing hiss of its gas cooker, and the crackle of meat on its oildrum grill, and floodlit columns of grey smoke rising among them on the breeze, beyond all that stood a tremendous wall of masonry. It had holes for beams, and holes where windows had been and, with the moon shining from behind, the wall took on the aspect of a row of giants standing arm in arm; a row of paper men. They pertained to a different scale, standing there above the merrymaking of the humans.

Jackson stopped Sarah with a touch on the arm. They both looked for a while at the strange monument, dark blue in the midst of a spill of milk along the horizon from the lowering moon.

Sarah chuckled. I forgot to mention that. Chachapoyas's own ruin. No one knows what in God's name it is. A temple, a meeting house, a barn—no one has a clue.

They were making their way down the rocky slope on the far side of the brow, thrown into blackness by the bright field of lights ahead, when a small figure appeared to one side, scuttling down the scree nimbly as a goat. He ran diagonally down to cut them off, and stopped in front of Jackson. He was breathing hard.

I don't believe this, Jackson said, and slapped his forehead.

It was Ignacio.

I had to get away. *El gato* needs something to eat. I've been looking for you everywhere, then I thought maybe one of the señoras at the fiesta will give me something.

Jackson sighed. Does the padre know you are here?

Ignacio stared at the ground.

Don't go leaving the padre now.

The boy didn't move.

I mean it. And I'll talk to the padre about food for your cat.

Jackson was reminded of a dog they'd had when he was a boy. Whenever he tied it outside a shop it would lurch toward him on its leash, its whole body yearning to follow him. He would bend down and nuzzle it, and whisper that he'd only be a moment. The boy's showing up here stirred the same tender feeling he used to have then. Jackson didn't want to think about it. He didn't see what else he could do than leave Ignacio with the padre.

Beyond the ruins the rooftops on the edge of town showed as a watery gleam in the moonlight.

The padre is a *strange* man, the boy said with an exaggerated inflection.

He is? Sarah asked.

He says he will make me clean the altar in the church every day. Two times all over, until everything is nice, he says.

Ignacio frowned seriously. I think he is *un poco loco, señor.*

Jackson glanced at Sarah, and she at him, and they both smiled.

Do you promise to stay with him even if he is crazy?

Ignacio stared at his feet.

Promise?

The word *Sí* dropped from his lips to the ground, as if by itself.

As they went down into the fiesta Sarah said under her breath, He's one resourceful kid, that's for sure.

And Jackson realised this was true, and that he hadn't recognised it before.

They bought Ignacio a meal of pork sautéed with onions and tomatoes, along with an extra slice of meat that the woman at the stall wrapped for him in greased paper. They sat at a table under a canvas awning. A kerosene lamp hissed above them, hanging from the wood frame of the makeshift tent, dazzling them and seeming to make everything outside its reach even darker than it already was.

Later, they watched some folk dances on a makeshift stage under two spotlights. Men wearing fans of feathers blowing four-foot pan pipes swayed between women in billowing skirts. The dances seemed to lay bare a simple truth: here the men were, weaving between the women, showing off their prowess with the pipes, and eventually the two sexes paired off into couples, and trooped offstage. Soon enough, another dance would begin all over again. Whatever one thought, that was what life consisted of: having the skills to subsist, procreating and exiting. Meanwhile four men beat drums and shook gourds at the side of the stage. On and on the beat went.

They walked Ignacio back to the padre's. Jackson hugged him at the gate into the alley, and promised to return soon, when he had finished his work in the cloud forest.

Ignacio said nothing.

It will just be two or three weeks.

Still Ignacio stood there silently.

Jackson bent down and embraced him again. The boy didn't move or say anything. Jackson's face grew hot. He touched Ignacio's hair. Look after yourself.

Still the boy didn't move. Jackson felt suddenly that he might either sob or laugh, and bit the inside of his cheek.

In the end they had to walk him down the alley and all the way up the stairs to Beltrán's home.

8 · Journey

1

It felt so different to be travelling with someone. It was lucky too, a help. For example, Sarah knew there was a corner a few blocks below the market where the trucks left for Tingo.

There was something about her. She was fearless. Look at her now, heading toward the supposed no-go zone without a second thought, even if her uncle did live there. Things had changed since she'd last been there. And she travelled so light, with just a small pack, and lightly too in the sense of not laying down hard and fast plans, being ready to skip about and change them. Like the way she had come up to Chachapoyas so soon, so unexpectedly, to help him with Ignacio. It made the world feel both broader and simpler.

Tingo, three hours to the south, wasn't much of a town: a single main street with a couple of restaurants, a bar and a tumbledown hotel. The driver pulled up outside a café. Behind it the valley fell away, but you couldn't see it for the thick verdure behind the houses. In the early twilight the dust of the street had turned pale, and the waxy subtropical leaves of the trees seemed to grow both stronger in colour, and darker.

Sarah and Jackson climbed out and paid the driver.

You can stay at the hotel, the driver said, lifting a hand listlessly from the steering wheel.

It was already too late in the day to set out on the hike into the cloud forest.

As they strolled down the street with their packs Sarah said, I guess we might be able to get to Uncle Alfredo's in a day from here. If we leave early enough. It's a big climb to the pass but after that it's pretty easy.

How high is the pass?

Thirteen thousand feet.

Jackson groaned, and felt a little as if he were acting. They seemed to have become quite formal with one another. He was nervous too, and wanted to get back to the easy calm way of being with her.

We're pretty low here, too, she said. As you can tell.

They were talking like a pair of climbers who had just met, and were planning some assault together. But it was true, the air of lower altitude was warm before nightfall and quite dank. Odours came now and then of blossom, fruit and a faint acridity of urine.

From my uncle's place it'll be another couple of days to where you're going, I think, Sarah added.

The hotel had only one room left, an L-shaped one they had to share. Jackson spent half an hour pacing round the walls with a towel, swatting every faint shadow he could detect by the light of the dim bulb hanging in the middle. Some of his blows yielded smears of dark blood. Others released a faint whine in the ear that quickly became inaudible, and he would continue his stalking.

They decided they would rest, have a shower, then find some supper and a drink. Neither of them had eaten all day, except for some crackers Sarah had brought along for the journey.

Jackson would normally have liked to be alone. Half of him in fact did feel alone because he no longer had Ignacio with him. It was strange to be without him. There was a sense of freedom, but also of emptiness, of something missing, of it being no use to have one's hands empty. Before meeting Ignacio, he had enjoyed arriving in a new town in the afternoon, finding himself a room, opening a shutter and looking down on a street in solitude. But the last few weeks had given him a taste for company.

He was calm, excited and nervous all at once to have Sarah in the room too.

The room's shape gave them each some privacy. His part was eaten into by a partition that stopped short of the ceiling, behind which was the bathroom—a little corridor of blue tiles, seatless toilet and a single pipe emerging from the wall at the end, which was the shower. Two small towels lay folded on a chair. Above the toilet two squares of mirror tile had been glued to the wall.

Jackson showered first. He was reluctant to. But once the thin stream splashed his chest he felt grateful to it. The water ran warm for a while, heated in its pipes by the day's sun, then cooled. He scrubbed himself with soap from his plastic soapbox. While he was drying he caught sight of his darkly stubbled cheeks in the mirror, and decided that now would be a good time to shave. He lathered himself with soap, all he had, and ran the shower onto the blade of the disposable razor that had come with him from Chiclayo, and laboriously, painfully worked his way through ten days' growth.

The towel was too small to wrap round his waist. Holding it close he peered out and saw that Sarah was hidden, as he had hoped, in her part of the room, and paced to his bed. He couldn't think what else to do but get under the covers. A wave of fear hit again. He didn't like being shy with her, he felt it was already somehow unnecessary, and therefore disappointing. But on the other hand, they hardly knew each other, and here they were having to share a room.

How is it? she called.

He could tell by her voice that she was lying in bed. A flatness in the tone. He could also tell that the strange stiffness and formality hadn't cleared between them. Perhaps it was just something to do with having spent half a day in an open truck, rolling through so much terrain.

It's a pipe, he said. He pulled the towel from his waist and pressed the damp cloth against his chin. He had cut himself in several places.

What else? the voice responded.

I mean it's just a pipe. I think I used up all the warm. I'm sorry. There was about ten seconds of it.

He heard her bed creak. She didn't reply for a moment then said: Of all the selfish, thoughtless things to do.

He could hear the smile in her voice. It's nicer cooler. Honestly.

Sure. She laughed. Her bed groaned and rattled. She appeared walking past the foot of his bed in her white T-shirt and jeans.

What's this? she asked, picking up the remaining towel from the chair.

We call it a towel.

She glanced at him and smiled. I see. It's a barber's flannel. Then she frowned. What happened to you? Safety razor didn't reach England?

He pulled the towel off his face and saw it was stained with blood.

He shrugged. You'd have a hard time shaving yourself with that thing. It was like mowing hay with a . . .

He hesitated.

You seemed to do all right, she said. Is there any part of your face you didn't cut? Let me see. She walked across the room, leaned over him and ran her hand over his jaw, then patted it with the damp cloth.

Keep the towel on, I'd say. She wiped her hand on the back of her jeans and went into the bathroom.

Jackson was paralysed. The image of her face just above him, and of her hair, and the smell of her, thick, sweet, light all at once, and the touch of her fingers on his face. And now the sound of her showering fell on him like warm water. He not only felt the water on his own skin, he sensed her standing right next to him, wet, naked, warm, shining. His heart jumped into his throat. The drubbing water. The steam. The gleaming skin. The hair blown flat by the stream. And she was just there, on the other side of that little incomplete wall. Here he was, naked in bed, all of seven feet away. He opened his eyes and looked at the pockmarked ceiling and made himself breathe deeply.

When she came out she did not worry about the skimpiness of the towel. She held it over her breasts, with her clothes over her loins, walked without a word to his bed and sat on the edge with her back to him. She put an arm behind her back, as if trying to reach her neck, and said, I've got this sore muscle. Right here. Under my shoulder. Could you press on it?

The skin was hot. Jackson couldn't believe how soft it was. And there was the chain of her vertebrae swelling under the skin. His heart knocked like a spoon in a tin cup. Every part of him was hot. Her shoulder blade opened like a wing as she raised her arm. The skin stretched like an elastic membrane, and although Jackson did not hear what she said he did what she asked; he pressed into the fissure under that snowdrift of skin, felt the tendon beneath the bone. Then his mouth was on her shoulder, open, breathing in the hot air her skin gave off. He heard her laugh, close by his ear, then her arm rose up round his far cheek, and pulled his face close.

Shall we . . . ? Do you want to?

His heart stretched like a piece of elastic. They were on the pillow now, her face before his, her smile, her small teeth, her pale, pale lips. Her light-brown cheeks. Her green eyes, that were gold just now—he had never seen such a colour. His heart was carrying so big a load it would surely pull itself from its socket and drop through the floor, into the dry earth of this unknown country.

He felt he had never kissed before. She moved her lips exactly as he hoped. His mind was silent as their lips spoke to each other. Every time he thought about breaking the kiss, something would fascinate him all over again.

He was pinned down by her weight on the covers. He tried to move his hand to her face but couldn't get it free. All the feeling he would have transmitted to his hand he sent into his mouth.

He didn't stop to ask himself where so much feeling came from.

It was as if he had lifted the lid of a box and instead of finding what he expected it had turned out to be a treasure chest, one new thing after another.

Outside the window the world turned translucent blue.

He stared at her eyes, which stared back. Do you always kiss like this?

She smiled. They say the kiss tells you everything.

The gaze went on.

I'm basically not—I mean, I didn't think I was—

He didn't have the heart to finish, not because he feared to, but because gazing at her was too interesting. Far from needing to stroke her with his hand, his eyes caressed her.

Up for this? she asked. I know. Me either. Does it matter? I mean, we seem to be enjoying ourselves.

When he next became aware of it, the street outside was dark, lit here and there by lights and lanterns. When a vehicle drove by he noticed that he had not heard a car pass in a long time.

She closed her eyes, opened them again. What is this? Her stare rested on his heart like a hand.

Then she said, I'm getting cold, and it was a relief to think about something ordinary. She lifted her T-shirt but held it without putting it on.

Should we go out and get dinner? We haven't eaten.

Now that she was sitting up he pulled his hands free. He looked at his watch. We've been doing this for an hour.

A sixty-minute kiss.

It's only just beginning. I mean the kiss. Doesn't it feel that way?

How can a kiss be so interesting? I'm a biologist, a geneticist. I know about nature's little tricks.

The situation—a woman sitting next to him contemplating whether or not to pull on a shirt, in a room of their own, in a country in which both of them were free—stirred a vague memory. Sometime long ago a woman had sat beside him on his bed and he had known she loved him.

She smiled down at him. We could go out and discuss it over dinner, or we could keep trying to find out. More research.

She said the last word quietly, bending toward him. He closed his eyes and felt the warmth of her face and knew without looking when her lips would reach his. She rested her weight on one elbow and steered herself under the covers.

The way Jackson later saw it was that he had been too over-whelmed to get erect. Simply too much feeling. That her body could be so hard and soft at the same time—he couldn't under-stand that. There were hidden depths in her that you only discov-ered once you touched her. A man's body wasn't like that, it was forthright, everything was on the surface. Then she pressed her length against him and he felt the at once soft and abrasive quality of the hair at her middle. When she opened her mouth, the blood pumped into him.

In a little while she said, You must do this all the time.

He pulled a frown into his face. But you must.

I'm not a nun, she said. But that's not what I mean. It's this feel-ing. I sort of knew I liked you. I thought you were cute. And inter-esting and bright and everything. But—I don't know. She frowned at him in mock anxiety. Is it—now I'm embarrassed to ask. Is it just me? Doesn't it feel sort of weird?

He said: I keep expecting to worry then not worrying. Yes.

Even though they were naked in bed, for hours they only kissed. When they tried to amplify things sooner or later they would come back to just kissing. Everything else seemed an acces-sory.

She said: The earth isn't supposed to move when you're just kissing.

He felt like the earth had evaporated. There was nothing but her and the room. But what amazed him more than the sensations, more than the sheen of her skin, the softness of her mouth, and its strength, elasticity, the erectile tenacity of her tongue that would suddenly become soft and giving, like a change of movement in a piece of music—as if together their mouths were engaged in some kind of ballet, and understood what move the other wanted to turn to next—more than that was the fact he felt no fear. Every time fear loomed he would remember who was here with him, and it would vanish.

Her breasts were small, barely distinguishable from the musculature of her torso. He was amazed how her nipples grew when he sucked them. The first time he did, when he stopped he felt her hand on the back of his head pressing him to carry on.

The feeling it roused in him was like a taste, so her nipples seemed to him to have a taste.

Later, dinner forgotten, sleep forgotten, dressing forgotten, there was the smell of her, and the briny, milky taste of her, and the feel of her pubic hair stiff and silky at the same time, and the sleek-haired cleft. He kissed it and felt he was being unfaithful to her mouth.

How could a person be so hard, but soft too? He felt he had never seen a woman's body before. He had been too afraid. Afraid that whoever she was she would go away, wouldn't let him do what he wanted, afraid he'd be too rough, too gentle, too quick, too slow. Afraid that afterward he'd find himself bound. Somewhere he had learned to think of women as allayers of lust, he saw now. People talked about men treating women as sex objects all the time. But he had never thought how it applied to him. It was a sorrow. He had been indoctrinated, had accepted the hateful idea that women's chief interest to men was their curvaceousness. No wonder he had been afraid of them, if that was all they were.

Now the sense bloomed as never before, of a woman as an allayer of fear, who slaked loneliness, not lust. He told her this.

In the middle of the night she asked: Do you want to go to my uncle's tomorrow? He's not expecting me any particular day.

Shortly before dawn the frogs fell silent and the two of them fell asleep.

Jackson's last thought, as he lay with one of her warm legs resting across his, and an arm encircling her rib cage—and her face right in front of his on the pillow, as if ready in a dream or a moment of waking to kiss again—was that his life had just changed. He neither minded nor feared it, because part of the change was the reawakening in him of courage. He could feel it prowling like a tiger round the cage of his chest. And that was his last sensation before he fell into happy rest.

2

They stayed in the town three days. Each mid-morning Jackson woke with a smoothness in his limbs, and stretched.

One night Sarah said: So of course I'm curious about your former loves. And I want you to know about mine. I mean, what amazes me is that if we had met any other time I don't think this would be happening. I split up with Hayden four months ago. That's part of the reason I came down here. I wanted to get away. I was kind of thinking I might have a holiday romance or something.

Holiday romance, eh?

She smiled. Mmm.

So that's what this is.

Isn't it?

Does it feel like it?

Does it?

Like Celer?

I guess. Though that didn't exactly work. She stared at him. As soon as I met you, and we danced that night on the beach, I felt something. Even if you didn't, I did. It was like I was spontaneously interested. I recognised something in you. Whatever it was I wanted to know it better.

He asked her about Hayden.

He was older than me. A post-doc. We lived together for three years. Strictly speaking he was my teacher, he supervised me in class—that's how we met. But the student-teacher thing vanished immediately. We were just two people, you know? He's a nice, clever man and he was good to me. But more and more I started to feel different from him. We did the same things we'd always done, we went to brunch on Saturday, we went to the beach sometimes, like in Newport, we hiked, we saw friends. Everything was the same, and we were always nice to each other too, we hardly ever had fights. But I began to feel more and more alien. We were different kinds of people. In our souls or something. Right from the start it had been about work and kindness. Those two things. What could be better, you might think. But something was missing. We worked differently, for a start. He's mathematical, I'm intuitive. I have a flash, then I can be methodical about proving it. But he doesn't. He works through experiments and slowly builds his conclusions. Except that's not it. It wasn't really about work. It was more fundamental. And yes, a lot of people might say it's good to be different, you can appreciate each other's strengths. That's what we thought. And we did. But I wanted more. I couldn't have stayed with him for the rest of my life—which he wanted to do—without finding out whether there was something else. She paused, then went on: And I had such a stable home as a child. I think I felt strong. Kind of brave about this stuff. I wasn't going to cling to one relationship in case I never got another. If I never did, so be it. She frowned regretfully. Is that bad of me?

He pulled her close. Very.

But what about you? She pushed him away. You had some goddam *man* in your past.

What do you mean? You mean Connolly? My friend?

That was his name? Well, he was obviously a big deal for you. So what was it with him? I mean, you said on the beach you were here basically because of him. It must have been one hell of a friendship.

I don't want to waste my life. I want to do the best I can with it. I want to live right.

You will. It's better not to worry about it. You can screw up if you do. But what does that have to do with this Connolly guy?

I lived right, when I was with him. He thought for a moment. I don't know if I'd count him as a former love, but there's nothing like it, that kind of time together. The stuff we did.

What kind of stuff?

Jackson was going to tell her about their times exploring

together, and the fun times, but the words stuck in his throat. He
hadn't meant to introduce anything else but suddenly found himself on the brink of an unexpected confession, and couldn't see
how to stop.

Stuff a lot of young men do. I don't know. Especially if they're
cooped up with a lot of other young men.

She pulled herself up and hugged her knees. That kind of stuff?

It wasn't much. It didn't matter, it wasn't what our friendship
was about.

It must have made you closer, I bet.

Maybe, in a way.

She shook her head. Oh my God. What have I got myself into? I
mean, how do I know you're not gay? How do you know? It can
be hard enough without bringing that whole deal in.

He hesitated. I've never really told anyone any of this. Sure you
want to know?

I better know.

It might sound sort of naïve, or callous even, but there wasn't a
lot of choice—for me anyway. It was just a phase. I mean, boarding
school, then the army, living with only men twenty-four hours a
day. You get love where you can. And Connolly was—he was
unusual. You'd know what I mean if you'd met him. He didn't fit
the pigeonholes people have. He used to say we were souls clothed
in human flesh. Gender didn't seem to matter with him. Well, he
had a cock of course. But he was beautiful in a sexless kind of way.
His face could almost have been a woman's. High cheekbones. You
know how Bowie is? He looked a bit like that. He loved Bowie. Listened to him all the time. He was the man.

Or woman.

You're catching on. He used to sleep with girls too sometimes.
He wasn't exclusive.

She screwed up her face. But I mean, what did you guys do? Did
you like do it all? I mean, shouldn't we be using condoms? Oh God.

It's OK. We didn't do anything you and I couldn't do. Provided
you were willing of course.

Are you sure you're OK?

Totally.

How do you know? You had a test?

He nodded.

He tried to put his head in her lap but she held him off.

It's weird, you seem like this uptight Mr. Englishman, but you're not really. You like trying stuff. You're into living on the edge. Did you know that? Otherwise why would you be down here, really? I thought you were all sort of meek and mild. You never even made a pass at me when we were sitting on the beach that night.

I'm shy.

Sure. She sighed. Well, I hope that's what it was. Was it?

You mean you think I might not be into this? Into you? Now I wish I'd never mentioned Connolly. It was nothing. Just some kind of late-adolescent thing.

Then why did it all mean so much?

Jackson inhaled and held the breath a moment. I don't exactly know, he said finally. But he understood me. I felt understood.

She stared at him, her eyes large and lambent in the dark. A walk on the wild side. I can see that. She reached out and touched his hand. That's good. It's good you're brave. But you're sure it's safe? Please?

Yes, yes.

She let herself gently collapse as he rolled onto her.

Me and Hayden tried it. I couldn't see the point.

It gets better. So they say. There's things you need to know.

Like?

You don't want to know.

She rubbed her nose against his.

Teach me?

For real?

For real. She began to roll over and he stopped her. No need to do that, for a start.

***

Later that night Jackson awoke to a vivid memory of Connolly, of the first time they'd touched. They were staying in the little house lent them by the *corregidor* in a village. Jackson had just washed in an icy stream, and was basking in the glow it had left. Afternoon sun was flooding the room. When Connolly's hand landed on his belly he jumped like a fish. The touch seemed to reach inside him. He couldn't breathe, his legs stretched apart by themselves. Then he was at Connolly's belt. What happened next he could only feel, not remember. There was something in Connolly's smile that dispelled all fear. When he thought it was over, there was more. He remembered how they lay side by side laughing, one arm behind each other's neck, shaking on the little bed that now squeaked hurriedly to the rhythm of laughter. He had not known human coupling could confirm you to the depths of your being. He had wanted to say something, but a thing like that, you could only get confused if you talked about it. No questions. The soul's surgeon had been at work. What you did was good because it felt good. You needed no other reason. They never talked about it.

What he felt now, with Sarah breathing silently but perceptibly under the sheet beside him, was the same thing. He had nothing to hide. Once again, all of him was known, and was acceptable. He folded himself against her.

On their last day in town they planned to get to sleep early so they could make an early start and try to reach her uncle's in one day. But they stayed up talking again till four.

She wanted to know what had happened to him when he was sent home from Belize.

The doctors called it a breakdown. They don't really have enough names for stuff like that. They should. It's not like there's just one thing that can happen.

He sat up on the bed and tweaked the curtain. There was no moon. He shrugged and rolled himself a cigarette.

I don't mean that, she said. I just mean what actually happened. Where were you? Was it a sudden thing? What caused it, do you think? I mean, what made it happen? Tell me about it. And tell me

why you are here. Why you left England. Tell me again. Tell me
everything.

He twirled the cigarette, neatly made, and sighed. It was a subject
he didn't like to think about. He had once done so too much.

I don't know where to begin.

Well, how come they sent you home from Belize?

Like I said, a breakdown.

How did you get home?

I flew.

Alone?

Yes.

Did anyone meet you?

Not at the airport. Off the train. I got a bus then a train.

And they knew what you'd been through? They knew you were
coming?

He didn't answer, but sighed, and lit his cigarette.

It's a weird, broken family, I suppose. He shook his head. It was
pretty awful actually.

Slowly, with pauses to draw on his cigarette, looking sometimes
at her, sometimes at his feet crossed in front of him, sometimes out
of the crack in the curtain at the end of the bed into the quiet, dark
street, he took himself out of that warm bedroom and told her
about that other time, two years earlier, just now seeming as irrelevant and strange as someone else's dream.

In a while his throat tightened and he closed his eyes. He tipped
forward onto the pillow and felt a warmth behind his eyes. Her
hand was on his shoulder.

I was so lost, he mumbled.

Whatever happened, it wasn't your fault. It wasn't. Christ, how
old were you? Nineteen. You're still only twenty-one. What are
you asking of yourself? You can't have everything sorted out perfectly. How can you?

But I did then, he blurted into the pillow. I lived perfectly before.

She inhaled and exhaled slowly. All this, all of it, is called growing up. Eventually it'll be over and you'll have embarked on some
kind of regular life. It might be a little less perfect than those

golden days you seem to think you had, but it's OK. That's how it's supposed to be. You have to stop blaming yourself.

He wiped his nose and mouth with the back of his hand, and lifted his face from the bed, and felt a sheepish smile break out. He was both embarrassed by his tears, unsure how they would be received, and also somehow pleased. He sniffed, and blew his nose.

I tried stuff. Well, after a while. I spent three weeks in the hospital, they told me, when I first got back. I hardly knew. Time just didn't exist. Nor did age. I could have been nineteen or a hundred and nineteen. It didn't mean anything. Then I had group therapy, loads of stuff. I can't fault the army. They couldn't have taken me back; you can imagine how they feel about mental-health issues, that kind of thing. And there was Connolly. They knew about me and him. The combination was too much. He shook his head and said again, I was so lost.

He remembered walking down an alley in the City once, in London, in search of a café he had seen advertised on a board out on the street. At the end were fogged-up windows, evidently steamed up by the heat of a kitchen and damp bodies. He went in. Over the tables the smell of vinegar and tea and steam hung in the air. A few chairs were occupied by figures bundled in coats. Because of the misted windows, the light was dim. He felt he had walked into some forest hovel, the home of a race who liked to huddle in dark places round a fire.

You could get to like this kind of life, he remembered thinking, amid rain and cold and sunlessness, but only if you erased the other kind of life from your brain cells, of sunshine and street life, a sense of moving toward a bright destination. Here all you moved towards was a damp grave.

He remembered scanning the shelves of off-licences to see if they had Casillera de Montezuma, because somewhere someone must have it, and walking the rain-splashed streets near the barracks, once he was out of hospital, past the curve of the Albert Hall and the Royal College, necklaced with BMWs, Rolls-Royces, Mercedes—all the gleaming diplomatic money. He thought of the vendors in Belize with their trays of cigarettes at the corners of dusty roads. Where could you buy a single cigarette round here? You had to come into some hot pub thick with carpets and gin, where a landlord with a belly stretching his city shirt would grudgingly give you change and you'd go to the machine at the back that would swallow up all the fun of the impulse, and emerge with a whole pack. How did you have fun here? Amid the daunting grandeur of houses in the rain, other things, snobbishness, ambition, swelling bank accounts, pride in one's newest car, one's chillingly sumptuous flat, one's latest screw with her short black skirt, took the place of fun. But those things weren't fun. They were a poor substitute.

What kind of stuff did you try? she asked.

He told her about his desperate search for a church.

A church?

Yes. I was living in London, and signing on, and I was miserable.

Signing on?

I didn't have a job. And I was drinking too much, and not knowing how I was going to get out of the state I was in. I read the Bible, all of it, and I tried to find a church. And I found one. One that lived up to Saint Paul and the New Testament, to salvation—the idea that salvation has happened, it's here for us now if we take it. The only church that really believed that was this crazy evangelical place. It was huge. It was humming. People loved it. All races. People got out of their skulls. High on prayer. It seemed great. But then I started going to Bible classes and they taught us about the devil and the powers of darkness that were out to get us. I couldn't buy it.

I'm glad to hear it, she said with a smile.

Whatever God is, he's not that petty. She gave this talk, the teacher, about the devil not being red with a forked tail but more like a beach boy with a tan and firm pectorals. She got so into her description of this devil of hers—well, that was it for me. I couldn't go there. I mean, what is so wrong with a hunky beach boy?

Well.

OK, beach babe.

She smiled.

A bright thick silence fell in their hotel room.

But what about men? I mean, did you love them?

He shook his head. There was only the one. I didn't know what I wanted.

Sarah sighed. They lay in silence for a while.

You know what I think? Sarah asked, staring at the ceiling. I think men are all looking for their fathers. You found a kind of father in Belize, in the army. Then he let you down.

Jackson let out a dry laugh. I don't know if he let me down or I let him down. He was silent a moment. Connolly used to say that's what Homer wrote about. Fathers and sons. I never read Homer. Connolly loved him. Jackson frowned. That was weird too. The rest of us were reading adventure crap, thrillers and stuff. And he was reading Homer and Prescott. Biggest adventure stories in the world, he used to say. The Trojan War and Odysseus, and the conquistadors. Were they all looking for their dads?

Maybe. Maybe for their dads' approval. It's the big wound of Western civilisation, someone said, fathers and sons.

Jackson shook his head. It's all weird. Now I feel sad and kind of warm at the same time. Is this called self-pity?

She nuzzled his shoulder. Maybe it's called being happy. Could it be?

9 · Sage

1

The mountains glittered in the early light. Two rivers of black scree flowed down from a crest, gleaming like coal, like jewels.

Jackson turned round to point it out to Sarah but she had fallen back.

He was hot from the climb, his thick blue cotton shirt wet against his back. Boots pale with dust. Legs strong and warmed up now. Loose. Trace of dust in the nose. Glitter of rock in the eye. A heavy back. All you needed on this earth. High above the treeline: anytime you were sick at heart, this was where you should come for healing.

When he reached the pass he crouched and waited for her. Connolly had told him never to sit while covering ground, it made it harder to get going again.

As soon as Sarah arrived she slung off her pack and lay down on the dry earth.

Oh my God. That is so intense. This crazy altitude.

He had an urge to go over and kiss her right there on the ground. Instead of questioning it he did it, and she kissed him back. He couldn't imagine ever again needing the mountains' healing. Below lay the cities of the globe, blazing in sunlight, brooding in rain, always at knee height, always manageable.

From the pass the trail crossed a broad bare shoulder of mountain then dropped onto a moorland of short grass. He could see the whole land they were about to enter. He had never seen anything like it. The land was a pile of heaped-up hills. Valleys fanned down to the east. Over all the hills lay a carpet of green, so they looked cloaked, like beasts smothered in a green sheet. Except here and there where a bare peak rose clear in a litter of grey rock. Above the fissures in the land hung a web of cloud. It was like aeroplane wake in the sky; cake icing puffed out by a baker—an inverse shadow of every water course in the land. As if the whole water-web of the land had left its breath on the morning air.

This was the land the Chachapoyans had favoured, that had favoured them. Beneath that tegument of green, for a certainty, lay the ruins of their cities, unremembered, unseen for more than half a millennium.

Here and there a whole valley was swallowed in a tide of cloud. Cloud and land went together. The cloud lay in tatters, in long ropes, in sheets, in lakes and seas. Clouds drifted and grazed and made their home here.

They traversed a huge forested valley, a deep green fissure of incomparable scale, in which all the valleys of the world seemed to meet—the kind of valley Jackson had thought you could find only in Sumatra or Malaysia, a huge flank of sparkling green, a wave of prehistoric verdure that faced them the way a tidal wave would face the village it was about to swallow.

They didn't talk much as they walked, each letting their thoughts roll.

They came to the brow of a hill and rested. Over other forested hills below them clouds passed; big unruly cumulus clouds that pulled blooms of shade across the carpet of foliage beneath so the whole dappled land seemed to be moving as if it were seething smoke that blew by on its own mission, travelling under the clouds which looked idly down.

Jackson pulled out his sketchbook and a thick pencil and began to draw. He worked fast, laying down a depth of shading, then cutting into it with his fingernail. It was amazing how you could bring something to life if you had the shading right. Light would start to emerge from all over the image. As he drew, the landscape on the page seemed to start flowing, just as the real one did.

The thought came to him: one day perhaps I will have the use of a studio, and paints, and time, and I will be able to work uninterruptedly at a canvas. It seemed an incomprehensible, scarcely supportable luxury. Then he wrote: *The land is an animal. The land is a human being asleep. Or awake but incapable of movement. Freely moving but we don't look right so we don't see the movement.*

He did not notice Sarah coming up behind him.

That's wonderful, she said.

Instinctively he covered the sheet with his arm, and glanced at her face. It was empty of expression—no smile, no archness—she meant exactly what she said. She had no agenda, he thought. It was nice. It was somehow a surprise.

So where did you train? she asked.

He looked up at her a moment. Well—we started at Sandhurst. Then out to Belize, I suppose. What do you mean?

I mean art college.

He frowned. I'm just a doodler.

But as he said it he felt uncomfortable, as though he was hiding something.

Come on.

It's true, he said, hearing himself sound defensive.

You're beyond doodling. She let out a laugh. You should be studying art.

Connolly used to tell him he was good at drawing. He'd never really listened. Nor had he ever contemplated going to art college. But now when he heard her suggest it he felt one day there really might be a chance to do something like that. Even as he allowed the possibility, he experienced a kind of dizziness. As if some land within him were shifting, and he could no longer tell what was firm ground.

Then she said, I guess the army showed you films about tanks and war planes, right?

He glanced at her, then looked away. You think the army are going to show opera films? He snapped shut his sketchbook. Anyway, what's that got to do with anything?

I swear to God, she said. You were wasted in the goddam army. Whoever the hell persuaded you to sign up? Thank God you got out of it. Now you need to get it out of you.

He didn't look at her but put the book back in his pack. He felt stung. She didn't know what she was saying.

Then with a weight of dread he remembered Brown's mission, and Brown's money, and the glistening eyes of Major Buckley at the Ritz, and whatever it was he was going to have to do for them up here. He had forgotten all about that the last few days.

It's more complicated than you think, he told her.

She shook her head in silence. Eventually she said, It's just that you're good. You should take care of it. It's a gift. I wish I could draw like that.

Time was moving on. It was already the ninth of the month: eleven days until his rendezvous. His heart sank. Why was it so hard to leave all that behind? He glanced at her. Her face was open, questioning, the sunlight making her eyes glow. He couldn't help smiling. Thank you, he said.

Friends? she asked.

Friends.

They embraced. Then she disengaged herself with a hum. We better be careful not to get too into this. There's a long way to go.

They sat in silence a moment, then started to walk on. Just then Jackson heard a low buzz in the air. He glanced around in case it was a wasp or hornet nearby, but saw nothing. The buzz had a depth to it, constant and steady, and grew louder, thicker. His heart was suddenly racing, and he stepped quickly over to Sarah and took her hand, looking all around. The noise acquired an edge now.

What is it? Sarah asked.

Hurry, he said, and pulled her toward an outcrop of rock nearby, but too late. The buzz opened out into a roar, and with a snarl a green helicopter floated rapidly up over the brow of the hill and along the ridge they were on. It rode over the crest of the next hill at a stately pace, where its sound became muffled again, and faded.

Jesus, Sarah said. What was that? I mean, what the hell are they doing here? Did they see us? she asked.

Jackson squeezed her hand.

Does it matter? she asked.

I don't know. Must be some old instinct of mine, to hide. From Belize. You don't want to be seen from the air. His heart was still thumping. Unless you know it's friendly.

Who *was* that? I mean, it's not like the Peruvian army has hundreds of helicopters.

Maybe the Americans? The DEA?

They heard a helicopter again later on, either the same one or another. By then they were back in the forest and didn't see it pass, and that was the last he heard of any helicopter for many days.

In the afternoon he noticed high up on a shoulder a patch of alpine meadow bathed in golden light, smooth as if grazed by chamois. On it stood a two-storey wooden house. As he stopped to look at it he heard the constant roar of a river below, like something echoing in the back of his skull. Up there in that house, lifted above the depths of green, the inhabitants would live on God's open palm. Higher still, the wave-face of green went on.

He wondered about that alpine scene. Who lived there? It could be local farmers, Indians like the rest of them. Or else it could be some Swiss or Swedish émigré perhaps, a man with a local family; barefoot children chasing sows in the yard, whose dugs swung as they hopped away across the dirt—some man for whom the word émigré would hold too much sense of a station in life.

Sarah caught up with him. That's it, she said, meaning the house. Another two hours and we'll be there.

As they threaded down toward a bridge across a small torrent, they ran into a long file of Indians with mules and donkeys coming the other way. The last two animals were still crossing the bridge, a pair of asses each with a young girl riding on its back among bundles of goods. The girls in their turn each had a baby tied to her back in a blanket.

Two men in pale grey ponchos walked at the front, sticks in hand, making sure the lead animals followed. Jackson sensed that at first they were reluctant to stop and talk, probably out of fear the animals would be stubborn about starting again. But they halted the dozen beasts anyway. Some started cropping the greenery on either side of the track.

Where are you going? one of the lead men asked. He had narrow eyes in a heavily wrinkled face, and squinted at Jackson from under thick eyebrows.

Up there, he said. The other side.

The man sucked his teeth: *Malo.* It's bad up there. We—he gestured behind him with a plump leathery hand that looked as if it might have been hurt—we are leaving until things are calmer. *Más tranquillo.* Now is a bad time up there. Don't go. *No te vayas.*

Through his narrow eyes the man was looking at him intently.

Gracias por la palabra, Jackson said. Thanks for the advice.

He and Sarah stood aside as the long file passed them, poultry crooning from sacks as they went. Then they carried on down to the river.

When the afternoon had passed its zenith and the air was beginning to thicken they emerged from the dark side trail they had been following onto a steep field, and climbed the last half mile in open view of the hills all around, which lay smouldering at the end of the day like the world at the end of an earthquake, as if just now finding rest from the tumult and cataclysm that had thrust them from the earth.

2

Alfredo gave them a one-room hut attached to the end of a barn to sleep in. During the day Jackson helped out Don Alfredo—

once Alfred—and Sarah hung out with the children and one or other of the mothers; by night, they were alone in the hut.

The main house had one big room downstairs, with a long table of rough, warped boards, and a kitchen at one end beneath a sleeping loft. A door at the opposite end led into the yard.

The days slipped by. One morning, sitting alone with a steaming cup of tea on the portal overlooking the valley, Jackson realised he had already been here three days, and had not had a moment of unease. Everything made sense here. The burbling chickens, the squealing guinea pigs, the bleating goats and sheep, all of them diminutive and scrawny; the small fields, or *chacras*, of corn and wheat, potatoes, onions, peppers. Around the house grew the tomato, tobacco and garlic plants. The way one spent the days—a few hours of weeding, planting, turning the dry soil, fetching firewood with the mule, or repairing the bamboo conduits that carried the stream water to various barrels and sinks around the compound so it could be at hand in different places—made time pass so you hardly noticed. Then talking with Alfredo over lunch. And resting through the heat of the afternoon. Then there'd be other things to do—painting a shed, working on the carburettor of Don Alfredo's beloved Enfield motorbike that he had once managed to ride all the way up here, except for the last two hundred yards, he said, where it had died and he'd had to push it into the compound, which it was perhaps fated never to leave.

Both during the afternoon rest and at night, he and Sarah would have time together.

They felt like children. How was that possible, when they were doing such adult things? Once her uncle had almost caught them making love on a flat rock by a little waterfall and pool where they bathed. As luck would have it, they had just got into a dog-style position, somehow graphic and ridiculous with an audience, when they heard a crack in the undergrowth. They leapt into the water. A second later Alfredo appeared asking if they'd seen Nellie. As soon as he left they swam together and fell into giggles.

Other times it would be deeply serious. He'd look into her eyes and they would seem to look so deeply back into his they stole into a recess of his mind he hadn't known was there.

❧

You're talking about the most powerful empire on earth, and what do they come up with? Truck stops, Arby's and cable TV. The same shows night after night. There has never *been* a civilisation with a lower level of culture.

Alfredo was a big man, a heavy American in scruffy jeans, with a warm-looking bulk to him. He wore plaid shirts and his beard reached to his chest. The ruddiness of his sun- and wind-worn face was emphasised by the silver-grey whiskers. His eyes were pale blue, almost alarmingly pale. It was a while before Jackson saw any family resemblance between him and Sarah. He thought their noses might once have been similarly fine, only Alfredo's had pitted, weathered and acquired a bump.

But don't the Indians here tell each other the same myths not just night after night, but generation after generation? Sarah commented.

Over a dozen of them were sitting at the table in the big room, which served as kitchen, dining, living room and bedroom at night for some, and children's classroom and their play area when it rained. Alfredo, his second wife Dolores—a slender local woman in her forties who must once have been a beauty—Sarah and Jackson sat at one end of the table, with the older children down the sides, the youngest at the far end. Among the children sat Nellie, a large woman from Lima who had always lived with them, who was in fact the mother of Alfredo's eldest children. With the rudimentary wood table, the wooden floor and the wooden shelves all around the walls the place had a rustic alpine feel on the inside as well as from the outside.

Millennium upon millennium, Alfredo said. We cannot quantify the age of their myths. They reach back to the beginnings of the human race. See this rock, how come it's here? See me, see this body, how come it is here? That tree, why does it grow? These are the questions the myths ponder. They *think*, these people.

Jackson slowly stirred the cup of tea he had been given. The spoon scraped and clinked dully.

Alfredo smiled. You know the way to possess life? Have nothing. Have enough to eat, keep warm and have a partner. Only what the species requires. A house doesn't need a lot of wires coming into it. It needs a stream nearby, good soil and firewood. *Leña*. By the way, that's what we called our first girl, Leña. Nellie and I. After all the trees round here. And our first boy was Sol.

Jackson sipped his tea. You mean all one has to do is lead an isolated life and happiness will follow?

Who says isolated? We see people every day. All the farmers up and down the valley. Tell me who wins: the guy on Wall Street on ten million a year with an ulcer who worries all night? Or a fisherman in Cuba who's lucky if he makes three dollars a day, which is enough to feed his family, who sleeps well and wakes up looking forward to the new day?

You're assuming infinite choice.

I'm not. He smiled in his white beard. All I'm assuming is that we are responsible for our happiness.

Jackson shrugged but somehow couldn't seem to let his shoulders drop. He stirred his tea again, took another sip. The brew had cooled to a good temperature. The splash of goat's milk was just enough, and the rough local sugar added an interesting tang. The tea itself was just the right strength. In fact, it was an ideal cup of tea.

Well? What do you think? Alfredo was eyeing him. We got the seeds from a friend in Norway. Real Darjeeling. It's taken pretty well. We're the same altitude as the tea gardens of India. But I never had an Englishman try it. The real test, eh?

Jackson smiled. Bloody nice. Haven't had a decent cup in months. Real milk too, not the canned stuff.

The tea made him feel hollow and spacious.

After a moment he asked, So what about all the troubles people talk about here?

A good man is invisible. They don't bother a good man. You put the right word out, you get by, Alfredo said, and fell to sipping his hot drink, musing.

They never touch us. No one has even threatened us. Except maybe the odd drunk at a fiesta. Why would they? We don't ask for much. Look, back in the sixties a lot of guys came down from the West Coast and tried this sort of thing. Around Machu Picchu, the Urubamba valley is littered with old communes, homesteads and such. They are ruins now. They wanted too much. It wasn't enough for them just to live. To sow, harvest and eat. They expected all that to make them feel wonderful. It didn't. So then they take all their shit, their mushrooms and San Pedro and whatever, to kick-start their brains so they *do* realise how wonderful it all is. See? Never enough. The white man is never satisfied. He's like a species that can't get comfortable on this earth. That's why I'm here. Because one day aged twenty-one when I was down here working for the Peace Corps, I was looking down a big valley toward the jungle in the late afternoon, and the light came pouring down, turning all the trees gold, and this feeling welled up. Like I was looking at my natural home. I had never felt that before. Not anywhere. I knew then what it really means to belong.

Alfredo scratched his leonine beard. Leastways, that's what I think, he added in a mock-redneck sing-song, as if embarrassed at the preceding rhetoric.

Came down here and never looked back, he added. He smiled at his wife and closed his hand over hers. Just knew I had found something a million times better than anything back home. And I still think I'm right, for all its faults. Is there, can there be, a greater human happiness than to live where you belong, and be in love with your wife?

He smiled at her, and she looked up from the table.

Jackson frowned. What about Nellie down at the other end of the table? he wondered. What did she think?

But come on, Uncle Alfredo, Sarah said. You can't seriously mean that the whole Caucasian race is just, well—fucked?

Nellie looked into her tumbler and laughed, making her big shoulders shake.

There was a pause during which the candle in the middle of the table fluttered to itself, softly clearing its throat.

Not by definition. But we have become disconnected for so long. That's why we have to work so hard to reconnect.

He smoothed down his beard and swigged from his mug.

For example, people take it as a foregone conclusion that the world's wealth ought to be spread around, that the peasant woman with a few blankets and llamas to her name wishes she had a car and garage, a new villa and household appliances. That's one hell of a supposition. A lot of people round here, they're not poor, they're just living a different way. You think anybody has actually thought this through? It's just a lot of businessmen trying to shift product wherever they can. That's what it's about.

We saw all these people leaving the other day. Fleeing the area. How is it here? Jackson asked.

How is it? Alfredo got up to fetch more hot water from the low stove, and paused in his stooping to glance back at Jackson, his pale eyes and pale lips gleaming in his white-whiskered face. He raised the grizzled bushes of his eyebrows, catching Jackson's eye. Then he put a hand in the small of his back and pushed himself erect.

You really want to know? You know what the preferred weapon was back in the days of Sendero?

Dynamite strapped to dogs. I read about it.

He shook his big white-fringed head. The stone. Rocks. Kids did it. They used to get eleven-year-old boys to pelt you with little rocks, you'd tell them to scram, and before you knew it, you had a mob stoning you. Like the Middle Ages only just arrived. Anyway, it's not like that now, that level of craziness couldn't last. But it could always come back. It's chaos, it's lawless. Mayhem, you could say. Anything can happen.

3

Sarah was sitting in the doorway of their hut. The moon had risen clear of the mass of hillside above, and beyond the silvery dirt of the compound the trees were dark like an inky lake. The sound of the river had become distinct and near.

He talks so much. I'm sorry. I'd forgotten that.

I like it. I like big ideas, Jackson said. Maybe not a lot of people are living like this, Western people, but it's real. Here we are.

She let out a little sigh that was also a laugh. The end of her cigarette glowed, a red star in the dark.

Come and sit here, she said, touching the wood of the doorstep beside her. Jackson settled his head into her shoulder, and her hair fell across his eye, filtering and fracturing the moonlight.

When they went inside Sarah wanted to know more about Connolly.

What must be hard to understand is how we grew up hating ourselves, as men I mean, assuming all women despised us. At least I did.

Come on.

Seriously. I remember going to the beach as a seventeen-year-old—fit, OK-looking, not a complete moron—and seeing the girls in bikinis and just kind of trying to slip past hoping I wouldn't disturb them.

Everyone feels like that at the beach. You should get a glimpse inside those girls' heads. Can he see the mole on my back, how does my ass look, no guy will ever want me, et cetera. After all, they're the ones who have to lie there like meat at the market waiting to be chosen.

The women you're talking about are American. There are all these hunky American guys walking past who are confident enough to pick and choose, who don't think any girl who gave them a second glance would be doing them a grudging favour. You have no idea what it's like to be an English male in single-sex education.

Maybe. Anyway, tell me more about the mysterious Connolly.

She rolled onto her side and wrote with a finger on his chest, reminding him that he was a man and had a man's chest, and that she was a woman and that it was good to lie naked together.

He sighed. I've been sort of trying to.

She said nothing but looked at him, her eyes pockets of shade containing a star each. The room was quiet; a creak of wood somewhere came and went. Silence pressed in on the ears. He felt he needed to break the quiet before it became oppressive.

I guess there is something else. I don't know what happened that night in the jungle. When Connolly died. For a long time I was convinced—well, in the rain and with my leg in such agony, and the fire coming in and everything. I just don't know what happened. I think I fired some rounds. I think I did. The doctors told me I was wrong, the army said we had fire coming in all around and Connolly got hit by it. But I used to think it was me.

She was silent. She propped herself on an elbow. I understand how that could happen. How you could think that. But even if it were true, you'd need to forgive yourself.

The candle in its glass bowl hanging overhead swung in a stray breeze coming from the window, turning long spokes of shadow about the room, making it seem that the room was a wheel and was slowly turning in the night. Or else that the whole dark valley outside was rotating on an axis that came down like a rod through the heart of their bed.

I didn't realise my life had got stuck, he said.

They talked some more, then the talk gave way to lovemaking. Then she fell asleep.

Jackson's mind was in a strange, calm state. Moments of memory from around the globe, what he had seen of it, came and went. He remembered sitting in a café on the Euston Road in London, watching people come and go at a smart office building opposite called Interfocus, and seeing then that all of them, everyone he could see, was going to die. Life was a glass capsule with night pressing in on all sides. It was just a matter of time until it broke.

As he lay beside Sarah the spokes of the lamp turned across the roof beams above, as if it were a lighthouse scanning the darkness. Its beams found substance, shapes brought into brief form by their touch as they revolved. As if light itself were no different from the touch of a blind man's fingers. As if all were darkness but the touch of light conjured the illusion of sight.

Sarah lay with her cheek on his breast. He felt the warm tremble of her exhalations. Her head rocked gently up and down on his own breaths. Outside the hills rose and fell and the rivers tumbled down to Amazonia. Somewhere beyond that the black ocean lapped at the iron shores and the quays of gantried ports, at the citadels with stone seawalls. Across the sea rode giant container ships, iron on iron, black hull on black water. That was all far away. He thought of the Chachapoyan people and their bones, piles of pebbles lost among the hills, forest and cloud. They seemed close and far at the same time.

He got up and went to the window. The shutter was simple and homemade but fitted well. It swung open silently when he unhooked it. A bleary yellow moon, a chip off an old plate, was floating above the black line of hill. He could see all the black land reaching away in furrows, smeared with a funnel-smoke of yellow cloud running up and down the valley. Immediately under the window was the bare earth of the yard that sloped away then dropped down the grey meadow to the line of trees where the forest began. Something cried, a short dull cry of boredom or despair like a question. It might have been a bird or small mammal.

A pale figure came out of the trees onto the meadow. Jackson thought it was a man. He wasn't visible for more than a few seconds. He took a few silent steps in the moonlight, paused and stepped back into the forest. He had seemed to be wearing a long coat that caught a sheen of moonlight, as if made of a shiny cloth. But that was improbable up here. As was a figure emerging like that out of the trees.

Afterward Jackson came to believe the man had been wearing a long white smock such as the Indians used to wear, and the figure became ever more of a puzzle and a preoccupation.

A big bird flew by, appearing out of nowhere above the roof, and swept away to the left on broad pale wings.

When Jackson turned back into the room Sarah was lying still with her eyes open. He reached up on tiptoes to the guttering candle and blew across the top of its glass jar. The candle went out in a cloud of smoke, releasing the scent of wax.

When he woke, grey light seeped under the eaves, turning the table, the chair, the bed itself with its thick white counterpane into ghosts.

4

Nellie had an indeterminate place in the household. She had been there from the start, yet she didn't exactly fit in. She kept to herself. Her daughter Leña had grown up and left, and the sullen teenage Sol spent much of his time swinging in a hammock on the porch reading. Often Nellie would sit nearby in one of the crude wooden chairs that looked like rockers but didn't rock. She looked after the other children too, even when Dolores was around. Dolores was more likely to do farm work—getting maize for the pigs and the two cows, bringing them hay, filling their water pails. She did the milking too, although it was Nellie who milked the goats. The goats were hers. She was the one who locked them up at night and let them out in the morning.

One day Jackson had been helping Alfredo plough up ground creepers. One more time, Alfredo said, and it would be good for planting. Jackson walked into the refreshing dark of the house and found Nellie kneeling on a plastic sheet with two of the younger children. There was a wooden box filled with gourds, bowls and pots of paint. She had a tub in which she was mixing small amounts of colour with a long brush.

Jackson watched from the end of the room. Nellie's skirts spread wide, and she was leaning forward to give a brush to one of the little girls. Her long black and grey hair hung on either side of her face. Jackson turned and left. He felt suddenly sad, or difficult. He wasn't sure what he felt. He walked round the building and went into the kitchen by the door at the other end, and dipped a cup in the bucket of sweet water, as they called it—the spring water for drinking—and drank two cupfuls straight down. Then, from the far end, he looked again at Nellie and her art class.

A girl was pulling a thick line of blue paint across a newspaper. In the daylight from the windows the wet paint glistened like blood. You could see the grains of it like wood grain. It seemed to Jackson a knife opening a broad wound, the blue blood welling up and shining stickily.

He couldn't watch. He went out and helped Alfredo turn in the mule that had been pulling the plough. While he was unbuckling the halter he realised that what he was feeling was envy. He was envious of the child with its carer and its paints. He felt sick, and bent down behind the mule's neck.

That evening he asked Nellie if he could have some paint.

Of course. She frowned. What for?

I'd like to do a picture of the family, he blurted without thinking. Of everybody, he added, just in case there was any confusion.

Over the next two days he did charcoal portraits of each of the children and adults from different angles, and a sketch of them all at the table together. Then he pasted several sheets of newspaper back to back, to make them thick and strong, then stuck together four of these thickened sheets to make one giant papier-mâché board which he nailed against the barn wall outside under the eaves.

Nellie's paints were powders, oils and gluey pastes that she said she made from roots and onion skin, herbs and rocks. She had plenty of limewash, and he painted ten coats of white over his big sheet to get a good base. Then he sketched in the family at the table. He had never painted on such a scale before. He used the little portraits to get the faces right. Then he started with the colours, working in layers from paler to darker. He built it up like reverse archaeology, giving himself time to see what he had done, letting the picture tell him how it wanted to be. He grew to like it more and more as he worked. He let the colours, the paint itself, determine its own harmony and balance, so it became no longer a matter of simply rendering reality, but the reality of the paint became its own force too.

After lunch he and Sarah would make love then fall asleep. He'd wake from a deep oblivion to find only ten minutes had passed. He would creep out of bed and work through the heat of the afternoon while the compound slept.

Then one day, just before evening, Alfredo gathered everyone outside the barn. He had covered the picture with a canvas tarp. He seemed to have a genuinely humble attitude toward art, which touched Jackson. Ceremony was called for. He asked Jackson to unveil it.

The kids drank juice and the adults had home-made wine. People pointed and grinned and the kids went up close and Jackson had to tell them not to touch it. Some of the paint was still not completely dry. Sarah linked her arm in his and squeezed it tight.

Alfredo said they'd hang it in the big room as soon as it was dry.

A true artist, he declared.

5

One afternoon Jackson and Sarah were resting on the rocks after swimming in the river pool, and heard a rustle in the undergrowth. They looked at each other. Neither was wearing anything, and they instinctively sat up and hunched over. The sound came from just above the pool where the path turned uphill toward the compound.

The silence was thick. Jackson could see in Sarah's eyes that she too thought there was someone there.

He had mostly dried off and pulled on his trousers. In the quiet as he buckled his belt there was a crackle above them. Again they glanced at each other. Sarah moved to her clothes and hurriedly put on a T-shirt.

Jackson climbed up the rocks out of the gully and paused behind a bush where he could see the path sloping up. It was empty except for a few twigs. He waited, and began to think maybe it had been nothing after all, perhaps just a bird, and walked a little way up to make sure.

The boy was squatting between two laurel bushes, staring at a length of bark in his hand, tapping it on the ground. Beside him his cat skipped and pounced on something, then looked about intently, having missed whatever it was, surprised to find nothing in its paws.

Jackson laughed, he couldn't help himself. You! he cried.

Before he knew it, he'd grabbed the boy in his arms and lifted him off the ground. He weighed nothing, and smelled of straw, farm animals and faintly of cheese.

My God, he said. What the hell. How did you get here? What are you doing here?

Ignacio hung limp in his arms. When Jackson set him down he looked sheepishly at the ground but Jackson could see a smile on his face. The boy always seemed to be embarrassed by his own smiles.

No sé, señor, he said. I came.

Jackson shook his head then held Ignacio by his little shoulders. How did you find us? Who brought you?

No, he said, *no es difícil.* It's not difficult. No one brought me, señor. I come with *el gato.* We find the way easily.

But how? It's a long way. Does Padre Beltrán know you're here?

The boy didn't answer, but picked up his woven shoulder-bag, put it round his neck and stood waiting in silence.

Sarah was already dressed and had Jackson's shirt and boots in her hands when they came back to the pond.

I swear, she said. I swear I thought it was him. I could hear you talking and I thought maybe it was Charro or one of the other kids, but then I just got this feeling.

She stepped up and ruffled Ignacio's head then pulled him against her.

Who brought you? No, don't tell me, you came by yourself. Right? She smiled at Jackson. I told you he was a resourceful kid.

As they walked up to the house Jackson kept questioning Ignacio.

I asked the women in the market where you went. One of them saw you getting on the truck and she knew the driver, he comes every week from Tingo.

But how did you know where we'd gone from Tingo?

I heard you talking about the man, the gringo, the señora's uncle, who lives in the forest, *la selva.* I ask in Tingo and a woman tells me the way. It was easy. And I see your boots sometimes in the mud on the path.

It was true, Jackson's boots did have a distinctive tread, he'd noticed it himself on the paths around Alfredo's farm. But he was surprised to learn that Ignacio recognised it too.

As they walked slowly up the hill, the question in Jackson's mind was why. Why had he come? But he felt he couldn't ask. Even if Ignacio knew the reason, he wouldn't like to say. Instead Jackson said, How is it at Padre Beltrán's?

He is strange, señor. The church is big and cold and that smoke the other boy has to make in the silver bowl, it smells funny. And I have to wear a red dress. And he talks and talks, the padre, and people come to listen but most of the time they sleep. I see them sleeping, señor.

But you didn't have to leave, did you? Jackson said.

Ignacio said nothing but pouted slightly as they climbed up the steep field below the farm. Then he said: Why stay? I don't live there.

But where do you live? Jackson found himself retorting.

Again Ignacio was silent. Then he said, Not there.

Another pause.

I know you señores are in the hills, in the forest, and I think maybe the señor needs my help. I know the mountains, but he is from far away. And I never get lost in the mountains, but maybe he will, and he won't know what to eat in the forest.

Jackson listened and didn't know what to say or think. For a moment once again he couldn't imagine how he had fallen into the company of this Andean orphan, or what responsibilities he had toward him. The boy not only baffled Jackson, but also shook his own ideas about who he himself was. Whatever he thought his life might encompass, this boy was outside it. Yet a warm feeling started up in his chest when he was with him, he couldn't help it. Right now he was very happy to see Ignacio again, and that was the thing that surprised him most.

How did you eat? Sarah asked as they crossed the last yards of meadow, partially shorn to bare dirt from when the goats had last been penned here.

Ignacio nimbly picked his way among the clods and the remaining tussocks. It is easy. Some plants you have to cook and some you can eat cold. And *el gato*, she is good at hunting.

The cat hunts? And lets you eat what she catches? And don't you mean *la gata*, if it's a she?

He stared open-mouthed at Sarah a moment. Then he said: She catches birds and manicou and mice.

And you cook them? Sarah let out a laugh of incredulity. You know how to make a fire?

Of course. I cut them and smoke them. Here.

He pulled a twist of dried brown flesh a few inches long from his pocket. It looked stiff and unsavoury. He offered it to them both, and they politely refused.

A woman on a farm gave me eggs. She tell me the way to Don Alfredo's, the gringo.

At the sight of the farmhouse up above Ignacio stopped. Jackson took his hand and led him on.

Later, standing in the kitchen at the end of the big room, with Alfredo quietly washing crockery in the sink, Sarah asked: What are we going to do?

I'll have to take him back to Beltrán's.

Jackson was aware that Alfredo was listening.

They had given Ignacio a cot in a long low attic room where six of the children slept, including the older Sol, who was supposed to act as a kind of dormitory prefect, although his adolescent sluggishness kept him from exercising any authority.

At the other end of the big room Nellie was playing a cassette about the Inca empire on a tape machine. The speaker was talking about the mighty fortress of Sacsayhuaman in a deep, dramatic voice. The children were sitting cross-legged on the floor, dutiful and quiet. Nellie, slumped in an armchair, had a toddler in her lap, a girl who was holding a toy car to her thick lips. Ignacio stood with his back to the French windows.

At any rate, said Sarah, we better let Beltrán know he's here.

Alfredo shook the excess water off a baking tray and held it a moment to dribble into the sink. He glanced over his shoulder and said softly, You think he'll be worried? I'm not so sure. He knows the kids in this country. They grow up young. He doesn't take them in so much to shelter them, you know, but mostly to give them an education. He doesn't want them if they don't want to be there. That's what he once told me, anyway.

Sarah was standing with her hands behind her, rocking herself gently, thoughtfully against the counter. She said, So what do you think?

Alfredo inverted the pan on the drying rack. Let's wait and see. I want to get a sense of who he is. My view would be, education aside, the boy would be better off with a home at least for a few years. If he's not going to stay at the padre's—well, bad things can happen to a kid on his own here.

Beyond Alfredo, outside the kitchen window, Jackson could see a blurry three-quarters moon above the trees. Late mist had spread across the sky, and the moon was a pale smudge. For some reason it reminded him of the desert, and just for a moment he could feel again how the desert felt, and realised he had assumed the desert hills and canyons were some kind of natural home to Ignacio, even though he'd worn the dress of a mountain *campesino*. It still baffled him that Ignacio should have managed to travel through the forest by himself, with no money, food or help.

Ignacio had his hands clasped together in front of him, staring across the room, his big eyes looking glossy in the lamp light.

At supper he sat between Sarah and Jackson.

Afterward, Jackson walked him over to the cabin where he and Sarah were staying, to show him the room, then over to the sheds where the goats spent the night.

There are mountain lions here. They have to lock up the animals at night.

Of course, Ignacio said. Then he added: The Incas ate the hearts of lions.

They did?

Without cooking them. And they built all the roads and the big buildings.

Jackson put his hand on his shoulder. You were listening to that tape?

Ignacio hesitated. The man you couldn't see was talking about it.

They walked back to the main house. So you're not going to run off in the night?

Ignacio shook his head seriously. *No, no, señor.*

6

Dawn draped the hills in dust sheets like old furniture in a vacant house. Out in the fields a column of smoke was rising dreamily upward. There was no sky yet, just a pervasive grey. Jackson stood in the stillness listening to the rustle of his urine falling on dry ground between old maize stalks.

It was good to be up at this hour. The pre-morning was mauve, latent with possibility. A few days before he had been reading a book plucked off the sitting-room shelves, a fantastic story of an Englishwoman's induction into a Zen temple in Japan, her nights without sleep in the silent dark of the meditation hall. Now he felt he could understand the desire to do something like that.

The farm stood at the bottom of a long slope of harvested corn, and beyond it another field tumbled down to the trees below.

Jackson heard a footstep behind him. It was Alfredo.

Don't mind me. He drew up beside Jackson and nodded. Me, I've gotten used to this view. Don't get me wrong. Would I rather have this outside my door or some city? Though now and then, you know. We went to New York once years ago, Nellie and I. What a place. I loved it in some ways, but how do people live there? He shook his head. What say some breakfast?

They moved into the house.

Jackson blew on his tea. A hen appeared in the doorway, took a curious step into the house. Alfredo waved an arm and shouted. The hen grumbled and lifted a foot, then withdrew.

Through the door Jackson could see unblemished hillside, first the near one falling away dry and yellow, then the far side rising blue, stippled with early light. The air was already bright and dry. Light made palpable. Happiness, almost, made palpable.

Alfredo's radio was hissing out a salsa tune, in which the only clear sounds were the fast notes played by a pair of trumpets, and the sonorous clack of a cowbell. The spirit of the tune communicated itself to the chest and acted like a key, opening up the ribs. The dawn sun, the cheerful music, the high farm with its orchestrations of clucking chickens, bleating kids and lowing cows—life was too short not to see the joy in it.

Soon he would have to leave. He knew that. It was already the sixteenth. Jorge, the man at the hotel pool, had said to be in Choctamal on the twentieth, when someone would contact him and tell him what to do. The thought of it weighed on him more and more.

Some people have part of their souls missing, Alfredo was musing.

It seemed incredible how tirelessly the man thought about big questions. Perhaps it was because he had two young foreigners for company; or perhaps it was an aspect of his hospitality, as if he thought it was rude to waste one's breath on small talk.

That's what I think, he went on. Some people are missing a piece of their soul and can't function without God. But give them God, or spirit, whatever you want to call it, and they're OK. The trick is to know if you're that kind of person.

Jackson wondered if he was referring to him. He swigged his tea.

I have to go to a village called Choctamal, he said after a pause.

Alfredo was at the sideboard looking big in his loose shirt. Jackson thought he could see his broad shoulders rise. He paused a moment in his preparing of sandwiches, but said nothing.

Jackson took another swig. The drink was hot and tasted good, rich with sweet molasses. He looked up at the man's back. Is it far?

The big man flinched. What do you want to go there for? he said to the window. It's not much of a village.

Well, these ruins I'm trying to find are beyond there. That's what I'm here for. I've got everything ready, my maps, my compass and sketchbook and so on, a new camera.

Alfredo turned round, holding two slices of home-baked yellowish bread with a thick slice of white goat cheese on each.

A couple of days maybe. Makes a good breakfast, huh? Cheese sandwich and a cup of tea.

They sat at the table eating in silence. From outside Jackson could hear the chickens as they pecked at the dirt, and the ticking of a collar as a dog scratched itself. Far below, the river would be rushing down.

A small frown settled between Alfredo's eyebrows. He finished his sandwich, brushed crumbs from his beard, and raised his mug of tea in both hands, resting his elbows on the table.

I was sort of hoping to avoid this. You're Sarah's friend and I like you. But really, I have to urge you not to go. This is a peaceful valley. You go over the valleyhead and it's a different story. It's dangerous. There's a man. I guess you'd call him a drug baron. He rules it. You must have heard of him, Señor Carreras. Ruthless doesn't come close. He's a monster. He'll do anything, and the whole place is in his pay. You can't go near his domain unless he invites you. It would be worse than irresponsible of me to let you go.

Jackson had left a corner of crust on his plate. He chewed it and swallowed it with the remains of his tea. I don't want to create problems. His heart was heavy. But then he thought of the ruins, and said: But La Joya has never been found. It's right here, within a hundred miles, maybe fifty miles.

Have you any idea what kind of miles? It can take a truck a whole day to go fifty miles here on what they call a road.

But I'm here. I know where it is, more or less. This friend of mine actually saw it. La Joya is possibly the biggest city of ancient America. The archaeologists think civilisation couldn't have come out of the jungle. It had to have developed in the highlands, or the coastal desert. This is going to prove them wrong. How come there are jungle motifs on the coast dating way back? I found one myself at Caballo Muerto, a jaguar carved on a rock, a jungle animal. How could that be, unless some kind of culture or trade reached from the jungle to the sea? All this history is just lying there like the pages of a book written for all to see, but no one bothers to read it.

Alfredo sipped his tea, with his big arms on the table. Well, to each his own. I've never quite seen the fascination of piles of rock myself. But there's the boy too. What are you going to do about him? You're just going to leave him? If he'll stay.

I wanted to talk about that.

I bet. You're certainly not taking him with you. Not if I can help it. I don't know what hare-brained quest you're on, but let me tell you the reality is there are two people right here who care about you, hell, even I care about you, don't ask me why, a crazy Limey obsessed with some lost and forgotten ruins. Not to mention all the family and friends back home. Just think of them. If you cross the pass at the valleyhead, you shouldn't expect ever to come back. I mean it.

He picked up his tea then set it down without drinking. There isn't anything else going on, is there?

Without waiting for a reply, as if sure he wouldn't get one, he took the plates to the sink. There was a small window above it but vines obscured most of the daylight.

Anyway, let's get going while it's cool.

Outside, the valley was blue and smoky, dewy-misty in the morning. The chickens squabbled as Jackson followed Alfredo round the side of the house.

Look at these. Alfredo squatted by a patch of rubbery tobacco leaves. The seeds came from Cuba.

He folded the tip of a leaf and sniffed. Gonna be good.

They went into a shed where he picked up a shovel, a hoe and a hessian sack tied with string. He gave Jackson the hoe. They walked across a half-cleared field littered with the stumps of saplings smothered in creepers, through a small strip of wood into a further field where the ground had been charred. It looked like a battlefield, with the broken trees silver and the ground black, covered with a lacy film of burnt underbrush.

Alfredo reached into his sack and gave Jackson a handful of nickel-sized seeds.

These are squash, he said. Just bend down and push them

under. About eighteen inches apart. But first you hoe. Put them in
your pocket for now.

Alfredo started at the bottom of the field and sent Jackson to
the top.

The sun drew clear of the low-hanging mists and rose above the
valley. Jackson unbuttoned his shirt, then soon pulled it off. His
back began to ache from the bending and swaying.

After an hour Alfredo stopped digging, pushed himself upright
with a hand to his back, and wiped his forehead. He waved and
called up.

A corpulent man with a mane of grey beard and a ragged shirt,
Alfredo made an appealing figure down below. He looked like he
belonged just where he was, in a field on the side of a valley planting squash. He looked humble. He had really been absorbed by this
valley. Jackson thought he would like to draw him alone. He was
in some way genuine. By some quirk of acoustics, up on this
height the river was audible. With the water rushing in the margin
of hearing and the broad green of the valleyside gleaming in the
first strokes of sun, and the man's brow red and glistening above
his beard, he made a moving sight.

He beckoned again. Come on down.

Jackson could smell him when he got close, a fresh tang of
work-sweat.

Here. He pulled two rolled cigarettes from the pocket of his shirt
and held them out. Home-grown tobacco. Last season's.

He gave one to Jackson and lit it for him with a Zippo. Jackson
smelled the petrol in the air.

You know, it's not like it used to be. I've been thinking. Why do
you want to do this? Really.

Jackson looked away down the valley toward the misty light
over the land beyond.

No one's sending you, are they? Nothing like that? You're talking about a forest the size of Kansas, in mountains filled with mist,
fog, cloud. There are cities in there supposedly, and no one can find
them. Whoever rules it can do what they like. Except you can't

really rule it. People have tried to get me involved. Nasty people. Bribes, blackmail, threats, they've tried everything. You know what it's really about? The governments, especially our government, I mean America, doesn't like to see people running this highly efficient and profitable business they've got no piece of. They can't stand that. So they send in the DEA choppers, they burn all the crops they can find, they spray indiscriminately, they kill, they make arrests. They make a war. It's just pathetic. They stomp around like frustrated bullies in the school yard. Look at you. You're young, handsome, talented. I think you're in love. You'll never have it so good. Yet you think you can just go and risk it all. What about Sarah, what does she think?

Jackson sighed. I've come a long way for this. I'm so close. I have to try. Imagine bringing an old city to light. I had this friend who came down here. He came three times a few years back, trying to find La Joya. The last time he reckoned he did.

So why didn't he come back again?

He died.

I'm sorry. But he was here? What was his name?

John Connolly.

Connolly? Alfredo thought a moment. A British guy? We hear about people coming through now and then, foreigners. But I most likely wouldn't have heard the name. He was really an archaeologist? There's military stuff going on too, you know, undercover, a lot of it.

Not Connolly. He was after the ruins.

Well, it all makes me sad, as I say. Here you are in this beautiful place. Look at all the experiences you must have had. Be satisfied. But I don't expect you to listen to me, so I'll tell you one thing only, because if I don't you're certainly going to get in trouble. Go to Carlos Cruz. He lives just over the pass. I'll tell you how to get there. Tell him you're a friend of mine and of Padre Beltrán. He could take you to Choctamal. Whatever he says to do is probably though not necessarily right.

Jackson trudged back up the slope to where he had left the hoe, and resumed hacking at a patch of stubborn lumpy soil, whacking the rock-hard clods with the instrument until they cracked, splintered and ultimately shattered into dust.

7

That afternoon Alfredo came and knocked on the door of Sarah's and Jackson's hut. You better come and see this, he called.

They'd been having a siesta. Jackson was sitting at the table writing a few sentences in the journal he'd recently revived.

They trooped across the yard to the big house, from which the sound of tropical music was drifting. Trumpets and congas, and a chorus of excited voices. The French windows were open and Alfredo paused outside.

A dozen children of all ages were having a dance in the big room. Nellie and Dolores were dancing too, each swinging a toddler in their arms. Amid the music Jackson could hear the children's laughter. Every now and then one would throw back its head in a grin and drop to the floor, then get back to its feet and jog once again to the music.

You see? Alfredo said. Dance class. It's a good, rounded education they get here.

It was a moment before Jackson picked out Ignacio, bobbing up and down with a smile such as he had never seen before on his face, screaming and laughing with a younger girl who was jumping around in front of him.

Look at that, Jackson said. Somehow he felt both happy and sad at the sight.

Well, Alfredo said, he's enjoying himself. It could just be you've brought him to the right place. Or he brought himself. You want him to stay for a while? See how it goes?

Jackson smiled. You're a kind man.

In the late afternoon Jackson paced downhill, the sound of the brook rushing beside him so he didn't notice the splashing from the pool until he was right above it. Through the leaves he made out a flash of pale skin. He instinctively crouched, in case it wasn't her. The leaves stirred. The flesh reappeared, moving. There was a flash of gold above it, then he saw a long hank of hair flowing down a gleaming back, and he stepped out.

The pale cloth of sky rippled over the pool. He stripped off and sank into the chilly water with its tang of clay. The stream came down dark and clear, turned white where it slipped down the fall over a boulder, then in the pool itself was dark red.

They swam for a while, then rested on the rocks, half in half out of small patches of sunshine, moving from rock to rock as the patches moved. They showered in the cascade and floated on their backs beneath the green and yellow leaves fissured with blue sky. When a cloud came over and brought a sudden drumming of rain overhead on the leaves, he rolled up their clothes and shoved them beneath an overhanging rock, then joined her again in the pool, which gradually began to feel the rain on its skin as the cloudburst forced its way through the overhanging trees. The surface turned silver like the fur of some Arctic animal blown with wind. A crack of thunder alarmed them, and they climbed out and sat, wet on wet rocks in the rain, and waited. Soon the rain stopped and the sun shone again, and the shrubbery began to steam, sparkling in the high air.

She sat on a stone in the sun with her head tipped to one side and her hair twisted into a rope over her shoulder.

I don't know what to say. I don't think you should go. That's all. Don't go. Not for me but for you. I'm scared. I don't think it's going to be like you imagine.

He pushed himself onto a smooth submerged rock near her, and knelt on it, his legs underwater, his torso clear. One week, ten days at the most, he said.

She squeezed the rope of her hair. A few drops sparkled as they fell onto the dark stone beside her.

The words of a song ran through his mind: *It wasn't the moon or the stars, it wasn't the pearls of the sea, or the salt on your dark skin, Xadinha, it was just your eyes.*

In the late sun her skin was gold, and on it the water drops were clear as glass.

I don't think you've told me everything. I don't mind. But I mind if it gets you hurt and I don't—

She stopped. She was staring at him. A drop travelled down her cheek, that could have been a tear or water from her hair. Her chin wrinkled and she wiped her face. I don't know how to let you go, she said, and hunched over.

He had his arms round her and felt her body quaking and shuddering. The sun went behind a cloud and it was as if the whole valley turned to ash.

10 · Cruz

1

Jackson could see a corner of rusty roof among the trees. A white flash in a bush startled him. He stopped, and after a moment picked out a diagonal line of taut rope. A white goat's face appeared in the foliage and stared at him.

The river gurgled. He climbed onward up the valley, found a footbridge, crossed and came back down through the trees on the other side. The yard of red mud was hidden by the trees until he was almost in it. Something made him stop just before entering.

There was no one around. The shutters of a long adobe building were closed. The only living creature seemed to be that white goat hidden in the trees behind him.

He cleared his throat. Then he took his pack off, then wondered if that was presumptuous and pulled it on again. He heard a rustle up above; the goat again.

The place looked deserted but he didn't think it was. Something about it was alert. It was odd to see one of these farmyards with no chickens pecking about. Just a small almond tree and a yard of smooth packed dirt surrounded by banana and brush.

Hola, he tried, not loud.

Silence. The fluttering of the stream. A silent cat's yawn of sunlight came out and went in again.

He called louder.

He thought he heard a scuffle within the house, then a sharp human whisper. He called once more, louder. *Por favor*, I'm looking for Señor Cruz.

A nut fell from a tree onto the metal roof with a tap, rolled a little and stopped. Right afterward a man's voice barked from inside the house. *¡Quítate! ¡No está!* Go away. He's not here.

Silence filled the farmyard again. Jackson looked up and down the building, along the four shuttered windows, wondering where the voice had come from.

Soy amigo.

He heard a click, perhaps a catch being released. A panel within the door creaked open and a pole stuck out. It took him a second to realise it was a gun barrel. He stepped back. *Soy amigo*, he repeated.

Aquí no tenemos amigos gringos, the voice stated. Here we have no gringo friends.

I am a friend of Don Alfredo and of Padre Beltrán.

There was a short silence, an exchange of whispers. The gun withdrew. Then a squeak of rusty metal, a knock, something heavy clanking to the ground. The door swung open, and a man wearing dirty beige trousers and a white shirt stepped part way out, his shoulders and head still in shadow. He held the rifle across his chest.

Ven, he called.

Señor Cruz?

Sí, sí, the man answered impatiently.

For the first time Jackson felt afraid. Supposing this wasn't Cruz, and Cruz had been kidnapped or killed? His heart knocked as he stepped forward. *Soy amigo de Don Alfredo*, he mumbled again.

He did not walk but floated across the sunlit yard. He had not seen a gun raised against a man in a long time. His legs were shivery, and the sunlight blazed, the shadows burned.

The man stood still. Even when he was close Jackson still could not see his face. He beckoned Jackson nearer, then quickly frisked him, running a hand down and up either leg, and said, *Pase.* Come in.

At first Jackson could make nothing out in the dark. There was a smell of cooking chickpeas. His shoes scraped on the grit of a dirt floor. A rustle. Light on the hem of a skirt showed where a woman sat, her face in gloom.

The man stood the gun against the wall and unfastened a shutter, letting in the light. Three women were sitting round the cooking pit. A boy lay on a pile of sacks, the pale soles of his feet tipped up. A cloud of white guinea pigs flowed among the women's bare feet. Two murmuring hens strutted indecisively toward the door, then stopped, then rushed out, hopping over the plank across the bottom of the doorway.

You're a friend of Padre Beltrán? The man had a mild face, Jackson now saw, friendly-looking, smooth-cheeked. His eyes were puffy, suspicious.

That's right. He sends his *felicitaciones.*

The man smiled slightly, as if with pride. And of Don Alfredo? How is he?

Good, good.

Well, you've come to the right place. What do you want?

Jackson slipped his pack from his shoulders but kept holding it up by the straps. I need a guide. To Choctamal. I'm looking for ruins.

The man looked down and said, *Pues*, noncommittally. I know some ruins. But we'll have to talk. *No es fácil.* It's not easy.

Jackson rested his pack against the wall. One of the women made coffee sweetened with slightly sour molasses, and the two of them settled on a bench outside.

It's not so good where the ruins are, Cruz said. His face darkened. Choctamal is no problem but if you want to go into the forest—I don't know, señor.

He looked at the ground, his elbows on his knees.

Is it about money? I have money, I can pay.

There are the other gringos too, I have to fetch them from another village. Cruz shrugged. *Pues*, he said, and shook his head.

You won't find another farmer who knows where to look for the *ruinas*. But we have to be careful. Very careful. *Quinientos dólares, no más.*

The figure shocked Jackson. Five hundred. He had expected to pay maybe a tenth of that, and to keep the man in cigarettes. He breathed in. *¿Sí?*

Cruz nodded his head. *Sí.*

He could pay it but it wouldn't leave him with much.

Cruz also wanted to be paid up front.

Sí, señor. I leave the money here at the farm. For my wife. Just in case. You never know in *la selva*. Anything can happen.

It felt reckless to Jackson. How could he know he would ever get what he was paying for? But he didn't see what else he could do. Also, was it really so dangerous the man would prepare for his own possible death like this? Or was that normal thinking here? Or just an excuse to get his money?

Jackson also wanted to know who the other gringos were, but when he asked, Cruz simply looked away.

He spent a night there. He woke early from a dream. All he could remember of it was someone asking who you could trust. The answer had been you could trust the rivers, the ground, the trees, the quiet mountains.

Soon after dawn he stood in the yard by the door. From the hut came the clear voice of a girl singing to a wide-eyed baby, her voice seeming to soften the air within the chamber of baked mud. Clear, pure, all echo smoothed away, her voice was like a candle flame in the dark mud room.

It was hard to keep up with Cruz's mule. The trail wound steeply up the hillside, and the mule didn't seem to notice the climb. Jackson felt as if there were nothing in his body but his pounding heart. This was the crucial climb of his whole journey. In crossing the giant green barrier ahead, passing that portal, he might finally find what he needed. As he walked, he had the sense that already he was moving into different territory. It was possible that what he had thought to be his whole life was only a chapter. He saw that now. Once you saw that, it was likely to become reality, he thought.

When they came to the last switchback at the top of a long slope, the shrubbery opened up like in a garden. Sunlight filtered through, casting a confetti of dapples over the path, as if they walked on petals. The trail was broad and pale. The river that had formed the valley ran beside it for a few hundred yards before the path swerved away and climbed again.

They walked a long time through the twilight of the cloud forest. Fog hung in the canopy, with the foliage floating like tea leaves, black specks in white mist. Sometimes they trampled across falls of large crinkly leaves curled on the ground beneath some gaunt trunk whose autumn was in season, and sometimes through spreads of small purple fruit, their pale insides bitten open by monkeys, parrots, manicous.

Seen on a map, the cloud forest didn't look big—the country between the peaks and the jungle, between the brown shoulder of the Andes as they swung west toward the Pacific, and Amazonia: a jumble of hills that didn't know if they were moorland or jungle, where the greenhouse air of Amazonia blew up the valleys and met with the chilly blasts from the peaks and grey glaciers. The two winds, not knowing what else to do, turned to cloud. Cloud that hung in rags on the brows, and in tufts like the wool you found on barbed wire in northern latitudes. Which hung like a veil of vaporised snow among the trees, a white-grey mist like whey. It was the rain factory; the place the rain was born. The big ragged thread of the Marañón river ran through it like an ice-crack.

Once, Cruz pressed a hand against Jackson to stop him. He stood a moment looking at a bush ahead, then moved so fast Jackson did not see how he got to the bush: a feral pounce his muscles were still acquainted with. When he stood again he was holding a large dirty white rat. He had it by its neck and rump. It drummed with its feet and bent its body up but the man's fingers were a strong clamp.

Cruz's eyes were bright. *Cuchillo*, he said, his voice quavering. Quick, quick.

Jackson came round and fetched the knife out of Cruz's belt.

Cruz was on the ground with his knee on the animal, the big blade sawed down to the ground through the neck with a muffled crackle. The plump body flexed with two powerful beats then went still. Cruz gutted the animal right there. The intestines broke out of the incision he made in the belly in a purple bubble, smelling of dung.

He flayed the beast, spread out the skin and used the moist inner side as his butcher's block. He took off the legs and cut up the racks of ribs, making a stack of miniature joints, added a couple of the organs to the pile, and flung the rest away in a dark string that spun through the forest and landed with a splatter in the undergrowth. He wrapped up the good meat in the skin and folded the parcel in his *mochila*. The aroma of offal hung in the air.

Cruz didn't walk but glided over the fallen leaves, the smooth-picked earth, the fan roots of the mountain manioc trees. He moved like a shadow, silent and smooth, through the forest world in which he and his forebears had long lived.

Another time he said: Come on, let me show you something.

They strode down off the trail and came to an empty wooden house that would once have been white, standing in what might once have been a clearing, now already drowned in new growth which plunged the house into gloom.

Cruz leaned against the door and played its catch. It opened. Inside, the house was not empty. A heap of burlap sacks, an old print of a map on a tongue-and-groove wall, a sideboard with a dusty brass pot.

Whose house is it?

Never you mind. *No te preocupes.*

They picked their way through the abandoned belongings. The man clicked the latch on a far door and they went up a bare wooden staircase, careful to place their feet to the side of each step. *Cuidado.* You never know with these abandoned houses, Cruz said. These people left seven years ago.

Jackson's boots seemed heavy against the wood. At least if the stairs gave and he fell he would have something strong on his feet. If he were lucky enough to land on his feet.

Upstairs were two bedrooms, each with an iron bedstead with springs but no mattress. A portrait of a girl hung in an oval frame. She had blonde hair and appeared to be wearing a nightie. It wasn't clear if she was family, or whether it was simply some cheap picture bought in a market. Still, she must have been family to someone.

Alemanes, Cruz said.

Missionaries? Jackson asked.

He nodded. Of course. *Por supuesto.* Who else would come here? Yourself aside, Cruz growled.

Why does no one raid the house?

Ah. Cruz's face lit up. Some places are dangerous. You don't treat them right, they can be bad. He tapped his temple. You have to know how to come. The original inhabitants may be gone but you don't know who's living here now. This house, it doesn't come from here. It comes from another world, and could be people from another world who you and me can't see are living in it. People round here don't like to take their chances with something like this. That's why they won't visit the *ruinas* either.

A once-white crochet tablecloth covered a small round table. A crucifix protected a wall. A fantastic pattern of spiders' webs coated the windowpanes, so only a haze of light came in.

Me, I don't mind, he added.

Outside, when they pressed on through the forest, Jackson asked, Where did they go?

¿Quién sabe? They left. They saw the times and left.

But they left everything.

That's how it is, Cruz said. *Es así.*

On another stretch of trail Jackson grew aware of a foul smell.

Cruz tied a cloth over his face and motioned to Jackson to do the same. He pulled a T-shirt from his pack and tied it over his mouth. It was warm in the forest, what with the air being close and still, and with the exertion of the hiking, but now to have his own hot breath trapped against his cheeks by that thick cloth, and with that hard stench on the air—it wasn't pleasant.

The smell became fiercer, almost like ammonia, and seemed to knock some other kind of dreadful reality awake in him. Then he heard a loud, intense humming, like a swarm of bees. Cruz kept his head down as they walked, but Jackson glanced toward the source of the noise. Beyond some glossy-leafed shrubs he could see a cloud of insects fluttering and buzzing in the twilight of the trees, all drawn to some great gathering of their kind.

Cruz quickened his pace and Jackson hurried to keep up, still looking to see what had attracted them all. Between two bushes twenty yards away he saw a man's boot pointed upward. Instinctively Jackson crouched. A black wing rose up, and a big bird fluttered a few feet into the air then dropped down. The buzzing intensified. Then he saw a dark trouser leg that seemed to be shifting by itself, the cloth flexing up and down as if in a breeze, although there was no breeze. He realised what all the commotion was about, and the smell, and rapidly turned to follow Cruz, but it was too late, his gorge was already rising, and he had to rip the cloth away from his face as the first retch heaved out of him.

Later he asked Cruz if he had any idea who it had been, and why the body had been left there.

Es así, he said in his soft, lugubrious, matter-of-fact tone.

Then he added, It's quick. The birds and the insects, they clean it in two days.

So that man— Jackson began.

It happens like that. He made a mistake. Here you can't make too many mistakes. You have to know what is OK and what is not. With the *jefes*, the *patrones*.

Later, Cruz slowed and picked his way among underbrush. He indicated to Jackson with lowered palms to be quiet. The two crept forward. It was a moment before Jackson realised there was brightness ahead, a clearing.

They paused behind the last trunks. Ahead lay a field of chest-high bushes planted in rows. Cruz was still a moment, then stepped out and broke off a few of the small leaves from the nearest bush, and stepped back into the cover. He worked the leaves between his fingers, then gave some to Jackson. He bundled the rest between his cheek and gums. Jackson did the same. He recognised the faint bitter taste, a little like spinach, and the tingle in the mouth, then the gradual chilling of his cheek.

Cruz dropped into a crouch and made Jackson follow. They crept away from the plantation, back into the forest gloom, then Cruz touched his leg to be still. As soon as they stopped moving Jackson heard voices out in the daylight, the crunch of footsteps, the swish of clothing.

Three men were walking along the perimeter of the field, right past where Jackson and Cruz had been hiding. Jackson could see them through the bushes. One was dressed in what looked like a dinner jacket, dusty and stained, another wore a khaki fishing waistcoat and oval sunglasses, and the third baggy white *campesino* trousers. The man in grubby evening wear had a semi-automatic rifle over his shoulder, and the *campesino* wore a rustic Winchester tied across his chest by a rope. They were having an animated discussion as they passed. They had the air of men who had just come to a decision and were heading off at once to carry it out.

Their footsteps receded, then their voices vanished into the stillness of the forest, and Jackson and Cruz were alone again.

They continued up a long slope among the tall bare trunks. Now and then Cruz would let fly his machete at a tree, slicing three or four blows quickly to make a notch, the little *chocks* sounding like an animal at work in the murk. These marks were not so much to know as to confirm the way back.

Se pierda, Cruz said. *Facilmente se pierda en la selva*. It is easy to get lost in the forest.

It was an area that the outside had messed with, Jackson could feel that already. Something was in the air, something from outside that didn't belong, that made everything unstable, uncertain.

They slept under a tarpaulin at night.

2

This love spans continents, Jackson wrote in his notebook. *A resonance in the world when I'm near you.*

He took to writing his journal whenever they stopped.

As he walked, Jackson would be surprised every so often by such a vivid memory of Sarah it would wind him. His eyes would sting. Memories rose unbidden, as if his muscles were full of her. He would suddenly smell her in the midst of passion, and a great sadness would rise up as if his body grieved her absence. He did not know how long he would be here, if she would still be at her uncle's when he returned from the ruins, if he found them, if he might somehow be able to visit her in America. Dread would come over him and he would feel he was walking the wrong way.

Sometimes her face would loom up before his eyes so vividly he wouldn't notice what was in front of him. Once he came close to stepping on a small snake on the path. He could feel her arms resting on his shoulders, warm against his neck, her smiling face just in front of him. A stick moved on the path behind the veil of her face. Cruz shouted. He stopped in his tracks, and the snake slithered into the undergrowth a step ahead.

He would feel her light, strong thighs against his. And hear her breathing, the hard breaths deep in lovemaking when she was panting and groaning at the same time, while sweat bloomed on her chest, and her stomach went hard, and she would hold her breath, except little pants would leak out, as if some of the pressure couldn't help but escape. Then the achievement, the attainment—right against his hand, his mouth, his face, there she would be, open, warm, tense all over. He'd hear the moans and cries, and eventually laughter.

Several times he decided he had to draw her, and was mostly disappointed by his attempts. But one time a face stared back at him from a bed of shading, drawn by someone more skilled.

To love someone is to want to know them, he wrote. *Their body wide open—and their mind too, talking, revealing their past, thoughts, feelings, and their philosophies—and their heart, their longings and hurts, wounds and wants, hearing them and experiencing them—discovering them as they do you through the talking.*

He felt there was something else to be known, some essence he was really after, which had nothing to do with appurtenances, lovely though they were.

Within the forest the trackways were avenues of gloom where giant blue butterflies like pieces of sky fluttered in company with bats like spirits, whirs in the murk, disembodied movements that stirred through the grey air, immaterial. Here, bats came out by day.

As they walked he wondered: what was this intense feeling? Craving, yearning, longing. Excitement and calm at once. What exactly was love? While he was pacing further away, every step made heavy by wanting one thing more than anything else, he knew she was wanting the same thing to the same degree.

Is to love simply to be happy while with someone? He thought back to Connolly and decided that yes, that was as good a description as any. And the converse too, to be miserable while apart.

When they first emerged from the forest Jackson felt a thrill at the opening into broad daylight, the sunlit valley. It was good to see the sky again.

They went down a silvery hillside of harvested maize stalks before what must have been one of the most remote views on the continent. The land of hills, mountains and canyons ahead, crimson and misty-blue, as if crumbling like old cheese in the smoky light, looked like it went on forever. It seemed the outer reaches of a whole new hinterland with secret savannahs, lakes, cities all its own.

A long slope led down to a handful of straw roofs that glittered in the sun like puddles.

Is that it? he asked.

Cruz nodded.

Beyond the little village the land fell in a gathering depth of green for miles and miles, settling into a canyon that must have been thirty miles in breadth. Then a faint wall of mountain rose up which Cruz told him was the canyon of the Marañón. Five hundred miles on, that river would become the Amazon.

They descended the broad slope of silver maize, acres and acres, provender for a small town, more than enough for the little homestead of five or six dwellings below.

Jackson commented on the abundance.

Cruz said, It's different here. If you have protection you can do what you like. Get paid well too. And if you don't have permission you can't do a thing. There are a lot of people to feed, *hombre*.

Who gives the protection?

Cruz ignored the question. He continued down the broad blond path in his light jog. Like a horse nearing its stable Cruz had been steadily speeding up for the last hour and now could barely hold himself back from running down the hill. Jackson, nearer now than he had ever imagined to coming to his goal, had a weariness in his limbs. Doubts weighed on him: that he wouldn't find what he was looking for, that it wouldn't be what he hoped, that even if it was, he wouldn't be able to do anything about it. Also, he had assumed all along that his jungle training in Belize, what he could remember of it, would equip him for this region. For the first time, he wondered about that.

He had no idea what Mr. Brown wanted him to do in exchange for his miserly dollars. What had he signed up for? It was 19 July, he was going to make the rendezvous at Choctamal. Whatever it was, he'd see everything through then get back to Sarah as soon as he could. In a way, what lay ahead was all just the journey back to her. This thought made him feel better.

Eventually they came into a compound of mud homes. A shriek came from one of the huts, followed by an elderly woman with a bowler hat and salt-and-pepper plaits who walked by pressing on her thighs as if manually pumping herself along. She hobbled up to Cruz and threw herself against his chest, which was where she came up to, talking away in Quechua.

With a sheepish smile Cruz said, This is my mother. *Te presento a mi mamá*, putting a lot of celebratory emphasis on the final syllable.

Jackson shook her hand. It was wrinkled so you could hardly tell it was skin, and tough as wood. She clamped him fiercely.

They ate a meal of chickpea soup, then Cruz disappeared.

Later, in the evening, Jackson went up to the hay loft where he and Cruz were to sleep and read by the light of a candle stub.

It felt good to be a guest in a peasant home on these remote slopes, with the fields of dwarf corn reaching up to where the trees began.

He thought of the hills around, cloaked in woods—an ocean of dark swells. Through these forests, over these fields, along the same paths he had been walking, ancient feet had trod. The field outside might have been milling with peasants a thousand years ago. And among the trees lay old cities of silver, malachite, gold, with their temples and plazas, shrines and pyramids. *Ubi sunt* was a cliché until you were somewhere like this, and then it wasn't, because really it didn't mean: where are they now? but: where will we be? With the landscape outside pummelled by dusk so the grey ground seemed to be falling apart, and the black line of trees above about to pour down the farmland like ink, he wondered: if today we could walk through the woods and pause to drink water among the trees exactly as a thousand years ago, who were we exactly? Identity was a matter of circumstance. We relied on the substances around us—chrome, ceramic, glass, steel—to know who we were. But they misled us, or we misled ourselves. They were mute, and told us nothing.

He heard a little flurry of squeaks—guinea pigs being tossed scraps—then a door closed and all was silent. A bird called in a deep *whoop-whoop*. Someone spoke among the farm buildings.

Cruz, he guessed, would be along to bed soon. But by the time Jackson fell asleep he had not come, and in the morning when he woke, there was still no sign of him.

Part Three

CLOUD FOREST

11 · Traffic

When the rain first arrived the mule pricked up its ears. Then it bowed its head, lifted a hoof, thought about taking a step, but replaced the hoof with a toss of its mane. The load on its back tilted from one side to the other. It looked like falling off but held, as the conspicuous, bony hips tipped the other way. One rose, one sank.

The rain fell like rotten fruit in dark splotches on the dirt of the yard. The thatch of the hut began to hiss like white water after a wave has broken, and the valley was suffused with a yellow marine light, like the ocean after a storm. No sky. Greyness filled its final V. Long grey arms, arm upon arm, reached down to the cleft where the cause of the valley thundered, a chalk-green torrent threading among boulders, leaping cliffs on its way down to the brown roads of water that shifted slowly across the green continent.

The river's roar was suddenly lost in the drubbing of the rain. Spurts of dust lifted from the yard. Then the dust was replaced by a knee-high cloud of spray and the yard turned silver.

Stryker, a small blond man with hair to his shoulders, blue eyes and dark brows, skinny-legged and abrupt in his movements, who did not look well, stood watching from under the eaves, his back against the rough mud wall. Morris, the American kid he'd picked up a few months back in Colombia, who'd proved himself useful, was sitting with his legs crossed, also watching.

Cruz was out in the yard, busy with rope, tying the load to the mule's back. His hair hung in a lank black mop over his brow. The rain made his face shine like polished wood. His lips moved as he struggled with a knot.

You be careful with that, Stryker called. Can't have any getting wet.

In fact a plastic sheet covered the whole load, and anyway Stryker knew the canisters were watertight.

Can't have any going missing either.

Morris added his laugh, high, out of control and loud, and brushed the wet hair back from his eyes which were clear and brown, the colour of sugar. He had a short beard.

Morris sang: Got an eye on you. He paused a moment, perhaps waiting to see if Stryker would say something, then let off his laugh again.

Cruz bent down to catch hold of the rope and drag it under the mule's dripping belly.

¿Vamos? Morris ventured.

We're heading out? Stryker called.

Cruz stopped what he was doing and looked up. He shook his head. *Hombre.* A worried look crossed his face. Look at it.

The land, the world, was sodden. Water poured off everything— off the fat waxy leaves of the ceiba tree in the yard, off the bare ends of twigs in the fat almond tree, off the edges and folds of the dirty plastic sheet on the mule's back.

It's too late anyway. Choctamal is three or four hours from here.

Stryker didn't respond. He wasn't sure what he thought.

They tell you anything about the Limey we have to meet? Morris asked. Will we make it?

He'll be there. Some young archaeologist guy. He won't be hard to find. Maybe in Piccadilly yes, but not here. But that's between you and me. No one else.

It's just that little thing?

Stryker looked at Morris, who was smirking.

I mean it. No one.

The afternoon was drawing on. The rain poured. The world darkened in an unnatural metallic dusk.

Cruz came under the eaves too and stood looking out.

We're going to Cienfuegos, Stryker said.

Cruz shook his head. *No, no, señores.* We can't go there. We go as far as Choctamal.

What's with fucking Chocfuckmal, Stryker said in English. We're expected at Cienfuegos. We're cool to go.

Cruz looked at the ground, pouting like an unhappy schoolboy. I don't know anything about that, he said. *Yo no sé nada de eso.*

The rain lessened to an even fall of large coins that drummed on the brown mud of the yard.

Stryker said quietly to Morris, Well, one thing's for sure. At the right age these native girls have great tits.

Morris laughed approvingly, exaggeratedly.

Gimme a shout, Stryker said, and got up and walked along behind the string curtain of raindrops coming off the roof. He put his hand on the latch of a door and pressed it down.

No borders, that was the thing. Stryker had noticed early on that the real money wasn't in smuggling. That was pocket money, it was just a way in. The people who got rich were either side of the borders, in the supply chain at either end—the one that took it from the producers, and the one that took it to the market. In between was the gap you had to get across, that you could pay for with many years of your life. Miserable years. Staying put, there was less to fear, and the money came in. People would be surprised to learn where from. He had been surprised. Not from crazed addicts missing teeth or slick dealers in black-windowed limousines, but from well-to-do families who sent their kids to college in the States, who had businesses and drove foreign cars and had a *finca* in the hills outside the capital where they went for barbecues on Sunday. They were the people who floated the business. They invested in the consortia, the shipment schemes. They only needed to have one shipment in ten come off and they still turned a huge profit.

Stryker had become one of the transports who brought the stuff down from the mountains. It suited him. He liked the rough and ready life of the country's cities, where you could buy just about any pleasure, and without any raised eyebrows. But also he liked the hills. He liked the scale of the country. Coming from Holland, with its narrow houses and streets, it felt good every time you came back to the mountains. And the forest, all the things that could happen within it, and no one knew. This region he had come to know, the Upper Marañón, the cloud forest, what locals called the eyebrow of the jungle, it was wild, free. If a man was willing to take some risks, he could do a lot here, and make a lot. So he'd taken to bringing in ammunition, make the trip profitable both ways. And meanwhile, he was helping something happen, something big. Señor Carreras had big plans. What could be bigger after all than starting a new country? He and the *guerrilleros* were working together now, and Stryker was helping the alliance with every load he brought up.

It had all begun with a backpacking trip. He'd been twenty-one. He'd saved enough from a shitty job burning old pallets at the Rotterdam docks to buy a backpack, sleeping bag and a ticket. A kid looking for adventure, that's all he'd been. But you made one move and it led to another. Cartagena first, where he'd helped a hopeless old hippie from Bogotá grow grass in the Santa Marta mountains. He'd lifted five grand from that operation and moved down to Peru, where he'd first fallen into company with *basé*, the paste that was so good to smoke. It had become a problem, he'd had a few hard years, but then he'd got himself in hand and become useful again. It had been the prospect of returning to Europe that had forced him to clean up: no way was he going back to that dismal place of lost souls drifting through lives they hated.

The Upper Marañón had opened up to him. It became his region. He went in and out with ease. He'd never actually met Carreras but the man knew of him. As did someone on the other side too. Not strictly DEA but linked to them. Now and then Stryker did a little reconnaissance for them, which he figured might be useful if things ever turned bad. At least he'd have someone on his side in the so-called authorities. And even this work could get boring, that was the truth. Having just a little doubleness, a hint of duplicity, kept it alive. Like with this beacon he was bringing in for the Limey now, which he wouldn't want found by the wrong people. You needed to have two sides to your life. That was the key.

The cooking hut was a building of thick red mud blackened by the cooking fire at the end. He blinked as his eyes adjusted to the dark. A line of blue smoke rose up to a hole in the roof.

Stryker closed the door after him and dragged a sack across to lean against the door.

Viento, he said, and hugged his shoulders with an uneasy laugh.

The girl was sitting on the rim of the earth stove. She glanced at Stryker while stirring a big pot.

Stryker settled himself on a lopsided chair with his hands between his knees, fingers dangling toward the floor. A huddle of fluffy white guinea pigs gathered between his boots, under the shelter of his legs, chattering softly to themselves.

The room was dark. Beneath a pot over the fire the embers had a rich hue. He could see it shine on the girl's cheek. The rain clattered overhead like handfuls of gravel.

They had been stuck on this farm two days now waiting for Cruz, and he was sick of it. The farmer they normally used was no longer around. The girl, dressed in a cotton skirt and woollen cardigan, was the one thing that offered any relief from the boredom of these dim country people.

These local Indian girls: as kids they were pretty, as women they were fat. It was that simple. But how they got from the first to the second you never could see. At least not until right now. This was the first one Stryker had met who was right on the edge. She was springy, as if her flesh was waiting to explode but her skin was still too stiff to allow it. Under her unbuttoned blue cardigan she wore a pink T-shirt, beneath which he could easily make out the volume of her bust. The cardigan hung on either side like a pair of parted curtains.

He had worked on her all day, imagining the feel of her skin under his fingers, and had got nowhere.

Lluvia, she said. *Mucha lluvia.*

That was the kind of thing these people said. They just had nothing in their heads, nothing at all. Rain. As if he didn't know.

He grunted. Which for some reason caused her to smile. He had been waiting a long time to see her smile. Ah, he said. *Gracias.* It's good to see that pretty smile.

He pleaded with her for a cup of coffee. *Por favor.*

She smiled another sudden bright smile. This was the moment to strike. What's your favourite colour? Stryker asked, unable to think of any good questions but determined not to lose the moment. Anything would do, stupid questions, it didn't matter, the important thing was to hold her attention, not let her off the hook. And dumb questions were good for kids. They couldn't resist answering.

Blue, she declared, grinning expectantly, waiting for what he would say next.

She was fifteen at most. Her teeth were still bright white and gleamed in the gloom of the room.

The girl reached for a metal tray on the side of the mud stove, and shook it. The beans on it rattled and shushed. She poured a palmful into the handmill.

The flock of guinea pigs travelled across the floor like mercury, coalescing into a single white fleece, breaking into pieces then flowing together as they kept up their constant search for crumbs.

The girl already had the water on the cooking pit.

Stryker took a chance he did not know he had been so close to. He walked across the floor. The moment he stood the guinea pigs all decided to shift from one side to the other. Like a spreading litter of overgrown chicks they flowed past his boots, squealing lightly as they went. For a moment Stryker was confused, felt he might lose his balance, as if he were standing in a fast-flowing river.

He settled himself on a corner of the stove, the girl within reach.

He picked up the can of condensed milk to make it appear that he had come over to be useful.

The month is July, no?

She agreed.

So if you're not getting married till Christmas, well that's a long time.

No, she cried delightedly.

At which point he reached out and touched her Andean hand. He was surprised how it felt. Strong and soft.

Your hand is cool and warm at once, he said. *A la vez.* Cool on the outside, warm within. It has night in its skin but day in its bones.

Even at this age they liked the poetic stuff.

She didn't remove her hand.

The clattering on the roof had become a sporadic drubbing, as if nuts were landing on it, now it redoubled its intensity and became a roar. The sound inspired him. While letting him hold her hand the girl swivelled toward the pot of water. The water crackled against the hot sides when she lifted it. Leaning away like that, her breasts pressed out the front of her T-shirt. He ran his tongue along his dry lips and settled himself closer.

Careful, she said, you'll burn yourself.

He didn't hear what she said. Because she was twisted toward the pan, he was able to reach straight for her chest. Before she had time to respond he pressed his mouth over hers, forcing her lips apart. Ah, but she tasted good, slightly salty, and she soon got the hang of what he had in mind. Without removing his lips he steered her off her perch and rummaged among her skirts. He fastened one arm round her waist and steered her onto him, grappling at the same time with the front of her T-shirt. She gasped. At least it sounded like a gasp. He spat into his hand and reached round to loosen her, fastening his lips once more on hers. He hissed, Quiet, quiet. That's nice. Nice. You're a good girl, aren't you? So good.

When she said, No, and tried to break free, he ripped up her T-shirt and gagged her with it, then gripped her by the firm balls of her young breasts and proceeded to unleash three weeks of frustration into her.

12 · Choctamal

1

Jackson woke with a start. Outside he could hear a cockerel going hard at its morning alarum. A young girl cried out. A footfall slapped on the dirt. When he put his head out of the loft a few scrawny hens were pecking about the yard murmuring to themselves, and a dog under an almond tree had its snout buried in its rump, nibbling an itch.

He settled back down in the warmth of his sleeping bag. There was a dreamy stiffness in his body after the days of uphill walking. His mind was as sluggish as his frame. He fell asleep again.

The next time he woke it was to a grunt. He opened his eye on the barrel of a rifle slanting over the edge of the loft. A grinning, stubbled face followed.

The newcomer had nicotine-stained eyes. The gun must have been fired recently, though Jackson had heard no shot. He could smell cordite in the air.

The man cackled. Jackson smelled alcohol and sweat. Don't worry, the man said. *No te preocupes.*

I'm not worried. Who are you? He sat up.

The man laughed again and heaved himself up beside Jackson.

Good question, señor. Let's say I am a friend and I have come to give the señor a friend's advice.

He slumped on the rough boards, pushing his leather rifle strap back onto his shoulder. He looked hot and uncomfortable. He let out a groan as he settled from the effort of climbing the ladder.

He smelled bad. Stale sweat, stale alcohol, and something else sweet and unidentifiable. He was a picture-book Latino villain—teeth brown, stubble like iron filings, shirt and trousers filthy, buttons all undone: a grown-up toddler who had not learnt to take care of himself, had instead learnt to drink *aguardiente*. You didn't see this type of person ordinarily down here; Jackson guessed they were more of a Central American phenomenon.

The man wore old patent-leather slip-ons that had fissured to a weave of cracks. Between the cracks some of the leather had flaked off, leaving rough patches of hessian. His shirt was black satin, but so faded and dusty it looked like canvas. They were the clothes of a thinner, elegant man, and only exacerbated his stupendous scruffiness.

It occurred to Jackson that he ought to be scared. Why wasn't he? It was a wonderful circle: for some reason you weren't afraid, and because of that, such a menacing figure became something of a cartoon, and consequently you felt you could deal with him, and therefore perhaps could. But what made you unafraid in the first place?

The man sat with his legs dangling over the edge of the loft. He hawked ceremoniously and spat through the open front of the building into the yard below. He laid his gun across his lap. He seemed excited and out of breath, as if he had just walked a long way while drinking at the same time.

Jackson watched him pull a small wooden-handled knife from his trousers, not one of the usual farmer's machetes, but a thin blade. The man couldn't seem to close his mouth. He held the knife in his lap alongside the gun, and either sneered or grinned at it. He stroked the blade with a dirty thumb, a thumb imprinted with grime.

The man shook his head, drew in a noisy breath and said: The señor doesn't understand that there is plenty of business—*negocios*—

going on round here. This place is all business. This region—*toda la región*—you can't just walk in any more than you could just walk into my house.

He didn't look up from his knife.

Other gringos they come on business. But not you. That's why I wanted to have this friendly talk. So the señor knows I am his friend and he should do as I say.

Jackson said nothing. He experimented with the feeling that this man was indeed a friend and had only come to help him. That way lay fear. He wondered who the other gringos were.

He said, Perhaps I can explain why I am here.

No me entiendes, the man whined, as if trying to apologise, as if he had done something bad. He was like a despondent little boy, whining into his lap. *No me entiendes*. He shook his head. You don't understand.

So explain, Jackson said. Any minute now he would remove himself from his sleeping bag, pull on his boots and clamber down the ladder and see about breakfast. But he didn't want to be rude to the man. He was smellably drunk and it would be better to work things out nicely. And he was after all playing with a knife in his lap.

The man shook his head and whined, I'm trying to explain so the señor understands me, but he doesn't understand.

He was talking now as if apologetically explaining some past event not to Jackson but to a boss. I try and I try and the señor doesn't hear me. No, no, no.

Jackson sat still. He didn't like to be so close to the man who could easily have seated himself further along the loft, closer to the eaves. Instead he had placed himself right in the middle, between the two sleeping bags. Jackson wished he had his own knife to hand. He leaned himself back on his elbows and reached behind his head with one hand, fumbling for his boots.

He had just made contact with the limp tongue of one of them when the man was on him. He felt something warm just under his chin, his shoulder hurt where the man was forcing it back.

The man said nothing but breathed heavily, up against Jackson's face. Jackson no longer smelled him at all.

You fucking gringo, he said in English, you fucking leeesten. I don't tell you again. The man hissed, straining to keep his voice down. We don't tell you again. We don't like no fucking gringos coming down here. People say you OK, you just here for looking at the *ruinas*, you haven't come to bother no one. But anyone who comes here he bothering us. You pack you toothbrush, you go away before you can't go away.

The man talked softly again, and dabbed at the front of Jackson's shirt, as if trying half-heartedly to brush something away. I just friend and help you.

Jackson opened his mouth to speak but his heart was thumping and the words wouldn't come. He forced himself to say, I've got work to do here. It'll take me a few days, then I'll be gone. That's all. Two or three days.

The man carefully and heavily turned himself around. The daylight glinted on his moist cheeks, his wet lips. As he positioned his chubby hefty body on the ladder Jackson noted how heavy the man had been on top of him. We got work to do too. Gringo, *gringo*, you can't come in here where we do our work just like that. We don't talk again.

Ponderously, like a comic corpulent gent, or like the overweight clumsy peasant he was, he let himself down the ladder, his shoes making dainty *chips* on the rungs. With his face turned down, Jackson could see that he was all but bald on top. He was reminded of a hi-fi salesman he had once attempted to buy a Walkman from in Miami, a slick hard guy quite different from the bumbling drunk this man had at first seemed.

He ducked out of sight. Halfway down he called up, Remember, gringo.

Jackson couldn't help himself from saying, Remember what?

He moved to the edge and looked over. The man was standing at the bottom with one hand on the ladder, adjusting his gun strap with the other, panting. Without looking up, he said, *Ts, ts*. You shouldn't ask that, gringo. I don't explain again.

Then he walked out into the electric mountain sunshine, where he briefly became a figure radiant with dust.

Jackson laced up his boots and buttoned his shirt. He went down to the kitchen hut where he had eaten the night before, half expecting to see the man in there. But only two old women sat in the dark.

A strong smell of sweat, animals and stale milk hit his nostrils.

The two women began chatting to each other rapidly in Quechua. One of them got up with a bustle of her skirts and foraged among the pots and pans piled against the wall, until she found a piece of ragged home-made string. Cruz's mother, still seated by the fire, tore up a rag. She came over to Jackson and shook her head and pressed the rag against his neck. Only then did he look down his front and see in the gloom the dark paint splashed down his front. Reflexively he sat down, feeling sick to his stomach.

Then both women were close, and he could smell the ancient stench of their clothes. Their hard sinewy fingers were on his arms, and the soft cooing notes of their Quechua were in his ears. One of them bit off a piece of the home-spun string, which was not string but a twist of dried fat, Jackson now saw, and Cruz's mother lifted away the rag she had been holding to his neck. The cloth was dark all over. She folded it again, getting a clear patch ready, and ran the rind of fat over it, pushing his forehead back with a cool hand. She studied his throat then placed the rag under his chin and took one of his hands in hers and pressed it there. He understood that he was to hold the cloth in place.

While he sat back against the knobbly mud wall the women quietly tended the stove. He heard the shush as one of them shook a tray of coffee beans roasting over the fire pit. Then the crackle of a handmill turning. A wisp of dust rose into the air like the smoke of a gunshot. After a while Cruz's mother brought him a hot tin mug and a brick of molasses. She carved at it with a knife, shaving off dark granular flakes that curled and plopped into the cup.

Muchas gracias.

The coffee was sweet and tangy like caramel, with a sweaty aroma. He sipped carefully.

The sick feeling subsided. He would have to get a real plaster or bandage on this cut. He wondered how bad it was, thought it couldn't be too bad or it would surely have hurt more. He'd have to wash his shirt, or ask them to do it. He hoped they might do it without asking. He sat back, one hand pressed against his throat, the other holding the hot rim of the cup. He would have to be more careful.

He took the rag away, planning to take a look at it and judge how bad the bleeding was, but the women both shouted at him, No, no, gringo. He put it right back, gaining only an impression, in the murk, of glistening dark cloth.

It was unsettling that he hadn't felt the cut being made.

In a while Cruz's mother came over again with another cloth, applied a new smear of fat and pressed it in place. The two women had a concerned exchange of whispers by the fire. Then the other woman called out, in Spanish, You don't have a belt?

Sí, señora. Jackson touched his belt buckle with his free hand.

The two women nodded eagerly.

Jackson frowned, thinking he knew what they meant. They urged him, and he pulled the belt off and looped it over his head and around his neck. But the pin went far beyond the holes, and although he doubled the free end round he couldn't figure out, fumbling with it where he couldn't see it, how to attach it.

Cruz's mother came across once again, using her hand-pump method of walking, and fiddled with the belt, nudging his head this way and that.

When she had seated herself once again beside the stove, her friend asked, Gringo, where's your wife? She should be here to take care of you.

Why do I need a wife when you two are here?

The two women exploded in soft giggles.

His neck ached badly. Must have been a razor-sharp knife. He had felt nothing at all. He had better keep quiet, then. He rested against the wall. Were they going to bring him something to eat? Surely they would. They always liked to feed a guest. Just then he heard a seething of bubbles as a lid was lifted off a pot, and the aroma of bean stew reached him.

2

Choctamal may have been a haphazard homestead of dwellings scattered around the hillside, but it was neatly kept. The houses themselves with their smooth walls of red mud and hats of golden thatch had the air of well-groomed schoolchildren. Fifty yards away a stream babbled, flanked by smooth rocks on which clothes were spread to dry. It was different from Don Alfredo's compound, not only a lot larger but neater too.

Jackson looked around it and felt afraid. He didn't know how long he could stay, if he should wait for Cruz to come back, or just leave, go back while he could. Was guinea-pig fat going to heal the cut? He didn't think the man had meant to do serious harm, just scare him off. Maybe it would be a deeper cut next time.

The sun detached itself from the valleyhead. Dewy light streamed down the valley. The world looked newborn, damp in its caul.

Cruz returned in the early afternoon with a mule and two gringos called Stryker and Morris.

I had to leave, Cruz said. He smiled. Some people, I am not their friend and they are not mine, and they know it and I know it. But here I am. You ready? Tomorrow morning we go.

Some people are not my friend either. Look.

Jackson pulled the rag away from his neck, making it smart in the open air.

Hombre.

He told Cruz what had happened.

Cruz shook his head. It's OK. I can talk to them. They are not the ones we need to be careful of. Was he drunk?

Stryker and Morris carried their bags to the loft where Jackson slept, then they settled in the warm sunlit dirt outside the kitchen hut and called for food.

They ate together, sitting out in the yard with their bowls on their knees.

I ever tell you about the most expensive flush in history? the man called Stryker was saying. He had a lined, worn face and burning eyes. Something preoccupied him, Jackson could see that. He had an accent too, maybe Dutch.

Morris, the younger one, snickered. What do you mean flush?

Flush. As in toilet. This guy I know he owns this little East Village bar down on Tompkins Square, a place the models hang out, doesn't get going till one a.m. type of place. So one night he's getting raided and he dumps this big bag straight into the cistern of the toilet. It's part reflex, part thought. The idea being get rid of it, it dissolves, and then later he can siphon out the water, boil it and lose nothing. It comes to him in a flash. Sixty thousand dollars, a whole kilo, and you can make it invisible, then collect later. Brilliant, right? Wrong. This model, she needs to use the john. The cops are still around hoovering the sofas and chairs, whatever, and he doesn't want to draw attention so he tries to signal her not to use the john but she doesn't get it, she goes right on in, pees and flushes.

Morris laughed hard, rocking back and forth on his seat. The most expensive flush in the world, he repeated. Love it.

Stryker didn't even smile. He looked at the youth with no expression at all. Jackson wondered why he had bothered to tell the story, if not to raise a laugh.

Stryker glanced at Jackson. Don't mind him. He's just a rich kid from Massachusetts. Isn't that right, rich boy?

Morris was still giggling. He must be high, Jackson thought. Probably grass.

You know how he got down here? Stole a cheque from the back of his daddy's chequebook and bought himself a one-way to Bogotá. Looking for adventure. Isn't that right? And fuck me if he didn't find it. Isn't that right, Yankee boy? I found him making necklaces for gringos on the beach at Bocagrande. You look young and foolish, how about you earn two thousand dollars in ten days? But he was cooler than he looked. Could keep his head. Not every-

one can do that. Maybe he's just young enough not to have a fucking clue. Where are you from anyway?

England.

Stryker's pale blue eyes rested on him a moment. He inhaled,
but said nothing. Then he asked, What brings you here?

Jackson hesitated. Ruins. I'm looking for a ruined city.

He swallowed the last of his soup, draining it straight out of the
bowl. It turned out to be a larger mouthful than he had expected,
and hotter, burning his throat. It was like swallowing a hot golf
ball, and seemed to stick in his gullet. He put his bowl down on the
packed mud with a clink of the spoon.

He was aware of Stryker's eyes on him. He was not an ugly man
yet there was something ugly in his face. Blond hair, blue eyes, a
straggle of beard, a goatee gone to seed. While the boy had a glint in
his eye; he was high not only on grass but on something else, maybe
adventure. Yet looking at the two men now, Jackson felt that to have
grown careless about one's appearance could be a sign of having kept
the inner fires stoked, of having fuelled some dream or conviction.

It was obvious how much the younger man gained from the
elder, and the sight unnerved him. It wasn't so much a matter of
whether the mentor was false, whether the younger man was
being led astray, as of the intensity the elder fostered. There was
something wrong with that. Or was it right for a man to throw
himself into whatever made him feel good? Or could gentleness
compensate for the deadening of the spirit? It was as if there were
only two philosophies on earth, adventure or kindness, and you
lived by one or the other.

Stryker looked at Jackson. You think you're safe here?

Jackson shrugged.

Damn right. Here you're either in with someone, or you're out.
And if you're out you better not be here. I'm telling you like it is.
Take it or leave it, it's good advice.

What about you?

We're on business. We're OK.

You think that's OK?

OK? As in ethical? We're traders, man. If they want to make us rich by declaring our merchandise illegal, I don't complain. I don't stop either. Who are they to tell me what I should and should not inhale? It's none of their business. People do what they want. Somebody has to take a stand against these arms dealers.

Morris giggled.

Arms dealers? Jackson asked.

I'm talking about governments, man. They're arms dealers, that's what governments are, you don't know that? Big daddy the rocket salesman. They used to be drug dealers, like the opium in the East, and now it's arms. That's fine, that's all right, they can sell their weapons of destruction all over the world but God forbid anybody else should sell a good time. It's their own fault this business is a mess. Of course you get the negative elements once you call it illegal. They have nowhere else to go. But at least it gives big daddy a chance to sell a few more bang-bangs. Anyway, so you're an archaeologist.

Of sorts.

Stryker looked back over either shoulder then got up and came and sat beside Jackson on the doorstep. He rested his elbows on his knees, his hands clasped, leaning forward, and spoke quietly.

You know Mr. Brown?

Yes.

OK. So Mr. Brown—don't look at me, just listen. You don't know anything, you don't know where this comes from. Tomorrow morning, you go to the top of the *chacra*. You know what that is? There's a black old tree up there, totally burnt. Right at the edge by the forest, you can't miss it. Struck by lightning. Under the root you'll find it. Somewhere round here they think there's an airstrip. You find it, you hide that package, you turn it on, you leave. That's it. And if you don't find the airstrip find something else. An HQ or something. That's what they want. If you do it and it's all hunky dory Brown says you'll get five times what it was before. You understand? Don't look at me. You understand?

What do you mean, turn it on?

There's a switch on it I guess. He said you'd know the thing when you saw it.

Jackson guessed already that he would. It would be a standard military beacon with a one-hundred-mile range. They had used them in Belize.

One last thing. Once you flip that switch get the fuck out. That's what he said to tell you.

Stryker offered Jackson a cigarette, lit it and returned to where he had been sitting. I had to hide it, I couldn't just give it to you. Something like that, you keep it to yourself here. You ever been up here before?

No.

There was another Limey a couple of years back.

There was a friend of mine who came down here.

What was he called?

Connolly.

That's the one.

You knew him?

Sure I knew him. He must have come two or three times. We came up together once from Tingo. He was cool. In spite of everything.

You knew him? Amazing. Did you ever go to any ruins with him? He was trying to find La Joya. You know there's a huge lost city in the cloud forest near here? I can't believe you knew him.

Stryker didn't reply but drew deeply on his cigarette.

Then Jackson said: What do you mean, in spite of everything?

What he was up to. Stryker blew out a stream of smoke and inhaled again.

You mean looking for ruins?

Stryker sniggered, letting out small clouds of smoke.

Sure. He had the wool pulled so low over everyone's eyes all they were seeing was sheep.

Jackson said nothing.

But that is what he was doing, Jackson said. Exploring the ruins.

Stryker shrugged. Sure he was, he said again. And maybe that wasn't all he was doing. A military guy down here? You think he's just an archaeologist? Just like you?

It had never before occurred to Jackson that Connolly might not have been doing what he said; that there might have been more to him, other agendas. Whatever truth you thought you'd pulled something aside to reveal, beneath it might lie a further truth, and beneath that yet another. It was a dismal thought. He preferred not to think about it. But he couldn't help it.

So what do you mean? What else was he doing? He felt dizzy and slightly sick as he asked, and realised that it must be true, Connolly must have had some other agenda, most probably with military intelligence. That would be exactly why they had asked Jackson to work for them too. That was why back in London Major Buckley had called him.

Stryker drew on the end of his cigarette noisily, then threw away the butt.

Some deal the Brits got going with the Americans. I don't know. All I know is, some people got hurt. Bad shit happened.

Jackson felt himself frowning. What do you mean? Who got hurt? How?

Stryker shook his head. We don't speak ill of the dead, man. It'll be us soon.

He did something bad? What did he do?

Forget it, man, it's history.

Jackson started to feel angry. What do you mean? Did he betray someone? Kill someone? What?

Stryker looked away and brushed a knee, then stood up. Shit happens, he said. Especially down here. You be careful.

He walked away.

Jackson found a roll of tape in his bag and rigged up a bandage for his neck from a piece of cloth cut from one of his T-shirts. The bleeding had settled down, but the cut smarted if he turned his head. He took an aspirin.

Later, another Andean dusk laid itself out over the green and gold slopes. The hills settled down like blue dogs for a rest. You looked out and saw the hills could go on forever. The blood-red throat of the Marañón canyon disappeared into smoke.

He went and found Cruz and asked him if he thought they were safe to go on. Cruz reassured him. He smiled. *Muchas ruinas*, he said. You'll see.

He was worried too about that beacon. What would happen if he switched it on? Maybe they'd come in and strafe the whole area. People could get killed. Old women and kids. Even if they didn't, it would change things here, people could lose their livelihoods or worse. What did it have to do with him? This wasn't his war. He had no war.

Cruz touched his arm. It's OK. You'll see. That man, he was drunk, we don't have to worry about him.

Later, as he lay still in his sleeping bag, he fell into a reverie. He was in the forest. Figures in white were threading through the gloom. They walked up to a low stone pyramid, then beyond it to a plaza built of laid masonry. Houses in which lights were burning stood all through the forest, and outside the houses families were sitting round dim fires. A woman was singing somewhere, and there was the knock of a machete on wood in the distance. A man was repeating a cry, perhaps selling something. It was a city, you could feel it—the bustle, the restful safety, the human world going about its business within the shelter of the tall trees. And the human lights burning like stars through the forest.

He snapped awake, still seeing the dream, still half in it. Outside a dog growled, and it might have been lying in that same old city.

He looked out from the loft. At first all he made out was darkness and the thicker darkness of the forest higher up. Then a star shook into view, then vanished. A moment later it appeared again, twinkling and shifting and dropping down the black face of the hill, then it moved out of sight.

Below, a moth was batting itself against the glass bulb of a kerosene lamp hanging from a nail on an outside wall. He knew what it meant. It meant that you pursued what fascinated you again and again, even when you had seen through it. By then it was too late and you'd keep on doing it until it killed you.

But the moon was burning outside too, burning, burning, and the moth couldn't see it.

13 · Ruin

1

They set off up the maize field without the mule. The hills were still grey, the sky mauve. Cruz carried a machete, walking in his sandals. Jackson had his backpack. Before the sun appeared it touched the folds of the far valleyside. As they came alongside the forest they moved into a current of warm air.

Jackson looked back over the landscape behind: yellow trees upon green trees upon grey, arm after arm of vista receding. The black tree he had to find was unmistakable, a charred crucifix twelve feet tall.

Jackson walked straight past it keeping the rhythm of his stride. It was easy not to think about stopping, not to collect the device. He could imagine it—a grey metal box the size of a paperback, with a dial for a frequency that would already be set, and a black knob that you gave one turn to.

He walked right past and they entered the forest. Ten, twenty, thirty yards on he could still feel that tree behind him as if the tree had taken a run and jumped right onto him and he was giving it a piggyback.

Wait here, he called to Cruz, and ran back through the forest into the broad daylight at the top of the field. He didn't think about what he was doing but noticed the firm clods under his boots, and the tendrils of creepers with floppy basil-like leaves. At the tree, as he had expected, thick black roots like fat snakes curled down from the trunk into the ground. Halfway round he saw what he was looking for, a glisten in the dark under one of the roots. He stood for a while with his hands in front of him as if taking a pee in case Cruz or anyone else was watching then, without a second thought, he bent down, reached in and grabbed the bundle of black plastic. A small hard thing that weighed as much as a lightweight field-radio, the size he'd expected, wrapped in a black bag. He didn't look at it but stuffed it in his trouser pocket where it just fitted, and scurried back to Cruz, who was waiting quietly in the gloom of the forest.

¿Ya? Cruz asked. *¿Listo?*

Jackson nodded. He wondered if Cruz might have seen, and what it would mean to either of them if he had.

In the forest they could only tell the sun had risen by a slight brightening of the shade. Cruz marked their path by slashing at bushes with his machete. Birds called to one another. Monkeys shook the high leaves.

They threaded among the bald trunks, the canopy fifty or sixty feet over their heads. Then the underbrush thickened. Lianas hung down in thickets of fat rubbery leaves. Red star plants grew halfway up tree trunks as if pinned there for decoration, and sent long tendrils out into the air. Sometimes Cruz had to clear the way with his machete.

Stands of beautiful trees made Jackson think of parks and town gardens—red maples delicate as Chinese bamboo, blue-green pines with their flame-like cones, and flame-trees too. Once he saw a cedar with trumpet-like protrusions of leaves, bell after bell, horn after horn, all of them misty blue, like a case of instruments stored away, long handles protruding. He imagined he'd seen a tree like that in a park once, brooding over a lawn like a memory. He would have liked it then. Now it scared him. No other word for it. Here was a world that did not need man, had not needed him for centuries, indeed had only tolerated him for a few hundred years at most, then saw him off and returned to its habitual stillness, its hush of small sounds.

They came into an area where many shiny saplings occupied the forest, each with a few handfuls of young bright leaves high up overhead. They were like ropes, hard, pale, miraculously standing upright by themselves.

In the late morning they moved into clearer forest. Cruz stopped and leaned against a tree saying, *Ya*. They had arrived.

There was nothing to show it. The gentle undulations of the ground were not unusual. Shallow mounds of moss and ground ivy rose here and there. You could imagine that these were the remains of fallen houses, now overgrown, but you could just as easily not.

Cruz led him to a low cliff among the trees, just tall enough that its highest rocks glinted through the leaves in open sunlight. Cruz lay on his belly and squirmed into a hole low down, until only his feet showed. He scrambled back out holding a brown human skull.

He handed it to Jackson and disappeared back into the hole, and came out again with two broken pieces of terra-cotta.

Cerámicas, he explained. *Hay mucho, mucho*. He reached in again and came out with more to prove it.

Then he pulled stones away from another part of the rock face and reached in, disappearing up to his waist. When he wriggled out he had another skull.

Gente antigua, he said: old people. Just in case Jackson had missed it. He smiled at the grinning teeth of the skull, with its steeply receding brow, undamaged.

Cruz had clearly been here before. Jackson photographed the things, and stored the ceramics in a plastic bag.

They moved on through the forest. In an hour or so they came into an area where the terrain was steeply cut up by mounds and hillocks over which the trees and undergrowth grew.

While Cruz was busy cutting away vegetation on one of the mounds, Jackson pressed up through the shrubbery, shielding his face with his elbows as he shouldered between two dense bushes. Earlier he'd passed a similar bush, thinking it something like a laurel, only to find its twigs were covered with a ferocious armoury of thorns. These two were different, they didn't cling to his sleeves as he passed or scratch his cheeks.

When he came out from between them, he was facing another dark wall of creepers and ferns. It was impossible to know what lay behind it: earth, or rock, or perhaps more of those burial sites. He pulled on his gloves and began slashing with his machete at the sinewy, root-like stems of the creepers.

He heard a rustle nearby between blows and stopped. The tail of a lime-green snake disappeared into the underbrush. He wondered if it had been a fer-de-lance. One archaeologist whose book he'd read seemed to think the fer-de-lance liked ruins; at any rate, he was always encountering them while clearing sites. Jackson waited a moment, then resumed his cutting of the toughest stems. In a while he heard Cruz coming up behind him, the shush of his progress through the undergrowth, the occasional ringing of his machete as it cut through stalks.

Cruz arrived just as Jackson was ready to start clearing away what he had cut. Together they heaved out a mass of greenery more or less in one piece.

The sight behind it made Jackson's blood race. He had imagined that after centuries beneath forest growth any stonework they found, if they were lucky enough to find any, would be darkened and roughened by moss and soil, misshapen by roots. But in front of him now stood a wall of clean stone, neatly fitted with straight edges, and so pale it looked like chalk among the shrubbery.

He looked at Cruz, and both men smiled. This was something Cruz hadn't seen before. Jackson began to laugh, and as he did so swung again with his machete, cutting away at more and more of the mesh of creepers. Cruz did the same, standing up on what might have been the pedestal of the wall they had uncovered, and reaching up as high as he could with his blade. Jackson could hear him grunting as he stretched. He himself was panting. He couldn't have wiped the grin off his face even if he'd wanted to.

Again they stopped, and started tugging away armfuls of the forest growth, pulling away more and more. Soon they had exposed a
large section of wall some fifteen feet tall and twenty broad. The
stonework was good, closely fitted, and clearly extended to either
side beneath the vegetation, as well as upward. Jackson had hoped
they might be able to clear to the top of it, but it was too tall. They
decided to walk along in either direction and see if they could find
a corner, and gauge what kind of structure it might be.

It was strange how the massive mound of masonry blended into
the forest, with its camouflage of plants. Even just twenty-five
yards from it you hardly noticed it, indeed, hardly saw it through
the undergrowth. But now they were walking beside it, it seemed
inconceivable it could be missed.

Cruz said, You see? I bring you to the right place. I know where
to come. This whole part of the forest is full of ruins. Many many
ruins. I never saw this one before.

No one has ever cleared it?

Cruz rubbed his finger and thumb together. Who's going to pay?
All the money for ruins, it goes down to Cuzco, to the ruins they
already know. He pouted. No one wants to come here.

In about eighty yards, by Jackson's rough measure of his strides,
the hidden edifice ended. Then it ran away at a right angle, going
slightly downhill. They decided to follow it that way. What was this
massive thing? Here and there they could see undulations and
mounds Jackson guessed might be fallen houses, old foundations.
He would have to check them out later. But what was this huge
structure? A citadel? A walled plaza? A fortress? The second side
they followed he estimated to be a hundred yards long, and as the
ground steepened downward the top of the wall seemed to main-
tain a level height, as far as he could tell through the foliage, so the
masonry grew taller and taller. On the third side they found a
doorway.

At first glance it looked like a cave, a hollow at the foot of the
bank where the foliage hung down but did not reach the ground.
Jackson bent and pushed aside what turned out to be a thin curtain of one particular bush's stems. At first it was completely dark,

and he took the place to be a chamber, but quickly he realised there was a glimmer of daylight ahead, deeper inside. He called out to Cruz to follow.

They switched on the torch. Hundreds of pale roots hung down from the roof like dead worms. They stooped under them, and the daylight ahead grew stronger. Meanwhile the chamber narrowed, until there was a wall right next to them. A bush filled the path. Jackson slashed at one side of it, and pushed past. He found his foot landing on a higher level, then higher still: there were steps, and they brought him up to a doorway at a right angle to the flight of stairs. Through it he stepped back out into the forest.

Cruz emerged behind him, and they turned back toward the high wall. They continued following it, now on the other side. Finally it turned a corner again into a fourth side, and that proved it was indeed some kind of enclosure, and they were inside it, in a precinct, or a citadel. At the far corner there was another opening, much smaller than the other they had been through, and instead of leading them back into the forest outside the enclosure, a passage five or six feet long brought them out onto something Jackson could never have foreseen.

A stone terrace had been built right at the foot of the massive wall like an overhang. Beyond it, the forest fell away. This side of the citadel was built along a cliff. Below, crowns of trees mushroomed up then vanished as the ground dropped away. Far below lay a lake, its surface glinting grey in the gloom of passing clouds. All around the lake rose steep forested hills. It was like stumbling upon some beautiful ornamental lake in Europe, even England, with that cloudy sky overhead. It was like being in a dream. The feel of the place—the feel the original builders must have had for landscape and views and setting—was still right here. It reminded Jackson of being a child, or of some childhood dream.

Because the forest fell away, the stone terrace had been largely unmolested by growth. A pale parapet wall some three feet tall ran along the edge, and although the floor was covered in mulch and old leaves, Jackson could feel stone paving under his feet. The terrace was perhaps twenty feet long and six wide, and formed a kind of balcony. It seemed hard to imagine how he could be standing here enjoying a view no one had seen for hundreds of years. The scene—the drop down to the lake, the sense of the massive wall behind—filled him with a kind of peace. This must have been how the Chachapoyans felt too: this very sensation he was having.

The rest of that day passed like a dream. Jackson felt he had stumbled into a treasure trove, a private garden. He could hardly believe what he was seeing was real. He kept asking himself: how, in the end, did he even know it was real? How did one know anything was real? He thought over his past: how did he know any of it had ever really happened? It felt as though it could have happened to someone else, or never happened at all. How could you ever really know?

There were several mounds within the enclosure, the largest of which, in the middle, rose some forty feet. The trees were sparser here, and grew tall and thin: more of those self-suspended ropes. Except they were fatter than rope, more like immensely tall pillars. What with the mounds, which could have been the remains of pyramids, and with there being no trace of smaller edifices close together, which would have indicated a residential district, Jackson guessed that the place must have been a ceremonial centre. Perhaps there had even been rituals performed on that balcony, sacrifices to the lake gods. He had read about a site down on the coast where archaeologists speculated people had been thrown from a rocky ledge to the Pacific sharks, in a marine form of human sacrifice. Perhaps something comparable had gone on here.

They rigged a makeshift camp by the wall near the passageway. Cruz tied up the tarpaulin and spread a blanket under it, then set off in search of dry wood for a fire.

Jackson began making a rudimentary sketch of the site. Then he went back into the forest. Nearby he found a small area of what he took to be fallen houses—mounds some fifteen or twenty feet across—but then no more traces of any buildings. It was strange. What had this place been? Why had there not been more human habitation? Such an elaborate site must have needed a large local population to build it.

Further to the east he came across a single hillock under the trees. At first he took it to be part of the lie of the land. It was so much bigger than any of the other mounds he'd seen that it was hard to imagine anyone could have constructed it. But as he walked around and took in its symmetrical shape, he began to wonder. He decided to come back with Cruz later, or the next morning, and see if they could clear any stonework.

Afternoon was drawing on, and Jackson had forgotten all about lunch. His mind was racing. Was this it? Was this the lost city of La Joya? But it seemed impossible. There just wasn't enough here. Yet there was also too much not to indicate the existence of a big population. Where had they lived, if not here? And that overlook, with the lake: Connolly had talked of finding a cliff, and seeing the city stretching away below. Was this what he had meant? Could it have got muddled in his memory? Surely he'd have remembered seeing a lake. Perhaps he'd forgotten to mention it.

Jackson made his way back to the citadel where he'd left Cruz, then out onto the balcony once more. Way over in the east, low in the sky, a distant hilltop gleamed gold in late sun. Otherwise, all the hills were khaki. White and grey clouds moved over the open bowl in the forest. The water of the lake looked paler now, and a breeze ruffled it.

While he stood there watching, Jackson heard a hissing sound, a whistling in the wind. It seemed to be coming from below him. He looked down, but saw nothing. Then a huge black beast rose in front of him through the air. He jumped. It was a second before he even realised it was a bird. His first thought was that it was a monster, a creature not known to Western humanity. It was as broad as two men. Its head was bald but capped with a large red tassel the size of a tea cosy, and it had a ruffled white collar like an Elizabethan courtier. Its arms—its wings—were thick as tree trunks and shiny black. At the end of each wing five stiff black fingers twitched in the wind. It was they, Jackson thought, that made the hissing sound, as the breeze rustled through them.

It hadn't seen him. Or else it didn't care. It had nothing to fear. It rose just a few feet from him, riding a column of air up the cliff and over the forest. He could see its feet hanging, and the bulk of its seal-like body between the wings.

There was an outcrop some fifty yards away to his right. The giant bird swung up and over it. After it had gone, Jackson looked at the rock. Something drew his eye to it. It projected like a buttress from the face of the cliff. Then he saw a long stratum of stonework running like a belt across it. It was human stonework, he could see that at once. It wasn't any old masonry: it was elaborate, and every few feet there was a deliberate fretwork making a pattern. As Jackson stared, the shapes in the fretwork jumped out: condors, a line of them, standing with their wings spread. It was remarkable anyone had managed to build anything on the face of the rock with a sheer drop below. But that it should have been such careful stonework—how had they done it? With scaffolding? By letting themselves down on ropes? And why? The evenness of the stonework was inconsistent with the rugged rock. Most likely there was a space behind it, he guessed. Perhaps it was a kind of cliff-dwelling, such as had been found here and there in pre-Columbian America. Often such places were cities of the dead. Were there perhaps mummies, funeral urns and mortuary treasures just behind that wall? It was possible. The more Jackson gazed up and down the length of that band of stonework, which might have been around four feet tall—not tall enough for houses of the living—the more convinced he became that there must be cavities behind it, and most likely it would be a series of tombs.

He could not believe what he had stumbled into. It was like taking a drug and entering an enchanted land. There were treasures everywhere—of architecture, culture, history. And it was not just deserted and empty, but had surely never been found before. There were no traces of looters. Everything was intact.

He pulled out his sketchbook but before he could get started drawing a rustle and hiss caught his attention. A second condor rose on the same path as the first. There must have been thermals here that the birds knew about.

At night, when the light of their campfire licked up the stone wall beside them, turning it gold, the whole great enclosure seemed to fall open, as if it were a huge garden. The old temples or pyramids in the precinct seemed to grow taller, and darker, and their layout became clear to Jackson: there was one in the middle, and four flanking it, two to either side. Earlier, in the daylight, he had not noticed this perfectly simple fact. The symmetry was more evidence that this had been a ceremonial centre.

You never heard of this place before? he asked into the dark, his voice sounding dry and sharp.

We hear of many ruins.

Do you think anyone ever came here?

There was a gringo back in the sixties, he found a lot of sites. He started to clear some but the forest just grew back. This one? I don't know. What difference does it make? The archaeologists, they don't know about it. They don't come here. Cruz whistled. It's a big place, a big, big place.

Jackson lay awake a long time staring at the canvas weave in Cruz's tarpaulin, lit by the glow of the dying fire. Now he felt happy that he had temporarily parted from Sarah in order to pursue this search. Somehow he felt the two things went together: had it not been for her, all this would not be happening. And vice versa. This find seemed to confirm the two of them might have a future. For a moment he felt he had not left her at all; their lives were somehow one.

When he eventually drifted off he slept dreamlessly.

2

After breakfast of small loaves with hot sauce that Cruz's mother had wrapped for them, Jackson wanted to explore the large mound he had found outside the compound the previous day. He brought along his backpack in case they found anything they wanted to bring back, and also to keep the food away from animals.

Once they reached the hillock Jackson began pulling at the low plants covering it, and soon found stone. In one place a wall still stood to chest height, and beside it creepers covered a level area—an old plaza perhaps, with a wall of masonry enclosing it. He pulled at the ground-growth, uprooting weeds, clearing soft moist earth with his fingers, flinging handfuls and armfuls to the side. Again he got down to smooth stone, and groped his way toward an edge, worked along and down from it, tugging more vegetation clear, until he realised the edge of stone formed part of a wall running to the middle of the mound. He pulled out a great ball of tangled weeds, and took a step forward to pull the stuff clear, but his boot found nothing solid to land on. It crashed through a layer of twigs and roots into a hole. He had invested the step with all his weight, and ended up sitting on the edge with a bruised hip, one leg stuck through the vegetation in front, ·the other kicked awkwardly backward. He called Cruz over. Cruz helped him get up, and together they opened up a passage into the hole, into the earth under the mound.

Cruz frowned. This too was new to him.

Wait, he said.

While he was gone Jackson fetched the flashlight from his backpack. Cruz came back a few minutes later with a bundle of leaves and fronds that he had screwed into a torch. He pulled out his matchbox and lit it. The leaves blackened, gave off white smoke, and a neat point of flame appeared at the tip. He handed it to Jackson, who stuffed his own torch in his pocket, thinking this flame would give a broader light, and lowered it into the hole. Right away he could see a floor of blackened stone a few feet down. He climbed in holding the torch, and saw that he had dropped into one end of a tunnel.

There was a strange effect of sound—a quietness in the tunnel, or not exactly quietness but dullness, a plainness to sounds. His footfalls. Cruz's scuffling with matches in the entrance when the flare had gone out. There was a faint breeze outside which Jackson noticed only now that he was protected from it in this dark channel under ground. He could hear it whistling in the trees. When he coughed it sounded like there was no other sound in the world.

Cruz got the home-made torch lit again and took it off Jackson, who squeezed against the dark wall to make room for him to pass. Even that—the feel of his palms against the cold earth and stone—was strangely vivid, as if the stone had come alive. His hands began to tingle, and a wonderful excitement kindled in his chest. How lucky, he thought. How lucky to be here. It was more than exciting. It was fulfilling. The rest of his life seemed to fall away. There was just this: standing in a dark tunnel in the earth in the middle of the cloud forest of the big northern mountains. What was doubly odd—yet at the same time seemed the most natural thing in the world—was that the place felt so comfortable, so like a home.

Was it something about its design? Had its builders factored in certain imperceptible features that made it automatically a happy place for a human being? Was it something about being underground, that there was a native instinct still hidden in him that made the under-earth feel safe? Was it being where Connolly might have been, finding not just what he had perhaps found, but much more besides? He had managed to do what Connolly had done, and now was doing more. It made anything else Connolly had been up to irrelevant. This was the real thing: to be standing in the ancient edifices of a vanished race. To be in the blackness and cool of this passage, and hear the trees hissing outside, and the occasional soft moan as the wind blew past, making the opened-up chamber resonate like an empty bottle—all these things felt close and warm.

Cruz knocked at a clutch of roots hanging down from the ceiling. With two neat blows of his knife he sliced them off and stepped over them. He travelled down the tunnel with a flickering rim of light all around him. Then he stopped and said, *Ay Dios*.

He might have been fifteen or twenty feet from Jackson.

Mira, hombre, he called. Look.

Jackson wasn't looking anywhere else. He stepped deeper into the tunnel, toward Cruz, who lifted his torch and lit up a sheet of stone covered in intricate carving. Jackson pulled his torch from his pocket. What he saw first was a carving—a wide mouth, fangs, round eyes the size of tennis balls. A tangle of carved lines writhed like snakes over a flat face of stone. In each groove humus and detritus had settled, forming black lines so the design appeared in sharp relief. As Jackson looked closer he saw that the lines were indeed snakes: there was a stack of snakes' heads, each with two fangs in its wide-open jaws, on either side. Higher up was a bigger face, perhaps the central feature of the carving.

Cruz said nothing. He stood still, the bush lamp burning in his hand.

Jackson became aware of a bad smell. He wondered if it was some fetid air in the long-closed tunnel. Or else some animal that had died in here.

Cruz said, low and sheepishly, *Me voy. Tengo que irme.* I need to go.

At that, Jackson recognised the smell. Cruz had soiled himself. Apparently that deity was too much for him. The stench seemed to sink to the floor of Jackson's belly.

Jackson bent down with the torch then shone it higher, and saw that the multi-fold deity had been carved onto one single slab of rock some ten feet tall. Two tunnels branched away on either side of it, but they turned out to be only a few feet long.

For there to be a tomb like this, or a shrine, a temple, an altar such as this, there had to have been a big population. This carving alone was an undertaking, and the mound above was surely an old pyramid. It could only mean there was a lost city nearby. Perhaps they were even in it. Was this it? Was La Joya a series of smaller sites? Had the dwellings been small and temporary, leaving little trace among the bigger stone temples?

He wondered what else they would find. If there was a place like this, and like the citadel, if they had stumbled into them so easily, who knew what they would find if they searched the whole area.

His heart was in his mouth. Instead of joy or relief, he mostly felt fear. How to relay this. How to convince people to help him. How to find it again. He would have to plot the route back to Choctamal carefully. But worse than that were the dangerous, lawless people he had already run into: never mind coming back later with a proper expedition, would he even be able to stay here long enough to do all the preliminary charting and documenting? He was scared of going back to Choctamal for more supplies. Who might he run into this time? He might have to leave the area at once. But they'd run out of food in a day or two at most. It crossed his mind to set off the homing beacon, but he had no idea what that might unleash. Stryker had said to get away fast, once he did.

He fumbled in his pockets for his compass. He couldn't find it. He climbed back outside and rummaged through his pack. He must have left it at the camp. He had left a few things there although he didn't remember taking it out. What had happened to it? It was impossible to have lost it at such a time. He looked through all the pockets again, scarcely able to believe he didn't have it.

Of all the stupid things to have done. He racked his brains and searched right through the bag again. Careless. So careless. But he was with Cruz. Though that was part of the problem; he was dependent. Dependent and unable to chart properly. Even sketchy charting was OK if you had coordinates. Without coordinates, it was close to a waste of time. But he must go ahead and do what he could. He must take Cruz's vague notions, and his own, of north and east. East was the easiest, but you lost it quickly, by ten or earlier, or as soon as you entered the forest.

They could spend the rest of the day, and the next day perhaps, mapping it out, and seeing what else there was nearby. After that, he could come back by himself with more food supplies. He would find it easily enough, if they amplified Cruz's markings on the trees.

He climbed back down with his notebook and started a rough sketch by the light of his torch, resting the paper on the dark peaty floor.

Then from outside he heard Cruz shout. Muffled by the tunnel came another man's voice, then another shout, followed by a sharp snap. He knew what it was. In the depth of the tunnel, a shot would sound like that. There was a short cry, a grunt, then silence.

Jackson switched off the torch. He didn't move. As quietly as he could he stepped into one of the side tunnels by the stone god, squatted down and listened. Outside, two men were talking to one another, and he didn't think either of them was Cruz. Their voices

were harder. He waited to hear if they would go away. His pack
was out there. Would they guess someone else was here? He
waited to see if he could hear Cruz's voice again. He couldn't.

He would not make a move.

The two men were still talking. One of the voices grew louder.
There was a scuffle of falling debris. There was no mistaking what
was happening: someone was climbing down into the tunnel.
Jackson's heart sank. His belly tightened. What could he do? He
had no way of defending himself. No weapon, no nothing. He'd
even left his machete outside by his pack. All he could do was keep
quiet. Maybe, just maybe if he saw the man before the man saw
him, he could strike and grab his gun if he had one.

Caballero, a husky voice called. Come out and we won't hurt
you.

A flash of light stroked the face of the stone god just in front of
Jackson. They had a torch, but the light wouldn't reach him unless
they walked right down to the end of the tunnel and turned. His
heart pounded.

We won't hurt you if you come out. *Inglés*. We know you're in
here.

Jackson heard the hollow knocking of his heart. They wouldn't
go away. He knew they wouldn't. They would come in with
Kalashnikovs without even bothering to light the chamber and
spray it full of rounds. Even if a direct shot didn't get him, a rico-
chet would. He wouldn't stand a chance.

I have a gun, he called.

There was a pause. The voice said, *Hombre*.

If you try and get me I'll kill you. There's something here Señor
Carreras will like. I am an English archaeologist. If you take me to
Carreras he will thank you. I know something he wants to know.

The man let out a dry chuckle. Gringo. You're bargaining with
us? You cannot wait because we cannot wait. We have a hurry
now. So you come out now. Or we come in and we kill you with
your own so-called gun.

The other voice said something and they both laughed.

The first said: What kind of gun you got anyway?

Jackson didn't answer. He exhaled.

Gringo. This not warning, this is now.

He stepped out of the side tunnel holding his sketchbook first.

Archaeologist. These are my notes. The torch was in his eyes. Señor Carreras will thank you. I'm an archaeologist.

Outside were three men, two he had not seen before, and one the strange drunk in the black satin shirt who had accosted him the morning before.

They said nothing. Two of them held Kalashnikovs. The drunk came forward and frisked him carefully. He pulled the black plastic package from Jackson's trousers, glanced at it and dropped it into Jackson's backpack, which he then handed peremptorily to Jackson, telling him to put it on.

It was a moment before Jackson saw Cruz lying face down, half sunk in ground creepers. There was a dark stain on the seat of his trousers. The drunk noticed him looking that way.

He come too often. He did not set things right. You lucky, my friend. My *jefe*, he say you bring the young *inglés*. The archaeologist. Your *holandés* friends, they are not so good now. They played games.

The two armed men walked behind Jackson. He recognised death in the air, the shock, the feeling of a roof having come off the world and the true, cold daylight flooding in. He felt that surely something had to be done about Cruz, they couldn't just walk away and leave him.

But what about— he began, almost stopping.

The muzzle of a gun was in his back, and pushed him on.

Jackson's heart was in his boots. It was his money, his five hundred dollars, that had induced Cruz to come. Brown's money. His head swam, and he thought of Major Buckley and his champagne; of how Cruz had taken the money up front. Perhaps he always did, but when they'd passed that corpse and Cruz had been nonchalant about it, it seemed now as if he'd almost been prophetic.

They had only been walking twenty minutes when they reached a broad track through the woods. It was tidy, neat, as if someone kept it shipshape. A long black bean pod lay on the ground and Jackson noticed it particularly. Normally something like that would not stand out. The track consisted of short dry grass and two strips of bare earth an axle-width apart. It could only mean vehicles came down here. It was a shock to discover that. Jackson hadn't seen a car or anything to do with one in weeks.

Everything was strange, different from the way he had conceived it would be. The ruins found just like that, so easily. There they were, all it had taken was coming here. Connolly had been right. And now this. Cars, trucks, vehicles could get here. Nothing was as he had supposed.

Jackson's moment came when they reached the men's green Land Cruiser, waiting a mile down the track.

One of the two men with the guns opened up the driver's door and climbed in. Jackson thought he heard him clip his safety catch. The other one walked to the near side of the vehicle, and the dissolute dinner-jacket man, who carried no gun, went to the far side. That side, beyond the edge of the track, the ground fell away in a steep slope among the trees.

Jackson didn't think, he made no decision, he only noted that one gun was inside the truck and the other was the wrong side of it, the far side from the drop. He ran and jumped. He was in the air, falling, waiting only to hit the ground and begin running. A twig whipped his face, and he rolled over on his side once, twice, and back onto his feet on the leaf-strewn slope. He heard a shot—a flat sharp snap, as of a mallet on wood—then a burst of semi-automatic rounds.

He ducked and dodged, weaving between the trees, and slowed for nothing. He hurdled a bush, he jumped a stream, always going down; he leapt over a broken trunk that had tipped to the ground from the hinge of its break. There was another burst of fire further off, sounding like it had little to do with him, it could have been hunters or someone doing target practice.

Down. Down was fastest. He didn't run, he flew. The trees came to meet him, offering fleeting hand-holds which he ignored. The trees drew him on, showing him the way, deeper into the forest.

14 · Forest

1

They tracked him soon. They were on to him.

Water filled his boots. There were little stones in them too, and what must have been mud. Grit. Grit in his boots. He hardly noticed. The difficulty that absorbed his concentration was which rock to aim for with each step or, where there was no rock, which ruffled segment of brown or white-breaking water. Where would it be shallow, where deep. Lightning decisions. The stream was not running high, that was something, but still, it was hard to run down a stream with a pack on your back. But he had to keep to the water.

Early on he had been aware of the braying of dogs in the distance somewhere within the canopy of the forest. Now they had gone quiet. Either he had outdistanced them or they had been muzzled.

He avoided the pools; the clay-brown stillnesses of deeper water. Once he splashed straight into one only to find his boot slipping on an angle of submerged rock. The next thing he knew his shoulder hit a boulder by the bank. It still felt heavy now, badly heavy.

And he was being noisy. *Crunch crunch crunch.* Each step an echoing rattle of pebbles, a splash of spray. He didn't like it, but speed mattered more. There was no way to run down a stream quietly.

So many decisions. One after the other. No time. He could do it. No time. He could make it. He could rest his mind on what mattered, on the one thing that mattered. Step after step. *Splash splash*. Knock of his heart. Rasp of his breath. His lungs stretching out again. Fine, fine. Just keep on. Birds were calling somewhere to the side. One long high clattering cackle of a shriek, a frantic warble, had set them all off. Now something was whooping too. A deep whoop that went up and up and ended in a little tail of a whistle, again and again. *Whoop whoop whoop, whistle*—like a valve blowing. The sounds overlaid each other: the clattering of the birds, and the splashing of the stream and below that a deep rumble, as of big rocks knocking against each other. He was unafraid. The famous calmness born of danger. Why was that famous? Whoever had talked about that was right. If you acted well under danger, you could do no more and were therefore calm. Yes, they might get him. They might track him and shoot him. Or worse. Somewhere soon he would have to make the decision to scramble up out of the stream. Must be mighty high at times, this river, when in spate. The bank was a good six feet. So that was the answer: wait for a low section, a gully where another stream joined it. Even if they followed him this far they would not know where he had turned.

No sooner had he thought of it than just such a side gully appeared. The stream turned a bend where he had to slide down a smooth-backed boulder and splash into a pool, deep, deeper than he expected, the brown water coming up to his chest—not that he cared about that or even noticed, he cared only to establish that his boots had landed without cracking his ankle on the ridge of some submerged rock. He was OK, he was still travelling down, already leaping to the next rock and the next, going down a stretch of ruffled water where it flowed over a pebble bed—these could be the worst, big round pebbles that wobbled like a bed of giant marbles— but he got over that too back onto a steeper fall of rocks that he could goat-jump down. At last he had learnt to move like the locals,

like Cruz and the boy, like an Andean, running so his centre of gravity hovered above the ground, and his feet and legs kept it afloat.
Then down beyond a fallen tree he saw the gully he needed, which
cut up and into the dark wood. Water, water, let it have water. He
thought he heard dogs barking. Only when he was right next to it
did he see a stream of fine white water pluming down off a table of
rock, just like he needed, into a little pool like a waist-bath.

No contact, no contact: he took a step into the bath—up to his
thigh—then reached under the layer of water flowing over the ledge
above, now at head height, and in one big heave pulled himself and
the weight of his wet pack up onto the ledge. He sat a moment, surprised to be there, with the water flowing around and over his belt.
He swung himself straight round and stood, then had to perform a
similar manoeuvre over another giant step. Then he followed the
new stream, clambering and scrambling up from rock to rock, pool
to pool. It was steeper, this one, much steeper, and he was climbing
back up against the hillside into the trees, but that was fine as long
as he was fast, fast. Now his arms ached and his thighs too, but he
pushed on through the ache. The blood jumped into his limbs and
pumped them full of a smooth strength. Suddenly there was the
smell of diesel exhaust in his nostrils but he ignored it, it wasn't possible, or was it jet fuel? But he kept going, and the roar of the other,
bigger stream he had been following became a distant sound, then
vanished, and all he could hear was the light tinkle, the rush, the
gurgle of this new stream, plashing down lightly and easily over its
rocks. He would take no chances, he would go further, until he hit
some natural obstacle where he would cut off. No, he decided, he
would press on past the next obstacle, improbably up and over it,
then cut off later. And sure enough, just as with the gully—the cards
kept coming, he was in the hand of luck and the hand remained
open—soon, at least it seemed soon, he saw a small fall ahead, similar to the tables he had just climbed, only bigger. Over one big rock a
thin sheet of white water slipped. He jumped clean across the pool
at its foot without thinking, and plunged his hands into the top of
the falls and found purchase. His right shoulder and hip knocked
heavily against the rock behind the waterfall but he clung on and

got a leg up. Water in his face, all over his arms, all over him, his clothes drenched. How lucky, he thought, he was wearing his blue shirt, something dark to blend into the shadows of the forest underworld. His cigarettes in the breast pocket would be shot to hell, you could forget about them after a run like this. The stream came down a flat stretch and abruptly changed character to lazy water running among small round rocks set in mud, with low banks of black mud. He splashed and sloshed ahead planting his feet sometimes on the little rocks like stepping stones, sometimes between them, feeling safe and sure of the footing now. The rocks were dry, and you could see on them dark lines halfway up where the water must once have reached but had not done in a long time, leaving the top halves pale and dry, chalky in the gloom under the trees.

He heard another roar, and wondered if he could somehow be approaching a big torrent. But the roar quickly grew into a clattering that came tumbling down through the trees. It was overhead. Instinctively he curled against the bank, as far under a boulder as he could get. The clattering and snarling came closer, and hovered in the treetops nearby, moved on a little then came back. It had to be a chopper. They were looking for him. Leaves and pieces of bark, twigs and beetles came hurtling down from the canopy in a roaring gale, and swept across the ground toward him in a tumult of wind. The eye of the storm moved away, and the clattering quickly faded, though the roar lingered, becoming a hum, a purr. He waited a long time, until finally he could no longer tell if he could hear it. Only then did he pick himself up.

The trees were very high. The trunks rose up bare like pillars and the ground was black, silvery in patches. The stream gurgled through the trees' vault. He sloshed a little further up the stream, then stepped out of it.

As soon as his feet hit ground, as soon as he was standing on the earth, he realised he was lost.

⁂

Lost in the cloud forest. Which way to go? It was easy to follow streams. Not so easy to wander through dark woods that never saw daylight, that sloped this way, that way, deceiving the eye into believing that a slope was a valleyside, so you would follow it down only to discover it was a hill which led to another hill.

What time was it? He guessed around noon. He looked at his watch. The face was smashed, white. That didn't surprise but alarmed him—to have instead of the blue face this shattered thing tied to his wrist. He took it off and put it in his shirt pocket, then picked out the soaked limp cigarette pack and threw it away. Then he went and retrieved it and put it back in the pocket. No traces. At least not this soon.

He might be lost but they had not found him either. If they did he was surely lost.

He had rice and some oats, he had his cooker still, though he might not dare use it. He would dare if he built a shelter of leafy branches, he decided, if he could find any leafy branches. Perhaps he could find some hollow for the night and hide himself well. The truly unfortunate thing was to have lost his compass. To have no compass here in the forest, in the land without sun—it was bad, it was deplorable.

So began his forest days, the hardest he had known.

2

Sarah, Ignacio—he would not let himself think of them.

Was it a week? He did not keep a tally, not expecting it to last so long. He had thought he would be at least down on some river by the evening of that first day or at least by mid-morning of the next. There was after all only so long you could descend in this country until you hit a river. Head east, that was all. Toward the green. Into the green. But it was not so easy. The world was so big here. One could not conceive how big it was.

Several times he considered setting off the beacon but he couldn't risk it, not in the forest. They might immediately send in a couple of F-14s to fire off their rockets to test the ground, see what came back at them. If he could find some open ground—a high ridge, or a river broad enough to part the forest—so they could see him first, then he might risk it. But where to find that?

▲

Across the black ground he went, over the silver crust of dead leaves, over the spills of small rotting red fruits half eaten by ants, by bats, by monkeys, by the quiet rodents he heard sometimes at night cracking a dead leaf, or pushing a snout under a little pile of leaves with a rustle. Waking up sodden in a sodden sleeping bag on sodden ground. He began wet and never got dry. Six days, eight, ten days, whatever it was, in the land without sky. Sometimes through the trees he'd see a green side of mountain suddenly, and think he was about to reach open ground, then obtain no further view, and backtrack till he found the same glimpse again, the same tantalising sight of topography, and slump down.

Sometimes a noise would begin overhead, like a clacking of spoons, louder and louder—you could not believe rain could be so loud. He would quicken his pace and feel his heart rise into his gorge. Then he would either reach some hollow offering an illusion of protection, or not. It made no difference anyway. Before long the big coagulated drops would find their way through the canopy, falling with cracks, then thuds, then a rhythmic drumming onto the ground all around. He would pull up the hood of his jacket and hear the drops drumming on the cloth, feel them like little pebbles, like hail, so he could hardly believe it was not hailing. Soon enough they would find their way, they always did, into his eyes, down his cheeks, down the back of his neck. The thighs of his trousers would dampen blotch by blotch, and the material would become tight and stiff, and remain that way the rest of the day. Later, when the rain stopped, he would pull on the other pair from his rucksack, but they would be wet too, sodden and stiff. He'd change anyway. (Wasn't that the point—to keep going and do what was required, though it made no sense?)

It was not pleasant to walk through the rain. You had to give yourself up to wetness, to the endless fat drops. Your breath, even in that warm latitude, appeared before you in wisps among the raindrops.

On the first day he traversed the hillside a long time, keeping at the same height, pacing among the trees in the gloom. After he had travelled what he guessed to be six or seven miles he stopped, removed his backpack and sifted through its wet contents. Once he paused, thinking he heard the bark of a dog, waited, listening into the stillness between the callings of a bird which was singing a three-note scale. It would sing the little tune, wait a moment, then sing it again. Once, from far away the same call came back faintly. The bird stopped singing for a while. Some animal let out a *chip-chip-chip* like a chisel on wood, then fell silent. He couldn't tell if it was a bird or an insect or something else.

He was tired. He had got his breath back but fatigue engulfed his brain. His boots were heavy as rocks. He looked around for some clue to where he was. A slope of broadly spaced forest extended in all directions. It was like waking up in some subterranean ruin, a giant temple of grey pillars, grey floor, grey diffused light, grey ceiling, the ossified ruin of a city that had been destroyed by ash. Like standing a hundred feet below ground in the world's grave.

He sat down. The ground was dry. The layer of big silver leaves like some stiff ancient quilt gave beneath him with a series of reluctant crackles. He leaned back till the weight of the backpack eased off his shoulders.

He rose from an oceanic sleep through an emptiness of consciousness into the grey world. A sleep so profound he felt he had been to another world. At first he thought it must be dawn—the grey light in the woods seemed young and nascent—and that he had slept right through from the previous afternoon. But it could equally have been evening. Perhaps he had had one of those brief lapses into exhaustion that felt infinite.

He pulled out his watch, poked out the crumbs of broken glass, wound it. The hands said one-fifteen, which surely could not be right. He would have to wait till dusk, set them for six and see what happened. He held it to his ear. No ticking, but he wasn't sure that all modern watches did tick.

He extricated his arms from the shoulder straps of the pack. A shock of pain seized his right shoulder, made him cry out. He bent forward on his knees and vomited—a heave and groan that produced nothing but a dark string.

His shirt stuck tightly to his breastbone. He felt something was stuck to his cheek, and kept wiping at it but found nothing there although the sensation remained. At least his throat wasn't too bad. The tape had held, and he had more of it if needed.

The old bones of the thunder, its bare elbow bones, unfolded in slow motion.

All day the second day he walked through a thunderstorm. It was a lazy sleepy storm which must have spread itself over a wide area and grown incapable of moving on. The rain came and went. The thunder would forget about itself for half an hour, then remember its task and roll over in the sky sending down cracks and groans of trouble as it did so.

Jackson walked and walked. At first his legs were very stiff, and his shoulder throbbed with each step. He checked it as well as he could, and thought it wasn't broken or dislocated, just sprained. Dark bruises had appeared on his skin overnight. The hardest thing was getting the sleeping bag out of its bag, then packing it away in the morning. Inserting his arms into the straps of his rucksack made him sweat with pain. Once it was on it didn't feel so bad.

Jackson tried to make a compass out of a needle he found in a side pocket of his pack. He unstitched a piece of thread from the frayed flap and magnetised the needle with the magnetic handle of his dead torch and tied it to the thread. He propped both elbows on his knees, held one hand in the other for maximum stillness, and watched the thread unspiral itself. The knot needed sliding up then down. It kept unbalancing itself. Finally it held, and slowly turned this way and that like an eye searching for its home. Jackson stopped the slow rotation with a fingertip, then let it travel whichever way it wanted.

The needle ended up pointing the same way twice, and having no better guide he decided to accept this as north. As far as he could make out, he must have got himself into the next valley system to the north of Choctamal. The Marañón canyon must be to his west, travelling northward for another fifty miles until it elbowed over to the east. If he headed east, he ought by rights to work his way down into the valley of the Tingo and the Chachapoyas road which could surely not be more than seventy or eighty miles away.

But it was hard to keep the direction true. He made his way diagonally down the slope of the forest, and after an hour or so reached a creek. He followed the stream down as it ran toward what he thought was east. But when he checked the needle again, it seemed he was travelling either south or even north but not east.

He gave up on it, and resolved to continue only downward. Eventually the stream, which he kept to his left walking on the smooth slope above the bank, would have to join a bigger stream, then that too in its turn would join something larger. Sooner or later he would surely find himself on the bank of a river wide enough to permit a gap in the forest, and he would be able to wait there till evening or morning, when he might get enough of a glimpse of the sun to determine east or west.

All day he followed the same stream until he no longer noticed its long gradual turns around the invisible shapes of the hills.

In the evening he heated a pan of water on the kerosene stove and made a cup of tea. As he held the pan in front of his face, fine lines of light appeared along the edges of his fingers, lighting up like traces of yellow paint. He noticed them with mild pleasure, bent toward the cup and blew, making the dark surface tremble.

Sunlight. Sunlight on his hand. He looked around frantically before it disappeared, saw no trace of the sun anywhere, not a

wink. Meanwhile the light vanished from his fingers. He resumed
the same posture, elbows on knees, cup in hand, and rocked gently
back and forth until, suddenly, the sides of his fingers were illuminated. Immediately he leaned forward, moving back and forth
until he felt the sunlight on one eye. He squinted and turned
slowly, unable to work out where it was coming from, assuming
that it would be from his left, where he believed west to be.
Instead, the tiny chink of light came from behind his right shoulder. He saw it, a star in the gloom of the forest, weaving rays along
his eyelashes, and touching a tree here and there with a ripple of
light. The forest seemed to come to life, an entirely different place
now, as if all it had been waiting for in its slumber was the kiss of
light. Like a man in the desert longing for water, he yearned for
more light. He moved his head, passing the balm to his other eye.
Immediately the chink closed. He couldn't find it again. He stood,
then squatted and moved from side to side trying to find it, but it
was gone. But where he was looking was indubitably west. West
close to the opposite of where he had thought it to be. It was hard
to heave the conception round in his mind. It meant that the
stream he was following flowed not east at all but south-west. He
had spent a day travelling south-west, back into the mountains.

It made no sense. All streams round here went east.

He tried out his makeshift compass again. The needle twice indicated that north was east, once that it was west. The thing was useless. He tied the thread to the branch of a bush and left it there to
sort itself out, then set his watch for six, just in case it decided to
work.

Jackson had with him a plastic bag of oats and one of yellowish
rice, each the size of a deflated football, and one large white onion.
He'd lost his machete but had his pocketknife, and imagined he
might possibly find a way of killing something to eat—maybe a fish
or a wounded bird or a small mammal—if he could somehow trap
or spring on one like Cruz had done.

While he was cooking three palmfuls of rice with a quarter of
the onion sliced into the boiling foamy water the camping stove
ran out of kerosene. He pumped the pump, then picked it up with

his shirt cuffs and shook it. It gave out a faint metallic tinging, like in a broken light bulb—as if a grain of sand were running around within the metal walls.

It didn't matter. At least he still had matches, the local matches made of wax paper which struck well and didn't mind damp. And he was in a forest. A little later he had a fire going, made of dry twigs, and long, thin boughs that he found under a thick bush and broke up.

Oats in the morning, rice in the evening. But how much to eat? How many days should he ration for? He guessed on a week at the outside. He needed to eat enough not to be clawed by hunger. If he kept east from now on then surely he would hit the Tingo in a matter of two or three days.

That night the worst thunderstorm arrived. It brooded right over his tent. He dreamt of a man snoring. The sleeper guzzled his snores, and crackled them out. Jackson emerged into wakefulness and the crackles came too, and he realised they were real. He sat bolt upright, grabbed his knife, heart thumping, before he understood what it was. But the fear never left him.

It was a strange storm. All night it hovered over him, never travelling more than a few miles away. For a while it would slumber, then a peal of thunder would turn over like a question in the sky's mind. Then more quiet, then a distant answering rumble from far away, as if the rags of storm called to one another across the mountains. As if the giants had decided to slide down their beanstalks and lie for the night on the forest canopy.

Jackson lay on his back waiting for sleep to return, for the fear to loosen up. He told himself he didn't need to be afraid, certainly not of a storm in the night, until one of the giants guzzled a few more snores, smacked his lips and settled down. The trees flickered like a neon bulb trying to illuminate itself. Jackson's body went taut again. For a long time he waited in the quiet between the peals hoping he had heard the last of it, only to be disappointed by a long gurgle, a soft detonation in the distance. He felt like whimpering, his boyhood upon him again.

The rain arrived in an even hiss and he thought that might mean the end of the thunder, but it didn't.

He awoke to a morning of dripping forest. He looked up and could barely make out the leaves above. Eighty, a hundred feet up, mist hung among the branches. One way, up the hill, the mist lowered itself from the branches and closed off the view altogether.

The music of the water was all-pervading—the flutes and guitars, the xylophone of the water running over rocks. He first noticed it in the morning, when he peed, when the forest was grey as an old man's beard, and it seemed to groan at being awake again, filled with the reluctant duty of day. His own stream played a scale as it plopped into a pool. The birds wove a tapestry overhead out of their threads of song.

He searched, but found no dry wood for a fire. He ate a slice of onion for breakfast, and drank two cupfuls of stream water. It was a risk not to boil it first, but he couldn't do that now and he had to drink.

He struck uphill away from the stream. All morning he climbed, finally reaching a pass, except *pass* was hardly the word for the gradual flattening of the hillside.

Once he thought he was walking along a path, which at first reassured then alarmed him. He swung off it, keeping to what he guessed was north-east. He considered going back and waiting at the pass till nightfall in order to get another take at west from its vantage, but couldn't be sure he would be able to see the sun even from there, and preferred to press on.

Later he came upon a ring of stones. They could not have been there long, because no vegetation had grown over them; then he wondered if they had been there for centuries, their baldness preserved by the lightless forest. The circle, a few feet wide, was too broad to have been used as a fire-pit and, anyway, there was no sign of ash. Yet someone had arranged them. To what end? Who? When? It could have been that morning, last week or a thousand years ago. He stepped impulsively into the little circle, feeling anxiously that someone might be so close, that he was perhaps not alone. Then he reflected how ancient the stones might be and felt better for a moment, then afraid again, feeling himself suddenly close to ancient, unknown people. His own day had retreated. He was adrift in time. Who were they? Was it possible they still had living, unknown descendants?

Jackson heard a slight crack. He spun round. Something streaked up a tree so fast he never saw what it was.

Evening never came. On and on he went down through the gloom, sometimes under a thick roof of leaves and boughs, sometimes under a dismal ceiling of cloud. The clouds rested among the twigs while they decided where to go next. They were like lost souls wandering the mountains no longer knowing what they were looking for. Like him. He asked himself what had happened to his sense of purpose, and didn't know the answer, except that it had gone, replaced by constant dim worry. How had this happened? He was no longer advancing but escaping, no longer hopeful but fearful, no longer in control of himself. His legs pumped and pumped and got hotter and wetter within the sleeves of his trousers, and he feared more and more until finally he hit the floor of fear. Once, he dropped to the ground, not knowing he was going to do so until he did. He curled up and lay still, hugging his knees.

The only man in the cloud forest.

3

When he looked up, a forest rodent was standing a few yards off, driven close by curiosity. When he lifted his head, it moved across the ground like thread in a sewing machine, then stopped like a sculpture of a cat, nose in the air, make-up round its eyes, and stared at him.

Jackson stood and it flowed away like quicksilver.

That day he made camp early. Time dragged and more rain fell. Finally dark arrived. He tried once more to get a fix on west and failed, then tried to get a fire going, ripping damp bark off twigs and dead branches in order to get at the dry wood within, but he couldn't get the flames to take. Meanwhile his only candle was a tiny stub with just a prick of wick left, and he thought he should keep it for a time of greater need. His torch gave out a dull yellow glow, its battery partially revived, he didn't know why.

He ate the rest of his onion, and lay down in his sleeping bag.

Rain came again during the night, and more thunder ricocheted around the hills.

In the morning he couldn't remember where he was. He headed off downhill for a while then wondered if that was right and decided to go back uphill, then changed his mind again, and continued downward.

He tired soon and heavily. All the more reason to go downhill. He struck a stream bloated with clay-red water and followed it all day. It took him to a burial ground of some animal. He could smell it before he finally reached the littering of furry bodies almost blended into the leaves of the floor. They had congregated to die, or been massacred. He couldn't see what kind of animal they were until he turned one over with a stick and was greeted with a small man's face and saw then the small black human hands: monkeys.

There was something hard in his pocket. He had lost his backpack now, it was in his past, but it seemed he had taken some things out of it. He had that hard thing in his trousers. He remembered what it was but couldn't remember putting it there. It would help him, he felt that. How did he know? He couldn't remember. It would say hello, and they would come and find you. They'd send over a fixed-wing or a chopper to see where you were, and if they saw you they'd get you and bring you back to camp. If they didn't see you there was no telling what they might do. It was important they could see you.

A river was what he needed. To keep going down until he

reached a river big enough to part the forest, open up the sky. He'd get away from the tree cover maybe onto a sandbank, if the river was running low. If he could find a sandbank. He'd swim to it and set it off there, then lie back in the sunshine and wait.

The thought of sunshine was overwhelming. It was like a drink, a cool orangeade with misty ice cubes bobbing in it. He would lie back and his whole body would drink in the sun, up and down his limbs, through his chest.

That was all he needed: a river.

The stream went on and on. Around every bend he expected it to join another, bigger torrent, but it never did. The birds whooped demonically all around. Once a flock of parakeets came flying and screeching at him. They flapped around him and he covered his head in his arms, though they never hurt him. A sudden rainfall silenced them and he escaped; although he wished for company it was not theirs.

Mosquitoes whined around his ears. It's their home, he told himself, this is their home. There were clouds of them sometimes. He ran awkwardly on, his paces thumping through his body, shaking his bones. All water flowed down, and down had to end up being east.

Then a troupe of elfin monkeys were running along beside him, tiny strange fluid creatures that were not afraid of him. They bared their teeth and let out screeching barks. There must have been thirty of them or more, and at first they seemed merely moving parts of the forest floor, dark shapes that flowed along beside him born of the leaves.

He shouted at them and waved his arms as much as his sore shoulder would allow, but they only screeched the more.

※

It must have been the fourth or fifth day, he no longer knew, when he found himself in a stretch of forest where the ground was not level, but rose and fell in mounds and dykes covered in creepers. He had been walking through them for a while before he saw the unevenness. It unnerved him.

He didn't recognise them at first—the undulations and hillocks—and went along flatter stretches, straight ways the width of a car, before he realised what he had been walking among, and for how long. He looked around and clambered on top of a loose mound of rubble covered in growth.

It was strange how young the vegetation seemed to be—not the thick layer of old growth that five or six hundred years would generate in the Old World. From on top of a mound, he saw he was in a vast pavilion, a mosque of lofty bare pillars, reaching on and on as far as you could see, a flatland of grey columns. And the ground, also grey as far as he could see, was all chopped up with dips and furrows and lines of old walls, and here and there some tall corner of masonry that had survived. There was no telling how big the area could be. It had to be a city. An old city untouched, collapsed but intact, which the forest had descended on like a shroud.

He got down on his knees and saw among the creeper stems something hard and pale and flat. He felt and found a crack at the edge of it. It was straight and went on. He stood and followed it. There were others. Beneath the ground cover was a network of these straight cracks. It was as if the foliage lifted now and he could see everything under it: a great field of smooth paving stones spread all across the floor of the forest.

What time of day was it? What day was it? What was day? He had no idea. His first thought was to find a mound to crawl into and sleep. For two nights, maybe more, he had been sleeping without his bag.

He woke to dim light. Dawn or dusk. He would know in five minutes.

Must have been dawn. He dozed again.

Next time he woke he heard paper rustling nearby. He looked round. A grey monkey was sitting on the ground with its fingers inside a red fruit. It pulled them out, coated in sweet slime, and licked them, staring at him. Then it let out a plaintive whimper and hopped onto him.

He lay still as the monkey settled itself on his chest, curling its tail round its own neck like a scarf, and rested its head on his shoulder. He didn't move, but raised a hand slowly toward it, touching the back of its neck. It rolled onto its back and took hold of his hand and stared at his palm for a long time. He took one of its black hands in his, tiny, soft, leathery, and inspected its deep creases.

The monkey rubbed its little face and stretched out on his belly, staring up at him with its ancient black eyes as big as cherries. A curious, charmed old face looking up from immemorial time at the lost man.

When Jackson got up, the monkey scampered off and squatted a few feet away with its head in its hands, as if destitute. Jackson stooped and lowered his hand as if he had something in it, and the creature at once scuttled up his arm and wrapped itself round his neck. Wherever he was going, it wanted to come too.

He walked among the ruins for hours. Here and there he tried to pull away the creepers from large mounds which must have been pyramids, but they were too strong for him. Once he found himself in a room, unable to remember how he had entered it. It had a floor of black earth which he picked carefully through not sure what he was looking for.

Outside there were moths flying about, little silver ones like paper and giant black ones with furry antennae and cloak-like wings. They flew in daylight through the gloom of the old city. At night they vanished and the fireflies came out. Clouds of them, constellations that showed themselves, switching on like fairy lights, then vanishing and reappearing in different shapes—fickle, shifting stars of the forest.

Several times he passed a pair of large stone walls draped in lianas, with the smooth and intricate stonework visible beneath.

Somewhere in the city the monkey remembered itself and left.

When light came again into the doorway of the room he was in, he didn't rise to meet it. A square of dimness. The dimness was called light. All things moved to the light. He must get up and move too.

In his pocket was a handful of grains. Hard grains. He picked out a few and put them in his mouth and crunched them.

Later he found himself at a stream, drinking, his face in a gush of brown water. His stomach began to hurt badly. It tightened itself into a knot, and the knot made his head spin. His stomach heaved and a spill of white and yellow flecks appeared on the water in front of his knees.

4

Dark again. A moth had landed on his cheek and was hanging there. A giant moth with wings of velvet. He could feel it adjust its footing on his skin. Cool little feet.

Then a firefly chose him and beamed right in his eye. The ground began to rock gently, as if some being had taken hold of the forest floor and were moving it to and fro, back and forth, lulling him, making him go to sleep.

Another day, another friend. This one lying at the foot of a tree, dressed in rags, his teeth shining and his skull still pale. His hadn't browned like the other skulls. And it had hair on it, rusty-coloured, a reddish-silver necklace round the neckbones and the remains of a khaki shirt. Jackson could still make out the pocket sewn on the shirt.

It was quiet there. All the trees seemed extra tall, and very still.

So he wasn't the only man in the forest after all.

Tropical issue, that shirt, a voice said. Just the stuff for here. Lasted two years in the damp. Anyway, Sinbad, you get yourself going. You don't want to hang about here. I only did because the damn old leg went and broke on me. But you, look at you. Don't hang about now. You've got a way to go.

He began to feel immensely tall as he walked, as though he were wearing twelve-foot stilts or had become a stick man. The feeling was pleasant, but he felt he might topple at any moment and fall as straight as one of the tree trunks to the ground. He had to be very careful not to lose his balance.

Later, the ground trembled silently. It created a pleasant tingle through his body, so gentle it couldn't have been an earthquake.

He heard the hum of an engine, like the hum of a lawnmower in the summer suburbs. A road, there must be a road nearby. Where was the sound coming from? He couldn't tell. He stumbled forward, stopped, listened again, thought the road could only be ahead, down at the bottom of the valley. He lurched again, perhaps he could cut the vehicle off in time. Then he sank to his knees, confused, understanding without knowing he understood that what he was hearing must be high overhead, far above the trees. A twin-engine with two humming props.

A small man was walking at his side now. Very small, not more than the height of Jackson's chest. He had a cream-coloured hat pulled low over his eyes, and wore stiff pantaloons and a dirty poncho. The man didn't talk but walked briskly. Once he approached him and touched his hand and said: *Señor*. Nothing more.

His voice was high and clear.

Jackson remembered trying to ask the little man a question but the words wouldn't come. He was too tired to talk. Then he was too tired to walk.

His last memory was of the little man crouching nearby. Behind him a tremendous hillside carpeted in lustrous green shone and shivered. A tree flickered all over, a million lights flickering on and off. He couldn't remember why but knew he had a great reason to be happy. Something had pinned his shoulder down which made no sense if he were standing up. But he wasn't standing up. Then he was standing up, then he wasn't. A voice of thunder unfurled in his ear, and a sound of water rushed in on him.

I'm dying, he thought. That would be the right thing. I need to die now, this is the right conclusion. It seemed natural and obvious.

Sparks from the flickering tree bloomed and floated free like seeds. One of them landed right on his heart, and his heart lit up like fire. All he needed had always been right to hand. Every last molecule of the world was made of exactly the same stuff as he was, these floating sparks, he could not have been in a safer place.

15 · Consular II

1

Sarah's favourite spot on the farm was the doorstep outside her room, a broad piece of warped, shiny wood just wide enough to sit on. From it she could see most of the main house, and the huts for the goats and cows. She'd sit there when she had finished helping Nellie teach the kids. She was doing basic biology for them. Cells and reproduction. Respiration and ingestion. What it meant for something to be alive. (Is a stone alive? she'd ask. *Yes!* the kids would cry. A mountain? There'd be a pause, then little Juan pronouncing: *No, it's too big.* What about a tree? And so on.)

Jackson had said he'd be gone ten days at most.

At first there was the mix of pain and sweetness of missing someone. She didn't know how much she really loved him—or knew him, for that matter—but the whole natural reproductive process had kicked in. Every cell in her body longed for him. For the sound of his voice, the touch of his skin. She went through her days in a state of latent arousal, which sometimes converted into extreme sensitivity. She would notice little things the children did, and feel intensely grateful—how beautiful they were, how innocent, how alert. And she would notice acts of kindness, and be overwhelmed at the generosity of people. Then she'd wonder if old feelings for Hayden were reviving, now she'd been intimate with another man. She had roamed back to the shore of romantic feeling. She had never really mourned the end of her relationship with him, there was all this old attachment to work through, compounded with the new one forming. If it was forming. Perhaps it was also anxiety over that: was something serious starting? She felt she might want that, but did she really? Was it so potent merely because uncertain?

While she was teaching, Ignacio never said anything at first. But gradually he became less shy, and sometimes offered a comment, always so quietly that she would have to ask him to repeat it. Whatever it was, it would show that he had been thinking and trying to understand what they'd been talking about. She'd see him sitting on the floor with a toy radio, or with the building blocks Alfredo had made out of different kinds of local wood, so they ranged in colour from yellow to grey-blue to crimson, or with a crayon and a sheet of paper in front of him. All these things were new to him, and his curiosity gradually overcame his reticence.

She began to worry about Jackson. By the end of the second week she could no longer sit quietly on her doorstep. She couldn't sit anywhere. She started sleeping less and less. A few days on, she was sure something had happened to him. It had already been too long.

Alfredo told her to wait, they must just wait. There was nothing else they could do. It was inconceivable they go looking for him. If they did, they would surely neither of them get out alive. He had a large family to look after, he couldn't take the risk of going over the pass. And she was his niece. If anything happened to her his brother would never forgive him.

The one person she could think of turning to was Padre Beltrán. She thought somehow he might be able to help. He would have an idea what to do. At least he might be able to reassure her, calm her down.

Just wait, my dear, Alfredo said. All things come to one who waits. He is a competent young man. I have confidence in him. So she had waited another day.

Then one morning there'd been no sign of Ignacio. His bed had been neatly made, and he, his cat and his bag had all vanished. On top of everything else.

Somehow she was convinced he must have gone back to town, to Beltrán's. In case things didn't work out for him here she had been telling him now and then that he should think about staying with Beltrán just for a while if he needed to, how valuable a good education would be. She had mentioned it just in case, and partly so he didn't feel trapped here. Now she wished she had kept her mouth shut.

She waited another day, and another, to see if Ignacio would come back.

At the end of a night of not sleeping at all, relieved to see dawn arrive at last, she decided she had to do something; she could wait around no longer. No sooner did she realise that, and that she wanted to go to Beltrán, than she was packing a bag, and waking Alfredo to tell him she was leaving for the town.

She didn't walk, she ran back down the mountains. Instead of the usual twelve hours it took her only the morning to reach Tingo. Uncle Alfredo wouldn't believe it when he heard, she thought to herself: Chachapoyas in a single day. Tingo by lunchtime, where she was all set to hire a truck for herself straight away, if she had to. But she found a market truck packed and ready to go. The back was full of sacks of oranges, and about seventeen Indian women. The driver was just turning the key to start off. He said if she could find a space she could come.

It was better to be moving. The daydreams stopped, the ones where she didn't exactly see Jackson, but saw some crashing river in the forest and knew he was there, nearby. There'd be a horrible sense of danger and menace.

As soon as she walked up the rickety stairs and into Padre Beltrán's kitchen that night she burst into tears. The padre pulled her into his arms, and she pressed her face into his warm bulk. She felt his thick hand on her head, stroking her.

Now, now. Tell me what this is all about.

She heard his voice buzzing deep in his chest.

She started to talk and heard her own voice getting thinner and thinner. She wanted to stop, and cry more, it was hard not to, but she found a way to press on. She told him everything she could think of, getting scared again as she did so.

I just know something has happened to him.

The padre said, All things can be worked out. We can work something out.

It was then that she asked herself clearly for the first time: Why do I care so much? I've only known him a few weeks.

Standing in the padre's kitchen with the dark town outside, in that brightly lit room she'd been in a few weeks ago with Jackson, it hit her. Clarity welled up, a newness in the world. It was as if the room and the town, everything became new. She knew then that she didn't just want to find Jackson. She wanted to be with him. She didn't know for how long, or how exactly. But she had decided. Was it crazy? Then she'd rather be crazy, like the songs said. Before, she'd have thought it was all just another trick of the genes, a means of ensuring their own continuance, but it wasn't. She knew that now. She understood herself like never before, as though her whole nature was laid bare, just because of knowing that she wanted to be with that lost man.

Alas he is not the only one who is missing, Beltrán said.

What do you mean? And just then she remembered that she had not yet mentioned Ignacio.

But before she could say anything, Beltrán sighed, pressed his fist to his lips, and his words tumbled out: I don't know how it happened but he's gone. One morning, I call him to breakfast and he does not come, I call and I call, finally I go in the bedroom, and that woven bag he has hanging from a nail, it has gone. I look all around, I tell the boys to go and search for him, then I find he has taken some bread, and the little cat is gone too. Then I knew. I have been asking all over town, and no one has seen him. One woman in the market thought she saw him getting into a truck. If that is true then we may have lost him forever, I am afraid.

Sarah stared at him as he spoke, and couldn't seem to find a pause in which to interrupt him. Eventually he slowed down, and she said: I'm sorry, I should have said, he's with us. I'm so sorry. I mean, he was with us. He came up to my uncle's all by himself. But now he's gone again. I was hoping he'd come back here.

Beltrán's eyes were more shadowed than usual. He shook his head. Here? We have seen nothing of him since he left. I'm sorry too. I have let you down. I don't operate a prison. It has never happened before. I always try to make it so they want to stay. I mean, why keep them, if they are not happy here? He took some *dulce de leche* too, and I think a plastic water bottle. Who knows, perhaps he was planning to try to go home, wherever that is. If he even knows.

Sarah touched the padre's hand. It's not your fault. Obviously. And you know, he's a pretty amazing kid. I mean, he got all the way to Uncle Alfredo's alone. He says he knows how to feed himself in the forest.

Beltrán was silent again. We have to think, he said. He filled a pan and lit his stove, then pulled out a chair for her and they sat together at the table. With Ignacio we can only hope, and ask around. But with the young Englishman, perhaps someone might be able to help.

Sarah wondered if they should approach the police captain, the one she'd met in the café, who had offered to help if they ever needed it.

But Beltrán wasn't so keen on that. He frowned and said, That might be out of the frying pan and into the fire. I wouldn't trust him an inch. No, no.

Beltrán stared at the table a moment. An official of some kind, but someone outside it all. But who? And how? Anyway, what do you think might have happened? Perhaps he is on the trail of some great archaeological find, and can't turn back.

She shook her head. It's been too long. He promised. Either he's totally lost in the forest. I mean, that could happen. Especially as he was going into these remote parts where no one lives—

Certainly.

Or else he's fallen in with some of these drug traffickers or whatever, and can't get away. Or, or something else. She stopped.

I know, I know, Beltrán said. And the important thing is to know. To know which. *Ay.* I was not firm enough. I should have forbidden him to go.

Everyone was telling him he shouldn't. But how was anyone supposed to stop him?

The pan behind her was sizzling but Beltrán didn't seem about to do anything about it, so she got up to switch off the flame. There was a bottle of black coffee essence standing beside the stove. She unscrewed the top.

Coffee?

He sighed again. Please, please. There's milk on the shelf.

An inverted saucer covered the top of a can of condensed milk. And cups by the sink.

It was when she lifted the hot mug to her lips that she thought of the man at the British consulate in the northern city, who had been friendly to her and the Australian girl when they'd gone in one morning. He had given Sarah his card, and she still had it somewhere. At least she thought she did.

She told Beltrán. He is a Brit after all. Maybe they'll try to help.

He shrugged. That sounds like an idea, he said, rather glumly. He seemed to have plunged into an uncharacteristic despondency. Not that it will help us with Ignacio.

Ignacio knows how to look after himself. Honestly, my guess is he'll be OK. I just hope we hear from him again, that's all.

Beltrán nodded. Well, at least let us see if we can track down one of them.

She said to wait while she ran to look for the card in her bag, which she'd left at the hotel. She had taken a room there before coming over. She prayed the card might still be somewhere in her bag. She didn't remember throwing it out, that was all she could be sure of.

Beltrán's face quivered a little, oddly. The phone here, they won't come and repair it, he said. I'm sorry, I have given up trying to get them to. We'll have to go to the *kiosko.*

She was already through the door. I'll meet you there, she called back from the staircase, taking it two at a time.

2

The shower gave out a spindly spray of half-warm water. When Brown reached up to adjust the nozzle he got an electric shock. How the hell did people live here? And why? Normally you could count on the weather to be warm at this time of year, yet it was cold, cold in the town, cold inside the hotel, and cold even in the bathroom, which was a cubicle of ravaged brown walls whose tin door fastened with a twist of wire. It had warped so badly a chilly draught came under it, so taking a shower was anything but the chance to relax he'd hoped for. And the hotel had two stars. It was the best in town.

Brown had been in a bad mood all afternoon. The first thing that had set it off was to have had to come to this bleak little mountain town at all. Then he had discovered a pair of American anthropologists dutifully camped in the hotel, conducting "phase two" of their fieldwork right here in town. Shouldn't you be off in the back of beyond, in the jungle or up in the sierras? he had asked. And they had responded with some sanctimoniousness about human anthropology—a tautology surely, he'd thought—concerning itself with everywhere, not just so-called simpler societies.

So not only were you no longer allowed to say *primitive*, *simple* wasn't OK either. Though that was not what had disturbed him. Rather it was the notion that anywhere was a fit subject for anthropology. Anthropology was supposed to be about the exotic. If everywhere was exotic then nowhere was. And if nowhere was, then how could a man who had made it his mission to live elsewhere, beyond the reach of home, remain safe? So the shower with its forked fistule of thin spray, and its little canister heater that didn't work, and the man who had installed it—even they were presumably fit subjects for an anthropological monograph. Then why not Brown himself? The anthropology of a disgruntled diplomat.

He unwrapped a fiddly bar of soap as small as a butter pat and attempted to work up a lather in an armpit. There wasn't enough water. He raised his arm and tried to insert it in the tepid stream. The plumbing hiccupped, the metal heater let out a trembling hum and the temperature leapt by forty degrees. By the time he withdrew his arm, whipped and welted, it was too late: he was scalded.

In disgust he turned off the stopcock, getting another tingle of a shock, and began to dry himself with the rag they had given him.

His room was a tiled tomb with a bed so soft it bottomed out when he rolled over.

He dislodged the towel from his waist and commenced to masturbate half-heartedly. What else was there to do? Outside in the gathering night the hills were black as iron. Upon them, hidden in their gullies and coves, were the little mud homes of the Indians. Thin patches of grass grew where the skinny goats and llamas grazed, and the Indians scraped out patches for corn and potatoes in the thin soil with their machetes, from which they made their staple: freeze-dried potatoes. You could see them out in the fields, old barefoot women trampling the tubers into pulp then leaving them as broken white carpets to crystallise in each night's frost, and crumble in each day's sun. Of all things to eat. There was something so helpless about allowing even your food to be beaten to a pulp by the elements.

The thought of the black world outside killed his well-worn fantasies. A man his age needed a helping hand.

However, there was at least one good thing about having come here. Whether he could possibly fulfil his mission he doubted, but in a way that might not matter. He had travelled to the mountain town on what was at worst a whim, at second worst a job, but at best an almost heroic quest. He was trying to help someone. Two people really. But especially one. It was an act of chivalry, more or less. Except perhaps it wasn't after all; perhaps it was desperation, or fantasy, or plain foolishness.

He'd taken the call two days ago at the consulate. He couldn't have got here any quicker.

You won't remember me, she'd said in her breathy, warm, American drawl.

And he had known immediately who it was. That in itself had seemed extraordinary, a kind of omen.

Yes? he'd answered tentatively.

I was in the embassy about a month ago? Six weeks ago?

He didn't correct her, tell her it was not in fact an embassy.

You gave me your card? I told you I was going to Chachapoyas, and you said to call if I needed any help or anything?

Yes? he said. Then he added: I'm terribly sorry, just remind me . . .

Why couldn't he just be straight and honest like her? Why wrap himself in lies and disguises? Why be complicated?

I was with my friend Daphne. And I told you my uncle lives near Tingo.

Yes, yes, of course.

Then he had had to act out having his memory jogged, realising that of course, yes of course he remembered her. He was really no good at acting. At least it had been a phone call rather than in person so she couldn't actually see how bad he was at it. He sensed somehow that she guessed that he was being dishonest.

This friend of mine, he's a British citizen; I think he's got into trouble. He was looking for some old ruins.

And it all came pouring out. He could hear a quiver in her voice at the end of each sentence, and sometimes in the middle. Once the line went quiet for a moment, and he heard a faint liquid sound, then she sniffed.

The judge. Right away he thought of Judge Montoya—the judge in Chachapoyas that the German down on the coast had put him in theoretical contact with weeks ago. If the young fool was still alive, the judge would be the man to ascertain whether Carreras had him, and if so might be induced to keep him safe, and ultimately release him.

He had set off right away. Why, he wondered now as he lay on the lumpy, sagging bed in the lousy hotel in the cold town. The

267

answer was obvious: to see her. It wasn't every day you met someone who aroused such feelings in you.

He had thought about her many times over the previous weeks.
It was mad, of course; they'd only talked together for a quarter of
an hour. Yet he'd felt her eye looking into his and understanding
him. Something had happened. She had penetrated his consciousness in some peculiar way, which was why he kept thinking of her.
And now this: sure enough, she had tracked him down and sum-
moned him. So maybe it wasn't mad, but a mystery, a beautiful
mystery. When he had hung up the phone on that otherwise dreary
morning, he had found himself suddenly wide awake, trembling,
already thinking about what he would need to pack, and for how
long, and what exactly he would say to the under-secretary this
time about his need to absent himself.

It was she who had given him the name of the hotel. He'd
expected to find a note from her waiting for him at reception, but
there hadn't been one. He'd managed to get here a day early. Five
hours he'd already been in town, and no sign of her. He didn't
know where to look. However, he'd made contact with Judge Montoya, and would be seeing him later. Soon, in fact. A drink in the
bar, then he'd be off down the cold streets in search of him. If only
he could keep out of the way of the anthropologists.

He couldn't. They were in the hotel's little bar, a bamboo kiosk at
the side of the lobby done up to look tropical. He sat on a stool and
ordered a pisco sour with a beer back as the Americans called it.

Had a good afternoon?

He spun round. It was the woman anthropologist. She was smiling at him, a smug, self-satisfied smile. Her long straight hair, her
placid well-fed face irritated him. It was too broad, too happy; she
had had too easy a life. He could see it all over her. Here she was,
down from the Midwest, from some sunny dull place, and now she
had a grant and was able to come and spread her milk-soft goodwill about the globe, and perhaps take a message or two back
home about peasant values and natural parturition, that kind of
thing.

But you felt her goodwill. It was almost nice. He only just managed to suppress a smile.

All right, I suppose, he said. And you?

Immediately he regretted asking. He got a full dose of her delight at how well her project was going. On and on she went in her calm and agreeable voice.

· Then the man came along, bearded and serious, dressed in a climber's fleece and big boots. He had a toothy mouth. When he smiled his lips contorted in a sneer.

They were from Indiana: no surprise. It was an advantage to be a "mixed-sex" team. They hoped to submit their theses in tandem.

Your what? he asked, having misheard.

Our theses.

Excellent. Oh good, said Brown. Good for you. He said all the right things. What he was wondering was whether the woman had a big bottom—he hadn't had a chance to see—and if he could conceivably find a way of incorporating her into a fantasy. A broad pale behind, a tuft of light-brown curls, and himself bouncing against smooth midwestern buttocks. Old habits died hard, he thought with an inward smile, and let the vision go, remembering again who he would be seeing soon.

He nodded and said, Yes, yes, then realised she was asking him a question. He let out a good-humoured laugh. Oh me, I'm just on business, nothing much. Nothing half as exciting as you.

That was the stuff, turn on a bit of the old British charm. Something they'd never get in solemn Indiana.

It worked, sort of. The girl's face opened in a beaming smile.

We're looking at patterns of distribution of cultural capital, the man informed him.

Brown nodded. Then he asked: Cultural capital?

In towns like this culture is an asset. It's capital.

Oh God, thought Brown. Still, you had to take your hat off to the man for his faith in the so-called social sciences.

The little acculturated Indian behind the bar in his jeans and T-shirt and woven Andean waistcoat asked if they needed *algo*, anything.

The Americans both sent him a smile. Politeness was presumably cultural currency. He saw now that beneath his wispy beard the man was just a boy, a kid. Kids were taking over the world. Staffing the universities, running the businesses, making the money. He had actually got used to it, to ageing. There was only one answer: get on and have kids yourself. Sometimes he used to think the answer might be to do it randomly. Plug someone like this girl, for example.

Brown ordered himself a second round, and after much persuasion got them one too which he knew they didn't really want, and the forcing on them of which was therefore a minor victory, a small triumph over the featureless spreading of the blandest empire the world had ever known.

Then out, into the blackest mountain night.

Here and there a cock crowed invisibly. The odd dog skulked along the gutters. The houses all seemed shut up tight against the world. There was nothing happening, which might be helpful: no one about, no one to notice him. Except to think in these terms was to flatter himself that what he was doing was the least bit important.

Such a strange coincidence, he reflected: this young Englishman bringing him and her together. How did she know Small, he wondered. And what did she know of him? Presumably more than he himself did. All he knew was that Small had been cleared for low-level activities—a fancy way of saying they'd be prepared to use him—by a Major Buckley in London, and had happened to call just when Brown had needed someone going into that very region.

The thought crossed his mind: had the young man perhaps given her his name? In which case, would he have mentioned the nature of their connection? He thought it unlikely.

Judge Montoya lived in a house built round a cobbled courtyard. A mule stood in the yard. Brown nearly stepped in its dung. The animal was a strange black presence, standing very still and blowing softly as he walked past. He thought it might move its head to sniff him but it didn't.

A lanky girl of twelve or so showed him into the salon.

Instead of glass windows there were grilles, one onto the street, the other onto the courtyard. The room was tiled, cold, furnished with antique pieces, an odd assortment of rockers, a wicker chaise longue, and a marble-topped table on which a lone lamp burned. A wooden letter-rack stood beside the light, and a blotting pad lay open. It was like walking onto a film set. That was the provinces for you: Montoya probably had waxed whiskers.

He came in smoking a cigarette and carrying a pack of imported Marlboros and a gold lighter. They shook hands and he offered one to Brown. Montoya went and closed the shutter onto the street.

So, he said.

He was a man in late middle age. Silver-haired, face faintly puffed and pocked, thin-lipped, of bulky but sleek build. Hard to place on the graph running from integrity to indulgence. He had the gravitas of a good judge, but that might just have been an effect of the dignity of office. At the same time he had small shiny eyes; they, and the slightly swollen cheeks, suggested a life of pleasure. A thought which brought a kind of smile to Brown's own cheeks.

Let me understand, Montoya said, seating himself, puffing on his Marlboro. You have a man on the wrong side? And you wish to bring him back?

It's more delicate than that, Brown said. We've lost touch with him. But we think he's in Carreras's zone. We understand how well placed you are with authorities of all kinds.

Montoya glanced at him and looked away.

An elderly maid came in with a tray of coffee. She set it down with a soft rattle on the marble table.

Thank you, Marta.

She stumbled on the corner of the rug on her way out and paused to straighten it with her toe, then continued into the darkness. It seemed the whole house was only half lit. In fact, as if the whole town was only half lit.

After a moment he said, A young English *arqueólogo*, you say. Just tell me his name and I will see what can be done.

We'd like them to know in case they come across him. So they know we'd like him back.

I understand. But what is your own, shall we say, personal investment in the proceedings? Are you acting solely in your consular capacity?

I'm not unaware of the advantages of my position.

A silence followed again. Montoya brushed his crossed leg. This was not a turn Brown had anticipated. He thought he would do best to play it, though. He had a hunch he would get nowhere without some semblance at least of duplicity. After all in this war there were no sides, just an array of players. It wasn't really a war anyway, but a mess—a mess of the great bland empire's creation.

Might I ask why you sent someone down there? It is surely more the American line.

There were particular circumstances. The man had a good cover, and the Americans were keen to have someone on the ground. A couple of years back we had a similar situation that turned out well.

Montoya recrossed his legs and bent over them and smoked his cigarette. Yes?

He had reasons of his own for going. Plausible reasons.

And above all you wish to establish contact, of course. You say you lost touch. So you have heard nothing? No ransom demands?

We've no idea what's happened. Can we get a message to them? That's the gist of it. So they'd look after him, not touch him—you know what I mean.

Montoya shrugged. You understand these parties are unlikely to entertain, what you say, truck with you, other than as a party with a business proposition.

The man looked at Brown, who assumed he was meant to smile and did so.

The judge glanced away. You have something to offer? he asked.

We believe Señor Carreras would like talks with the government. He has asked before.

Montoya smiled. We can see. Though you realise he may well have been dispensed with already, this man. The smallest whiff of suspicion.

We know.

So all the efforts may be wasted.

Brown shrugged.

Montoya's eyes sparkled in their field of dough-like flesh. Not entirely wasted, I suppose. One might have the opportunity to turn a little profit. I do not need to say this conversation stays in this room. You better give me your hand on it, not that there is any surety left in this world.

Montoya leaned forward, half getting out of his chair, and reached across to shake Brown's hand. Brown had to stand up and take two steps to reach it.

Then they drank small cups of weak coffee flavoured with cinnamon and cloves.

A sharp frost had descended when Brown turned back up the street. His breath appeared in a white plume before him. He walked fast, relieved to be out of that house. The further he walked the more he felt the house and what he had done in it were coming with him; the unease could not be outwalked. His head ached, and his throat was dry. He had let too long elapse since his last drink. Once you started drinking of an evening you shouldn't stop. But it wasn't just that, it was that he might have stepped outside the shelter of his job into the big bad world. That was why we have jobs, he thought, to keep us safe. It was fine to attach oneself to a cosy core of cynicism as long as you had a roof over your head, so to speak. But what about when you stepped outside into the night? What could you cling to then?

Back at the hotel, just as he had feared, the hotel man was nowhere to be seen and all the lights were off. The little bar had its bamboo shutter down. He went back out into the street toward the plaza, where there would surely be a cantina of some description. Then he began to worry that they would lock the hotel, and anyway these local cantinas could be full of witless thugs who got into pisco fights and knifed not just each other but all and sundry. But the prospect of going to his room seemed terrible.

The plaza was a clean-cut affair with four dying trees, one in each corner, and a church and a *policía* and no trace of a bar. What was the point of a town if at nine thirty at night it was as dead as this? Why not live on a farm? He walked around the plaza passing one man on a bench who nodded to him, and went back to the hotel. The Indian was back. As Brown approached the misleading glass door—suggesting a level of modern comfort of which the place fell far short—the Indian had a ring of keys in his hand and was kneeling on the floor to lock the bottom bolt.

Ah señor, he said. Just in time. He laughed as if it was a joke, and he might really have locked Brown out for the night, and that would have been funny.

Just before Brown went upstairs, the man called to him.

Señor, here.

He handed him a small piece of torn-off paper, smiling and telling him that the American girl had left a message for Brown earlier. Brown couldn't help frowning. He assumed the man meant the anthropologist.

The American girl?

Yes. She call for you.

It was from her. Sarah. The note named a café and suggested nine a.m. the next morning, if he'd arrived by then.

He went to bed in the lightest mood he could remember in a long time.

There was another turn-up the next morning. He didn't have to go as far as the café. As soon as he came downstairs for breakfast, there she was, coming straight up to him across the lobby.

She was lovelier than he remembered. She looked a bit dishevelled, and it suited her. Her face was worn from worry, and her hair was a mess, but there was no avoiding the beauty of her face.

Oh my God, oh my God, she said with great rapidity. Thank you. Thank you for coming so quickly. I'm so grateful, I can't tell you. I didn't think you'd have made it yet, I was just coming to check. He's lost, he's totally lost. He left us three and a half weeks ago.

Wait, wait, Brown said, waving both hands and laughing. Slow down. He felt his face fill with a smile. Shall we go and have coffee and you tell me all about it?

The air in the hotel was brighter, and out in the street the morning was also bright, and full of charming bustle as he walked along with her beside him.

They found a café and sat down. She closed her eyes and sighed.

So. What was he doing? Brown asked. I mean, it's an out of the way place, to say the least. What on earth took him there? And it's a dangerous part of the world.

He wanted to know what she knew.

He was staying with us. With me and my uncle.

She looked at him. She had such lovely eyes. Just as he remembered. And not just her eyes but her eyebrows too were lovely, quite thick, decisive, somehow brave-looking.

Brown felt a heave of emotion deep down. He sensed his good mood giving way. If she would only acquiesce, if he could only get her to see his tender side and accept him, he would give her anything, there was nothing he would deny her. She could even have affairs, whatever she wanted, so long as she would only give herself to him, give him a home. He frowned in what he thought to be a concerned, caring way.

So what was he doing when he went off?

He's an archaeologist, she said. He's looking for ruins. He's hoping to organise an expedition next year. She sighed heavily. He left nearly a month ago. We're so worried, we don't know what to do.

Brown felt his face darken as she spoke. It was obvious Sarah was in love with this man. He could see that a mile off.

Do you know where he was going?

More or less. At least, I know where he started out from, and where he was planning to go, roughly.

He shrugged. Well, he is a British citizen as you say. We better see what we can do. Fortunately we have some contacts in the region. But really, it was reckless of him to head off into the forest like that. It's a terrible part of the world. He could hardly have picked a worse place.

She shook her head. What can we do?

He was buying time. Let me think about it. Let's go to the Ayuntamiento, shall we? They'll have some decent maps. And you can show me exactly where he left from. I take it he's gone into the cloud forest?

She nodded slowly. I must take you to see Padre Beltrán too. He met him. He knows the area.

They paid and left. He strung her along the rest of the morning. But it wouldn't do. He knew it wouldn't do. He would have to do everything he could. Maybe, somehow, if he did actually manage to help her, he'd have a chance. Maybe she'd sense his generous side and be grateful to him, and gratitude could lead to—well, to anything.

Except he knew it wouldn't. And he knew that wasn't the point.

Oh well, he thought. There goes another one. One day, one day.

16 · Flight

1

Jackson heard the rustling then a little *chink*.

There were lumpy things under him—several hard things, and all his weight was on them. He didn't mind, their pressure was warm. He turned his head slowly and blinked. There was a blinding dazzle that way. Even a brief glimpse filled his cranium with orange light. He waited and tried again. This time he saw rock and leaf, and on the rock a white object, close by. He closed his eyes. The white object remained in his mind.

It came to him slowly that it was a mug. A tin mug.

When he woke again he remembered it. He opened one eye and checked: still there, sitting on the rock. He knew it. It was familiar to him. It was a white tin mug with a blue trim. It seemed lovely.

It was then the burning started in his chest. There were embers inside him. They were crying out to be quenched.

He closed his eyes and rested again. The burning remained. He felt the burning and saw the cup in his mind's eye. The burning and the cup went together. It sat there on its rock, and the coals glowed and ached in his chest. Then, like a door cracked open in a dark house letting in a shaft of light, an eddy of clarity arrived, and he stirred. A flicker of memory. He was in the forest. He had been walking many days. He did not remember his name but he knew who he was. It was enough to prise his mind loose from the clay in which it had been fired. Enough to lift his head and raise a hand slowly toward his shoulder first, where he let it rest a moment, then out toward the cup.

He missed. He tried again, and a finger bluntly nudged the enamel. Then he managed to touch it with his fingertip. Slowly he let the fingers curl round the handle. He tried to lift it but only managed to drag it a little. He rolled onto his side and saw the glittering, twitching surface within the circle of tin. It was close. He moved closer still, closer, until his lips touched the rim, and he sucked, and felt the first spasm of coolness enter the fire. It was sweet, he sucked and sucked, and told himself to stop, to slow down, he knew to do that but couldn't remember why. He pulled himself away, and lay down again, closed his eyes and felt the beating of his heart.

As he lay back it came to him that while drinking he had seen something. Some sight was lodged in his mind. Something to look at. He turned his head again. There, some small distance away, seated on a fallen trunk with his hands between the legs of his stiff trousers, and his eyes large and dark, with a blinking sphinx seated beside him, also staring at Jackson like its master, sat a young Indian.

Jackson closed his eyes. Like water welling from a spring and making a broad mushroom cap on the surface of a pond, relief welled up. The feeling bubbled and swelled and all he could do was lie still and let it run through him.

The next time he woke the boy was sitting right next to him. He was holding the mug in his hand, close to Jackson's face.

Something warm was lying on Jackson now, something smooth and shiny, lying all over him.

Later, he realised it was his own sleeping bag.

The boy slept beside him. When Jackson could prop himself on an elbow he unzipped the sleeping bag and spread it out over both of them. The boy's body hardly touched him but he could feel his warmth along his side.

***

You brought the cat. All this way.

The words hurt Jackson's throat. He lay still, watching the boy after he spoke.

Look, señor, she caught us these.

He opened his *mochila* and pulled out a sleek folded grey bird, and some small brown squirrel-like mammal. The cat yawned, as if it knew it was being discussed.

How did you find me?

I followed you, señor. You walk round and round all over the forest. I could tell where you had been. I found these things.

Ignacio held up a box of matches and a plastic bag with some grain in it.

And your bag.

Rice, Jackson said. We can have it with your squirrel. His throat ached again.

Ignacio pulled out a pocketful of leaves that looked like watercress. Good, señor. We cook these, and this.

From another pocket he pulled out a white bulb with a green stalk.

We cut it. It makes you strong, señor.

***

The cat appeared periodically with its mouth stuffed with a small bundle of fur, and sometimes of wet feathers. It truly was a good hunter. It was as if it had found some secret store, some tame population it could plunder at will.

Ignacio had already made a fire. A circle of ash lay a few yards away beside the trunk of a tall sapling.

The first hot thing Jackson consumed was a mug of tea. A mix of tea leaves and other larger leaves that Ignacio must have gathered in the forest floated in it. Jackson sipped slowly. It was bitter and sour, but the warmth travelling down inside him felt so good he lay back and closed his eyes.

He instructed Ignacio on how to cook the rice. The boy brought the pan to him every so often, carrying it carefully from the fire with the edge of his poncho, and Jackson tested the grains with a spoon. When it was done he told him to bring the tin plate and he strained it, the hot milky water steaming into the ground beside his sleeping bag.

From the village it took four days to find you, Ignacio told him.

He was sitting on the tree trunk again, looking past Jackson down the hill into the trees.

I followed the signs. Once I found where you left the stream the rest was easy. I see where you stop and camp, and the cat helped find the way. She is very good. She catches the food, she knows the way.

What village?

The old woman there, she told me you had been.

Jackson lay still.

How did you know to go there?

I hear you talking about Choctamal. When we were at the farm.

They sat in silence awhile.

Jackson was full of a kind of silent brightness. It made it hard to think. He could feel the thoughts rising and getting in a tangle and falling away again before they could form in his mind. He lay still a long time.

I'm lucky, Jackson said after a while. Thank you.

I hear the señora talking, señor, Ignacio said.

The señora?

The *americana*. Sarah. Ignacio said her name quietly, as if embarrassed by it. *Sí*, he went on. So I think I must help you. She is very afraid for you. They talk about you, they say you are lost. So I came to find you. We must use the radio, señor, Ignacio said.

The radio?

Ignacio held up the transmitter-beacon.

I found this, he said. We can call for help.

Jackson's head began to swim. A worried feeling started in his belly and he lay back and closed his eyes, and the feeling subsided.

I found many things, Ignacio said. I found your bag, your sleeping bag, your food.

Later Ignacio brought him some small charred carcass on a stick. Half the innards were still in place, blackened by fire.

Jackson gnawed at the thing as he lay on his back, little flecks falling onto him. He didn't mind. The taste was rich and fierce. He pulled off little sheets of flesh from the ribs, and strings of meat from the limbs. It took a long time to chew.

We have to get to a river, he said. That's the only way it will work. A river. Somewhere we can be seen from the air.

From the air?

From the sky. Or a clearing. Somewhere without trees.

Ignacio stared at him, not understanding.

The next day Jackson was roused by Ignacio's voice calling to him.

I found a clearing, señor.

At first Jackson had no idea what he meant. Then gradually sleep drained from his mind.

Where? How far?

Jackson tried getting up. As soon as he was crouching he became intensely dizzy and fell back. When he came to, Ignacio was squatting beside him with another mug of his tea.

There was nothing for it, they had to move camp.

A day and a half now Jackson had been drinking Ignacio's forest infusions and eating the scraps of food he brought. He could sit up without fainting, and stand with the help of a stick.

They set off after breakfasting on the last of the rice. Jackson wore the pack, which they filled together, and Ignacio let him lean one hand on his small shoulder, while he grasped a stick in the other.

At first Jackson had to stop every few steps and crouch with his head in his hands to bring the dizziness under control. But he didn't mind. There was no need to hurry. Ignacio knew the forest and they could survive in it. He trusted that. Jackson was happy because the boy was with him. He had the feeling time was on his side.

But it was hard going, and took a long time. At one point Jackson had to lie down and at once dropped into a deep slumber. He woke to find Ignacio nudging his foot, breathing, *Señor, señor.*

They stopped often to drink water from a clear plastic bottle Ignacio had.

The trees' shadows were long, the ground striped all over with them. They came out onto a patch of hillside, a broad ridge where there were rocks and the trees stood back to let the stony ground rise up.

Here, señor.

Jackson saw it was a clearing, and the sky grew wide as they moved onto it, a hard sheet of metal overhead. It was too much. His heart began to race and his breathing came quick, and he lay down before he fainted again.

When he opened his eyes he saw that it would do.

Tomorrow morning, he said. Bring me the beacon.

Ignacio stared at him.

The radio. Let me see.

Ignacio made a fire and they ate a soup of water and leaves as the sun winked low through the crown of trees surrounding the knoll. At first light he would trigger the device.

First he heard a rhythmic knocking that could have been a woodpecker. Then it deepened to a drumming, then a kind of throb you could feel in your chest, and he knew for sure what it was.

Ignacio was standing and looking around. His cat crouched beside him, its eyes big and dark. Then they were both gone, Ignacio and his cat. They scampered down the hill and were lost in the forest. Jackson called after them, saying it was OK, but he couldn't have been heard. Already the noise was deafening, and the trees were hissing and seething. There was a whine in the air, and the machine rose over the nearest ridge of treetops, a red-and-white civilian helicopter. It circled the area, its tail swinging high, then hovered, and Jackson saw its door slide open. Against the bright sky he could hardly make out the man in the dark interior.

The wind was in his eyes and he had to look away. A storm of old leaves and dust and bark skidded past. He heard the engine pitch change and grow, and knew without looking that the helicopter was coming down. The wind lessened, though the pitch didn't drop. He shielded his eyes and turned to look.

Two men carrying automatic rifles were coming toward him. He let them come. There was nothing he could do, whoever they were.

He called out a greeting as they came close, and one of the men lifted his gun with the barrel down. Jackson saw the swing then the butt cracked the side of his head and made him bite so hard his jaw rang. Singing burst in his ears, and everything went still for a moment, then black.

2

On the morning Brown was packing up to leave Chachapoyas, his mission aborted, having failed to locate the young man, there was a rapping on his door.

The hotel man was there with a note in his hand.

On the note was a phone number. It was the consul's private line, except a digit had been taken down wrong.

At first Brown was tempted to leave, to ignore the message. He had half an hour to get to the bus station. It was Monday morning. If he caught the eleven o'clock bus he'd make it to the coast tonight, and be home tomorrow.

With a sigh, he locked the door and went downstairs to the telephone in reception.

The American anthropologist was down in the lobby seated in

an armchair with his head gravely inclined toward a copy of *Time* magazine. He raised his face, stared at Brown for a moment, then nodded.

Wanker, Brown thought. All that fake gravity and sageness. You're a grad student on the make, that's all. He nodded back.

The consul's voice in the receiver: I've had a message. Lord knows what you're up to, you mysterious fellow, but the message is, apparently, that they think they've got him. Surveillance picked up the signal of a beacon. But by the time they got the chopper together and on its way the signal was moving. On and off—consistent with a flight through mountains. Low level. They think someone else got to him first. You're to go back to your contact up there and try to find out.

For a moment Brown thought: why all the fuss? Why didn't they just let it be? In a country like this, you could count on things to muddle along in their own chaotic way regardless of what you did. And anyway, wouldn't Jackson surely be dead by now, after all those days and nights in the jungle?

Apparently the worry is secession, the consul droned on. The region is all but autonomous as it is. As you know.

Brown wasted no time and headed out into the street.

Montoya saw him right away. Yes, yes, he said before they even sat down in his stiff, ancient salon, before they even walked across its threshold. Montoya waved Brown to a hard wicker seat, and took his own place on a leather chair behind his desk.

Yes, I have had this message. Like you hope, I think. Carreras has the boy, the young *inglés*. He wants to know what you want to talk about.

Talks. The Americans are offering talks.

Brown said it abruptly, excitedly. His blood was pumping. He could feel a stool forming and pressing for release. At last. It was long overdue. He was suddenly full of excitement as if he really did care about all this. He felt for a moment that he actually did. He was beginning to see a way it might all unfold like clockwork. If the beacon wasn't going to lead them to Carreras then perhaps Jackson himself could lead Carreras to them. He could hardly wait to find Sarah and tell her the good news. At least the potential good news. Her side of the good news. And there could be a welcome party waiting for Carreras. Brown would be the hero of the moment, the one who managed not only to get Carreras but to bring Jackson Small back from the dead. He'd get the credit and the raise. It was true it might get hot, anyone might easily find themselves caught in crossfire. Nor would Carreras like it when he realised he'd been brought into an ambush. He might well finish the young man off then and there, if he had a chance.

He could see it all. I'm so sorry my dear, he'd say to Sarah. I did try. I *told* Jackson to keep down. And she'd look at him with her eyes washed clear with grief, and gratitude for his efforts. Everyone knew bereaved women were the most seducible. But it wouldn't just be about seduction—no, the gratitude would grow into lasting love. Yes, it could all work out like a dream.

Talks? Montoya asked. Really? You have their word? The Americans, they will press the government for this meeting?

That's what they're saying. Yes.

There is probably one minister they wish to talk with. Last time, Carreras demanded talks with the finance minister. My guess is it will be the same this time. If we're lucky, that is, and he agrees to ask for anything. I will see the message is passed on and try to make some arrangements. I'll call you at your hotel later.

Brown could hardly keep himself from breaking into a jog as he went over to the priest's flat to find Sarah. She had taken him there to meet Padre Beltrán, and he knew she could often be found there.

He knocked on the gate at the end of the alley where the priest lived but there was no answer. He called out, and heard no response.

Faintly he heard the sound of singing somewhere. Perhaps it was coming from the church. He walked into the little plaza and up the steps to the main entrance. He swung through the door, and heard a man speaking up near the altar, and a rapping of some kind that echoed through the cool dark of the tall edifice. The man's voice ceased, and after a little pause the singing started again—high clear voices, just a handful of them, singing some kind of hymn. They were presumably local women, and for a second Brown wondered whether any of them might be young and good-looking.

A church choir, for God's sake, he told himself. What's the matter with you? And at once he thought of Sarah with a spasm of longing so intense it would have floored any arousal instantly.

He walked up the aisle. Through the carved wooden screen behind the altar he could make out a man's arm moving. He walked around and saw Padre Beltrán with a music stand before him and a white candle in one hand, conducting a little line of local boys.

They weren't very good. Beltrán said loudly, No, no, no, and tapped his makeshift baton on the music stand, stopping them.

Brown coughed in the susurrating quiet that followed.

Beltrán glanced at him, looked away, then looked back.

That young man we were talking about? They've got him.

Beltrán turned to face him and raised his eyebrows. He had this way about him, this priest, slightly supercilious. It was as if he wouldn't quite trust you as an equal because he was so used to taking the moral high ground. He turned back to the choir. Boys, we must take a little break. Come back in twenty minutes.

Up in the flat, with Sarah in the room—she had been writing her journal, she said, on a terrace at the back—Brown didn't beat about the bush.

They have him. We don't know what kind of state he's in but we think he's alive, that's the main thing.

He couldn't help smiling as he said this.

He noticed the click as Sarah put down the cup of coffee she was holding. She stood up from the table where she had been sitting, and looked at him, her face bright. *Bright* was the word. It wasn't just shining, it seemed literally filled with light. Brown felt momentarily winded. What a catch, he thought. What a catch for that useless half-baked explorer, that drifter with all his life ahead of him.

It was just like a film, Brown thought. The three of them standing in the kitchen, no one quite sure what to say, not quite sure of anything. The padre stood with his back to the sink nodding.

He had missed the bus but it hardly mattered now. He had made her happy. He hád done some good in the world. Did it make any difference? Not really, not for him. After all this, what would he do but head back to the grindstone? But he felt that there was a certain kind of weary, familiar pleasure in that, in going back home having accomplished something; at least to some kind of home, however far flung.

3

Jackson woke in darkness. To the side of him he could see a single line of light.

He tried to turn his head to find out which way he was lying, on his back or his front. He moved a little and a fierce ache hit him. He was lying on a hard surface; it seared the back of his head. He must have a bruise there, a bad bruise.

A grunt escaped his lips and echoed. He wasn't sure if it was resonating in his skull or in some small chamber. The line of light was a little way away from him. He stared at it.

It all came back: the forest, the gale of a helicopter overhead, the roar, the snarl of it, and the two men, the crack on his skull.

He forced himself to swing his legs down, knocking something over with his shin. He felt around for it. As he reached out there was a sharp pain in his forearm, and something metal clanged to the floor. He felt his arm. There was a plaster on it, and beneath it something small and hard, and from it a pipe came out, bendable and soft.

He reached down with his other hand and found the first thing he'd knocked over: a plastic bottle. In the dark he unscrewed the cap and put the neck to his lips, and pulled in a mouthful. The liquid tasted bitter, salty, and he spat it out at once. It left a dry, chalky taste in the back of his throat.

How long had he been out?

He waited a moment in case the liquid burned. The sip had awakened a desperate thirst. He guzzled from the bottle until he choked. Then his stomach began to ache. He curled up again on the hard surface on which he had been lying, the pipe attached to his fore-arm no longer pulling painfully, until the ache in his belly passed.

He lay still in the dark, growing ever more conscious of that line of light to his side. He could hear sounds—the crowing of a chicken, a faint babble of running water, and the distant gurgle of an engine. These sounds were pleasant. Now that the water he had drunk had entered his body and he could feel it being absorbed, he felt at peace. He lay still, weightless on the bench. He floated, the bench floated, the floor floated, this whole world floated.

Into this peace arose the question again: how long had he been here? The question brought with it a tight, uncomfortable feeling in his belly, which he would rather not experience, so he put the question away. He was capable of doing that. Another question arose: where was he? That too he put aside for now. He was able to. He had never known it could be so easy to choose your thoughts.

He was surprised at how easy it was to lie still and feel his breath rising and falling, and feel the peace of the whole world, inside and out, rising like dough, all through the sounds he could hear, through the light filtering into the room, through his own breaths and the rustling of his clothes as his chest moved and through his entire body. He knew he had once worried a lot, and now he could not think why.

The line of light lay along the foot of a door. It was a door of ribbed metal. He considered getting up and trying it but that too could wait.

When the door opened the light broke in like the flash of an explosion. He rolled away and squeezed his eyes shut.

Two men came in and got him to his feet. One of them snapped out the pipe attached to his wrist, then whipped off the plaster and pulled out the needle that had been embedded in his arm. He felt the sting as they did it.

At first it was hard to stand. It was as if his legs no longer knew how to hold him up. He would have liked to sit back down but the men held him and kept moving, they turned sideways to get him through the door, the three of them shoulder to shoulder as they shuffled into blinding daylight.

White dust, white hen, white tree. He closed his eyes. A bloom of swimming bright orange filled his vision.

His toes dragged across the ground. Then his eyelids turned darker; they had moved him inside another building. He squinted and saw a wooden door frame, a stone floor, a long room. They pulled him up a staircase and along a corridor with floorboards and white walls and small framed pictures. One of the pictures was of men in red coats on horses jumping over a hedge.

I know what that is, he thought. But he couldn't remember what. He could feel the cold weather of a northern winter, frosty ground, sleet and bare trees, and it came to him: England. That was an English scene. He was in an English house. How had this happened? When had he come here?

He thought to look at the men who were escorting him now. Were they English? They both had brown faces and black hair.

The men took him into a bathroom and sat him down on a stool with a cork seat, like one he'd known years ago in the bathroom of his childhood home. He slumped back against the wall when they let go of him.

Put on the clothes after you wash, one of the men said, and they walked out, closing the door. He heard the click of a lock turning.

There was a window with a thin gauze curtain above a white bath. The bath was full of pale green water. Wisps of steam moved over the surface. There was a basin with a mirror above it, a large bar of brown soap, a sponge and a back brush on the side of the bath. Two plump towels were folded over a steel radiator. On the back of the door hung a grey suit with a white shirt folded inside.

He slumped back against the wall for a long time. Where was he? Was all this real? One minute in a cell, the next in a plush old-fashioned English bathroom. Who had put the cannula in his arm? And why?

He leaned forward to pick up a blue china mug that stood by the basin. He filled it with water from a tap, and drank. Then he sat still again.

After a while the door opened.

Hombre, one of the men said. He clapped twice. Come on. Get moving. The *patrón* is waiting.

Jackson heard what the man was saying. The voice was deep and smooth and seemed to touch a place way down inside his stomach. It was nice listening to it.

Hombre, the man said again.

Then he was at Jackson's side, kneeling to unlace one of his boots.

Hurry up, the man said, his voice now sounding soft, muffled, as he crouched on the floor.

We have to get you ready for the boss.

As the man began unlacing Jackson's second boot something woke up in him, and he automatically started unbuttoning his shirt.

The door closed again with a click.

The bath was hot enough to make him gasp as he lowered himself in. The water stung his skin. There was a smell of something sharp and bitter. Perhaps some herb had been added to the water. As he lay there his face began to sweat and he could feel his heart thumping. Through the thin curtains he saw beads of condensation on the windowpane. When he put his head under water he could hear the blood clattering in his ears.

He remembered again the thudding sound like rapid mortar fire coming down through the trees, screaming at Ignacio as the boy dodged and ran away, himself unable to move after the long climb to the clearing on the knoll. The big machine floating in the sky, clattering and thudding. The tremendous storm-wind blowing all around, leaves, twigs and dust scuttling across the ground in a blind panic, the trees bending and tossing. Then the men with guns, a shout and the smack to his head.

They had brought him here. How long ago he didn't know. Maybe yesterday, maybe much longer. Wherever it was he would have to wait and see.

Wearily, heavily, he reached for the big bar of soap and began to wash.

17 · *Carreras*

1

You soldiers are romantic. This *compañero* of yours who die, you think he want you to fly across the world to look for lost *ruinas* in a war zone? We are at war, you know. You don't see it.

The man rattled his drink gently, then tapped his head. This is estrange war. You have to see what you don't see. Both sides have invaded, but the people do not know.

The man uncrossed then recrossed his ankles. The cuffs of his slacks rode up enough to reveal the designer monogram on his cotton socks. The leather of his loafers squeaked faintly as they moved against the hide of the stool on which they rested.

He inhaled. We wonder what to do with you. What is a young *inglés* doing here? Why he have these notes on ruins? He must be a young explorer hoping to make a find, but why here, and why this radio beacon we find in your bag? Already many days ago we receive a message that the British consul he wants you. So when we finded you we keep you alive. Is a miracle you alive. How you survive? You are lucky. Yes, I like the English, lucky people. Across the world, is there any better life? Hunting and shooting, libraries and escotch. And polo, and ponies for the daughters. And your Caribbean countries, they are the best. Look at Cuba, look at Santo Domingo—just a mess. But Belize, Jamaica, the people have this quality in their minds, what you call, *wit*. Especially Belize, I have good friends in the jungle, with big *estancias*, big plantations.

I know Belize, Jackson said.

Carreras shrugged. You were in the garrison. The man swilled his whisky and eyed Jackson.

I see you are on the trail of the Chachapoyas. We call them the People of the Jaguar. Because of their jaguar-god.

Carreras settled his glass on his knee. I tell you an estory. I was one of five brothers. Now I am alone. That is what we mean by war. You were a soldier. You should know this. You talk of your lost companion who was searching for these *ruinas*. Look this. Look around. You have seen the paintings and Land Rovers and the hot water in the bath, and the televisions and antique furnitures. In our country such things mean hard work. Imagine this situation, so far from civilisation such as road or railroad. Everything it has to fly in. In the old days we use mules, donkeys, llamas. This table here—the man gestured at a large oak dining table on which stood a computer and a sheaf of papers—come on the back of three mules harnessed side by side. Seven days through the cloud, the rain, the mud. Anything that comes here it must come through the cloud. These days it all must come by air. How else? Even the vehicles. There is still no track over the pass of the Marañón. We used to have a Chinook, one of your British Goliaths, a wonderful machine, but we lost it. Now we use Italian Vipers. The airstrip was too dangerous, and too often the weather was bad. We lost so many planes.

Jackson said nothing but was aware of his own breathing. He was still trying to catch up. First he'd been starving in the forest, then locked in a cell on a drip, then made to bathe and put on a good suit, and now he was sipping whisky with one of the most wanted men in the Andes.

So with all these signs of hard work, why you do not see we are too busy to help visitors who come searching for a pin in a haystack?

Jackson hesitated. The man obviously intended him to reply. But a strange silence had come over him. The feeling kept coming back, as if an ocean of calm had opened just behind his back, and wherever he went, whatever he did, he felt it. Then it would slip away again.

Your friend who come here, he was Connolly, yes? You think we don't know? I tell you, only people who are doing businesses come here. You must know Belize is good for us. We do business with Belize many years. Your friend he was based there. He work with us. He was in the garrison. He help us. You understand?

Jackson listened silently. The fire rustled and shifted in the grate.

He understood that he had been lied to. By everyone. Everything he had believed, no matter the source, had been false.

Above a timber fireplace, a mask of green stone hung on the wall. It had almond eyes and a long nose, recognisably Andean but finer than the usual ceramics of Chimu and Moche. Its mouth was wide, with four fangs, just like the face he had seen in the tunnel. It was a beautiful piece, though frightening, and glowed in the half-lit room.

What do you know of that mask? Jackson nodded at the wall.

The man turned his head to the side but didn't raise it from his chair back, which he would have needed to do to look at the object.

You recognise this estyle. The man sipped his drink.

Are there more?

The man whooped and lifted up his glass, falling into the local idiom of gesture. More? Who knows?

Jackson sat forward on his chair. I know who made that.

The man shrugged and ran a hand through his hair. It made no impact on his severe coiffure. The hand, remembering itself, returned to the thigh.

Of course.

Then you know there are lost cities out there. They've been waiting hundreds of years for someone to unearth them. There might even be twelve cities. That's what some records say. We could reveal them all. I found one myself.

We? The man got up without waiting for a response and crossed to the mantelpiece. He took a cigarette from a wooden box and stood smoking in front of the fire.

There's a saying we have: you can't see your own estupidity when you are in it. My friend, you have an idea of the position you are in? We have no visitors. Although you have been told this you do not believe. The young believe themselves safe even when their *compañeros* die beside them. Yes, you are right about these cities. There are seven. You may have found your way to one. Let me tell you. One night early on when this house is just a barn, it was the night before my youngest brother die. He was the first to die. I walk about the farm, everyone else asleep, even the dogs had not woken to accompany me. Well, I saw a light in the trees above the *chacra*. I walk up there. I was troubled. Next day my brother and I we will fly from here with some precious things. I was always nervous before flying from here. You don't know who might send up a SAM rocket to say hello. Not just the Yankees, either.

Well, I didn't believe what I saw, coming down through the woods, a procession of men wearing white robes. They are monks? They are some tribe on a pilgrimage of which I do not know? They walk past me just a few metres away, but none even turn to look at me. They don't see me. Others appear, a long line of Indians winding among the trees. Last came a group carrying a *santo* on a raft, except it wasn't a *santo*, but this deity with the body of a jaguar and this face.

He gestured behind him with his cigarette, toward the mask on the wall.

I try to call them but they do not hear me. After that I shut up. You know why? The only person could hear me was that god or *diablo*. That thing turn and stare at me. I jump from my skin. And that night I learn the only lesson in this life. You know what I do? I ran at that raft they were carrying, I jump at the *diablo*, I was just crazy. I don't know what happen. I pass out. When I came to, it was dawn and I was cold and wet and had a terrible pain in my

back, a great pain. I didn't know where was I, is there an earthquake in the night and something landed on my back? I can't even
move because of this pain. Just I lay there wishing I had a cigarette
and some painkillers. Then finally I hear someone shouting on the
farm, and the dogs barking and Simón, our foreman, and my
younger brother found me. When they lift me—he gestured with
his cigarette hand, raising the palm toward the ceiling—this is
what they find. This mask. I was lying on it. What is it doing there
under me? Those Indians if they were just some dreams or visions
then why this thing is here? Still I do not know. I tell them bring
the mask to the farm. Your fears—you have to take them prisoner.
You must not be afraid of them. So now this demon, he work
for us.

The man moved away from the fireplace to a window. He
stooped a little to look out, then turned back to face Jackson.

You cannot imagine these mountains how confusing they are.
They have secrets. They confuse not only a man but a whole
people, they confuse even the ghosts. Time bursts its banks here,
and does not know which way to run.

But are you going to let the cities just lie there? The archaeological finds of the century?

That mask, I understood she was a peace offering. From the *gente
antigua*. I think there are more old cities than you and I could even
dream, lost in the jungle. But they stay lost. I take this mask, this
treasure, from their ancient hands.

Jackson listened. It occurred to him that the discovery of ancient
cities just here might bring all manner of unwelcome attention
from outside, whatever else Carreras was telling him. It was convenient for him that no one know about them, or come looking for
them.

You think I am crazy, but who knows what is crazy? Most
people, the way they live these short lives I think is crazy.

Jackson said, There's a friend I have, a priest. He says there are
terrorists again in this region.

Carreras tutted. There are *guerrilleros*. But not like before. They
are good people. That is one thing. And there are two-bit *traficantes*

who come from *la costa* and try to get some business, and they don't know what they are doing, just they get themselves killed. But they are no terrorists.

His face darkened slightly.

Let me ask you, why the government doesn't accept my offer? I offer to pay all the foreign debt. My business is strong. I could take care of the whole country. Why they say no? They are estupid. At least the revolutionaries, the *guerrilleros*, they are practical people. They need help, they ask for help. And they know they must offer something in return. Maybe we will have to become our own country here.

He tutted again. Today the business it's full of ignorant people who just want to get rich. My family, we have been in Peru three hundred years. We have responsibilities. We don't just make monies and drive fast cars and have *chicas* and loud music. As you see—he gestured around the room's book-lined walls—we read, we listen Beethoven. I have builded eight schools and three hospitals. Two soccer stadiums. Would the government do this? Would the Americans do this? They try to stop me helping my own people. This country she is so poor. Only the government has to accept she must use the one product the world will buy. First the world powers rape our land and make us poor. Then finally we find a market and they stop us. They come in and spray the farmers' fields, these Yanquis. They burn the crops and bomb the factories killing many many peoples. And I try to help, and they tell me I must not, I am criminal.

He shook his head, then glanced up at the wall above the fireplace, where the mask was glinting softly in candlelight.

So. You will stay one more night with us. Now you are talking again, and walking. The drip help you. Still I do not know how you are alive. You had no food many days I think. But you will have a comfortable bed, perhaps the first a traveller such as yourself has slept in in many weeks. Then in the morning you join me in the Viper and we go to *la costa*.

He paused and drained the melting ice from his glass.

Just you go to any police station tomorrow. They will help.

Jackson didn't move. Then instinctively he lifted his glass and put it to his lips. The smoky aroma filled his head and the sip he took was hot in his chest.

And we shake hands. Like English gentlemen, Carreras said, and laughed a short, dry laugh. His cheeks, badly pockmarked, creased up.

Outside the window the cobbled courtyard of the hacienda had turned blue-grey. The lights on the far wall burned brightly in the dim and misty dusk.

Jackson shrugged. It's like England here.

Is the cloud and the rain. Is cold here at night. So. Good.

The man set down his empty whisky glass and clicked across the tiled floor and out. The room was quiet. It was a long low-ceilinged room of tiles and antique furniture, with three steps up to a gallery at the far end. On one wall the fireplace, and in another a row of low windows giving onto the courtyard. Jackson got up and let himself out of a side door.

A dog lay curled on the broad steps at the end of the yard. It licked its rump then shook itself and wagged its tail half-heartedly. It stared at Jackson and slunk off down the steps. It was chilly out. Chilly, dark and misty. The whole world had turned grey and soft, as if things were losing their corporeality. As if the stones of this house and courtyard were nothing more than mist, and the only dependable firmness in the world was the points of light from the lamps fastened to the house wall.

There were lights high up too, on two pylons at either end of the compound. He looked, and saw they were watchtowers, and in either one he could just make out a figure standing and smoking.

Somewhere a horse nickered. Big dry leaves rolled across the cobbles. Jackson walked up to the stone gateway with a big stone diamond set above it, and out through the portal to where the paddock with the mules and horses began. Several cattle were lowing in a barn nearby. An avenue of tall spindly trees bent in the wind and a little posse of leaves scuttled past him rolling over and over.

He couldn't get what Carreras had said about Connolly out of his head. He had listened to so many people. He had believed in so many people: his father, who had persuaded him to join the army; Connolly, who had instilled this need for adventure and exploration in him, and more—he was here because of Connolly; even the priest, Father Beltrán, who had impressed him with his own notion of how to live; and likewise Sarah's uncle Alfredo, who thought he too understood what a good life was. He had listened to everyone. And now this killer drug lord Carreras—him too Jackson was listening to, being impressed by his take on the world, on what constituted a worthwhile life. But what did he, Jackson, think was a good life? What were his own choices?

He had no answer, none at all. But he thought of Sarah, and of Ignacio, and recognised them as two people he had not blindly believed. That was a start. He listened to them, and they to him.

He wondered if he would ever see them again. He wanted to know that Ignacio would be all right. He guessed he would be. If he had managed to come all that way alone through the forest then probably he could get back out too. How he had managed to find him, Jackson still couldn't imagine. It was as if he was like a homing pigeon with a lodestone lodged in his cranium. He would probably go back to Choctamal first, which he said had been only four days' walk from where he had tended Jackson. That still bothered him, that he had walked for so long and travelled so much less far than he'd thought, that he'd been so confused by the forest. Then presumably Ignacio would go back to Alfredo's. That was where Jackson would go too, if he could. For now, dressed in nothing but a flimsy suit, with the guards in the watchtowers, and who knew how many others he couldn't see, it would be madness to try and make a break for it. He would wait and see what tomorrow brought.

As he thought of that, of waiting, he felt again the ocean of calm behind his back. It stayed for a while, and all worries floated away. Then in a while it left.

He heard rain ping on a tin roof and felt the first drops on the backs of his hands.

It hit him that nothing mattered beside the fact that Cruz was dead. Jackson, because of listening to people like Connolly, had stumbled into this region as if it had something to do with him, and had caused a man to die. He and Brown and Major Buckley between them. What did they have to do with the Upper Marañón? He felt now that the misgivings he'd had about getting involved with the old major had been more right than he'd known.

He turned under the portal of the side door into a lobby. He would have thought there'd be boots, coats and tackle in such a lobby, but there was nothing, and the floor was clean. He could smell the wax polish on the wood when he stooped under the door frame.

In his new room there was a big wooden bed piled high with white linen. He lay on it—or floated on it—and waited. He could hear music playing softly. Then he noticed his backpack standing by the door against the wall. So they had allowed him that.

It was fully dark now. He set off across the cobbles and back into the main part of the house. At the far end of the salon three young women, pretty and long-haired, were sitting at the big table up in the gallery, slicing limes and chatting in Spanish. One of them glanced at him and nodded, and continued her chopping.

Jackson paused and said good evening.

Two of them, a brunette and a rusty blonde, looked up and sent him a smile, but said nothing. The third, another brunette, kept her head down. Jackson guessed they were all in their early twenties, perhaps a year or two older than him. They had an air of experience about them, as if they weren't too interested in a youth like him. He didn't mind. He thought of Sarah, of the real love he'd found, the first of his life, and felt something almost like pity for these women. For a moment the oceanic calm came back.

He made his way to the fireplace, where the fire was roaring, and helped himself to a cigarette.

While he was sitting in the salon a man with a moustache and mirror sunglasses walked in. Although he looked familiar at first Jackson assumed it was just his Latin accessories. But the man came across the stone floor, bowing courteously to the girls as he passed them, coming straight toward the big fireplace where Jackson was.

I did not expect to see you here, he said.

Jackson stood up. Something about the man's military bearing seemed to require it. He didn't know whether to salute or hold out his hand.

You do not remember me. We met in Chachapoyas. I am the captain of police.

Of course, Jackson blurted, as if it were necessary to be polite. That morning, in the café.

I see you have not listened to me. Here you are. Well, you must have a good night tonight. Make the most of it. Me, I am about to leave. I wish I could offer you a lift back to town but I'm afraid it will not be. When in Rome, *caballero*, you must learn how the Romans do things. I hope it is not too late.

He shook his head. With that, without a handshake, he turned his back, clicked past the girls, and up the three stone steps out the door.

Just then a servant in a white shirt brought Jackson a glass of whisky and led him across a carpeted hallway and up a short flight of stairs into a study. The room was lined with books, and there were two leather armchairs. A candle guttered on a big desk strewn with papers. Small shaded electric bulbs burned in an iron chandelier. Botanical prints of plants hung on spare spaces among the books on the walls. The room could have been a don's study.

In a moment Señor Carreras appeared in the doorway. He clicked his heels together, pressed his arms into his jacket pockets, paused a moment, then said: We go.

Jackson followed him through the big sitting room again. At the table with the beautiful young women, Carreras stopped. The three of them raised their eyes to him, and one by one Carreras caressed their cheeks with his thick hand. He bent down to kiss the lips of the third. He hummed as he did so and said, *Preciosa. Más tarde.* Then he straightened up and said to the others, *Y tú, y tú*, and bent down to kiss them too.

Then he turned toward the heavy oak door and walked away in

a manner that suggested he had forgotten all about the women, his attention now fully on something else. Jackson couldn't help noticing and admiring that.

Carreras led him through a swinging door into a stone-floored kitchen where a table had been laid with two places. Candles in pewter sticks illuminated the room, giving it the air of a farmhouse kitchen.

A black man with curly grey hair and a friendly round face held a chair for Jackson.

I tell you about my brother. Maybe you learn something.

Carreras snapped out his napkin.

That day after we finded this mask, my brother he was espooked as you say. He didn't want it in the house. I told him it had been sent to us God know how, and we should accept him. We leave it in a stable. One of our Indian *porteros* saw to my back—they are marvellous healers—and later we take off in the plane. We get out of the valley and fly into cloud. We climb and climb, usually the cloud here is thin, you get through quickly, but this morning we keep climbing and never come out. We fly through an electric storm. Twelve, fifteen, sixteen thousand feet. We learn after that, you don't fly in these mountains without a pressurised cabin. So we go west, get over to the coast.

The servant came back into the kitchen with two bowls of soup. He fetched a bottle of wine from a sideboard and filled the glasses. The soup was creamy. Jackson brought a spoon to his lips and the taste so overcame him for a moment he couldn't think of anything else. Celery soup. He had never tasted anything so good, and he had thought he didn't even like celery.

Well, we come out of the cloud, we see a huge green plain. A clear sky—usually you can see the coast from two hundred miles. First you have the mountains, then the desert, then the ocean. There's no green plain. Neither of us want to know what this means—the compass must be broken. Maybe because of this storm we fly through, maybe it change the magnetism, we don't know. So a brown loop appeared in the flat green land, and we knew was true—it was a river, and we had flown east, we were above Amazonas. Can you imagine? A precious load, a small plane, and we're hundreds of miles the wrong way. One good thing—we have a lot of height. But we can't stay high forever, we are using the oxygen and it will run out. We cannot risk going back across the mountains; we do not have enough fuel. So I scrabble with the map, I try to pick some landmark, maybe find a jungle airstrip. But in that land there are no landmarks. The one thing we see is smoke far far off. Maybe is a field. Maybe, who knows, is a town. So we fly that way. Is further than it looks. Finally our reserve tank runs out; we glide, come down. We have only one parachute and we decide we stay together, we don't use it. We are losing height all the time, soon we can see the trees. Then this river is beneath us. We turn to follow it, because the last hope is to land in the river, is better than the trees. We follow the river round a bend and there ahead is smoke, and is a field the Indians are clearing, a field of broken trees and shrubs. In the smoke by the river we see the Indians, real *nativos*, naked except for some feathers in their hair. Little figures down there between the smoke and the river, five of them staring up, and we're thinking fuck this, we have troubles now.

He finished his soup and broke off a piece of his roll.

Of course a plane like that has no avionics. She don't exist, you understand. We are gliding on flaps and are down to a hundred feet, so it must be, how you say, a belly-flop on the river. The tree-tops are flying past. Then in front, is unbelievable, we see the one thing could help us—a sandbank. We don't waste time. I slip down, full flaps, the stall alarm is going, and once I get all three wheels down I slam on the brakes but still the sand is too short and we fall off the end in the water. But we're alive. We grab the bags off the back seat and I'm thinking we will get out of here. We make friends with the Indians. We pay someone to paddle us to a village, from there another canoe to a bigger village, then to a town. You always can get anywhere if you have money. Thanks God.

We wait for those Indians to come. They must have a canoe. But they don't come. We wait and wait, we call, we wave a gun, we wave money, but nothing, no one comes. What to do? We're hungry. Night falls. Is a bad night, hoping there are no caimans, and the big tail of our plane sticking out of the river in the moonlight. And all the jungle noises. And the sandflies and mosquitoes.

The servant cleared away the bowls and brought in plates of steak and fried potatoes.

Well, the next day a big party of Indians arrive in canoes and they are not friendly, we think is some tribe of Shipibo, they wave their bows and spears. Lucky, at least one of them knows what money is, he grab it from my hand. So they take us.

The first village the Indians bring us, we get there and my brother he's acting estrange. Kissing his crucifix and showing it to the Indians, trying to get them to kiss it. Like he turn into some missionary guy. I looked him, I touch his face, and he is hot, maybe he have some fever. An *antropólogo* is studying this tribe, he is living with them. He dress like them, he don't wear any clothes, but we see is a Yanqui right away, he has a big beard and pale skin. I take my brother to him in case he has some *medicinas*. He give my brother something, I do not know what, a little yellow pill. Suppose to make him better. Then we travel to Tarapoto. Is a journey by canoe, several days, we eat manioc bread and monkey meat. Is a small town and when we reach it I am carrying my brother on my back, he has bad, bad fever. That Yanqui *antropólogo*, he poison him. I take him to a doctor but is too late, the fever it's on his brain. I tell the doctor and he say yes, yes, could be that pill make him much worse. The doctor couldn't say if is malaria or cholera or something else he never see. So fast, he said. So I flew to the coast in a charter with my brother dying beside me. He stop breathing over the *cordilleras*. You know what I did? He was a wild kid and I did what is right. I open the door, I make the co-pilot help me, I have to shout at him a bit, eventually I have to pull the gun. Finally he help and we get my brother to the door and I bended down and I kiss my brother's crucifix and tear it off his neck, and we let him go.

He had a swig of wine.

When someone has an espirit like this he should be buried the right way.

The man touched his shirt, then unbuttoned his collar and reached inside to pull out a silver crucifix.

Every day I wear it.

He pushed his plate to the side, half finished, and put an elbow on the table. I talk, this is my table, you must listen.

He drained his glass. The servant reappeared at his side and replenished it, then Jackson's, and to retrieve the plates. Once the servant had withdrawn Carreras said, Forget about these ruins. Leave them in the jungle. Life is now, not five hundred years ago.

He patted his mouth with a napkin.

You know how my next brother die? The Yanquis too. They shoot down his plane. No warning, no radio contact, just they shoot. And the next, and the next. They don't care about anybody, only how to get rich, and they don't mind how many people dies. Any business in the world, it must be their business. The British, they were not so bad as this, they have some *responsabilidades*, where they make the empire they builded schools and hospitals. But these Yanquis just they kill, they take the money, they don't tell nobody about it, and they leave. Then they come back and do it again. Sancho! Sancho!

The servant came in again and stood to the side of Carreras. *¿Sí? Uno Yonnie. Fuerte.*

As the man left the room Carreras snapped, *Por favor*, after him.

The servant glanced back with his eyebrows raised. He seemed unafraid of his boss, and that seemed momentarily comforting to Jackson. But then he wondered why was he being given this dinner. And why the bath ready for him earlier, and the fresh clothes? Why the comfortable bed for the night? It all felt unreal, and dangerous.

Now I look after my brothers' precious children, the ones their women will let me have. I take care of them, these especial girls. They are safe here. I look after them good.

When the Johnnie Walker arrived Carreras guzzled half of it straight down, then wiped his mouth again and said, *Chicas, chicas*, where are you? He pushed back his chair and left the table with the glass.

While he was gone the servant brought Jackson a dish of half-melted ice cream, perhaps made here on the farm.

He loves his polo, the *patrón*, the servant said with a high-pitched laugh. You are English. Very lucky. He knows the English are wonderful, they invented polo. The house is an English manor.

I noticed.

Ah. Yes, he like the English.

He stood at the dresser wiping down some willow-pattern plates.

Jackson asked him who the women were.

The servant tutted and removed the ice-cream dish. *No te preocupes.*

Outside in the courtyard a man was sitting on the mounting-block by the gate with a rifle on his knee. In the light of the nearest lamp Jackson could see the magazine and thought it was a Kalashnikov. The man was smoking. A trail of white smoke clouded up over his shoulder toward the lamp, as if drawn to the source of its visibility. Beyond him one of the watchtowers loomed. The man up at the top spoke, his voice clear and small, and the man down below murmured a reply.

Inside the house Jackson could hear music playing again. A solitary cicada was trilling in the night. It would sing for a while then pause and listen for an answer, then try again.

Jackson smoked a cigarette and went to his room.

2

Dawn was slow and partial in the forest. A faint drizzle hung in the air.

The two lights of the helicopter, one red, one clear, had each impregnated the air around it with a halo. The guard boarded ahead of them and settled into the seat beside the pilot. When they lifted up they rose straight into mist. The roofs of the farm below became dark slabs. The trees were the last thing to disappear, trailing in the atmosphere like black weeds seen through a depth of murky water.

The clouds were like snow slopes, poured across the turbulence of dark hills like some attempt to conceal the tumult of the land. The forests and hills were black beneath them, breaking out here and there in flashes of green so intense you hardly registered it at first.

Then they were flying through sunshine in a brilliant sky. Up there in the high air you rejoined the rest of the world; all nations met in the ether of jet fuel, air conditioning and blue sky. The pilot in his soft leather jacket with a gold zip at either cuff, Carreras sunk in his seat with a newspaper, a cigarette, a paper cup of coffee, the helicopter vibrating in the air over the hills as if running over rubber balls, then finding the smooth high cloudless air all seemed vividly normal.

Carreras leaned across and tapped Jackson on the knee.

Here, he said. This is you.

He handed over the radio beacon.

Of course you had it in case you got lost. You can do what you like with it now.

Jackson had forgotten about it.

Thank you. I never expected to see that again.

Carreras shook his head. We are not thieves. He stared at Jackson. You must know that. We buy, we sell. You do not listen the lies anymore.

He couldn't help flicking up his eyebrows as he spoke, and Jackson saw a glimpse of a friendliness, almost a vulnerability, as if he might really care what people thought of him and his trade. Then the face set hard again, and Jackson saw that that kind of openness would be the most dangerous thing in a man like him.

Would he really be able to walk away when they landed? They were not more than twenty minutes into the flight and already the other land—the coastal desert—was visible in the distance. Geographically, the *cordilleras* were not wide. Yet they held entire worlds.

The beacon was in his hand. It had a weight to it, he noticed again. He held it in his lap and turned it over. The battery cover was there, still screwed down with its four little screws. The thought occurred to him: if it weighed this much, it must still have the battery in it; it might well still work.

Carreras unbuckled his belt and moved to the door. He glanced up at the pilot, then reached for the door handle. In an instant Jackson saw that he was going to slide the door open, then he was going to get the bodyguard sitting up in front beside the pilot, and the two of them would come back and grab Jackson, and do to him what Carreras had done to his brother. The pilot began to climb and the hills fell away.

Jackson saw now there was no way out. To have no way out was to have no choices: meaning there was only one thing you could do. He had only one choice. In such a situation, if you saw any way forward at all, you had to take it.

It was obvious that Carreras couldn't possibly offer hospitality to a stranger who arrived uninvited in his domain, who had discovered the ruins there, which might attract all kinds of interest, then let him go. Holding the beacon pressed between his thighs he switched it on.

He felt the click. The chopper whirred and heaved through an air pocket, and although the device let out one squeak—enough to confirm it was working—no one heard or noticed. Keeping the side with the light face down, Jackson put it into his pack.

Meanwhile Carreras seemed to be struggling to unlock the door. Finally he managed it, and slid open the window a few inches. That was all. Not the door. It was sunny outside, but the draft that whistled in was icy.

Jackson sat still, shocked to find that he was not about to have to fight to stay on board. He had no idea what would happen now. Would anyone be watching for the beacon? It seemed doubtful, especially since it had already been triggered once before. That time, someone had indeed come running to see, but it hadn't been the military.

For five minutes nothing happened. Then beyond the low partition separating the pilot and the bodyguard from the passenger section with its four seats, Jackson saw the pilot lean to his right and look at the man next to him, then pull away his microphone, and say something. The man glanced back into the cabin, and the pilot pushed the helicopter into a downward swerve.

The big engine moaned as they descended, sweeping to the left. Then he levelled out again and they carried on.

A moment later the guard in front unclipped his seatbelt and stepped through to the back. He touched Carreras's shoulder and spoke in his ear. Carreras glanced at Jackson but sat still with his legs crossed.

The guard went back to his seat.

Carreras turned to his side and reached into his leather bag, which was standing open beside his seat.

Jackson knew what he must be doing. Again he saw what was about to happen. He could hear with great clarity the air rushing past the fuselage; the light outside seemed to grow brighter. He could feel the warmth of his seat pressing against his legs. All there was in the whole universe was this helicopter rushing through the air, with the sunlight streaming into it illuminating the fibres of the carpet like fine filaments and Carreras with both hands in his bag as if he was trying to clip two things together. It must be a gun with which he would force Jackson out of the aircraft. The great machine shook twice in the rushing air. Jackson could feel the weight of his seatbelt's buckle in his lap. The thought entered his mind to undo it, rise from his seat while there was still time, grip the white plastic handle of the door and leap out into the rushing air before anyone could force him to. Then before he knew what he was doing, he had left his seat, and fallen on Carreras.

He had short silver-and-black hair, and smelled faintly of bacon and coffee, and some eau de cologne. His elbow pressed hard into Jackson's chest. Jackson leaned right over him and grabbed his wrists.

Excuse me. What?

But Jackson kept on gripping him.

Excuse me, Carreras shouted.

Then someone had taken hold of Jackson's shoulders from behind, and forcibly tugged him away, and shoved him back into his seat. It was the guard from the front, who slapped Jackson on the chest now.

Idiot. He slapped him again.

Carreras was back in his seat. Is OK, is OK, Jorge. In his hands he held a diary and some folded papers, and nodded at the guard.

Jackson was bewildered. He couldn't believe the man didn't have a gun in his hand.

Is this what they tell you, the Yanquis? We save your life, we look after you good. What we have to do?

Then out of the corner of his eye Jackson saw something large and green outside in the air close by. It swung from underneath and rose up beside them, another helicopter, a green military one with its door wide open and a soldier sitting there with an AK-47 in his lap.

Carreras saw it too. He stood and moved between the two front seats and tapped the pilot on his shoulder. The pilot handed him a spare set of headphones. Carreras squatted there a while. He looked to his side at the helicopter, and when he did, Jackson could see his lips moving. He was talking into his microphone. Once he saw him smile.

Outside the window the big green machine rocked from side to side slowly, then veered away and pulled ahead, as if it had stopped by for a chat, given a farewell wave, and moved off. It rushed away over the green hills and vanished into a cloud, reappeared for a moment, much smaller, then turned away behind them.

Carreras removed the headphones and came back to his seat. He buckled himself in, then leaned forward and said to Jackson: You do not understand. Nothing at all. Estupid. You do not know this situation. We have friends. This is the DEA. Is not so simple like you think. I have been good to you, but you do not understand. You must learn, or everything is throwed away.

Jackson sat still. What did all this mean? Surely it wasn't really possible the man would let him walk away when they landed? Especially now.

But it seemed it was. It wasn't even nine in the morning when they touched down at a small airport in the suburbs of Lima. A two-hour flight, that was all.

They got out of the helicopter and went down its little flight of fold-out steps. The big blades were still turning briskly, and there was a strong breeze. The turbine hissed and whined as it slowed.

Carreras walked to a waiting black Mercedes without a word or a nod, without a backwards glance, as if preferring not to think of the clemency he had shown the stranger. A driver dressed in jeans and a T-shirt shut the door on him and climbed into his seat and started the car. Before they drove off a door opened and another man stepped out, said, *Sí, arreglado*, all arranged, and walked over to the small prefabricated hut that was the only sign of an office or terminal at the airport. The car idled in the sunshine.

Jackson stood still on the concrete ramp, his bag resting against one knee. Was this it? Was he free? The sun was strong already. Any trace of freshness there'd been had left the morning.

He walked to the wire gate out of the small dusty airstrip with his pack on his back. A few cars were parked outside the hut. A once-paved track, rutted and rotted, big flakes of tarmac scarring it, led out beyond the chain-link fence. Only a quarter of a mile away the buildings of Lima began. There would be streets there, and people.

Jackson paced down the track still hardly believing he was free, trying not to walk fast. As soon as he could he'd lose himself in a crowd. The first thing he'd do, if only he made it to the street, was take a taxi to the bus station and get straight on a bus north, back to the mountains, and find Sarah. He felt completely exposed. No cover at all. Any second there could be a pistol crack behind him and he'd drop to the broken ground. But there was nothing he could do except walk. He felt like a man crossing a wide flat desert. A line of spindly palm trees with yellowing fronds ran along the track, and halfway up there was the rusting wreck of an old bus.

The black Mercedes was still behind him, at the airport. The chopper was still whining.

He hadn't gone far when he noticed a man coming toward him. He wasn't more than thirty yards away, yet Jackson hadn't seen him before. He wore a pale baseball cap, an old light-coloured sports jacket and a pair of ancient trainers whose soles had shaped themselves into bows. He had white stubble and a creased face and was small and skinny.

Was it strange that there was no one around except him and that one man? The place seemed deathly quiet, unnaturally still.

They passed each other with a nod. Something made Jackson glance back at him over his shoulder. To his mild surprise the man had also turned back. He looked away again and walked on, toward the buildings and the city.

Then he realised what was happening. He spun round. The man was already on one knee with both hands cupped together taking aim.

Jackson dived off the track, and as he did so he heard the snap of the shot. He hurt his leg in the fall but didn't think he had been hit. There was nothing for it. He got up and jumped toward the old bus, ten or fifteen yards away, hunching and leaping from side to side. But the man didn't try again.

Jackson heard the Mercedes coming fast. He made it to the back of the bus in time to see another car appear, driving down the track from the city, toward the airport, a white limousine with something red and blue on the hood at the front, fluttering in the breeze as the car's tyres spat little puffs of dust out of their way.

Carreras's car stopped. He thought he heard a window being buzzed shut. The driver must have realised something was wrong. Meanwhile behind the white limo coming from the street, a dark green, heavy-looking jeep had swung into view, and was accelerating down the track after it.

Carreras's black Mercedes reversed rapidly back to the airport. As it went there was a crackle of automatic fire, and a couple of answering rifle shots. Then more fire, which seemed to be coming from other quarters. A round whirred past Jackson's head, and he heard the twang of a bullet striking the old bus. Someone must be aiming at him. He hunkered down into a rotted wheel arch.

There was another exchange of fire, then silence. The big engine of the converted jeep roared, and he looked out and saw it pass the fender of the bus and continue down the track, its engine whining high, as if straining in a low gear.

Jackson heard the chopper's engine again, hissing as it rose in pitch. There was a clatter of fire, and he looked back toward the airport. The big green jeep had stopped on the tarmac just inside the gate; all its doors were open. The white limo had pulled off the track, and the black Mercedes had parked by the helicopter. Above it, the blades were turning swiftly; the little flight of steps was still down. Another military vehicle roared across from the far side of the airport, its windscreen looking blue in the morning sun.

A man came down the steps of Carreras's helicopter. Jackson thought it was the driver of the Mercedes. He was carrying a Kalashnikov. Unhurriedly he lifted it to his shoulder and began spraying bursts of fire in different directions. There was a whoosh and a short screech. A cloud of smoke erupted just in front of him, and he was no longer there.

Then came a loud rasp, a roar, then a slapping groan. The whine of the big turbine dropped in pitch, then was smothered altogether by a series of bangs so loud they seemed to thump Jackson in the chest. Another bullet whined on the chassis of the bus, and the last thing Jackson saw before he huddled over was a flag of flame flapping up the column of the helicopter's engine, and two figures appearing one after the other on the steps with their hands on their heads. They stooped as they came out, and jumped straight down to the tarmac, as if sure of what they were doing, as if they'd just heard an order to do it. The second man straightened up, then amid another crackle of fire seemed to jump back, his shoulders hunching, and spun on his heels. Another jolt ran through him, and he fell to the ground. He must have been hit two or three times. Jackson could no longer see him, he was hidden by one of the parked cars, but he was sure from the black trousers and blue *guayabera*, as well as the man's carriage, that it had been Carreras.

Two rounds ricocheted near his head, and another thudded into the side of the bus. He ducked down again just as something struck his shoulder, the bad one, and for a second it stung so badly and felt so cold he didn't think he could bear it. His mind whirled just long enough for him to recognise the coldness in his body, to remember it from long ago, to know what it meant, before the prickly ground came up and struck his face.

Then he was lying on a smooth cool floor of linoleum. Men were talking above him. A siren sounded in the distance. Someone was lifting him, moving him, he could smell leather, and a gentle tremor ran through the earth. Now he could smell disinfectant. Sarah was walking away while looking back at him, or he himself was being carried away. He didn't want to be taken from her. He tried to shout to her to come closer, to tell her he would get back to her, that everything was all right now, he was safe, he had found incredible things and answered all the questions; he was coming back. But she couldn't hear anything he was saying. She moved further and further away.

3

The day before, Montoya had called Brown at the hotel as he had said he would. Brown listened. They were to send a car to the Miraflores municipal airport in Lima the following morning, and they would have what they wanted.

Brown was standing at the window of his lamentable hotel room wondering if he might go and see Sarah one last time before he finally made his way home. Down below, small bulky Indian women were skipping along with enormous bundles on their backs, no doubt making their way to the market. He felt something like a twinge of nostalgia to be leaving. It wasn't such a bad place after all, especially in the mornings with the sun on the mountains behind the town, and the streets bustling with life.

He went down for his coffee and omelette.

The phone rang at the reception desk, and Brown had a feeling it might be for him. The helicopter should have arrived by now in Lima. It should all have happened.

Sure enough, the receptionist appeared in the corner of the lounge waving at him and calling.

Brown picked up the heavy old receiver and listened. It was

good news. It had worked. What a relief, he thought. Except for Jackson, who was in hospital. Apparently he was lucky to be in hospital. The fool hadn't had the sense to get out of the way. But he had survived.

With a sigh of annoyance, Brown said, OK, yes, the San Porfirio Hospital, Lima Surco, and hung up, then settled down to his breakfast.

Now that it had come to it, he didn't want to go and see Sarah. But it was unavoidable, he would have to go and tell her. No doubt she would want to make her way straight to the young man's hospital bed. If he pulled through. Which knowing his luck—the same luck that had got him through the jungle, and got him this girl—he would. It was true, as Brown had once heard, there were only two kinds of people in this world, those with luck and those without. Jackson was the first kind. And perhaps he himself was too, in a different way. After all, it had worked this time. They'd got their man and Brown, more than anyone, had fixed it.

4

Jackson spent ten days in hospital. The surgeon took one bullet out of his thigh and another from his ribs. One centimetre more, he said, and it would have hit his heart. He slept solidly for the first four days. On the fifth he opened his eyes and saw Sarah sitting on the chair by the bed, her face furrowed in an expression that was both a frown and a smile, an expression that seemed to reside and rest on his breast. She came and put her head beside his on the pillow. Of all things, he'd started to cry. Then the nurse came in and told Sarah to sit on the chair again. He needed absolute calm.

She stayed in a hotel nearby, and came every day. Something had changed in her. There was a seriousness about her way with him, as if she had made up her mind that he was her responsibility. She had opened some gate and allowed him in, and he was fully in the garden of her attention now. He liked it. He felt that it would not be easy to slip out again, and he liked that too.

One morning before she came to the hospital the nurse entered with a telephone in her hand. Jackson rested it beside his ear on the pillow.

That all worked out rather well. Well done.

It was Brown, speaking once again in his fake officer's tone.

Jackson said nothing.

You know how this sort of thing is, you develop a plan as you go. But it was a good thing you set off that beacon the other morning on your way. We'd have been late otherwise. Anyway, I was just calling to say we want to express our thanks.

Jackson's head was spinning. This was the man who had sent him right into the fire without warning, with not a weapon of any kind on him.

If you go to the Surco branch of the Bank of Lima, the smooth voice went on, and give them this transaction number they'll sort you out. Got a pen?

There was a biro on the bedside table, and before Jackson had answered Brown began giving the figures, which Jackson took down on the back of a book. He didn't know what he would do. He couldn't think just now, so it was better to write them down in case.

What happened? Jackson asked.

Brown chuckled. All worked out splendidly, he said.

It was true, as he'd thought. Even the so-called keepers of the peace, these guardians of civilisation, had lied. That's what the army liked to call themselves. Civilised values are in our hands, gentlemen, one colonel had said during a seminar he'd attended years ago. But they were liars, professional double-crossers. They would do anything to get their way and call it victory.

Curiously, Jackson began to feel better after the phone call. His senses began to come back. He would certainly take the money. He remembered Stryker telling him it would be five times his first instalment. Five thousand dollars was something. And they would leave him alone now. He was sure of it. He may have unwittingly delivered another man, Carreras, into their net, but he himself had at the same time slipped out of it. He was free. No one held anything over him now.

They changed his bandages every day, and when he left they gave him a plastic bag full of fresh supplies. The nurse had shown Sarah how to change them.

He was concerned about the hike up to Uncle Alfredo's. He couldn't wear a strap over his bad shoulder, and bought a shoulder-bag he could sling over the other, but it wasn't something to hike with. Even walking along the street he felt dizzy and short of breath. They spent five days in Lima, then after the bus ride into the mountains they spent another four days in Chachapoyas, relaxing and getting back his strength. They sat in the cafés drinking sweet coffee and watching the sights. The sunshine, the bustle of the market, the sweet, rich *pollo saltado*, and the glistening beer bottles in the evenings, and the long afternoons lying in bed together, with the light falling in stripes through the window shutters—he loved all of it. He had rarely known what it was like to live without worry.

Except for Ignacio. He guessed that the boy would be OK, but he wanted to know.

On their first morning in Chachapoyas the sun was shining and a spring-like breeze was blowing through the market square. They were sitting at a table in the arcade outside the market hall. A pillar's shadow lay across the table and they sat either side of it, each in sunshine.

The heat of the sun filled Jackson's limbs. He took a swig from the glass of coffee in front of him, then added another spoon of sugar.

Good, she said. Have another. Go on.

That's three spoons.

Got to build you back up, remember?

He smiled. Look at me. I'm fine.

Sugar and fried things. Nice things.

They looked at each other a moment for no particular reason, and laughed. Her eyes were smooth and hazel in the morning sun, and shone like agate. The lovers' gaze only ended when they closed their eyes and kissed. He saw the flash of light on her smooth cheek, then the warm orange on his eyelids.

Big explorer, Sarah said, pushing him away.

They finished their coffee and left. She tucked her arm in his as they strolled among the small-time marketers selling no more than they and their husbands could carry, who lined either side of the dusty road. Jackson let the bustle of the little town wash through him. It was good to feel all that activity going on, all that salutary human endeavour. Humans were like bees, he thought. Most of them lived in these horizontal hives called towns, but some were out on the land itself growing things, gathering and foraging things they would then bring into the lively, sunny hive for exchange.

As they walked the streets became quieter and emptier, and the houses taller, more gaunt and elegant. Soon they came to the plaza and the church.

It was dark and cool in the nave. A choir was singing somewhere in the cavernous space, the voices thin and high. Then the chorus stopped, someone coughed, and a man said something.

It was hard to walk quietly in there. Your footfalls on the stone floor echoed all round the building. Behind the altar with its white, gold-embroidered cloths and elaborate candelabra, a screen rose up, carved in dark wood. The choir were behind the screen, four boys in red surplices and Beatle bobs of short black hair, singing a simple Andean hymn with Padre Beltrán conducting them. In the dark cool, knowing there was the dusty sunny bustle going on outside, it was a beautiful sound, water-like in its clarity.

Ay María, the father exclaimed, leaning back, opening his arms wide. *Ay Dios*. He kissed Jackson on both cheeks, then embraced Sarah.

We all thought you were dead, Beltrán said. He glanced at Sarah. Well, I never said it, but really I did.

He shook his head and grasped Jackson's hand. How they found you I cannot imagine. And our scourge is really gone? Beltrán cleared his throat with a smile. Anyway, what I want to know of course is what did you find? One day, who knows, perhaps it will even be safe enough to bring the ancient Chachapoyans to light. But later. You are invited to dinner at my home. I will hear all your adventures then. With one raised eyebrow he said, My choir is waiting for me.

Hand in hand they left the dark church and went out into the sunlit mountain town.

5

Alfredo cracked open a bottle of Chilean wine. Look at you. The wounded soldier and his girl. Does it hurt? You should have Nellie take a look at it. She's a wonder with her herbs.

Ignacio was there, he had been back two and a half weeks already, and in that time had learnt to write some of his letters. He could read three-letter words out loud. One of the older boys had helped him carve a toy rifle out of wood. Sometimes Nellie let him milk the goats. He was good at it, she said.

Over a dinner of roast kid, Alfredo said: Rumours are flying. Carreras is dead, he's wounded, he's in prison, they caught him but he escaped. You know what happened?

He's dead. I saw it.

That's what I was sort of afraid of, Alfredo said. I'll bet you'll start thinking that now you can go straight back in and get busy excavating your ruins, or whatever it is you do. But mark my words, the area will be worse than ever. At least for a while. Things will settle down, let's hope, but it will take time. I don't imagine you'd be too popular with any friends he left behind.

Jackson had been thinking about it. The first thing he ought to do was go home and organise a real expedition. There was no point wandering in again by himself, even if it were safe. He needed to find backers and colleagues; people who could help him. Perhaps he might even go to college for a while and study archaeology thoroughly.

Sarah was against that. If you're going to college, I know what you should study, she said. Art, obviously. All this other stuff, all this macho stuff, ruins and soldiers and explorers and all that—that's your past. I've been thinking about it, and that's what you're free of now. And just think what it would do to this whole area if some new Machu Picchu opened up here. It would ruin it.

When she said this he felt curiously relieved. He would see, he would see. Anything was possible.

In the morning he and Ignacio poured themselves glasses of lemonade from a pitcher standing by the sink, and took them outside. They sat on a bench under Jackson's portrait of the whole family. Ignacio sat upright on the edge of the seat, looking down into his glass, swirling the liquid around.

You like it here?

He nodded seriously and said, *Sí*, in a long, protracted syllable.

You'll stay?

Why not, señor?

You have no place you're planning to go?

No. Why do you ask, señor?

I just want to know you'll be OK. We'll come and visit you, you know. We'll be back.

Sí, he said again, in the same slow voice.

Who are your friends? Jackson tried.

My friends?

Yes. Which of the kids?

Ignacio lifted his head as if to nod at something he agreed with. Well, Charro and Juan mostly. But they are all fine. *Todos buenos, señor*.

After a pause, Jackson said, You're incredible, you know that? Without you I wouldn't be here. I want to thank you but I don't know how. On impulse he put his glass down on the ground, closed his good arm round the boy's slight body and pulled him close. I'm going to miss you.

Ignacio let out a little sigh that might have been a laugh. *Sí, sí*. I'll be here, Jackson heard him say over his shoulder.

In the late afternoon he and Sarah sat on the doorstep of the hut they were once again sharing and watched the shadows creep up the valley. Soon the shade would arrive and leach the colour from the world, but before it came the dirt of the farmyard seemed to turn gold. The phrase *field of the cloth of gold* entered his mind. He felt that he was himself on such a field, sitting on its lambent weave. For a moment it seemed this whole world was one big field of gold spun by him, as if he himself had created all of his life. A laugh of astonishment escaped him. He had never before seen to what extent his life was his own. Just his. Even his difficult past, that too he himself had spun, and now it lay woven into the same cloth.

Across the yard Ignacio's cat sat on a fence in the last of the light. It yawned and blinked. Jackson held Sarah's hand, cool and light, and that too seemed made of golden dust. Soon the shadows would reach the compound like an evening tide and climb the glowing walls, swallowing them in sombreness. But before that happened was the time of richest light.

Outside the Greyhound bus window, the lovely mix of pine and deciduous trees moved by. Brilliant rivers, carpeted mountains, white shingle houses with climbing frames and paddling pools in the yards, lawns strewn with toys—this was where he was now. New York state: refuge of exiles, of utopian dreamers, he thought.

Along sun-dappled roads, past a sign saying "Unfinished Furniture" (who the devil would want that?), past "Lowe's Knows" (what did they know?), over the green "209 NORTH," past Johnson's Steakhouse Motel, among all the tree-nestled good fortune, the effluvia of affluence come to rest among the trees, while the jewelled cars flowed down the smooth grey streams poured out for them down the green valleys of the promised land.

Green on green: in his bus window the emerald reflection of trees on the opposite bank of the thruway overlaid the actual green trees on his side. Here and there the sheen and dapple of water would show from some creek or a flooded copse, a marshy stand. Through all the trees flooded the light of the sun as though a glittering wash had been poured over them. They shivered, they shook their pelts, they offered themselves to the air and to the eye.

This was a healthy land, a good place to live. A team of power pylons came stomping down through the woods along their own private avenue, paused to look right and left, and crossed the highway arm in arm.

Just now Jackson felt suffused with good fortune. He'd met Sarah's parents in the house in Woodstock where she had grown up, where her father was an entrepreneur of the New Age, a holistic snack-producer, once prominent among the star-studded hills around Woodstock. Jackson had understood then how Sarah had grown up responsible, self-preserving, self-nurturing, globally minded, in a world of family and friends who knew to keep enough distance at crucial times. Whatever it was between him and Sarah had not run its course. It was good they arrange things so they could explore it, whatever it was. So he was in America. He would enrol in college, study both archaeology and painting and work part-time for Sarah's father, who had helped get him the student visa. When he was ready, he would see about going back down to the cloud forest. Sarah was teaching and doing her research at a charming clapboard university.

Then "NYC" ahead, and New York came into view. The towers all bathed in the light of the seaboard afternoon. To live with the healthy breeze of commerce on your cheek—that was the natural element of humanity today. If

sweat, leather, wood, iron and soil had provided humankind with its envi-
ronment until a hundred years ago, if they still did so in the backwaters, so
what? Did that make them any more natural than the fur, bone and rock
which had preceded them? Concrete and glass, steel and plastic made
humankind's home now, and that was fine. Every point of every building on
that shining skyline said the same thing: we are good, we are right, trust us,
we can take you to places of excellence hitherto unknown. They pointed to the
future, the only way there was.

Below the traffic crawling toward the mouth of the Lincoln Tunnel, a
parking lot lay framed by a seven-storey Days Inn on one side, a bank of trees
and suburban homes on another. Two trucks—South Hills Movers and
something he couldn't see—waited in the car park, among a scattering of
cars. A bus called Ex-Cart Services loitered too, empty. A flag flew, and the
breeze that rippled the flag also stirred the trees on the hillside. The glossy
parking lot with the gleaming vehicles left in its care, the grey block of the
Days Inn with its shiny scales of balconies, a house tattooed with the fine
shadow-lattice of a tree—it was all beautiful. He had not realised how much
he had resisted the modern world. Why had he? Through spurious notions,
through the damage of experience. You learnt early a way of living success-
fully, and you took that to be the only way. You could be intelligent and still
do that. Gradually, sooner or later, life could be trusted to divest you of your
fond illusion, to show you there were many paths. The mountain was riddled
with so many paths they smoothed one another's margins and could not be
distinguished from each other.

Finally they drove past some flattened traffic cones over which the small
cars bumped, and into the giant marble archway that opened the way to the
underground—to the tiled vaulted ballroom with its strings of bulbs and its
ceiling gleaming with reflected lights—down and down, ferried in the traffic
of commerce, until, with a growl of black smoke, the buses in front curved
upward, up the battered black ramps into the heart of today, alive with the
scent of hot dogs and burnt petrol, sentinelled by giant lamp posts.